CW01635276

GENESIS

ANCIENT ORIGINS BOOK FOUR

ROBERT STOREY

FUSE

In the blackest pits, or emptiest of voids, there is always a guiding light; it's just up to us to find it.

– Robert Storey

FACTS:

On the 31st of October, 2015, an asteroid (possibly a dead comet) with the designation TB145, passed close to Earth at eighty thousand miles an hour. This rock measured approximately half a kilometre in diameter and its impact on our planet would have had the power to devastate a whole continent. The worrying thing is, due to the unusual nature of this asteroid's solar orbit, TB145 was only discovered *three weeks* prior to its flypast of our planet.

That an object of this scale evaded our notice highlights the tenuous nature of our existence on the Earth's surface and opens up the questions, why is there no mechanism in place to detect these threats? Why aren't our governments uniting to combat them? And perhaps most importantly, how many more dark comets are out there waiting to strike?

On the 8th January 2011 an asteroid with the potential to impact Earth in 2040 was discovered by the Mount Lemmon Survey. This near-Earth object was given the designation, 2011 AG5.

TERMINOLOGY / MAP

USSB – United States Subterranean Base
GMRC – Global Meteor Response Council
Darklight – World's largest private security contractor
SFSD – Special Forces Subterranean Detachment (*Terra Force*)
SED – Sanctuary Exploration Division
Deep Reach – Special survey team working within the SED
Silver – An elite military unit available to the highest bidder
Sanctuary Proper – Ancient underground structure built by an extinct species of Hominid, Homo giganthropsis (the Anakim)

USSB
STEADFAST
NEVADA
UTAH
COLORADO
CALIFORNIA
Las Vegas
USA
Los Angeles
ARIZONA
NEW
MEXICO
TEXAS
MEXICO
USSB
SANCTUARY

YEAR:

2041 A.D.

PROLOGUE

'This is SED Command. We are a go for express shuttle launch Zulu–Seven–Two in T minus twenty seconds.'

The countdown timer in the Control Station sank under ten seconds and SED Command spoke again. 'T minus seven seconds ... five, four, three, two, one – launch.'

Another air-shuttle roared forth from USSB Sanctuary's Exploration Division, plunging down into the great shaft that cut down into the rocky substrate beneath. Soon after, rockets fired and the craft picked up speed, its blazing lights ploughing through the darkness like a tethered jet fighter as it twisted and turned through massive dark chambers and tight spiralling tunnels. On the same track, many miles south, another shuttle emerged from a transparent tunnel to cruise to a stop at an SED outpost. A unit of armoured Special Forces soldiers disembarked, their Terra Force insignias standing out against their grey and brown camouflage. Weapons and kit were unloaded, and with little ceremony the group of men struck out on a pre-planned route punctuated by waypoint beacons. Following this treacherous path, lines of shielded cabling had already been laid down by those that had gone before. These red conduits of electricity snaked up vertical climbs, down sheer drops and across the gaping fissures that littered Sanctuary Proper like a scaly plague. Deeper into the pitch-black void, teams of men and women tackled the unforgiving landscape of the ancient, Anakim, subterranean world. And further still, at the head of the far reaching expedition, hundreds of people congregated on a vast plateau, where portable floodlights lit up an enormous cavern, transforming the endless night into the dazzle of day.

Stripped to the waist, a couple of hundred men heaved on ropes, dragging up heavy pieces of equipment from a deep ravine below. Amongst these toiling souls, an armoured man bellowed out orders.

'Pull, you sons of whores! Put your fucking backs into it!!'

The efforts of those nearby increased and the Terra Force leader walked to the cliff edge and peered down, before unleashing a string of threatening curses at those beneath.

Further back amidst the masses, Deep Reach team leader Riley Orton heaved back on a rope. His muscles bunched and sweat dripped down his naked torso while around him blazing lights added to the heat of his exertion. Without sleep for forty-eight hours, Riley felt fit to drop and it seemed he wasn't the only one. Ahead of him, a man slumped to the ground in exhaustion, his grip failing. The rope's momentum slowed and stopped as two other men went to his assistance.

The incident drew the attention of their uncompromising mission commander, Colonel Samson, who strode to the scene. 'Leave him!'

'He needs rest,' one of the men said. 'We all do.'

'You'll rest when I say you can rest.' Samson pushed aside the unconscious man and picked up the rope. 'NOW PULL!'

Everyone leant back against the massive weight they were attempting to drag up from below. Hand over hand, the rope moved through Riley's gloves, slow at first but picking up speed as Samson continued to berate and push them, while his prodigious strength added impetus to the struggle.

A shout of warning came from the cliff edge and the ground beneath Riley's feet shuddered. Fifty feet away a section of rock disappeared in a cloud of dust and ten men vanished from view, their screams echoing into the chamber as they fell.

The rope snapped taut, dragging Riley forwards before shearing through his grip as the heavy load dropped.

'Hold!' Samson shouted. 'HOLD!!'

The man nearest the edge let go and rolled to safety. Samson, next in line, coiled his arms round the rope and activated his armour's inbuilt anchors. Two metal bolts fired into the ground, jerking the colonel to a stop with their attached cables.

Samson grunted in pain as opposite forces threatened to rip him in two, and Riley held on as others rushed to their aid. The unbearable weight lessened and, inch by inch, foot by foot, the tide turned back in their favour.

After what seemed like an age, their goal neared its conclusion and the equipment appeared over the ridge and continued up onto flat ground.

Riley released the rope and sank to one knee as the other teams around them finished hauling up their respective machinery. He breathed deep and not for the first time he questioned their conservation of power. It had been deemed prudent to conserve energy by limiting the use of winches now they were beyond the reach of an electrical supply. He could see the wisdom behind the decision, but it didn't stop him complaining about it.

As Riley contemplated passing out, Samson detached the cables that secured him in place and made a beeline for the man who'd abandoned his position on the rope.

The colonel punched the soldier to the ground. 'Disobey my orders again,' Samson said, standing over his victim, 'and I'll throw you over the edge myself. Do you understand me!?'

Silence fell on those gathered.

Dazed, the man looked up at his attacker before nodding his head.

Riley felt a pang of sympathy for the soldier, who'd done the only thing he could to save his own life. But as everyone knew, arguing with the colonel was like wrestling with a rabid bull; it could only end one way.

Samson swung round to glare at them. 'What do you think you're looking at? Get back to work!'

The noise of labour resumed, the incident forgotten, but Riley knew Samson had saved many more men below from being crushed to death, putting his own life on the line when no one else would. It was hard to accept such an animal could demonstrate such selflessness. *Although*, Riley reasoned, *he was probably more worried about losing his precious equipment than lives*. Whatever the case, he'd saved them from yet more losses, but there was one thing his actions could never change, it was the colonel's single-mindedness that had pushed their death toll to over forty and they were still only a few days out from base.

How many more will die in the coming days? Riley could only guess.

His hand strayed to the safety harness at his waist, the touch reassuring him he had options should *he* find himself freefalling to his death.

Samson wiped sweat from his brow and accepted a water canister from one of his commandos, and Riley caught himself glaring at the man who seemed hell-bent on pushing them beyond their limits.

'If he keeps this up,' a voice said from behind, 'none of us are gonna make it back to base.'

Riley turned round to his friend and Deep Reach team mate, the bald-headed Jefferson Church. The bear of a man took on some water, wiped the back of a thick forearm across his bewhiskered face, and passed the flask to Riley, who drank his fill.

'And it'll be for naught if Sarah has already made it to the surface,' Riley said.

Jefferson looked sceptical. 'If that's where she's going, she's headed the wrong way.' He lowered his voice. 'What's she doing down here, Ri? I still don't get it.'

Riley shrugged. In the spare moments he'd had to ponder such questions, the answers remained as elusive as the woman herself.

'One thing's for sure,' Jefferson said, 'whatever she's taken, they'll do anything to get it back.'

Riley murmured his agreement as the colonel turned in their direction.

'You, team leader,' Samson said, pointing at Riley, 'a word.'

The colonel stalked away as more soldiers and SED personnel flooded up onto the plateau from below.

Apprehensive, Riley picked up his gear and approached the intimidating presence of the Terra Force commander, who stood staring out over a deep fissure.

'How far until we intercept the route?' Samson said, his metal shod boots sending loose sediment skittering down into the abyss.

'According to our charts,' Riley said, 'after we cross the chasm, about three miles.'

'And no one's ever come this way before?'

'No, it was deemed too dangerous.'

Samson grunted. 'Where's your superior?'

Riley looked around. He hadn't seen Locke for some time. 'I think he said he was going to scout ahead. Ophion and his two ... companions, went with him.'

Samson's perpetual scowl deepened at the mention of S.I.L.V.E.R.'s chrome clad leader. He looked Riley in the eye, his ice-cold eyes burning intensely. 'You were close to this woman? You know how she thinks?'

Riley hesitated.

'Withhold information from me, boy,' Samson said, 'and it'll be the last mistake you make.'

Riley stared into the man's feral gaze and didn't doubt him for a second. He nodded.

'What are her chances?' Samson said.

'Of what?'

'Of staying alive.'

'Down here? It depends.'

'On what?'

'On how well she's prepared,' Riley said. 'She may be able to locate fresh water in Sanctuary, but there's no food. If she finds water and ekes out her supplies, she could survive for forty days maybe, fifty max.'

'Will she follow the waypoint markers?'

'If she's heading for the temple, she'd be crazy not to.'

Samson fell silent and Riley, not sure if he'd been dismissed, felt compelled to fill the uncomfortable break in conversation. 'Have you heard from the other teams?'

The colonel didn't reply, instead he flipped open a pouch and knocked back a handful of something to chew before swallowing it down.

'The second expedition has located their tracks,' said a deep voice.

Riley turned as the towering form of Ophion Nexus appeared out of the gloom, his chrome armour glinting in the light. At his side walked the smaller figure of Dresden Locke, the SED's facility commander. And following behind them both were two women encased in the same shining armour as their leader, Ophion's ever-present lieutenants.

'How many days does Sarah have on them?' Riley said.

Locke removed his outdated Deep Reach helmet. 'They think she's at least a week ahead,' – he ran a hand through short, grey hair – 'according to the latest report, anyway.'

Riley's hopes soared. *If that's the case*, he reasoned, *after we've found a route across the unexplored terrain, we'll get to Sarah first. If we can find a route across*, he counselled himself. The only problem was he wasn't sure that was a good thing. He wanted to be there when they caught up to her, but at the same time that meant the colonel and Ophion would be there, too.

Riley glanced at Samson and remembered the conversation he'd overheard between the colonel and the GMRC Intelligence Director.

'Tear Sanctuary apart if you have to,' Joiner had said. 'Whatever it takes, whatever the cost, that pendant must be retrieved.'

'*The woman?*' Samson had said.

'Secondary; alive is better, dead will do.'

Riley suppressed a shudder.

'How far ahead will she be when we make the transition?' Samson said, back in the present. 'A day? Three?'

Locke withdrew a knife and bent down to the dusty ground. He drew a line in the dirt and marked one end with the letter T. 'This is the path Morgan will take to the temple.' He looked up and then made a cross at its centre. 'And this is where the second expedition is currently located – along with just under half of our force. And they're at least seven days behind her, maybe nine.'

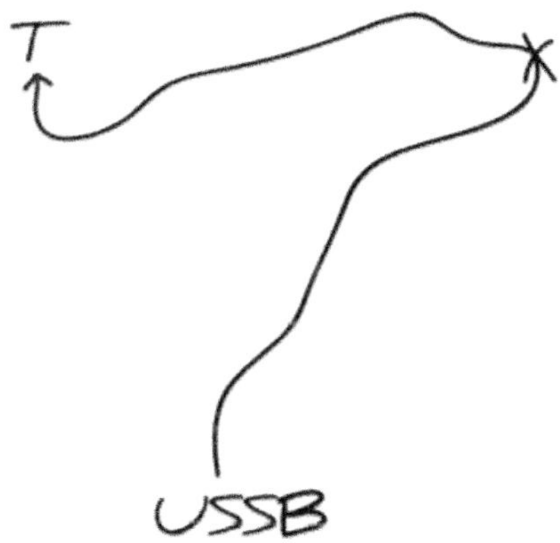

He drew another line with the blade and put a circle on it. 'This is us,' – he extended the line but left a gap in its centre, then drew in some more features – 'once we cross the chasm it'll put us right behind her. If she's experienced problems, we may come out ahead of her.'

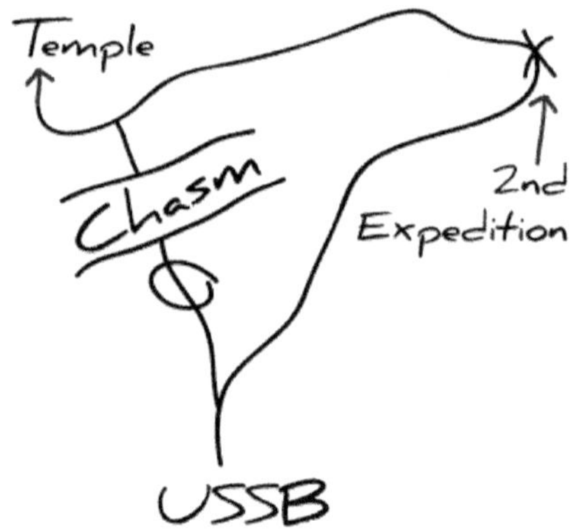

Samson sniffed. 'So how many days, old man?'

Locke's jaw tightened at the colonel's lack of respect. 'In my opinion, considering Morgan's abilities and with her two friends slowing her down, she'll be less than a day in front by the time we rejoin the temple route.'

Samson appeared satisfied with the answer, but Riley could tell Locke had been riled.

'We break camp at zero one hundred,' Samson said, scrubbing out the map with a foot. 'Tell your men.'

The colonel went to leave, but Locke moved to block his way. 'Zero one hundred? Are you trying to get my people killed?'

'If my men can keep going,' Samson said, 'so can yours.'

'I don't give a damn about your soldiers,' Locke said, 'and clearly neither do you. But if you think I'm going to tell my teams to keep going without at least a few hours' sleep, you've got another thing coming.'

Samson's eyes narrowed and Locke held his ground before the colonel's lip contorted into displeasure and a growl escaped his lips. The animalistic sound coupled with the man's ferocious glare made Locke take an involuntary step back.

'SED Commander Locke's position is valid,' Ophion said, in his stone cold baritone. 'Dead men do not make good time.'

'We've already lost over thirty souls—' Locke said, his tone placating.

'Forty,' Riley said, 'we just had another collapse.'

Locke looked at him in alarm. 'SED personnel?'

Riley shook his head.

'How many more need to die, Colonel?' Locke said. 'Another forty, sixty maybe, a thousand?'

'As many as it takes.'

'Then you go on alone,' Locke said. 'I won't help a madman.'

Samson's face blanched and he grasped the front of Locke's uniform. 'What did you just call me?'

Riley, sensing imminent bloodshed, stepped forward to intervene and Samson's manic eyes homed in on the movement, his expression stopping Riley in his tracks.

The sound of laughter made Riley turn to see one of Ophion's lieutenants had removed her sculpted helmet. The Chinese woman was stunningly beautiful and she moved past her leader to trail a beguiling finger up Samson's bulging arm.

'Maybe the colonel fears lost time,' she said, her Asian accent soft. 'Maybe he's afraid to stop.'

'Unhand me, woman,' Samson said, 'or lose the hand.'

The S.I.L.V.E.R. operative gave a throaty chuckle and let the colonel be, while giving Riley the once-over as she passed.

Riley followed the woman's seductive walk as she moved away, before turning his attention back to Samson to see the situation defused.

Samson pushed Locke aside. 'You've got three hours,' he said, and stalked off.

Locke shook his head in relief, gave Riley an amiable slap on the shoulder, then walked away without another word.

Meanwhile Ophion spoke quietly with the two women, before also taking his leave.

Riley sighed. *Three hours is better than nothing,* he decided and made to follow Locke back to his SED colleagues.

'Riley Orton,' the Chinese woman said, making him pause, 'we hear you were involved with this Sarah Morgan.'

Riley didn't know what to say to this armoured assassin, so he decided to stay quiet.

The woman approached. 'Your colonel is a dangerous man, is he not?'

'Much like you, I expect,' Riley said, looking into the woman's dark eyes.

She smiled, the effect dazzling. 'Forgive me. My name's Zhang Bai. I am merely interested in the man who can hold the attention of such a woman as Sarah Morgan.'

'Such a woman?'

Zhang ran her eyes over Riley's bare chest and then glanced down at the tattoos on his arm. 'You were in the military?'

'For a while.'

She moved closer. 'And you're a believer?' She touched the depiction of the crucifix over his heart with soft fingers.

Riley felt confused by her attention. 'I—'

Zhang smiled again, disarming him. 'You don't believe your Sarah is special?'

'She isn't *my Sarah*, and why such an interest?'

'Not many can afford our services.' Zhang touched the emblem on her armour that spelt out the word S.I.L.V.E.R.. 'And fewer still can afford our whole order.' She ran a hand through her jet-black locks. 'I've read Sarah Morgan's dossier, she is quite the woman. Beautiful, athletic, intelligent, but ...'

'But what?'

'But flawed. Her psychological profile indicates mental instability.'

'Is that so?'

'Have I offended you, Riley?' She tilted her head. 'May I call you that?'

Riley was too tired for games. 'Call me what you like.'

As he went to move past her she grasped his arm, her grip

surprising in its power. 'Strong women need strong men, Riley Orton; be careful where you tread, the darkness is full of peril.'

Riley gazed into her sultry eyes. She released her hold and let him continue on his way, while leaving him at a loss as to what she was going on about. *And she says Sarah's unstable. Was she propositioning me or threatening me?*

Rejoining his teammates, Riley settled down for some much-needed sleep and his last vision before he closed his eyes was that of the S.I.L.V.E.R. woman, Zhang Bai, who remained looking in his direction as her masked female companion returned to her side. As he drifted off to sleep, for once his thoughts weren't dominated by the mesmeric, blue eyes of Sarah Morgan ... the woman in the eye of a storm.

CHAPTER ONE

COLONEL SAMSON SAT STARING out into the darkness. He hadn't slept for days; whatever Joiner and his pet agent had pumped into him, it kept his mind whirring away like a never-ending nightmare. Pain lanced through his head forcing him to clench his teeth. His pills still had an effect, but it was like he wasn't there, didn't exist. The thought – the feeling – of not being, of not existing, terrified him. *Am I real?* he wondered. He clenched an armoured fist. It felt real. *I feel real. I just don't feel ... here.* He concentrated on the task at hand. *Find Sarah Morgan, retrieve the pendant. Kill Ophion. Kill Joiner. Kill them all, every last one.* Another thought wormed its way into his mind. He had something else far more important to do. *Find Brett,* he told himself, *find your daughter. And that went so well last time, didn't it, Colonel?* He shifted his position. *That was Steiner's fault. This time will be different. We'll do things our way, my way. Time's running out. The meteors are coming, or had you forgotten? Of course I haven't forgotten!*

'Sir?'

Samson looked up at a Special Forces officer.

'Sir,' the man said again, 'a communication's come through from the SED.'

Samson stared at the soldier, waiting for him to get to the point.

The officer grimaced in discomfort. 'You wanted to know if S.I.L.V.E.R. received any encrypted messages? One's just come through and they've sent an operative to access it.'

Samson stood up. 'Nexus?'

'No, sir, it's a woman, one of the two that follow him around.'

Samson donned his helmet and collected his rifle. 'Take me there.'

The soldier moved to the top of the cliff, connected himself to a line and dropped over the edge. Samson did likewise, abseiling down to the ground two hundred feet below.

At the bottom, the two men worked their way through the sleeping bodies of Terra Force and SED personnel to travel back the way they'd come hours before. Climbing up a steep incline, they passed by more weary troops who continued to filter in from the rear of the two mile long procession.

'You men,' Samson said, gesturing to a unit of five commandos with a sweep of his hand, 'with me.'

The soldiers fell in behind, with weapons drawn on their colonel's command.

Ten minutes later they entered a narrow ravine and the lights of the portable communication terminus came into view. Numerous cables snaked into its specially designed receiver, which filtered out the unwanted interference created by Sanctuary's foundations, the curious substrate the Anakim had manipulated in order to build the supporting structure of their underground world.

A chrome-clad figure stood next to the coms station, her slim form a sliver of light in the gloom. On the left a deep drop fell away below, while on either side high rock faces continued up into the distant darkness. A small contingent from the U.S. Army Signal Corps worked nearby, using robotics to un-snag the long lengths of cable that served as their lifeline back to base and the SED within.

The woman, her face concealed behind her mirrored visor, looked up as Samson and his small company approached.

'I hear we've been contacted,' Samson said, slowing to a halt some feet away.

The S.I.L.V.E.R. operative's mask shimmered into transparency to reveal the grey eyes of the Chinese woman within. 'We have. It is quite interesting. Would you care to listen?'

'Where's Nexus?'

'With my sister, Zhang.' She reached up and pressed a button on the side of her helmet.

'If you're trying to send a transmission,' Samson said, motioning at the walls around them, 'you should know ... this is a dead zone.'

The woman let her arm drop back down, but Samson noticed her other hand had slipped behind her back.

'What did it say?' Samson said when she failed to respond.

'It said S.I.L.V.E.R. is to resume command.'

'On whose orders?'

She hesitated, then said, 'Malcolm Joiner's.'

Samson gave a hollow laugh. 'I doubt that.'

The woman didn't reply, her eyes remaining fixed on Samson.

'Your precious Committee thinks it can control me,' Samson said, preparing himself, 'but they made one big mistake.'

The woman shifted her stance. 'And what was that?'

'Threatening my daughter.'

The woman frowned and Samson shouted, 'Take her!' to his men, and unleashed his rifle.

The assassin dived to her left, her arms a blur of motion and something whizzed past Samson's head, killing a soldier behind.

Suppressed gunfire echoed out and then the woman was among them, a flash of light in each hand whirring through the air as she leapt and spun in a dance of death. Samson fired and missed and fired again, his shots killing his own men. The woman's weapon licked out, cleaving his rifle in two. Rolling to the ground, Samson sprang up and seized her arm, and with a mighty heave propelled her into the cliff. Her body slammed to a stop with a jarring crunch and Samson picked up a dead man's gun and blasted the rock above her head as she staggered to her feet. Another soldier fired. The shots bounced off her armour and she sent a tiny drone exploding into his face, felling him where he stood. A great, cracking groan made her look up. The wall collapsed and the S.I.L.V.E.R. operative disappeared in a cloud of dust and debris. When the area cleared, all that was left was a mound of rock.

Samson looked around at the scene of carnage. Body parts lay scattered everywhere. She'd killed five of the men who'd been with him. Samson himself had killed one with friendly fire, along with three from the Signal Corps. Only one other person was left standing; the operator of the coms receiver. The man stood in stunned shock while Samson went about hiding evidence of the brief battle. After he'd dropped the final body into the ravine, Samson yanked the receiver from its stand and, along with everything else, tossed it into the deep rift.

'What are you doing?!' The operator said, staring down into the blackness.

Samson moved alongside him and placed a hand on his shoulder. 'There can be no more messages.'

'But we have a spare receiver,' the man said, looking up at him.

'And you're the only one who knows how to work it?'

The man nodded dumbly.

Samson grasped his arm and pushed him over the edge.

The screams of the operator's life-defying descent echoed through the chasm before ending in sudden silence.

Samson scoured the area with his visor and then climbed the landslip that had crushed the S.I.L.V.E.R. assassin. Removing a device from his armour, he ejected its spike and slammed it into the rock face. Moving back two hundred yards, he detonated it and a massive section of the ravine collapsed with an earth shattering roar. With the air filled with the mist of pulverised stone, Samson turned and moved back the way he'd come, satisfied with a job well done.

'No one's taking my command,' he said, wiping blood from his mask, 'no one.'

CHAPTER TWO

DEEP in the lower reaches of Sanctuary Proper, a river of glowing magma wound its way around the base of a subterranean mountain. Clouds of toxic steam drifted across its wide expanse, rock melted and the air itself burned as the scorching flow continued its unstoppable advance.

Close by this seething, oozing flood, scattered amongst the fiery pools of gas and flame, the remains of an all-terrain vehicle lay crushed and twisted. For so long this machine had provided those who utilised it with a vital lifeline in the dangerous depths of beyond, but now all that was left was a broken shell – the salvation it represented wilted and dead.

A large section of the mangled wreckage sank further into a molten tributary, its bright yellow carcass melting into a pool of liquid metal under the intense heat before disappearing beneath the silken surface. An instant later a jet of fire erupted into the air, propelling before it a cluster of sparks which travelled on an updraft into the dark. These floating sprites flared and died until only one remained. Up and up this lone wayfarer went, swirling past the jagged sides of the towering chasm and the giant peak at its centre.

Feet after thousands of feet swept by, while bridges and aqueducts crisscrossed the expanse in the dark. Nearing the mountainous summit, a steady gush of glowing lava spewed forth, sending waves of heat rushing up the cliff face to the three companions who struggled for survival on the precipice above. Finally, the single spark passed the lone man at the cliff's ragged edge, its light flickering out as it turned to a blackened carcass of ash.

Jason Reece gritted his teeth in agony. Someone screamed at him to pull and he leant back with all his might. The rope cut deeper into his lacerated hands and tears of anguish rolled down his cheeks. He inched back, but the weight below dragged him back to the edge. The pain increased and he held on. Seconds passed like hours before a despairing scream penetrated his mind and the pull on the rope halved. He stared down into the abyss, inches from death and saw the woman he loved fall burning into the darkness. Wracked with grief, Jason stood, transfixed in time, the streak of fire seared into his soul. Trish was gone and his world collapsed with her.

♦

Sarah Morgan reached out, grasped Jason's outstretched hand and was pulled to safety. Her burnt and blackened Deep Reach uniform smoked with residual heat. Her eyes stung with soot and tears. Burns covered her neck and hands, while her whole body cried out in exhaustion. But amongst all this, cutting through the pain like a razor, was the vision of her friend falling into the abyss below, her clothes and hair aflame.

All Sarah could hear was Trish's final heartbreaking words: *love you.*

'Love you,' Sarah murmured and opened her hand to look at the broken necklace nestled in the palm of her hand. It was the only piece of her friend she had left, torn from Trish's neck as she fell. The golden locket that remained on the chain glittered in the light from her helmet's torches.

Rough hands grabbed her shoulders and she gazed up into Jason's terrified eyes. He was shouting, but all she could hear was the ring of tinnitus.

He dragged her to her feet and shook her again. 'SARAH!'

Her hand closed around Trish's locket.

'Sarah, for fuck's sake snap out of it!' Jason slapped her round the face, shook her and slapped her again.

He went to strike her a third time, but she caught his wrist. The sensation of pain and loss sunk vicious talons into her heart and she slumped back to the ground in defeat.

Jason hauled her back up. He was shouting at her again, but what he was saying didn't make any sense. She shook her head, unable to make herself say the fateful words.

'Yes!' Jason dragged her away from the cliff edge. 'We need to hurry!'

Sarah let herself be pulled along before resisting. 'No! Jason, she's gone, Trish is ... gone!' She felt her legs go weak in realisation.

It was Jason's turn to shake his head. 'You're wrong, she's still alive!'

Fresh tears rolled down Sarah's face. 'I saw her fall.'

'So did I,' Jason said, frantic, 'but she hit the water, she fell into the aqueduct! We have to move. We have to find her!'

Brief hope disappeared to the crush of reality. 'Even if she did,' Sarah said, her speech robotic, 'it must be hundreds of feet down, the impact would have been like hitting concrete.'

Jason's expression grew angry. He grasped her arms, his fingers digging into bruised flesh. 'I'm not giving up on her!' He yanked Sarah forward through the darkness and into the pitch-black of a tunnel. And then they were running, and Sarah followed Jason in a daze.

The path leading to the Anakim transportation device that had been within reach vanished behind them, lost to the labyrinth of its foundations. The promised land of the surface was forgotten, the dream had gone and only nightmares remained.

CHAPTER THREE

SARAH RAN down into the dark. She didn't know where she was going. She didn't care. Jason was wrong, Trish was gone and nothing could bring her back.

The grey figure of Jason raced along in front of her, her visor keeping the never-ending black of Sanctuary at bay. But every stride she took ate away at her spirit; it felt like she was running through tar. The effort to keep going became overwhelming, the desperation of grief too much to bear. Sarah slowed and Jason disappeared into the gloom, his passage fuelled by the intense and deceptive silver tongue of hope.

Moments later, Sarah stumbled and fell sprawling to the ground. She lay there, unmoving, her breath rasping and shallow. It felt good to be still, to not worry; to not fear. *Just stay here*, a voice whispered in her mind. *There's nothing left for you, there's nothing left to fight for. Your place is here in the dark. The dark is safe; the dark is where you belong – the dark is your friend.*

'Sarah! Sarah, where are you?!'

The lights from Jason's helmet appeared around a corner.

The sensation of cold, wet stone pressing against her face made her roll over.

She groaned as Jason helped her to her feet.

'Are you hurt?'

'Go on without me,' she said, 'I'll only hold you back.'

'What are you talking about? We stick together. Come on, I've found the water.'

He helped her back into a jog, the movement jarring and abhorrent.

They rounded a series of bends and stopped as the path ended in a crumbling ruin. Water lapped at its lip, while further out a fast-flowing river powered from right to left.

'It heads out to the aqueduct, look.' Jason increased the power output from his helmet and focused the twin beams to highlight the start of the bridge of water that crossed the deep void below.

As Sarah wondered what he expected her to do, the torches on his helmet stuttered and went out. He cursed and banged the Deep Reach unit with the flat of his hand.

A memory from her SED training popped into her head. 'Switch to battery saving mode.' She leant forward as he fumbled with the buttons and flicked a concealed switch.

With his torchlight gone and only basic visor functions to guide him, Jason stepped into the shallows and held out his hand.

She mustered a sigh. 'What are you doing?'

'This river will take us to her.'

'You're afraid of water.' Sarah eyed the rapid torrent. Her visor displayed the temperature, two degrees Centigrade, thirty-five Fahrenheit; it was almost freezing. 'Jason,' – she grasped his hand and tried pulling him back – 'this is crazy.'

'She's alive, I know it.'

Sarah shook her head. She didn't know what else to say. *He's in denial*, she thought, *nothing I say will help.*

He tightened his grip and waded deeper and Sarah, too weary to offer much resistance, splashed into the water after him. Before she had time to think a wave knocked Jason from his feet, plunging them both into the rapids. Icy water swallowed her whole. Spun round, she resurfaced with a gasp. Jason bobbed up ten feet ahead as the two of them were carried out onto the aqueduct. Sarah's feet brushed the bottom of the bridge and she looked up to see the lava flow on the cliff that had claimed Trish's life.

A hand grasped her shoulder. 'Are you okay?!' Jason shouted over the rush of water.

She managed a nod as they were swept from the aqueduct and back into another tunnel.

Her lights and visor flickered as the freezing liquid fused its circuitry. The screen gave a final fuzz of pixels before flashing dead, thrusting her into total darkness.

'My helmet's failed!' she said, the terror of blindness intense.

'Mine's still working,' Jason said, 'hang on.'

'I can't see anything!'

'I won't let you go.'

Sarah clung to him, her fingers going numb with cold.

Their passage slowed as the water calmed and Sarah adjusted her vice-like grip. 'What can you see?'

'More tunnel.'

'What's that noise?'

A strange reverberating sound grew louder with each passing second and she felt Jason twist round to look.

'I don't know,' he said, 'my visor light's really dim.'

The river's flow picked up again and Jason swore.

Sarah tensed. 'What is it?'

'Waterfall,' he said, his voice full of fear.

Sarah felt panic swell within her. The voice had been wrong, the darkness wasn't her friend – it was her enemy!

Jason wrapped his arms around her as the thunderous sound engulfed them. 'HOLD ON!'

Sarah took a deep breath and went weightless as they were washed over the top of the waterfall. Seconds later they plunged into frothing darkness. Torn from Jason's grasp, Sarah's helmet clonked against hard rock and pain exploded in her back. Tumbling over and over, she was tossed round the seething cauldron like a rag doll. Lungs bursting, the submersion continued and the terror of death seized her. Moments later she surfaced and gasped for air as she flailed in the water.

'Jason!'

Swept onwards through the black, she heard no reply. 'Jason!!'

A faint shout came from far ahead. She tried to swim, but the sodden arms of her coveralls made it impossible. Concentrating on keeping her head above water, she called out again and this time Jason's answer sounded closer.

A wave caught her in the face. 'Where are you!' she said, spitting out water.

'Sarah, over here, this way!'

Sarah turned her head in the dark, trying to get a fix on his voice. More water covered her head and she went under. The sound of water filled her ears before she bobbed back to the surface.

'Sarah, I'm here, keep going!'

A hand grabbed her collar and she was pulled sideways into calmer waters.

'Put your feet down,' Jason said.

Coughing and spluttering, she did as instructed and found the bottom with her feet. She stood up, waist deep in water, and clung to Jason in desperate relief.

'There's a path,' he said, 'take my hand.'

Reluctant to let him go, Sarah hung on until she felt his hand grip hers.

Splashing forward, she was led into the shallows.

'Stay here,' – Jason prised away her hand – 'I've got to climb up.'

She grasped his arm. 'Don't leave me!' she said, pulling him back.

He touched her cheek. 'I'll be right here, I promise. Just don't move.'

Reluctantly, she let him go while the noise of the river continued to thunder past behind. Blind and freezing cold, she stood shivering in the dark, her arms hugged tight to her chest.

'Okay,' Jason said, his voice coming from just above, 'reach out and you'll feel a wall.'

Sarah put out a tentative hand and felt hard, crumbling sediment.

Something touched her arm and she yelped.

'It's okay,' he said, 'it's me. Hold out your hands and I'll pull you up. It's about six foot high.'

Sarah raised her arms and felt Jason's hands grasp hers.

'You ready?' he said.

Sarah said, 'Yes,' and was lifted from the ground.

When she was back standing by his side, she felt around for another wall to guide her, but found nothing.

'Wait!' Jason grabbed her. 'There's a sheer drop two feet away. We're on a raised walkway. The river on one side, nothing on the other, okay? I'm going to clip you to my harness. *Don't* move.'

Sarah heard the clink of climbing gear as Jason secured her to him.

'Right,' he said, and gave the short piece of rope between them a quick tug, 'where you go, I go. If you fall left, shout "*left*!" and I'll jump right and stop us both going over. Now the ground on the right also drops away, so if you fall right, shout "*right*!" and I'll jump left, okay?'

Sarah nodded. 'Okay.'

'And if I fall, I'll do the same and you jump the opposite way to my call, agreed?'

'Agreed.'

'Good – okay, the river carries on, but I can see more waterfalls ahead as this place opens out into a big chamber. The path's quite narrow so we're going to have to take it slow. Hold onto my harness with one hand and keep your arm extended, otherwise we'll get too close and you'll trip me up. Understood?'

'Yes,' she said, her teeth chattering.

'We're lucky; the air in this chamber's warm,' – he rubbed her arms vigorously – 'which means the sooner we get to safe ground, the sooner we can dry out and move on. If Trish was unconscious she'll have been swept downstream. Let's get moving.'

Sarah reached out and felt for his harness. Securing her hold, they moved out in single file. In the lead was the man who couldn't see the truth – and behind – the woman who just couldn't see. It was the delusional leading the blind, and both chased the dead.

CHAPTER FOUR

SARAH CLUNG to the back of Jason's climbing harness with an outstretched hand. Soaked to the bone, she trudged along one step at a time, led onwards by Jason, the two of them on a hiding to nothing. Her mind wandered as the noise of the cascading waters below echoed through the chamber around them. Three times she'd almost slipped from the edge, but due to their slow pace she'd managed to cling on and avoid taking the desperate action Jason had envisaged should one of them fall.

The thought of jumping into mid-air was bad enough, but to jump headlong into darkness sent fear coursing through her veins. She knew the rope that bound them together would prevent her from falling to her death, but it didn't make the idea any less daunting. Jason could falter at any moment and she'd have to react immediately or be pulled over the edge with him.

Step by step she felt the pressure increase, the wait for the inevitable almost unbearable. Some would say the darkness was preferable as you wouldn't be able to see the deadly drop below. Sarah, however, didn't need to see the hidden danger; she knew it was there and that was enough. Memories of past excursions – and of sanctuary itself – terrorised her mind, hinting at what would happen if she made a mistake, a fatal error of judgement that would kill them both.

Time passed and Sarah's fears remained until the path ended, bringing them out onto a flat plain that Jason said followed the river, which continued into the distance. Taking a quick time out, they shed their Deep Reach climbing gear, jackets, coveralls and underwear and squeezed out the water as best they could. Sarah also removed her Deep Reach helmet and shook out the liquid that remained inside while Jason decided not to risk disturbing his in case it ended in disastrous results; if they were both blind they were truly lost. After rubbing themselves down with handfuls of dusty soil from close by, they pulled on damp clothing and struggled back into their harnesses, Sarah operating by feel alone while Jason utilised the dim visor on his helmet.

With the river close by, they drank their fill and then moved on.

Sticking close to the fast-flowing waters, Jason scoured the landscape looking for signs of Trish. At first Sarah had held onto his hand, but as they continued she let go, trusting in his unwavering guidance and the rope that linked them together.

Hours later, Sarah's energy reserves finally gave up the ghost and she pulled on the rope to halt Jason's advance.

'I need to rest,' she said.

She'd been expecting him to argue, but he mumbled in agreement and they moved away from the river and lay down on the ground in exhausted silence. Sleep came easily, whisking the two friends off into the mystical realm of unthinking thought. The day had been long, but the night had only just begun.

♦

Sarah's exhaustion led her into the deepest of sleeps, the halls of darkness as unfathomable as the history of Sanctuary itself. Down and down she fell, tumbling into the abyss of nothing. Time vanished, giving way to a heady swirl of lights that drifted through an ocean of loss. A voice whispered to her and Sarah moaned in her sleep.

The Anakim orb, tucked away in a pocket on the leg of her coveralls, throbbed in the dark. Its corrugated surface shifted and turned smooth. A pulse of light shone within, its power glowing through the red cloth that held it prisoner against its will. Sarah whimpered in her sleep, fighting against the demons of her mind's own making. A roar of sound flashed through her eyes and she woke with a start. Still lying on her side, she looked down to see the orb resting on the ground next to her leg. It continued to glow with an eerie light and Sarah wondered how it came to be where it was. Had Jason removed it from its place of safekeeping? She looked up to see her companion gone. Heart racing, she sat up. 'Jason?' she said, turning round to gaze into the darkness. 'Jason?!'

There was no answer. *Has he gone and left me? Is his desire to find Trish so great he would leave me all alone in the pitch-black?* She picked up the orb, which felt light in her hand. 'At least I have you to keep me company;' she muttered, 'at least I have light.'

The orb's glow brightened in response; it was if it could hear and understand. Sarah held it aloft to light her way.

'Jason!' She took a few more steps and called again. 'Jason!!'

She listened. There was still no reply.

Attempting to quell the panic within, she tried to think. If he didn't return she needed to do something. *I could go to the temple and wait for him there.* She touched her chest where the pendant dangled. *And if he never returns I can try and get to the surface using the transportation device.* She wandered through the dark, continuing to call Jason's name.

What seemed like days came and went, and she slept twice more and each time she woke the orb was waiting for her, its light a blessed oasis in the dark.

Deciding the moment had come; she drank from the river one last time and made her way back to the temple. All the while the

Anakim orb remained bright, lighting her passage through dark chambers.

When Sarah finally found her way back to the place where Trish had fallen, she felt a deep sense of despair. Trish and Jason had left, each by their own choosing. Never had she felt so alone, so lost.

Leaving the scene of torment behind, she climbed stone steps and worked her way to the centre of the temple's ancient complex.

'I thought I'd find you here,' a voice said out of the dark.

Sarah's heart constricted in fear and she held the orb higher to reveal a shadowy figure standing before the transportation device.

'Jason?' she said, knowing the voice wasn't his.

The shadow turned and Sarah felt her world lurch sideways.

'You were just going to give up and leave me?' Trish said, walking out of the gloom. 'And now you're leaving Jason, too?'

Sarah stumbled back, the vision of her friend warping the reality around her. 'You died, you're not real!'

Trish strode forward and grasped Sarah's face. 'Not real! You left me to die. You brought me down here to die! And you knew what would happen. You knew, and did nothing!'

Sarah tried to shake her head. 'I didn't know ... how could I know?!'

Trish's hands grew hot and her eyes shone bright. 'You dreamt of fire and smoke. You were tormented by dreams. But it wasn't your mother who burned, it was me! You could have saved me,' – wisps of smoke poured out from Trish's hair – 'you could have saved us all, but you chose to be selfish, you chose to risk our lives for your own gain.' Fire ignited to consume Trish's torso; the tongues of flame licking at Sarah's horrified face.

'You caused your mother's death,' Trish said, 'and now you've killed me and Jason, too!'

Sarah tried to break free of the inferno that held her, but the fire had taken hold. Pain seared her skin and dark smoke choked her lungs.

'You're a selfish bitch, Sarah,' Trish said, her eyes filling Sarah's mind, 'A SELFISH FUCKING BITCH!!'

Sarah let out a squeal of terror and sat up, her head reeling. Darkness surrounded her and she put out a hand and felt Jason lying a foot away.

Relief flooded though her.

She hung her head and wiped a tear from her face before reaching out to touch him again. Reassured he was real and that she was actually awake this time, the reality of her situation returned to crush her like an anvil. *How has it come to this?* She looked back over her life wondering what she'd done wrong to deserve such torment. Events that had seemed major at the time offered up little in the way of explanation. *I've never been an evil person. I've never intentionally gone out of my way to hurt anyone. So how has this come to pass? Is it just fate? Is it my destiny to suffer?* The memory of her mother's death reared its ugly head and she knew that's when it had all started to go wrong. *That was my fault. I deserve everything I get. But how do I make amends?* she asked herself. *Do I need to die? Do I need to sacrifice my life to redress the balance?*

Fearing more dark dreams, she decided to stay awake while her questions continued without answer. Jason murmured in his sleep and Sarah wondered if he was having a nightmare too. She pulled her legs up to her chest and remained that way until he woke some time later.

The mood was as dark as their surroundings as they set out once more. Jason, still refusing to accept their loss, kept scanning the river and Sarah walked in silence by his side. *Is there no end to the darkness?* she thought. She removed her helmet and tried turning it on. The visor glowed to life before dying to black a moment later. She switched it to battery saving mode, also to no avail. And so she remained – entrenched in the bleak pit with only the faintest of illuminations escaping from Jason's visor to light her way.

The sound of white water drifted up from the depths, its urgency growing louder with each passing moment and Jason halted their progress.

'Another waterfall?' Sarah said.

'Yes.' He sounded weary. 'There's no way down.'

'Perhaps we missed her; perhaps ... she survived and is wandering around lost behind us.' Sarah didn't believe a word of it, but it was all she could think of to say, and even that was an effort.

'No,' he said, 'the current is too strong and you said her arm was broken, she wouldn't have been able to swim to shore.' Jason's voice broke. 'I don't know what to do.'

Sarah found his hand in the dark and squeezed it. 'I should never have brought us here. Neither of you deserved this. Trish didn't deserve to die, it should have been me.'

Jason snatched his hand away. 'She's still alive.'

'She said she loved me,' Sarah said, holding back tears, 'she was my best friend and I failed her. She died because of me.'

'She's not dead.'

Sarah didn't have the energy to keep up the façade any longer. A sob escaped her lips and tears flowed. 'It's all my fault. I killed her. I killed Trish and I've killed you, too!'

Jason shook her. 'She's not dead, do you hear me?!'

Sarah was crying now, 'I killed my mother. I deserve to die, I have to die. I want to die!'

'I said, she's not dead!!'

Jason pushed her away and Sarah felt the rope that tied them go slack. She reached out her hand but her fingers closed on nothing. 'Jason,' she said, 'Jason?!'

He didn't reply.

'Jason!!' she crumpled to the ground, sobbing, her hands searching in the dark. 'Jason, I'm sorry, don't leave me!'

Her stricken voice echoed around the cavernous chamber, but Jason still didn't respond. He'd left her, and it was what she deserved.

The noise of the gushing waters grew louder, filling her mind. Still crying, Sarah found the edge of the abyss and knew what she had to do. Standing up on wobbly legs, she took a deep breath and stepped out into nothing.

CHAPTER FIVE

SARAH TOPPLED FORWARD into the welcoming arms of death – then something yanked her back. Propelled into reverse, she crumpled to the ground in a heap.

Jason pulled her into a sitting position. 'What the hell are you doing?!'

Sarah shook her head in despair, her sobs renewed.

Jason wrapped her in his arms. 'I'm sorry,' he said, stroking the back of her head as she clung to him, 'I'm so sorry.'

They stayed that way for some time. Jason offering soothing words while Sarah cried herself out.

'Do you know why I follow you?' Jason said, breaking the silence.

Sarah wiped her eyes. 'What?'

'Do you know why you lead and I follow?'

Sarah shook her head.

'Because you have passion, a goal – a goal better than any I can find myself.'

Sarah sniffed. 'My goals get people killed.'

'And yet without them my life has less meaning, without you it has less meaning. Some things are worth dying for, Sarah, and purpose is one of them. You know what you want and go for it. It's what I admire most about you.'

'I thought that was my bum.'

Jason managed a laugh. 'That, too, but don't let Trish hear me say that.'

Sarah's mirth died at the mention of her friend.

'One thing is for certain,' Jason said, 'you don't deserve to die.'

Sarah felt tears well again. 'You would say that; you're a nice person, a strong person.'

'Am I? Do you know how I used to think when I was young? I wasn't strong; I grew up a coward, my thoughts twisted by the fear of physical threats. I started having evil thoughts about the bullies that surrounded me and those thoughts took root and spread and caused me to wish bad things on others, others I loved. I became a pathetic shell. But you know what? I saw what I'd become and knew that wasn't me. I decided I wasn't going to live like that, I wasn't going to let that be who I was. I'd rather have died.'

He paused for breath before continuing. 'I know how you feel when things get too much. You think you might as well give in, end it all, but that's not what life is about. If you give in to death, the dark, you're only giving in to those people who put that darkness in you, to those bullies and bastards who don't deserve to take your light – *our* light. You didn't kill your mother, the people who set the fire did, the people who stole your maps. They're probably enjoying life right now. Is that fair? Hell no! What are you going to do about it? Look at yourself, Sarah, and know this is not you. Do you hear me? This is not you.'

Sarah nodded.

'You don't deserve to die,' he said again, 'and Trish needs us, needs both of us, needs you. Do you know what I said to myself when I realised what I'd become, when I reached my lowest ebb, when I thought about ending it all?'

'No,' Sarah said.

'I said, "I'm not living my life like this, other people do not make me who I am, I make me who I am, ME!"' He held her hand and placed it against her heart. 'You! You decide who you are and if you don't like what you are, you damn well fight back. Never give in, as at the end of the day, when there's nothing else left, that's all we have, that's who we are.'

Sarah stayed silent, thinking about his words and the power they promised.

'And do you know what else?' he said after a while. 'I'm not giving up on you, even if you have. The same as I'm not giving up on Trish. Now get up,' – he hauled her to her feet – 'and let's keep moving. I think I can see a way down.'

◆

Some hours later, they'd made it down to the base of the falls using a honeycomb of sloping tunnels that criss-crossed the wall of the chamber through which they travelled. After they'd taken on some more water, the two friends carried on a while longer before stopping to rest. Sarah slumped down and then lay back on the hard ground, not speaking, just listening to the distant roar of the waterfall.

Thankfully Jason's visor had remained working, which not only enabled them to stay alive for a little longer, but also let him continue his search for Trish.

Now that they'd stopped he turned the power off to prolong the life of his helmet's depleted battery pack. With all light extinguished the darkness was truly complete. Newer to this sensory deprivation than Sarah, Jason came up with a novel suggestion to combat it – although considering her recent nightmare, Sarah knew she should have thought of the idea herself. There were two problems, however.

'What do you mean?' Jason said, turning his visor back on again. 'You can't or you won't?'

'Won't.'

'Why not?'

'Because of all of this.' Sarah gestured around her. 'Everything that's happened is because of me and because of this.' She held out her pendant. 'I won't use it again ... ever.'

'What happened isn't that thing's fault, it isn't your fault either, it's no one's fault.'

'It made Trish ... fall.'

'That was the rope, or that light chasing us, it wasn't the pendant.'

'Wasn't it? As soon as we activated the bridge that light appeared. It must be attracted to Anakim technology, like we thought.'

'If you won't use it, how are we going to get to the surface?'

'You can use it.' She unclipped the metal artefact from her neck chain and held it out in his direction. 'In fact,' she said, 'you can have it, it's yours. I wish I'd never found it.'

'What?' Jason sounded shocked. 'You're serious?'

Sarah remained silent in her conviction and he didn't pursue the matter further, perhaps due to her determined expression.

'Shall we try it, then?' he said, taking possession of the pendant. 'If my helmet goes completely we'll need it.'

An inner voice of warning made her hesitate.

'It might be Anakim,' he said, 'but the light didn't turn up when you turned it on last time.'

He was right, it hadn't, and Sarah was well past caring. She withdrew the Anakim orb from the safety of her coveralls and placed it on the ground between them.

Only able to see the tiniest glow from Jason's visor, Sarah heard the rustle of clothing, but nothing happened.

'Are you touching it?' she said.

'Yes.'

'Then why isn't it lighting up like before?'

'I don't know.'

'Are you doing anything differently?'

'I don't think so.'

'Try one of the parchments.' Sarah passed him one of the ancient documents.

He tried a second time and again nothing happened. 'Perhaps it's because I'm tired.

'I don't think so,' she said. 'It should still work, it would just make you even more tired.'

'Then I'm doing something different.'

Relieved to have something else to occupy her mind, Sarah thought back to when she'd activated the orb before. A thought struck her. 'Have you got any more of those stones?'

Sarah heard the slap of skin hitting skin.

'I'm such an idiot,' he said.

More rustles of clothing followed and then a bright blue glow appeared.

Jason held out the crystalline brick he'd unearthed before they'd been chased by the dreaded light. 'We don't need the orb at all. We have this.'

The crystalline stone shimmered in the dark like a magical cerulean pearl, its light bright enough to see by.

Savouring the renewal of sight, Sarah gave Jason a tired smile, but rather than return to thinking about their situation, she took the opportunity to study Trish's locket.

'She always wore this,' Sarah said, holding it under the crystal's illumination, 'and I've never seen inside it, not in all the years I've known her.'

'She always *wears* it,' Jason said. 'Not wore, *wears*.'

Sarah nodded and clicked back the catch and opened it up. Inside was space for two oval photos. The photo on the left was faded and old. But Sarah recognised the two people framed within it. One was Trish and the other was Sarah herself. It was taken back when they'd first met at uni so they were both a lot younger, fresh-eyed and smiling. Sarah wiped a tear from her eye. The other photo confused her. It was the image of Christ on the cross.

She showed it to Jason. 'Do you know why she has this in there?'

He shrugged.

'She's not religious,' Sarah said. 'I've never seen a cross at her home and she never talks about going to church or anything like that.'

'Perhaps that's because she knows how you feel about the Vatican.'

'With good reason, they helped cover up the Anakim's existence for millennia. They killed to protect their doctrine, destroyed priceless artefacts, stole ours ...'

'You don't have to tell me.'

She frowned. 'I don't understand. She knows what they stand for, what they've done and yet she still carries around their symbol.'

'Everyone needs faith in something,' Jason said, 'some more than others. Does it matter?'

'It matters to me.' Sarah felt betrayed by her friend's secret perversion. It was like there was a whole other side to her she'd never known. She stared at the locket and then realised something was underneath the photo of the Redeemer. She prised the photo out and something clinked to the ground. Sarah picked up a golden cross to hold in the palm of her hand. It glinted under the blue glow of Jason's rock, but the sight of it served to reinforce the sense that her best friend had not been what she seemed. How many times had she spoken to Trish about the church, of how she loathed its power and influence over history? Until recently Sarah had believed they'd been solely responsible for her mother's murder, too, although as things turned out they were now no longer the only organisation under suspicion.

She passed the cross to Jason, her thoughts melancholy, but as she placed it in his hand she saw the rent in his glove and the congealed blood beneath. She grasped his wrist to inspect the wound. 'This is bad.' She leant forward and looked at his other hand. 'If you don't get these seen to they'll go septic.'

He touched her neck. 'Your burns need treatment, too.'

'We're both right, but without supplies there's nothing we can do.'

Jason mumbled his agreement, his attention turning back to Trish's cross. 'I always thought,' he said, stroking the metal surface with a finger, 'if God created us, the universe, everything, he did it so he wouldn't be alone. It must be very lonely to be omnipotent, don't you think? If I was omnipotent I'd make a universe so complex that it could produce things I couldn't even imagine.' He smiled a curious smile and handed it back to her.

Sarah stared at him for a moment and then returned the cross to its home and snapped the locket closed. She held it out to him.

He shook his head. 'You can give it to her when we find her.' He stood up and held out his hand. 'I know you still think otherwise, but she's alive. I can feel it. I will search for her, and I *will* find her.'

Sarah grasped his wrist to be pulled to her feet. 'How can you be so sure?'

'I believed in you; now it's your turn to believe in me.'

Sarah picked up her helmet, pulled on her gloves and re-pocketed the orb and locket. Jason collected his stone and adjusted his visor.

'You're going to use it as a torch?' she said, looking at the glowing rock in his other hand.

'No,' he passed it to her, 'you are. I have my visor.'

She accepted the stone and held it higher to help light the ground ahead. It didn't produce much of a beam, but it was better than nothing.

'You can also have this back.' He held out the pendant to her.

'I told you, I don't want it.'

'Just keep it safe for me.'

Sarah couldn't be bothered to argue, so fixed the pendant back onto her chain alongside its smaller sibling.

All set, they moved out once more, friendship renewed and situation slightly improved. *All we need now*, Sarah thought, *is divine intervention and we might just last a few more days*. As it was there was little left in the way of hope, for her, anyway. Jason seemed convinced of a miracle, but she knew it would take nothing short of a resurrection to turn things around, and as far as she understood it such things were in short supply, even for believers. She was just pleased to be alive for a few more days, to be able to keep Jason company, and then, when all was said and done, she could rest. The thought was a comforting one. She was tired, bone tired, but most of all she just didn't want to fear anymore. Sarah linked arms with Jason and they carried on into Sanctuary's black vaults, searching for the elusive that might never come.

CHAPTER SIX

A LOUD EXPLOSION sent a grappling spear and attached nano-cable arcing out across the mile wide chasm. Seconds later the titanium tip bit deep into the ancient Anakim building that had been targeted for impact. Large chunks of masonry fell into the abyss below before a smaller charge ignited, sending three bolts drilling further into the stone façade, securing the anchor in place.

The cable pulled taut and Samson gave the nod to three of his men, who edged out in single file onto the nano- rope's narrow surface utilising wire tethers and specialised equipment attached to their feet, like some kind of human-powered monorail. Far below the faint glow of orange lava revealed the immense depth of the mighty expanse that blocked the way ahead.

Twenty feet away Riley Orton, in sombre mood and with Locke and Jefferson for company, watched the scene unfold through his Deep Reach helmet's visor.

'No regard,' Locke muttered.

'Sir?' Riley looked to his superior.

'They have no regard for Sanctuary,' Locke said, 'none. That's priceless architecture they're destroying, it can never be remade.'

With a final shake of the head, Dresden Locke turned and walked away.

'He's taking this hard,' Riley said.

'He cares as much about Sanctuary as he does about the SED itself,' Jefferson said, 'maybe more.'

Riley returned his attention to Samson's men, who'd made it past halfway, the equipment they pulled behind dragged along using a clever configuration of wheels and pulleys.

As the possibility of crossing the divide and the reality of closing in on Sarah loomed ever closer, Riley's concern for his one-time lover grew in combination. He knew she had to be found, the orders from on high were unequivocal, but he also knew he couldn't see her locked away for the rest of her days. The thought of someone with such a passion for life being confined behind bars made his skin crawl. He could imagine what he'd feel if the same happened to him. There's no way I could live like that, year after year with no hope of salvation, I'd rather be dead. And if Sarah felt the same way – and I know her well enough to know she would – after failing to escape her prison she'd resort to the only thing that was still in her control, the taking of her own life. I wouldn't wish such a bleak outlook on my worst enemy. To exist for the sake of living was not life. And yet what can I do to help her? She has nowhere to go. And if she resists, which she will, they'll kill her to retrieve what she has.

When he'd shared such thoughts with Jefferson, the Deep Reach archaeologist had counselled distraction. 'Try not to think about it,' he'd said, 'Sarah has made her bed, there's nothing you can do, there's nothing anyone can do to save her now, except maybe Sarah herself.'

Back in the now Riley broached the subject again. 'I can't let them take her, Jeff.'

Jefferson put his hand on Riley's shoulder in a gesture of comfort and shared understanding.

'When the time comes,' Riley said, 'can I count on your help?'

'Ri, I'll always back you, you know that, but don't do anything stupid. These people won't think twice about taking out anyone in their way, be that Terra Force or Silver. For us, they're one and the same.'

'I have to do something.'

'We'll figure it out when they get her back to base. In a few years things will have calmed down, she might get parole with good behaviour. She'll never be allowed back in the SED, but she'll be alive, and that's better than the alternative, isn't it?'

Riley grimaced, Jefferson knew as well as he did that Sarah wouldn't make it out of the military prison for a third time. And Sarah had said it herself, '*They'll lock me up and chuck away the key this time. Three strikes – I'm out.*'

'And besides,' Jefferson said, continuing his ineffective pep talk, 'they haven't found her yet; she might make it out of Sanctuary. God knows how, but in the short time I've known her, if anyone can find a way, it's her.'

Riley remained silent, deep in contemplation, while in the distance Samson's men neared the far side of the enormous chasm.

'It's a goddamn witch-hunt,' Riley said, growing angry. He looked behind at the formidable array of armoured troops on display. 'She doesn't stand a chance.'

A distant shout brought his focus back to the chasm. Zooming in with his visor, Riley saw the Anakim building breaking apart, and the three men who'd been sent across screamed as they were consumed by the falling mass that carried them into oblivion.

The cable spanning the colossal void stretched tight, dragged down by the massive weight of the structure that had torn loose on the opposite side.

'It's gonna go!' someone shouted.

Shrieking in protest, the sound of failing metal ended as the cable snapped.

Jefferson knocked Riley sprawling to the floor as the severed cable tore past to decapitate those standing behind.

More screams filled the air and chaos reigned as people ran here and there trying to administer medical assistance to the injured few who'd survived the disaster.

Riley got to his feet and gazed at the carnage before him. Along with those that had lost their heads, some soldiers had been cut clean in two; the grisly sight was not for the faint of heart.

Through the carnage – parting a sea of Special Forces soldiers like Moses himself – strode the tall figure of Ophion Nexus, with Zhang Bai and nine other S.I.L.V.E.R. operatives in close attendance.

♦

Samson cursed his luck. Suppressing an urge to lash out, he instructed the team in charge of the mortar canon to reload another grapple and to secure another cable. Busy with restoring order, he'd failed to see the S.I.L.V.E.R. operatives that had crept up behind him like the cowards they were.

'What do you want?' Samson said, in no mood for games.

Zhang's hand went to the hilt of her sword.

Ophion held out his arm to stay his companion's intent and raised his visor. 'It is said you were one of the last people to see Tien Bai alive.'

'Who?'

'My sister!' Zhang said, between clenched teeth.

Samson remained cool. 'I heard there was a collapse at the transmission station.'

Zhang's eyes narrowed to slits, her blade sliding from its sheath with a sibilant hiss.

Ophion turned his head a fraction in her direction and said something in Chinese, his tone angry.

Samson laughed and in the blink of an eye the point of Zhang's sword hovered a fraction from his throat, the hand that grasped it shaking with rage.

Samson didn't flinch. Around them fifty commandos, witnessing the exchange, trained their weapons on the assassins, the sound of mechanical actions being readied producing a muted yet threatening cacophony of noise.

'I'm ready to die, Nexus,' Samson said, leaning onto the blade to draw a spot of blood, 'are you?'

Ophion moved forward to whisper something in Zhang's ear.

The woman slammed her sword back into its scabbard and let loose with a string of curses aimed at Samson, before stalking away in fury.

'Do you find it convenient our communications are down?' Ophion said, after Zhang had gone.

Samson considered the man before him. He didn't doubt he could kill him if he had to, but he was liable to get injured in the process and he could ill afford such a hindrance if he was to secure the Committee's precious pendant.

'Sanctuary is a dangerous place,' Samson said, 'landslips happen all the time down here.'

'Our scans showed traces of explosives at the scene.'

'Did they?'

'And the back-up receiver has mysteriously disappeared.'

Samson didn't care what they thought, they couldn't touch him and they knew it, not with the thousands of soldiers at his back.

Ophion stepped alongside him and lowered his voice. 'Don't go anywhere alone, Colonel.'

'Threaten me again,' Samson said as Ophion walked away, 'and I'll chop your fucking head off.'

Ophion paused to glance back over his shoulder. 'Advice is not a threat, nor is the fact that you won't make it out of Sanctuary alive.'

S.I.L.V.E.R.'s leader strode away leaving Samson fighting the temptation to shoot him dead. *Why shouldn't I?* he asked himself. *Nexus would be the first to attack from behind. Assassins are born cowards. Just do it.* Samson reached for his replacement rifle, which was attached to his armour's back-plate.

'Colonel,' an engineer said, breaking Samson's preoccupation.

Ophion drifted out of sight and the chance had gone. *Why not give the order to kill them?* Samson thought. *Thousands against twelve.*

He liked those odds. He'd heard the stories, though, much like anyone else who'd served for long enough. S.I.L.V.E.R. never went down without a fight. At least one of them would be carrying enough explosive to collapse two square miles, so even in defeat they made sure their job was completed; either that or retribution was served. Samson's anger rose. *They lack honour as well as courage.*

'Colonel,' the man said again, 'the mortar's ready to go.'

'Then what are you waiting for?'

'This is the third attempt. From our visual scans and the previous failures, we believe the target zone is too unstable to withstand the impact and sustain the weight of the cable.'

Samson focused on the man before him. 'And?'

'We also think a third strike might bring down the whole structure. It's too risky.'

'Alternatives?'

'We could go over one at a time.'

'How long would it take?'

'A few days, considering all the supplies we'd need.'

Samson shook his head. 'Unacceptable. What else?'

The man swallowed. 'There are no other options. It's the only place in range with access to the next chamber.'

'You're saying give up and go back?'

'We can't see any—'

'Fire the damn mortar.'

'Yes, Colonel.'

The man saluted and hurried away while Samson stood by, waiting.

Soon after, an explosion thundered out and another spear soared out into the dark to punch home into the Anakim building over a mile away. The massive winch whirred into reverse, bringing the nano-fabricated cable taut, and the engineer gave the all-clear.

Samson frowned and summoned one of his Terra Force captains.

'Sir?' the man said.

'What's the hold up? Why aren't our men ready to cross?'

'Word is the anchor's not stable; no one wants to go over.'

'Want? This is the U.S. Army; there is no want, only do.'

'Yes, sir, but the engineers are predicting the same result. We've already lost many men,' he indicated the mounting body bags from the most recent incident, 'morale is low – would it not be wiser to try an alternate route?'

'So you're the hold up?'

'No, sir.'

Samson glared at him.

'Yes, sir, but—'

Samson pushed the man aside and moved to the nano-cable. He gestured to an engineer. 'Hook me up.'

The man bobbed his head and clipped a small line from the large cable onto the inbuilt harness of Samson's armour and the exoskeleton within. Giving the connection a couple of yanks to ensure it was secure, the engineer then handed Samson two attachments for his boots. 'These will allow you to walk on the cable; each step you take will slide your foot forward on either side. If you need to unhook, just use your visor control system.' He stepped back to allow the colonel to mount the thick, wire rope.

Samson clipped his boot adapters onto the cable and gave the signal to load up the equipment behind.

A multi-wheeled rail rolled forward and another two lines secured him to the rolling stock. Samson braced himself against the resistance.

'Colonel,' the chief engineer said, moving to his side, 'the equipment sled is designed to be pulled by two people, preferably three.'

Samson leaned lower and grasped the cable. 'Release the brakes.'

The man's expression was dubious, but he nodded and gave the signal. Samson leant into the harness, tensed his stomach and gave a mighty heave with his arms, while forcing his legs straight. The sled inched forward and Samson repeated the process and, like a strong man completing a truck pull, he dragged the weight behind him slowly gaining momentum. By the time he was halfway across, he was labouring. Sucking in air and expelling it in a cycle of pain, he grimaced and used his visor to redirect power into the exoskeleton to help him continue. Minutes felt like hours and he gritted his teeth. *I will not fail. I will not fail! I WILL NOT FAIL!!* A picture of Ophion's face appeared in his mind, fuelling his anger and propelling him on.

More agonising moments passed before the crumbling architecture of the Anakim monument came into view.

Loose sediment fell from around the cable's anchor point and the engineer spoke through Samson's helmet speakers. 'Colonel, it's holding, but the closer you get, the greater the shear factor. The load is reduced, as there's one man instead of three, but you need to act fast.'

A crack appeared in the building's stone façade and every step closer increased its size. Warning symbols danced across Samson's visor and he slowed to a stop, his chest heaving.

'Sir,' the engineer said, 'you need to move ... NOW!'

The cable shuddered and a web of smaller cracks spread out from the first. Samson stood up, detached his safety cord and secured a winch line from his armour to the cable.

'What are you doing?!' the engineer said.

Another shudder set the cable rocking; Samson clipped another winch line to the sled and redirected all the power from his armour into the exoskeleton. A loud rumble swept over him and the rock face gave way with a tremendous groan. With nowhere else to go, Samson powered forward into falling chaos.

CHAPTER SEVEN

ALONGSIDE DRESDEN LOCKE and Jefferson Church, Riley Orton watched Samson's distant form disappear in a cloud of debris. 'The man's insane,' he murmured with a shake of the head.

Locke huffed. 'Don't say that to his face.'

'No chance of that happening,' – Jefferson adjusted his visor's settings – 'he's a goner.'

Riley spotted movement in the haze. 'I wouldn't be so sure of that.'

♦

Stones clattered off Colonel Samson's armour as he fired a grappling hook into the Anakim structure and leapt from the sinking cable and onto falling rock. As he plunged down, his line snapped taut and he swung out into nothing before dropping down onto dusty ground. He rolled to a stop and activated his radio. 'Release the clamps!'

On the other side of the chasm the engineer pressed a button and the freefalling equipment separated from the cable. Leaping up, Samson wrapped the screaming winch lines around a massive pillar and braced for impact.

'Colonel,' the engineer said, 'the weight's too great, you'll be dragged over the edge!'

Samson ignored him and activated his amour's anchor protocol. Ten high tensile cables lanced out into the ground, locking him in place. The two winches reached maximum extension, halting the sled and cable's downward plummet, and yanking Samson backwards as the cables extended from his armour to dampen the sudden weight from below. Pain tore through his body as he was spread-eagled by the intense load, his every fibre and sinew stretched to breaking point. Like a pendulum, the equipment sled cut an arc through the air to smash through the wall of the Anakim building six storeys down. Released from half his burden, Samson detached a winch line using his visor and secured the second that held aloft the cable spanning the chasm.

With his muscles on fire from his brush with dismemberment, Samson worked his way down to the sled and unpacked the kit it had been transporting. Using the inbuilt manual, Samson set the system up while accounting for the increased gradient. A mile away, the chief engineer let out some of the giant nano-cable and prepared the mechanisms on their side.

'The cable's reattached,' Samson said and pulled down a red lever on the platform he'd erected. Twenty pneumatic screws whirred into motion, burrowing down into the bedrock beneath. A red light atop each screw switched to green and the main cable pulled tight. 'Land-locks deployed and secure.'

'Stand back, Colonel,' the engineer said, and gave the signal to his men to start the turbine. 'Cannons firing in three – two – one ... fire.'

Two thunderous blasts sent two rockets powering into the air, and behind them wires unfurled to drag a large, rectangular prism across the cable. The oblong device sped over the chasm, pulled along by the rockets. As it moved it deployed a flat platform in its wake, decreasing in size until the rockets fell away. This strange contraption continued to hurtle along the cable, reducing in size to a cube, before it slammed into the buffers on Samson's side, then rebounded back the way it had come, its momentum undiminished. As it shot back across the divide, two sets of interwoven cables created sides to the newly formed base, and by the time it returned to its starting point, its function completed, the device had reduced to nothing.

Samson stepped onto the bridge they'd just created and gave the signal for the crossing to begin. A hundred commandos at a time made the trip across and after a thousand had passed over, a convoy of all-terrain vehicles followed, their snake-like yellow hides trundling along with the supplies that fed and watered the six thousand strong host. SED personnel came next, with the Deep Reach teams at their head, and close behind them followed Ophion and his S.I.L.V.E.R. mercenaries.

'Time for dead weight to earn its pay,' Samson said, as Ophion stepped down from the bridge.

S.I.L.V.E.R.'s leader swept past with his retinue and issued his commands. The elite team activated their advanced camouflage systems and slipped into the shadows like wraiths. Zhang Bai was the last to vanish from view. The Chinese assassin held Samson's gaze with hate filled eyes, and a sneer of contempt twisted his lips as she pointed at him before following her colleagues into the black.

An officer approached. 'Colonel, we're ready.'

Samson pressed a button on his helmet and patched through to the reconnaissance units. 'Send out the drones!'

On cue, a whir of electric motors buzzed to life and a horde of flying machines filled the air with tiny flashing lights. As one, they zoomed off into the pitch-dark corridors of Sanctuary, accompanied on the ground by their human masters.

'If she's out there,' the officer said, 'we'll find her, Colonel.'

Samson rubbed at the stubble on his chin. 'Send word to your men, ten thousand credits to the operator who finds her before S.I.L.V.E.R..'

The man failed to conceal a smirk. 'Yes, sir, I'll pass it on.'

'Dismissed.'

The officer saluted and left Samson to his musings. *When the woman is found*, he thought, *S.I.L.V.E.R. will try to take charge of her and the artefacts she holds*. And he knew if he was to secure the pendant, he couldn't allow that to happen. 'Lieutenant.' Samson called over a veteran Terra Force commando, a man he'd fought beside in years past. A man he knew he could trust.

'Colonel?'

'Handpick a hundred of the best killers in the detachment and rendezvous with the drone operators in teams of ten. If they get the opportunity to be alone with any S.I.L.V.E.R. operative, take them out.'

'Yes, sir.'

'Make it clean, no traces.'

'Their leader?'

'No,' – Samson stared out into the darkness – 'he's mine.'

CHAPTER EIGHT

A WHITE LIGHT pulsed bright in the dark, a tiny star in an ocean of night. A man knelt down next to it and scanned its transmitter with a sweep of a handheld device.

'Well?'

Riley Orton stood up and faced Dresden Locke, his expression mixed. He nodded.

Locke turned to the SFSD commando at his side. 'Go tell the colonel the waypoint beacon is confirmed. We've intercepted the route to the temple.'

The man disappeared back down the tunnel to inform his commander and Riley removed his helmet as Jefferson drove a Centipede up alongside them, its main beams lighting up the rocky terrain.

'Now all we have to do is find the needle in the haystack,' Locke said.

Riley turned to Jefferson. 'Any news?'

The Deep Reach archaeologist shook his head. 'Not yet.'

Riley sighed and rubbed his hands over his face. *How long has it been since Sarah passed this way?* he wondered. *Has she even made it this far? Is she hurt somewhere, alone and lost?* The thought distressed him more than he cared to admit.

Residual scans had revealed nothing, but that meant squat, Sanctuary was notorious for playing havoc with human tech. No, it was up to the old fashioned trackers to locate her trail. So far none of the reconnaissance teams had reported back and no one had seen hide nor hair of the S.I.L.V.E.R. operatives.

Riley gazed up at the ceiling of the tunnel, which sparkled in the light, and the memory of a conversation he'd had with Sarah played back through his mind's eye.

'Have you noticed how the ceilings of the chambers sparkle when the light catches them?' he'd said.

Sarah craned her neck to look at the phenomenon. 'I suppose so, yes.'

'It's not a result of the geological composition of the rock, but because across virtually every chamber ceiling, tunnel and cave roof a translucent material has been applied.'

'What sort of material?'

'The scientists aren't sure what it is, only what it does, or did.'

'And what's that?'

'Produce light; in fact they think it functioned much like our dome back at base, but instead of being localised, like the dome, it provided light for the whole of Sanctuary.

'What, on every level?'

'Yep, every level. Well, every level we've surveyed so far has the same feature, so it's assumed it goes everywhere.'

'That's incredible. So gigantis had the ability to create huge swathes of plant life underground, along with simulated sunlight too.'

Riley gave her a strange look. 'Gigantis?'

'Sorry – yes – that's what I, and many others who theorised and promoted the existence of the Anakim, named them, Homo gigantis. And yes, I know, everyone down here calls them giganthropsis or Anakim.'

'Gigantis,' he said, trying out the word again. 'I like it, rolls off the tongue better than giganthropsis.'

'I know, doesn't it?' she enthused, pleased he agreed with her own viewpoint.

'It wasn't just plant life, though,' Riley continued, 'many small animal fossils have been found down here, too, and there are still many insects and different types of algae clinging onto life in certain places we've surveyed.'

'Amazing,' Sarah had said, excited at the prospect.

Riley smiled, remembering the look of wonder on her face. Such unadulterated passion; he'd never met anyone that felt the same as he did about archaeology, it consumed her as much as it did him. Yes, perhaps he was biased by their mutual physical attraction, but it was more than that, or at least he'd thought so at the time. On his side of the – *was it even a relationship?* Their time together was so brief, it didn't seem to be the appropriate term. *A fling, maybe? A friendship*, he decided, *yes, it was a friendship first, of that I'm certain*. On his side it had been more than lust, he'd felt a connection he'd never experienced before. He'd been with his fair share of women, but all paled in comparison to Sarah. That she had broken the sanctity of trust between them had bitten deep. She'd risked everything he'd helped her achieve in her short time in Sanctuary, flinging it back in his face with a metaphorical slap; and stealing his multi-function card to carry out her misdeeds had sealed the deal. *Did she care so little for me?* He didn't want to believe it, but there was no other alternative. She knew what the consequences of her actions would be, for her and for him, but none of that had deterred her. She'd had her way with him one last time, a farewell lay before leaving him to suffer the consequences. Anyone else would be forgiven for hating her, for cursing the day they'd ever met, but Riley couldn't bring himself to be consumed by such negativity – by hate. It wasn't in his nature. He just felt a pervasive sadness that had left an invisible scar on his soul.

He thought he'd known her, understood her. And in many ways he had, but her actions had confounded him. Perhaps I never knew her at all. Perhaps the real Sarah was never unveiled and remained hidden behind a carefully tended wall of deceit. No, I can't believe that – won't believe that – I know genuine when I see it, hear it ... taste it – he could almost feel her lips on his.

A fuzz of radio chatter brought Riley out of his reverie.

Locke put a hand to his helmet and cocked his head to listen.

'They've found her.'

'What?!' Riley said, suddenly anxious.

Locke held up his hand as he concentrated on the garbled message. 'No – wait, they've found ... something. They're calling everyone back.'

Grumbling, Jefferson manoeuvred the Centipede back round and Locke hopped onto the back, catching a lift, while Riley walked behind, his stomach clenched in fearful anticipation. And there he remained, trapped in his trancelike state, until they rejoined the masses congregating in a large chamber a mile from where they'd bridged the chasm.

The press of troops created a sea of armour before them and Jefferson parted their stationary forms by using the Centipede as a slow moving human plough. The soldiers who were shunted out of the way offered up a variety of colourful insults and curses, all of which went over Riley's head as they worked their way to the military command group.

Locke jumped down from his ride and joined Riley, who pushed past a number of Terra Force officers surrounding the indomitable figure of Colonel Samson.

'Do you doubt me, soldier?' Samson was saying as they shouldered their way to the front.

The officer he was addressing, a brute of a man, shook his head. 'I only meant '

'I know exactly what you meant,' Samson said, glancing in Riley's direction. 'Get back out there, I want no stone left unturned. Come back empty-handed again and you'll see how far I'm willing to go.'

Suitably chastened, the reconnaissance soldier snapped to attention and left to carry out his orders, his leader's words ringing in his ears.

Another commando appeared and passed Samson a crumpled map.

The colonel smoothed out the paper chart on a supply crate. 'Where did they find the trail?'

The man pointed at a section of the map. 'Two clicks south east.

There were three sets of tracks and those of a multi-wheeled, SED RV.'

Samson squinted in thought. 'So there's no doubt, then?'

'No, sir, it's definitely them.'

'How far ahead are they?' Riley said

The commando looked up. 'Over twenty-four hours,' he said to Samson as if it was he who'd asked, 'but no more than thirty-six.'

Locke peered at the map and gauged the distance with his hand. 'They're moving quickly.'

'But not fast enough.' Samson picked up his helmet and rifle.

'Who's on point?' Riley asked, fearing the answer.

Samson didn't reply as he stalked away, oblivious.

'Colonel!' Riley said, his voice ringing with authority. 'Who's on point?'

♦

Samson tensed at the challenging tone. He stopped and turned to fix the Deep Reach man with ice-cold eyes.

Riley Orton looked like a rabbit caught in the headlights as Samson moved back towards him.

'Who found the tracks?' Orton said, staying resolute.

Samson studied him. 'You fear for the girl, the terrorist who murdered your friend and colleague?'

A grumble of discontent came from the assembled officers. Orton was lost for words.

Samson leaned in close and whispered, 'You should fear, boy.' He gave the Deep Reach team leader a final scathing look before moving back amongst his troops.

Samson's thoughts turned to Nexus. It was S.I.L.V.E.R. who'd found the girl's tracks. *Who else?* he thought bitterly. *Who fucking else? Not the incompetents that are supposed to be the cream of USSB Sanctu-*

ary's military, that's for sure. No, it had to be Ophion. So much for my incentive; it seems I'll have to deal with S.I.L.V.E.R. the hard way. Although, having said that, Samson knew not all the recon teams had checked in. Perhaps some of the men he'd sent to accompany them had further depleted Ophion's ranks. He could but hope. The fewer there were, the easier it would be to prise the pendant from them, and the less chance they'd have to fight back. And Samson was nobody's fool, despite what some might think of him, particularly Malcolm Joiner. *Did the man think me so intoxicated by his drugs not to realise he'd double-cross me as soon as he was able?* Samson wondered. He'd known before he'd set out that as soon as the intelligence director had what he wanted all bets were off. Samson was on his own and, when it came down to it, he could trust no one, and that's the way he liked it. He had no masters, which meant the law was as he made it.

Standing amongst his legion, Samson called for a floodlight to be turned onto him. A crate was dumped at his feet and he climbed onto it. Under the spotlight, he removed his rifle from his back-plate, chambered a round and fired off a shot.

The noise drew everyone's attention and thousands of eyes peered at him, the sound of chatter dropping to a murmur.

Now he had their attention he surveyed the faces of those closest. Their expressions were grim, tired ... weak. The curse of command was that no one ever lived up to his expectation. No one ever reached his standard. He was destined to be surrounded by the inferior.

'I've been told morale is low,' he said, his voice raised. 'I was told you were tired. Do you know what I said when I heard this? Do you know what I felt?'

A few men shook their heads and further back someone shouted, 'No,' and another said, 'Tell us!'

'I felt sickened; and I asked the question ...'

Samson paused, waiting for someone to respond.

'What question?' a man shouted.

'Are these the men I've heard spoken of? Are these the men I've been told were the best of the best, the finest soldiers in the Subterranean Detachment, those that stand above all others?' He hesitated and shook his head. 'Perhaps I was mistaken. Perhaps it wasn't the men of USSB Sanctuary they spoke of; perhaps it wasn't Terra Force at all!'

An angry murmur rippled through the crowd.

'Do you know who said you were tired, said you were *weak*?'

Shouts of 'No,' and 'Who?' came from the crowd.

'No?' Samson said, cocking an ear, 'I can't hear you?'

The discordant shouts of dissent were music to his ears.

'S.I.L.V.E.R.!' Samson slammed a fist against his chest in sudden fury. 'Assassins – cowards – called you weak! They said they would find the target first and they're out there now, doing your job! I say fuck S.I.L.V.E.R., I say we are Terra Force and we are masters of Sanctuary!'

The soldiers shouted their agreement.

'Who are we?!' he shouted.

'Terra force!' came the response.

'Pathetic! I said who the *fuck* are we!!?'

'Terra Force!' shouted the soldiers. 'Terra Force! Terra Force!! TERRA FORCE!!'

He brandished his weapon. 'We have a terrorist to catch, are you with me!'

The men roared in response.

'I SAID, ARE YOU WITH ME!!'

The sound swelled to a crescendo and Samson jumped down from his crate and pulled on his helmet. A group of officers fell in behind him, their masks and visors sliding over faces and weapons readied.

'The way ahead is flat and unbroken for a solid mile,' one of his men said.

Samson activated his visor and broke into a jog. His men followed in formation and the legion parted to let them through. Drones lifted into the air, lighting the way, and Samson upped the pace to a run. Behind, row upon row of soldiers followed him out into the dark of Sanctuary; the hunt for Sarah Morgan was on.

CHAPTER NINE

The steady drip drip drip of water echoed through the cave and Sarah tightened her grip on the glowing crystal that lit her way. By her side, Jason continued his endless search in the fading hope they'd find Trish alive, the power supply from his Deep Reach visor dwindling further towards nothing with each and every second that passed.

Having made a detour away from the river in order to keep moving forward, they traversed an adjoining chamber looking for a way back to the water's edge. And as they persisted with their lost cause, Sarah tried to keep her mind occupied and came to an interesting conclusion, albeit one that failed to relieve them from the dire nature of their plight.

'I think Trish was wrong,' Sarah said, her voice sounding loud as it pierced the dark.

Jason frowned. 'About what?'

'I don't think the pendant increased in power because we're in Sanctuary.'

'Then why?'

'I think it has something to do with this blue stone.' She gave the crystal a waggle. 'Do you remember when we activated that tunnel through the arch?'

Jason shivered. 'Yes, that's when I first saw that thing ... the light.'

'I know, but before that, the tunnel of water only formed when you and Trish laid your hands on me.'

'Did it?' Jason said, his tone weary.

'Yes, and after that you said your smaller stones stopped glowing. And then when we activated the bridge, you were the only one that touched me.'

'So?'

'So, that bridge must have taken a lot of power to work, but we didn't feel tired afterwards and it was only you and me charging it, unless—'

'Unless the crystal was doing the powering,' he said.

'Why not? If your small stones went dull after we created the tunnel through the arch, then they could have been drained of power. But as this crystal is much bigger, it enabled us to power the bridge with ease.'

Jason didn't respond.

'Don't you think?'

'We should have found the river again by now,' he said, distracted.

Sarah knew he was worried, but that was because he thought there was something to lose. Sarah had accepted their cause was lost, she was at peace. She'd felt emotionally wrung out after the incident at the waterfall, but she knew now that was just a transition. She'd been moving from the world of hope to the world of defeat, it was bound to be a bumpy ride. 'We'll find it,' she said simply.

And after another hour's walk they did. The river had returned and now wound its way through a narrow cavern, its flow reduced to a slow meander.

Stopping to rest, they lay down and both drifted off to sleep in quick succession. However, despite her waking state being one of numb tranquillity, Sarah's dreams were once again filled with visions of flame and terror. But unlike before, the apparition of a shimmering light chased her though dark halls, through searing lava and over the edge of a hidden cliff. As Sarah tumbled down through the dark recesses of her mind, the same voice that haunted her waking life whispered to her in a silken hiss. *Why do you fear me?* it said, as Sarah gazed into the creature's shimmering light. *Am I not what you desire?* Succumbing to its siren call, Sarah stepped from the ledge and drifted into its deadly embrace as blackness consumed her. Frightening images bombarded her mind and she twitched on the ground, her body responding to the unfolding nightmare within.

A hand grasped her mouth and Sarah awoke to the dark with a muffled cry.

'Shhh,' Jason said in a hushed whisper, 'it's me.'

Wide-eyed, Sarah quietened, but Jason kept his hand in place.

She felt his lips press against her ear. 'Something's down here with us.'

Sarah's heart beat faster and she tried to speak.

'Shhh.' Jason slowly released his grip.

'What is it?' Sarah said, her voice as strained as his.

'I don't know, but it's taken the crystal.'

'What?'

Jason moved her head in the direction he wanted her to look.

Some way away, the blue glow of the crystal swayed from side to side in the dark.

'Can you see it?'

She nodded.

'I'm putting my helmet on,' he said.

Tense moments passed as the glowing stone continued its eerie dance, and Sarah thought she could see something reflected in its light.

Jason switched on his visor and the blue glow vanished.

'Trish!' Jason shouted.

Sarah heard Jason scramble to his feet.

'Jason, what are you doing?!' she said, jumping up.

'It's Trish!' He grabbed her arm and dragged her forward.

'What?! Jason wait, it's not Trish!'

It was no use, Jason wasn't listening and he pulled her onwards through the black.

Sarah stumbled and Jason called out again. 'Trish, wait!'

The blue glow reappeared moving erratically in the distance.

'Jason, it's not Trish!'

The light dropped and bounced as if the stone had fallen, and Jason led them towards it. Seconds later they came to a stop over the glowing crystal, which spun to a halt on the ground.

Jason bent down to pick it up and Sarah grabbed his hand. 'Wait!'

'We need to keep moving,' he said, retrieving it, 'she's close.'

'Jason,' – Sarah held him back – 'it's not Trish. I saw something, pale skin, or – I don't know. It's not Trish.'

'It must be. I saw her.'

'You're tired; you saw what you wanted to see.'

'No, it was her ... I'm sure it was.'

Illuminated by the blue glow, Sarah saw him shake his head in confusion.

'Trish!' His shouts echoed through the system of tunnels. 'Trish, it's us, come back!'

A faint buzzing noise like a distant swarm of flies made Sarah look down. A small light on the side of her Deep Reach visor blinked on and off and she pulled the helmet on to listen. 'I'm picking up a signal.'

'What?' Jason said, still scouring the area with his visor.

'My visor's still down, but I'm picking up a radio signal.' She tried focusing on the transmission, but it was an intermittent garble of white noise.

He passed her the crystal and wandered off. 'We need to keep searching.'

'Jason, stop – wait.' She hurried to keep up before a distant sound stopped them in their tracks.

'Did you hear that?' he said, ears pricked.

The noise came again. It sounded like a woman's scream.

Jason ran off again. 'It's Trish!'

Sarah cursed and followed, the glowing crystal held high.

They passed into a dense structure of interconnected passageways, the ins and outs disorientating, like a maze.

Jason ran on and Sarah tripped and fell. She called out for him to stop, but it was too late, he'd disappeared into the dark.

'Jason!' Sarah slowed to a stop. 'Jason!!'

She shone the stone before her, its light barely illuminating the narrow tunnel ahead. A noise behind made her spin round. Nothing was there, just a darker black of the opening she'd just walked through.

Another sound made her whirl left.

'Jason?' she said, her voice shaking. She held the crystal higher and moved into another passage.

The scurry of movement made her flesh prickle in fear. Following the sound she stopped at a junction and listened.

A noise behind, made her freeze in place.

Her eyes swivelled left to try and locate the source. She could hear it close in on her, the sound of its movement stealth-like slow. The closer it came, the more terror she felt. And the more terror she felt, the less she could move.

It was right behind her; she could hear it – she closed her eyes – *oh my God, I can hear it ... I can hear it breathing.* Something touched her back and she span round. A white face full of teeth and eyes shrieked loud.

Sarah screamed and the apparition vanished.

Sick with fright, she stumbled back. The shock left her wheezing for breath, her chest tight with pain.

A hand grasped her shoulder and she screamed again.

'Sarah, it's me,' Jason moved into the light. 'It's okay, it's me.'

Sarah hugged him close; she'd never been so pleased to see anyone in her life.

CHAPTER TEN

'I THOUGHT you were right behind me,' Jason said, I heard you shout and looked round and you'd gone. I rushed back and couldn't find you.'

Sarah regained her breath and looked behind her. 'I saw it, it was right here.'

'What was?'

'I don't know, but it's not Trish.'

'The light?' he said, trying and failing to keep the tremor from his voice.

'No ... maybe ... I don't know.' Sarah remembered the horror when she'd confronted it. She shut her eyes to try to dispel the memory.

She failed.

A buzz of noise came through her helmet's speakers. The same signal as before. 'I think I can hear a voice,' she said, listening.

'What does it say?'

Sarah held up a hand. It was difficult to tell. It sounded like ... it sounded like—

Sarah looked at Jason in disbelief. 'I think it might be Trish.'

'What?!'

She moved her head and the signal faded. She moved it back and it grew louder. She stepped to her right, and then did so again. 'This way,' she said.

'What's she saying?' Jason said, overjoyed.

'I don't know, it sounded like Trish, but I'm not so sure now.'

'How can you not be sure?'

'It's a weak signal, it keeps breaking up. It sounded like her at first. I'm sorry, Jas, I don't know ... I might have been wrong.'

Jason didn't say anything else and Sarah questioned what she'd heard. It had sounded like Trish's voice. She knew it had. *I couldn't have been mistaken, could I?*

Walking through twists and turns, Sarah followed a path that kept the signal as strong as possible. Occasionally it stopped, only to start again. It still sounded like a woman, but who that woman was remained to be seen.

Weaving through the darkness, they eventually emerged into a central chamber. The floor dropped away below, but Jason said he could see the entrances to many other tunnels above and below, each one connected to the rest by a network of narrow paths. As they worked their way down, the signal drew them onwards, taking them further into the structure.

Sarah had a worrying thought. 'What if it's a trap?' she said, slowing.

Jason shook his head. 'It's not. It must be Trish. You said it yourself. And instincts don't lie.'

'I don't like it.' She stopped walking and shone the crystal in his direction.

'What if it is her?' he said. 'We have to find out, one way or the other.'

Sarah knew he was right, but he hadn't just seen what she had.

A strange sound echoed through the passages behind them and Sarah looked at Jason in disquiet.

'Let's keep moving,' he said.

She nodded in agreement and they set out at a faster pace.

Reaching the bottom, they clambered over a fallen statue and followed a narrow stream into another warren of tunnels.

The signal got stronger and Sarah pressed a button on her helmet. 'Trish, is that you?'

She waited a moment before a distorted reply came back.

'Well?' Jason said.

Sarah shook her head. 'I don't know, it's still breaking up too much.'

They carried on a little further before the signal grew much louder and a high pitched feedback whistle made Sarah wince in pain. The torches on top of her helmet stuttered to life before her visor also blazed forth, it's plethora of digital dials and readouts lighting up like a fighter jet's head-up display.

Stowing the crystal in her coveralls, Sarah's elation at being able to see properly again took a back seat as a familiar voice came through her internal speakers.

'Can anyone hear me?' the voice said. 'Is anyone there?'

'Trish,' – Sarah glanced at Jason, her eyes widening – 'is that you?'

'Oh my God – Sarah?!'

Sarah felt like her heart would explode with joy. 'Trish, yes, it's Sarah! Are you okay? Where are you?'

'I don't know,' she said, her voice breaking with emotion, 'I've been following you for ages. It's so good to hear your voice. I thought I was going to die down here, alone in the dark.'

'Is your helmet working?'

'Yes; it's pretty smashed up, one torch doesn't work, the other blinks a bit and the visor's cracked, but yes, it's been working ever since it dried out.'

Despite Sarah's soaring spirits at her friend being alive, she frowned, stopped and held up a hand to Jason who smiled while wiping away tears from his cheeks. 'What do you mean, you've been following us?'

Trish didn't reply for a moment and Sarah thought she could hear her friend crying. 'I've been following the light from your torches,'

Trish said, sniffling, 'but you've always been one step ahead. Why didn't you hear me calling you? Why didn't you—'

'Trish, stop. How long have you been following the light?'

'I don't know, it seems like forever. Hours, days maybe, I don't know.'

Sarah glanced at Jason. 'Is it a faint blue light?'

'No, it's quite bright, and more green than blue. I can see it now. Why?'

'Trish, I don't want you to panic, but whatever you're following ... it's not us.'

Silence ensued before she replied, 'What?'

'My torches haven't been working for a long time and Jason's are down. That light isn't us.'

'Then what is it?'

'Don't worry about that, just walk the other way. Describe where you are.'

'It's that thing, isn't it?' Trish said, her voice wavering. 'I'm following that ... that thing.'

'Trish, calm down.' Sarah gestured for Jason to keep moving. 'Where are you?'

'I'm ... I don't know. It all looks the same. Tunnels. There's a river next to me.'

'Good!' Sarah said. 'That's good. Did you just see a statue of an Anakim warrior?'

'I think so; there was a statue that had fallen down. I had to climb over it.'

'Yes,' Sarah said, increasing her pace to a jog, 'you're close. We're behind you. Follow the stream back to the statue.'

'Okay, keep talking to me.'

'Where are you now?'

'The stream's on my right,' Trish said before letting out a shout.

'Are you okay? Trish? Trish?!'

'I'm fine, I fell over. My light keeps going out.'

'Okay, don't worry; we'll fix it, just keep going.'

'I heard something behind me!'

'Keep going sweetheart, keep going!'

Sarah ran faster and Jason sped up too. 'What's happening?!' he said.

'It's following me,' Trish told her, 'oh, God, I can see the light!'

'Trish, run! Just run!!'

A surge of adrenaline flooded her body and Sarah flew down the stone clad tunnel with Jason on her heels. Moments later they turned a corner and saw a flickering white light appear round a bend fifty feet away.

'I see you!' Trish said.

Sarah ran forward and her torchlight revealed an out of breath Trish, leaning against a wall with her arm in a makeshift sling. But before Sarah could say anything, something moved in the dark behind her friend. Sarah shone her light in its direction and a white shape skittered away into another tunnel.

Trish screamed and Jason cried out in alarm.

'What the fuck was that!' he said.

They ran forward and grabbed Trish.

'I don't know,' Sarah said, 'let's move!'

They ran back the way they'd come and Sarah glanced back to see the glow of light growing brighter in the dark. 'Faster!' she said.

They ran down the tunnel, but Trish's injured arm slowed them down.

Another light appeared ahead and Sarah skidded to a halt.

'Jesus Christ.' Jason looked behind as the other glow approached. 'There are two of them!'

Sarah froze, incapacitated by terror.

Trish grabbed her arm and pulled her sideways. 'In here!'

They entered a narrow passageway and ran through it in single file with Sarah leading. A myriad of turns and bends led them into a labyrinth full of leering statues and hidden drops. Sarah jumped over a deep fissure and ran on. A terrifying screech echoed through the maze. Sarah looked back to see Trish and Jason dropping behind and she stopped to encourage them on.

Moving off once more they rounded another bend and Sarah screamed.

'What is it?' Trish said, terrified.

'I saw something!'

Another fearsome noise made Jason glance back. 'Keep going!'

Sarah ran forward, forced to follow whatever she'd glimpsed. Jumping over another fissure, she hurtled round a bend and fell tumbling into a deep pit. She hit the ground with a thump and her visor and torches blinked out

'Sarah!'

Dazed and hurting all over, Sarah looked up with blurred eyes. Twenty feet above, Trish's visor glowed in the dark and the single light on top of her helmet flickered in and out of existence.

Sarah groaned and sat up. 'I'm okay, but my helmet's stopped working.'

'Use the stone,' Jason said.

Sarah struggled with her coveralls and withdrew the glowing crystal and shone it around to see she'd landed on soft clay.

'Can you climb back up?' he asked her.

Sarah stood up. 'No, it's too high and there's no hand holds.'

A strange clicking noise made Trish and Jason look round.

'Go,' Sarah said, 'there's a tunnel down here, I'll find a way up.'

They hesitated before another horrific noise echoed out.

'GO!' Sarah said.

'Be careful!' Trish jumped across the hole.

'We'll find you!' Jason said and followed.

Sarah moved off into the tunnel in the same direction, the crystal held aloft to light her way. A wall loomed before her and she stumbled left and then right into yet another passage. Time passed and she found herself climbing up a slope. Up and up it went, higher and higher until she came out into yet another strange Anakim building. To her left the floor disappeared into nothing and on her right tall pillars led into shadow. She crept forward, listening out for Trish and Jason and anything else that might be following.

Minutes passed before she heard a curious clicking noise echo up from below. Pulse quickening, she paused to listen. The noise ceased before a guttural growl sent spine-chilling tingles rippling through her like a wave. She shoved the crystal into a pocket, plunging herself into total darkness.

She waited, ears straining, eyes wide and breathing shallow. Her heart felt like it was beating out of her chest.

Down on the next level, a familiar, shimmering light grew brighter, its curious blue-green glow bending and bulging as it moved.

It's stalking me, Sarah thought, hunting me down!

The light floated forward, before pausing. The clicking grew louder before its illumination vanished and a nightmarish bark made Sarah tense. It barked again, once, twice, three times, and her senses screamed at her to run, but, like before, she couldn't move. Fear held her rooted to the spot. The creature's barks echoed once more and she managed to step back from the edge before a noise behind made her freeze.

It had come for her and she couldn't move!

She wanted to scream, but her mouth wouldn't work. Paralysed, she saw a dim glow of light appear out of the corner of her eye. A shadowy form reached out around her, its dark mass visible in the faintest of lights. Sarah knew the end had come, but instead of peace, she felt pure, unadulterated terror.

The cast of death closed in and a powerful force clamped over her mouth. Something else grasped her body and she was lifted off her feet and sucked back into the void.

CHAPTER ELEVEN

SARAH WAITED for the final blow that would end her life, but the sensation never came. The thing that held her was keeping her alive. For how long, she didn't know, but whatever it was, it was far too strong to escape from. The hold on her mouth was unyielding and her body hung suspended in mid-air.

She whimpered in fear and struggled. It squeezed harder, its limb constricting like a snake. The grip on her mouth tightened and the faint glow of light she'd seen before grew closer to her face. She managed to turn her head a little and her eyes widened in horror as two fearsome blue eyes turned to look at her.

'Quiet,' a deep voice whispered, 'it's down there.'

The blue eyes turned to look into the hall below and Sarah followed its gaze. The shimmering blue-green light had reappeared and the clicking sound began again as it moved along from where they watched.

The light stopped and coalesced into something transparent that glowed from within. Its form twisted and expanded, rippled and contracted. Whatever it was, it wasn't stable. It had no single shape – at least, not then. More clicking echoed out and the strange vision dissolved back into the oscillating light and continued away into the dark.

Minutes passed after the light had disappeared from view before the thing that held Sarah relaxed its hold and she was lowered to the floor. Something was tied around her mouth and then her arms and legs were bound. Hoisted into the air, the darkness transported her through silent halls and down hidden stairs.

Finally the motion ceased and Sarah felt herself lowered to the ground. Still captivated in fear, she looked up into burning blue eyes. A sound to her right made her turn to see another demon appear from the ether. And then another behind that. She looked left as more glowing eyes hovered in the black, and light blazed forth to blind her.

Blinking against the sudden illumination, she saw tendrils of lightning ripple over the entity before her. A tall figure materialised, his body encased in black armour and bristling with weaponry. Either side of him, more of these dark knights emerged from the shadows.

The being reached up and removed its helmet. A man, with a jaw like granite and a wicked scar down the centre of his face, stared down at her. He reached out a hand and Sarah let him remove the gag from her mouth.

'Who are you?' she said in wonder.

He didn't reply and Sarah glanced down at an emblem on his chest which bore a single word:

DARKLIGHT

And close to that were two more words, spelt out in white block lettering:

Cmdr. HILT

CHAPTER TWELVE

SARAH STARED up into the impassive eyes of the man before her. Standing well over six foot, his Olympian physique bulged beneath his armoured suit, the overdeveloped muscles reminding her more of giganthropsis than that of sapiens.

Movement to the right drew Sarah's focus. Two more black-clad soldiers appeared out of the gloom and deposited next to her the struggling forms of Trish and Jason.

Her two friends were wild-eyed and spoke with muffled voices through their respective gags. When they saw Sarah their volume increased.

The man leant towards them. 'Quiet,' he said, his deep voice full of power, 'or I'll put you back where we found you.'

Jason and Trish fell silent and huddled closer to Sarah.

He studied them for a moment and then switched his penetrating gaze back to Sarah. 'Deep Reach, S.E.D.,' he said, touching the emblems on her arm. 'U.S.S.B. Sanctuary.' He slid a large knife from his armour and held it before her.

Sarah watched the point of the blade hover in the air ... and then drop down to slice through her bonds. She rubbed the circulation back into her wrists. 'What about my friends?'

'In time.' He beckoned forward a female soldier. 'Search them.'

The masked woman hauled Sarah to her feet and patted her down. First she removed the Anakim parchments and passed them to her leader. Then she found the Anakim orb, Trish's locket, and finally she located the glowing crystal.

'Sir.' The woman held up the blue rock.

The man's brow furrowed as he took the crystal. Turning it over in his armoured gloves, he held it up to Sarah. 'Where did you find this?'

Sarah stayed quiet. She had no idea who these people were, but they were armed to the teeth and stank of authority, and while they were a welcome respite from the wilderness of Sanctuary and the thing that hunted them, they were also two things Sarah couldn't abide.

'Who are you?' The man slipped the glowing stone into a concealed pouch on his belt. 'How far is the base?'

Sarah remained in silent defiance.

The man's eyes narrowed. 'What do you know about the light – the creature?'

Sarah felt her throat tighten in fear and she looked around into the dark. 'Are we safe?'

He followed Sarah's gaze. 'No,' he said, his eyes searching the pitch-black beyond, '... no one's safe.'

Sarah's anxiety increased.

'What do you know of it?' he said, turning back to her.

'Release my friends and I might tell you.'

'Answer my questions and I will do.'

The female soldier, who'd been searching Sarah, noticed her pendants. 'Sir.' She parted Sarah's jacket and held out the chain with its two pentagonal discs.

Sarah tried to keep calm as the man stepped forward to study them. He glanced at her with calculating eyes. *He can't know what they are*, Sarah thought, *there's no way*.

He let them drop back against Sarah's chest with a clink and she relaxed.

He gave a nod to the woman. 'Take them.'

'What?!' Sarah said, alarmed. 'No!' She grasped the pendants as the woman tried to remove the chain from her neck. Sarah continued to resist before the woman grew angry and pinned Sarah's arms behind her back. The leader grasped the pendants and gave them a sharp tug to break the chain.

'Start talking and you get these back.' He pocketed the pendants and the woman released her hold.

Sarah glared at her captors, but there was nothing she could do except comply. She glanced down at Trish and Jason, who looked back at her with worried expressions while the woman searched through their coveralls.

'My name's Sarah, Sarah Morgan.'

The leader's expression remained unchanged.

'We're exploring Sanctuary. That's what we do; we're an SED Deep Reach survey team. Do you know what that is?'

'Where's the rest of your team?' he said. 'Where are your supplies?'

'We got separated.'

His eyes bored into hers. 'You're lost?'

'You could say that.'

'How far is the USSB?'

'A long way. A hundred miles, as the crow flies – with Sanctuary's terrain, maybe three times that.'

'The light?'

'We don't know what it is.'

The man considered her anew and moved her face to one side with a finger. 'How did you get these burns?'

'Lava.'

'Commander,' another soldier said, 'we've reacquired the target.'

'Heading?' he said, still looking at Sarah.

'Due east.'

'Saddle up!' He straightened and pulled on his helmet.

The black-garbed soldiers shouldered heavy rucksacks and

readied weapons, and one by one they activated their camouflage and disappeared into the gloom.

'Wait!' Sarah said.

The leader's face appeared as his helmet's mask retracted and visor rose.

'You can't just leave us here,' she said.

'Why not?'

'Our helmets are low on power, mine's stopped working. We have hardly any food and no climbing gear,' – she pointed to Trish and Jason – 'and my friends are injured.'

He remained unmoved.

'Because we'll die,' Sarah said.

'Sir, we need to go,' one of his men told him.

The commander acknowledged him with a grunt while holding Sarah's gaze.

'I told you what I know,' she said. 'At least give us our things back.'

He turned to his subordinate. 'Cut them loose and see to their headwear.'

The soldier looked like he was about to dispute the order and held his commander's gaze. Something seemed to pass between them and he gave a nod and went about his tasks.

The leader approached and held out his hand. 'A gesture of good faith.'

Sarah caught Trish's locket as it fell, and Trish and Jason were released, while another soldier chucked them some ration packs before attaching a device to their helmets.

The commander moved past Sarah and grasped Jason's hands and turned them over to inspect his palms. Apparently satisfied he wasn't in any immediate danger, he moved to Trish and manipulated her arm which made her cry out in pain.

'Stop!' Jason tried to pull him away.

The leader turned to him. 'I have to reset the bone.' He looked at Trish. 'This is going to hurt.' He grasped Trish's arm and she closed her eyes as he nodded to the soldier who'd been seeing to Sarah's helmet.

The man positioned himself behind Trish and held her tight while covering her mouth with his hand.

With a sharp twist, the leader pushed the bone back inside her body. The corresponding crunch and Trish's muffled scream made Sarah feel sick.

The Darklight commander sprayed the bloody wound with a cleansing anaesthetic, which he also used on Jason's hands. He then injected Trish's arm and applied a special battlefield wrapping to it before lowering his visor. 'We're moving out,' he said from behind his glowing mask, 'keep up, or get left behind.'

The leader and his remaining soldiers melded into the gloom as they activated their armour's cloaking devices.

Sarah pressed a button on her helmet and she was relieved to see it power up, its battery back to quarter charge.

'What do we do?' Jason said, coming to stand next to her.

'Can you move?' Sarah asked Trish.

Her friend, looking pale, gave a tremulous nod.

Sarah kissed her forehead and gave her a hug. 'Then we follow.'

The three friends, weary, reunited and patched up, activated their visors and followed the warriors into the realm of night.

CHAPTER THIRTEEN

Commander Hilt, private contractor and operations leader of Darklight's North American Division, strode through the abandoned ruins of Sanctuary. Behind, the three explorers from the USSB hurried to keep pace. As Hilt listened to incoming messages from his reconnaissance unit, another part of his mind ran through a myriad of questions. *What is this Sarah Morgan hiding? She's a good liar, but not when she's under duress. And if they aren't exploring, what are they really doing in Sanctuary Proper? Have they been sent to find Goodwin and his civilians? Where did she find the blue crystal and does she know more than she thinks she does?* He vaulted over an obstruction and continued his advance. *Do they know the crystal attracts the creature? Obviously not,* he thought, *considering she was waving it around like a sign saying 'free all-you-can-eat buffet'. And her English accent is out of place.* Hilt knew USSB Sanctuary was U.S. citizens only – or at least ninety-nine point nine nine per cent were U.S. citizens, according to Sergeant Alvarez, anyway. Despite this, something about her seemed, *what is it?* he thought, *unprofessional? No, desperate, perhaps, emotional? Something ...*

A garbled message from one of his men made him pause. He sent out a signal for his unit to halt and for line of sight transmission to be recalibrated.

Hilt scoured the close quarter terrain with his rifle scope and glanced back as the three civilians rejoined them. 'Say again,' he said.

The message came through once more, still distorted, but coherent. 'Target has stopped,' said the operative, 'I say again, target has stopped.'

'Any sign of secondary?' Hilt said.

'Negative.'

'Distance?'

'Ninety yards.'

'Activity?'

'I'm not sure, it seems to be—'

The signal cut off.

'Talk to me, soldier,' Hilt said, adjusting his radio.

The crackle of static buzzed through his helmet's speakers before the voice returned. 'Target gone, target gone!'

'Fall back and regroup,' Hilt said, 'we're coming to you!'

'Roger, that.'

'RV on point,' Hilt said through the com, 'boost power to signal relays, roving spectrum UV gamma, move out!'

The unit broke into a loping run through the never-ending labyrinth.

After leaping over a drop, Hilt passed two of his men who'd stopped to cover a T-junction. 'Protect the civilians,' he said as he ran past.

The operatives nodded and hung back to allow them through.

♦

Sarah pursued the ghostly outline of the Darklight leader round a bend and over another deep drop. Trish and Jason followed and now, behind them, two fearsome, blue-eyed demons shadowed their every move.

Sarah leapt over another obstacle and marvelled at the agility of the man in command. He carried a massive backpack, an arsenal of weapons, and yet he was still able to move with a cat-like fluidity that belied his size. Coupled with his measured demeanour, he exuded strength like some god of war. But considering what they were up against, Achilles, or even Ares himself, would have been hard-pressed to fight off the thing from the deep. Just thinking of the monstrosity made her legs go weak and she almost stumbled and fell.

Willing herself forward, she couldn't help but wonder if they'd be safer on their own. These people seemed hell bent on chasing the thing they feared the most. It was a feeling Sarah could relate to, but not one she wished to replicate. The only problem was, their leader had the one thing they needed to return to the surface.

Sarah's views on the pendant hadn't altered, but her faint hope of getting out of Sanctuary alive had resurfaced at the same time as her friend's miraculous return from the dead. She glanced back to see Trish doing her best to stay close and Sarah held out her hand and helped her on.

♦

Hilt saw his unit secure the area ahead – a small plaza overlooked by multiple levels. Not the best defensive position in the world, but far better than being stuck in a narrow passageway.

Hilt slowed and moved to the centre of their formation. He knew they could ill afford any more losses. They'd started out as seventy-five; they were down to fifty-two. Fourteen MIA, presumed dead, the rest KIA. He thought back to the confrontations and wondered if he could have done anything differently, if there was something he'd missed that might help him combat the beast that seemed destined to end them all.

He breathed deeply, sucking in Sanctuary's dank, musty air, and expelled his negative thoughts with a slow exhale. Professor Steiner tasked me with protecting Steadfast's civilians and that's what I'll do until they're safely tucked up in a USSB, be that Sanctuary or otherwise.

Hilt had never let the professor down before and he wasn't about to start now. It helped that the man he now took orders from was someone he liked, not just because he was the professor's friend and protégé, but because he was principled and would do anything to help those under his care. What's more, he was one of the few that didn't do it to boost a fragile ego. And since Richard Goodwin was Steadfast's director, that made him Hilt's director. But so far he knew he'd been a disappointment, a feeling he was unaccustomed to. A feeling he loathed. Hilt had let the entity take the girl through incompetence. He'd been lax when it came to defending the camp and he'd also failed to locate Sanctuary's USSB. Goodwin had been vigorous in Hilt's defence, but Hilt knew it was up to him to redeem himself. Goodwin had told him to find Susan and bring her back, and that's what he was going to do – or die trying.

Hilt glanced round as the civilians moved into his unit's ring of steel and weapons. He'd known they would follow, what choice did they have? And he hadn't enjoyed taking their possessions, either, but time had been of the essence and Susan was more important than three strangers. He'd needed information and he needed it quick, and so he'd acted accordingly. Plus, he had bigger things to worry about. Bigger things like killing the creature and finding the woman it had taken. Susan – *that poor woman* – mentally disabled and taken by some *thing* beyond a nightmare and beyond understanding. He couldn't imagine the terror she must have endured, and not for the first time he wondered if she still lived. They'd seen her tracks six days ago, but nothing since.

Why the creature hadn't killed her long before he didn't know, but it was one of many worrying aspects about the thing they hunted – or was it hunting them? Hilt wasn't sure, but he had a strong suspicion it was outthinking them at every turn. They'd set up traps, mines, ambushes ... none had worked, the creature using an eerie sixth sense to avoid all danger. And yet, was that what it wanted them to think? That it was vulnerable when it wasn't? On the two occasions they'd got it cornered, their weapons had been ineffective, regular rounds and even beam weapons having little impact. They'd still to hit it with their limited supply of high powered missiles, but he held out little hope of even a direct hit causing much damage. And even if it did, such a blast could bring the crumbling ruins of Sanctuary down upon them. Of course, they still had a small number of thermal swords, but getting close enough to use them was one thing, inflicting any damage was a whole other ball game.

A piece of falling masonry hit the ground twenty feet away and Hilt looked up, rifle trained.

'Stay alert,' he said, scanning the area, 'this thing might have decided to stop running.'

◆

Sarah heard another rock hit the ground with a dull, crunching thud. And then another to the left.

Tense moments passed as silence reigned.

The Darklight leader moved forward to stand outside of the defensive ring. His massive rifle glowed with suppressed heat, its power cell humming quietly with stored energy as he swept it in slow, sweeping arcs. 'Watch the flanks,' he said to his unit, 'all elevations.'

'I've got a bad feeling about this,' Jason said, from close behind Sarah.

A sudden roar of sound echoed through the ancient buildings and Trish grasped Sarah's arm with a trembling hand.

A glimmer of light appeared above and the Darklight soldiers unleashed their weapons.

Sarah put her hands over her ears to block out the deafening noise before the commander shouted, 'Cease fire!'

The onslaught ended and the fall of empty shell casings tinkled to silence.

A second later a large section of the structure gave way, falling with a muffled crash onto the plaza's periphery.

Nothing else moved except for the dust that now hung swirling in the air.

A soldier who knelt on one knee sprang to his feet. 'There!'

The roar of gunfire thundered out once more, muzzle flashes sending shadows cavorting through the dark.

Eventually the barrage ceased and more stonework collapsed into rubble.

Hollow silence fell again and Sarah felt Trish tug at her sleeve.

Her friend was looking down and Sarah followed her gaze. A few feet away, stones and dust vibrated across the ground. The tremor increased and Sarah took a backward step.

The surface distorted and swelled like liquid. One of the soldiers shouted a warning, but it was too late, as the light emerged within.

♦

Gunfire and screams filled the air. A roar of sound and a flash of light and Sarah was thrown to the ground. Ears ringing, debris rained down around her. Staggering to her feet, the world spun into slow motion. Sarah whirled round, hair flailing as Jason ran towards her, his mouth open in a protracted shout. Behind him the Darklight soldiers shot at the shimmering light, beams of energy and muzzle flashes blasting out like dragon fire.

Someone grabbed her arm. 'SARAH!'

Normal time whooshed back into reality and Trish dragged her into a passageway, with Jason close behind.

'Run!' he said, pushing them forward.

Sarah followed Trish as they fled from the carnage, shouts,

screams and rapid gunfire driving them onwards. Twists and turns flashed by and the sound of the battle faded. But the three friends didn't stop and more frantic moments passed, ragged breathing and mindless direction only ending when Trish faltered and their flight slowed. Sarah leapt over a deep fissure and skidded to a stop beside her friend, who leant against a wall, panting and gasping for breath.

'What now?' Jason said, appearing beside them.

Sarah shook her head; she had no clue.

He looked at them, waiting for an answer. When none came, he glanced behind and then moved past to see what lay ahead. 'We need the pendant back,' he said, coming back to them, 'so we wait it out and then go back and see if we can find it.'

'He won't just give it to us,' Trish said, nursing her broken arm.

'You think he's still going to be alive? That thing cut through them like they weren't there. And besides, what else can we do?'

Sarah made a face. 'Not much.'

'Then it'll have to do,' Trish said.

With their plan set, they headed off once more with Jason leading the way.

Another minute passed before sporadic gunshots echoed down the passage ahead.

Jason swore and turned them back the other way.

The twisting turns continued before they ran into a Darklight soldier.

The woman swung round, eyes glowing and rifle raised.

Jason held out his hands. 'Don't shoot!'

The woman relaxed, shook her head at their stupidity and turned back round before being dragged with a scream into the dark, gun firing.

Seized by terror, they ran back the way they'd come. Another heart-pounding minute later, they stopped again, out of breath and eyes wide.

No one spoke as they listened for signs of pursuit.

None came.

Running out of options, they worked their way further into the labyrinth.

A while later – with Jason still leading – they halted for a third time when he held up a hand.

'What is it?' Trish said in a whisper.

He shook his head. 'I don't know; go back the other way.'

They did so, the decision putting Sarah in the lead. She heard a noise to the right and so she turned left. Creeping forward with stealth-like care, she let out a shout as three Darklight soldiers ran past, weapons firing.

'Go back!' Sarah said, pushing Trish in the opposite direction, as the screams of dying men chased them along the passageway.

Running again, tense moments turned to hushed minutes and they found themselves emerging into a large void, the passages and tunnels giving way to a whole new chamber. Escaping from the confined space would have been a blessing except that in the distance a sheer rock face rose high to block off any chance of escape. The new area was one vast, dead end.

Movement to their left made Trish scream.

Poised to flee, Sarah spun round to see something crouched huddled against a wall.

Jason pushed Trish behind him. 'What the hell is that?!'

The small figure raised its head and Sarah took a step towards it. Covered in dirt and clothed in rags, Sarah stared into terrified eyes. 'It's a woman.'

CHAPTER FOURTEEN

'What the hell is she doing down here?' Jason said.

Sarah didn't know, but one thing was for sure, this newcomer was more frightened of them than they were of her.

The woman scuttled back as Sarah approached.

'It's okay,' Sarah said, switching on her helmet's torches and holding out a hand.

'It won't be for long,' said a deep voice.

Sarah turned round as the powerful figure of the Darklight commander strode out into the area behind, followed by the remnants of his unit, their torches blazing bright.

'What do you mean?' Sarah said. 'Who is she?'

'She's the woman I've been searching for.' Hilt switched out a magazine from his rifle and loaded a new one. 'And where she goes, the light follows.'

'What?!' Jason said in alarm.

Hilt ignored him and beckoned to the woman. 'Susan, come here, child, I'll take you back to Rebecca.'

The woman whimpered in fear and edged back along the rocky wall.

Trish moved to Sarah's side to bar his way. 'I don't think she wants to go with you.'

'Then it's lucky I don't care what you think.' The Darklight leader strode forward and pushed Trish and Sarah aside.

On his approach the woman sprang up and Hilt made a desperate grab for her, but she scampered out of reach to cower behind Trish.

'You're scaring her,' Trish said, laying a tentative hand on the half-starved creature.

The woman flinched at the touch, but remained where she was, eyes darting this way and that.

Hilt's mask and visor retracted into his helmet. 'This is no time for games; that woman is under my care.'

Trish stroked Susan's grimy hair. 'It doesn't look like you've done a very good job.'

The commander's face darkened.

'Sir!' one his men said.

Hilt paused and his eyes went distant as he listened to a communication. His mask and visor slid back into place and he cocked his weapon. 'The beast approaches.'

CHAPTER FIFTEEN

ALL WAS STILL in Sanctuary's depths as the Darklight soldiers formed up behind their leader to await their fate.

Commander Hilt stood facing the entrance to the black labyrinth like an immovable force attempting to hold back the unstoppable tide.

He glanced right to see Susan still clutching the woman's leg.

A fearsome bellow of noise gusted through the chamber. *This is it,* Hilt thought, refocusing on the passage ahead. *No more running. No more hiding. No more chasing. It ends here, one way or another.*

The last surviving members of his recon team came steaming out of the dark.

'It's right behind us!' one of them shouted.

Hilt flicked the switch on his reserve rifle to full auto and the shimmering blue-green light burst from the black.

'FIRE!' Hilt roared.

Weapons blazed. Bullets and beams of energy tore into the light, but the creature shrieked and flew on.

Hilt dived right and kept firing as two of his men disappeared in an explosion of blood.

The creature attacked again and Hilt slid a mine into its path. The detonation rocked the ground beneath his feet, but the light persisted. Hilt rolled aside as the creature smashed one soldier from his feet and then pinned another to the ground, before dragging him screaming into the labyrinth.

Hilt signalled to one of his men. The man nodded and loaded a tactical missile into his rifle's launch mechanism.

'As soon as it reappears,' Hilt said through the com, 'take it out.'

'Sir,' the soldier said, 'no one will survive the blast.'

Hilt glanced at Susan and the three civilians. 'It's for the best,' he said, with a heavy heart, 'this thing can't be allowed to return to camp. Director Goodwin would understand.'

The soldier nodded and took aim.

♦

Sarah watched in horror as the Darklight soldiers fought the creature and died without even slowing it down. With over half his force massacred, only the leader and less than twenty of his unit remained. And when they'd fallen, there would be just four, unarmed civilians left to face it alone.

Sarah hoped – prayed – for another miracle and her hand clasped Trish's locket in unconscious desperation. A lull in the fighting allowed her short relief before the light came again.

♦

The creature reappeared inside the entrance before blinking out of existence. Hilt cursed and the man with the missile launcher glanced in his leader's direction before a gush of blood burst from his lips.

The dying form of his lieutenant was lifted into the air and Hilt's helplessness turned to rage.

'SWORDS!' Sprinting forward, Hilt drew forth his thermal blade.

The light vanished again and the mangled corpse slumped to the ground.

♦

Sarah saw the Darklight leader slow to a stop, his glowing eyes turning this way and that as he sought their hunter. In his hand, a bright shining blade pulsed in the dark like a weapon forged by God. Around him seven other swords shone out with the same white brilliance.

Sarah held her breath, but as the seconds ticked by only darkness stirred.

'Where is it?' Trish said, her voice shaking.

Sarah didn't know.

After a minute of deathly silence the Darklight leader separated himself from his unit and approached.

'Has it gone?' Trish said.

'For now.' The Darklight man switched off his white hot sword, retracted his mask and held something out to Sarah.

She opened her hand and he dropped her two pentagonal pendants into her palm.

He then passed her the Anakim parchments, before withdrawing the orb from another compartment. 'What is this?' he said, holding it up for inspection.

'Just an artefact,' Sarah said, making sure she kept her tone as bland as possible.

He studied the orb before tossing it to her. He glanced at Trish. 'She seems to like you,' he said, indicating Susan, who cowered behind her. 'If you can keep her from running off, I'll do my best to get you safely back to the USSB.' He removed a small pouch from his armour and held it out to her. 'For the arm.'

Trish reached out and accepted the offering.

'You haven't told us who you are,' Sarah said, hurrying to keep up with him as he walked back to his unit. 'Who is Susan? Why are *you* down here? What is Darklight?'

'They're used by the GMRC,' Jason said, 'peacekeepers for hire – mercenaries, right?'

'There'll be time for answers soon enough,' Hilt said, 'for now, we concentrate on staying alive.'

'You intend to keep chasing it, don't you?' Sarah said. 'You mean to kill it.'

Hilt looked like he was about to reply before a rumble of distant noise made everyone turn. The Darklight leader's sword glowed back to life and he strode to the fore. His troops fanned out behind him, their own blades drawn, and odd-shaped shields slid from concealment to mechanically expand in preparation for another round with the phantom.

Coming from the opposite direction to the labyrinth entrance, a light was growing on the escarpment high above. The sound grew louder and Sarah glanced behind, wondering if they should make a run for it. She swapped glances with Trish and Jason, and they edged toward the passage that led into the sprawling maze.

Blazing light appeared over the rise, flooding the chamber and turning night into day. Sarah squinted as her visor image flared due to the sudden change in spectral input.

A powerful voice rang out into the chamber. 'SARAH MORGAN!'

Sarah stopped and turned to look up at the top of the escarpment, which was now lined with row upon row of Terra Force commandos.

In their centre a single man stood atop an SED all-terrain vehicle. He retracted his helmet's mask and pointed down at her. 'I've come for you, Morgan!' he said, 'there's nowhere else to run!'

CHAPTER SIXTEEN

COMMANDER HILT LOOKED BACK at the SED woman, who stared up, open-mouthed, at the force arrayed before them. Whatever she was doing in Sanctuary Proper it seemed it was as he suspected; there was more going on with her than met the eye.

'Sarah Morgan is under my protection,' Hilt said, raising his voice and zooming in his visor on the man above. 'What do you want with her?'

The SFSD Colonel turned his attention to Hilt and his expression changed to one of recognition. 'If it isn't Steiner's pet merc. I heard you were all dead.'

'Then you heard wrong.'

'Keep standing in my way, Darklight, and I won't have.'

Hilt glimpsed a glimmer of movement and thrust his blade left. 'Take another step, assassin, and it'll be your last.'

A shimmer of light distorted the air and a chrome-clad figure appeared, with Hilt's glowing blade resting at its throat.

Something tapped against Hilt's armoured chest.

'Think again, Commander,' a woman said.

Hilt glanced down to see the tip of a slender blade and he

followed the length of the sword to where its owner emerged from the background.

He gazed into the mirror-like visor of another assassin. 'Where's your leader?' Hilt said, glancing at the woman's S.I.L.V.E.R. emblem and the gun she held in her other hand.

Motionless moments passed before she turned her head to look towards the labyrinth. 'Hunting,' she said, her voice distant.

Hilt studied her. 'He seeks the light?'

The woman's visor retracted to reveal beautiful Asian eyes. 'He seeks Sarah Morgan, as do I ... we all seek the light,' she touched his Darklight emblem with her sword, 'but the dark is always just one step behind.'

'You know of what I speak; the entity – the creature.'

The woman didn't reply as more of her colleagues materialised to confront Hilt's beleaguered unit.

The colonel's voice rang out again. 'Can you hear me, Morgan?!' he shouted. 'You have something I want, the pendant; give it to me and you get to live!'

♦

'They know about the pendant,' Trish said in hushed despair.

Sarah's heart skipped a beat. Their secret was out. They knew what she possessed, the key to the Anakim's past, the key to their technology, the key to everything. And they'd sent an army to reclaim it.

She glanced at the chrome-plated warriors who'd appeared from nowhere to force the Darklight commander and his unit into a stand-off. And then her eyes were drawn up to the escarpment and the troops surrounding the Terra Force leader. Virtually all of them had their weapons trained in her direction. She felt her throat run dry and automatically licked her cracked lips in response. She wanted to run, but she'd be lucky to get two feet.

♦

Colonel Samson ground his teeth against a sense of building impatience. S.I.L.V.E.R. had taken it upon themselves to secure the woman. Nexus had disappeared and his Chinese bitch had switched off her radio. If they get their hands on the pendant first, he thought, the only way to get it back will be to prise it from their dead hands. The only problem with that – they'd take everyone else with them by detonating their failsafe device. I have to act, but how?

'Do you know what this woman is?!' Samson said. 'Does Darklight know who it protects? This woman is a thief, a murderer and a terrorist,' – he paused for breath – 'as are any that stand with her!'

'Says the man that murdered Steadfast civilians,' the Darklight leader said. 'I know who and what you are, Colonel Samson!'

Samson had had enough of this charade. He called over one of his captains. 'Get down there and retake control from S.I.L.V.E.R..'

The man saluted and gathered together four squads. The soldiers each fired a climbing anchor into the cliff and then dropped over the edge to abseil down to the ground below.

Samson gestured to one of his men. 'Bring him.'

♦

Sarah felt sick. She'd known what she'd done was right. She'd taken back what was hers. She'd defended herself and escaped false imprisonment, but now the stark reality of her choices had come back to haunt her. Being called a thief she could live with, but a murderer and a terrorist? Hearing the words spoken, and with such malice, made her feel numb.

Movement above made her refocus her attention.

'Sarah Morgan,' the colonel said, 'you have something I want, but I have something of yours!'

Sarah's eyes widened as a man was dragged to the edge of the cliff. A man she'd grown to admire, a man who'd become a friend, a man whom she loved. 'Riley,' she whispered. She went to move forward, but Trish grasped her arm.

The colonel jumped down from the Centipede on which he stood, removed his rifle from his back-plate and pointed it to Riley's head. 'The time for talking is over, Morgan! Surrender yourself to my men—'

Sarah saw more Terra Force soldiers reach the bottom of the cliff face.

'—or this man dies. You have ten seconds!'

♦

The commandos disconnected from their descent cables and approached Hilt's position.

'It looks like the colonel doesn't trust you,' Hilt said to the assassin.

He could tell the woman wanted to look behind to see what was happening, but she kept her discipline, her sword remaining near his armour's weak point and her sidearm aimed at his face.

'Eight seconds!' Samson shouted.

Hilt knew Samson had massacred his men back in Steadfast and he was as likely to kill them all as let them go. He tightened the grip on his sword, his muscles tensing for action.

♦

Sarah adjusted her visor and homed in on Riley, who struggled in vain against his captors. Seeing his face again brought memories flooding back and her heart lurched in anguish and longing in equal measure.

The colonel's voice boomed out again. 'Six seconds!'

Sarah opened her hand and looked at the two pentagonal pendants. *How can such a small thing cause so much trouble*? She touched the larger of the two artefacts. No one could have guessed at the power it held, and yet it might be the most important find in human history, beside Sanctuary itself. Much like the Rosetta Stone was to Egyptology; this pendant could do the same for the furtherance of revealing the Anakim's past, but at the same time it could do so much more – it had the power to shape the future of humanity. *I should have known such a thing couldn't stay mine for long*, she thought. *It doesn't belong to me, to anyone – it belongs to all mankind.* Which was why giving it up to those that would hide it away for all eternity went against everything she stood for, went against everything she ever was and would be.

'Four seconds!'

Sarah looked at Trish and Jason with sad eyes. 'I have to go; I can't let Riley die because of me.' She gave Trish a hug and slipped the bigger of the two pendants into her hand and whispered, 'They'll never know the difference until it's too late, if you get the chance – *run*.'

'Three seconds!' Samson said. 'Two seconds ... one sec—'

'OKAY, STOP!' Sarah turned back and raised her hands. 'You win! I surren—'

Something powerful grasped her from behind and she felt something sharp nick the skin on her throat.

'Do not move a muscle, Sarah Morgan,' a voice like death said in her ear, 'very slowly, give me the pendant.'

Sarah glanced down. A chrome-clad hand held a knife to her throat and she unfurled her fingers to reveal the smaller of the pentagonal discs.

'Do not play tricks with me,' the voice said, 'for I will not hesitate to kill you.' The knife's pressure increased. 'The other pendant, now.'

Sarah swallowed and felt a trickle of blood run down her neck.

♦

Samson swore as the large form of S.I.L.V.E.R.'s leader appeared behind Sarah Morgan.

'Nexus,' he said, his eyes flaring with rabid hate.

Samson removed his gun from Orton's head and took aim at Ophion. 'Time to die, assassin,' he said, and pulled the trigger.

CHAPTER SEVENTEEN

A GUNSHOT RANG out and Sarah felt the knife leave her throat. Everything that had been held in suspension snapped to life. Rapid gunfire exploded like a storm and all hell broke loose.

'Go!' Sarah grabbed Trish and ran for the passageway.

'Look out!' Jason shoved Sarah left.

Something whistled past her head and Jason was spun round, his wrist pinned to the stone entrance by a strange device.

Sarah's visor revealed the shimmering form of a man bearing down on them, gun raised. Bullets ricocheted from the assassin's armour, forcing him to take evasive action and giving Sarah the chance to prise Jason free, just as more bullets tore into the stone inches from her head.

♦

Hilt parried the thrust of the woman's sword while ducking a projectile that whizzed over his head. Falling back, he grasped his shield and deflected a hail of bullets that peppered the ground around him. The chrome assassins vanished from view and Hilt joined his men to form a shield wall, like the soldiers of yore. He glanced round to see Susan running into the labyrinth, followed by Morgan and her friends.

'Fall back!' Hilt said.

Under relentless assault, the Darklight unit retreated on command, shields interlocked. Hilt sheathed his sword and scooped up the missile launcher dropped earlier by one of his men. With another order his team broke formation and entered the passage at a dead run. Bringing up the rear, Hilt continued for fifty yards before skidding to a stop. Turning, he armed the weapon – took aim – and depressed the trigger.

♦

Colonel Samson chased Nexus with a hail of bullets until the man vanished from sight. With the clip depleted, Samson threw the gun to the ground and held out his hand to receive another. He cocked the weapon and fired at the retreating Darklight mercenaries.

Seconds later a message flashed up on his visor:

WARNING!
HIGH YIELD MISSILE LAUNCH DETECTED

'Incoming!' Samson shouted and sprinted away from the cliff edge.

♦

A trail of smoke shot out from the entrance to arrow into the base of the cliff. A blaze of light blossomed into being as the missile struck and the earth shook. Sound built and stone shattered as the detonation erupted in a cataclysmic shockwave that flashed out like a supernova.

Inside the labyrinth, Sarah stumbled as the ground shuddered around her. Trish screamed and a wave of light swept down the passage. Sarah glanced back and saw Darklight soldiers following. Behind them a cloud of dust burst into the passageway at breakneck speed.

'Keep going!' Jason said.

Heart racing, Sarah ran faster, and the small form of Susan disappeared around the next corner.

They emerged into a large channel that cut through the centre of the labyrinth and Susan waited for them fifty feet away. Reaching her side, with Trish and Jason at her back, Sarah slowed to a stop, breathing hard.

The sound behind faded before a tremendous rumble built above.

Sarah looked up as the topmost level of the labyrinth collapsed onto the level beneath. In a chain reaction floor after floor came down with a successive boom Boom BOOM!

Sarah's eyes widened and she was running again as the collapsing floors chased them down the central avenue.

The vibration underfoot grew stronger. A glimmer of silver made Sarah glance left to see chrome-clad forms on the level above fleeing before the same storm.

Susan angled right down another passage.

'Where's she going?!' Trish said.

Sarah didn't know, but instinct told her to follow and so she did, while behind them, the Darklight soldiers ran past the entrance, carrying straight on.

The thunderous noise continued and they were running through a maze of tunnels again. Tiring, Susan slowed, allowing the three friends to catch up.

'Which way?!' Jason said.

'Right!' Sarah ducked into the right of three passages.

'Sarah, wait,' Trish said, 'Susan's gone left!'

Sarah slid to a stop and ran back to follow Jason and Trish, who were hot on Susan's heels.

The ground beneath Sarah's feet lurched and she bounced from one wall to the other, and staggered on. The levels behind continued to collapse and the roar of falling stone filled the air.

Jason glanced back. 'Sarah, watch out!'

Sarah looked up. A massive ceiling block plunged towards her. A force smashed into her from behind, flinging her from her feet.

Hauled up by armoured hands, she was pushed forward.

'Move!' The Darklight commander said.

Followed by the bulky form of Hilt, Sarah ran for her life as giant blocks thudded into the ground behind them.

They reached another intersection. Susan hesitated, and Jason and Trish took the lead, but the collapse was on them. The entrance to the tunnel crumbled. Susan covered her head with her hands, but Hilt was there again, leaping forward to hold up the massive load. Trish dragged Susan onwards and Sarah crawled beneath the Darklight officer as his left leg buckled under the weight, forcing him down onto one knee.

Sarah grabbed his arm. 'Come on!'

His helmet's mask retracted. 'Go,' he said, grimacing in effort, 'keep Susan safe.'

Sarah looked back at the tsunami of rock seconds away.

'GO!' he roared.

Sarah scrambled to her feet and ran.

The ground beneath Hilt gave way and the Darklight leader was carried into the depths in a cloud of dust as thousands of tons of rock came crashing down.

The rumbling continued and Sarah sped through twists and turns after her friends. A large crack appeared in the ground, its black maw splitting the ground in two and lancing down the tunnel through which they ran. Sarah found herself with nowhere to go. With a scream she fell into turmoil, to be joined soon after by Trish, Jason and Susan. With a jarring thud, Sarah slammed into a slope and was swept down in a sea of debris. Down and down she slid, into the black. Surrounded by chunks of tumbling stone, she was washed along on a wave without water. Gradually her descent slowed and the noise from above petered out to distant tremors. The labyrinth had ended and they'd escaped its final death throws by the skin of their teeth.

Standing up, Sarah sidestepped some smaller rocks, which bounced past, and looked for her friends.

Trish came clambering over the boulders, her injured arm cradled against her chest. 'Where's Jason?'

Sarah shook her head and searched for him with her visor.

'Jason!' Trish called out.

A slew of stone and dirt trickled down to the left and the small form of Susan appeared, the mute woman stumbling towards them before stopping close by.

Trish cupped her hands to her mouth. 'JASON!'

'Over here!' he said, his voice coming from the right.

Sarah and Trish worked their way over to find Jason lying on his back. He turned his head and looked up at them.

'Stop messing around,' Trish said, 'we need to keep moving.'

Jason pointed at his leg. 'That might be a bit of a problem.'

Sarah looked down to see Jason's leg trapped beneath a large piece of masonry.

'I can't feel my foot,' he said.

Trish moved round to the other side of the obstruction and Sarah followed to where Jason's foot was twisted back at an abnormal angle.

'How bad is it?' he said.

'Not good.' Sarah crouched down to see if they could free him.

'Can we move it?' Trish said.

Sarah thought they could, but she wasn't sure and she didn't want to make things worse. She stood up. 'I don't know. You take a look.'

Trish bent down and felt around with her hand. 'If we can lever it from the other side it should roll off without doing any more damage.'

Sarah nodded and after a couple of minutes of struggle they managed to remove the block of stone from Jason's leg.

He looked down at his injury. 'That doesn't look good.'

'It might not be that bad,' Trish said.

'Not that bad!' He gestured at his foot. 'It's pointing the wrong way!'

'Can we twist it back?' Trish asked Sarah.

'I don't know.' She looked at Jason. 'Do you want us to try?'

He nodded and dropped his head back to the ground. 'I can't go anywhere with it like that. Do it.'

Sarah looked at Trish and saw her incapacitated arm left the job up to her. However, as she considered the task she realised she could do more harm than good, especially if her track record on poor decision-making was anything to go by. As she delayed, her doubts continued to mount and she shook her head. 'No, I can't do it, I might make it worse.'

'How can you make it worse?' Jason said. 'Look at it!'

Sarah glanced at Trish for support.

'I can't do it,' she said, indicating her injury.

Left with little option and despite her own anxiety, Sarah bent down and grasped Jason's ankle with one hand and his foot with the other.

'Okay,' she said, feeling queasy, 'I'm going to move it on three, all right?'

Jason nodded, unable to watch.

'One,' Sarah said and wrenched his foot round.

Jason screamed in agony.

Sarah felt resistance and twisted harder.

Jason screamed again. 'Stop! Fucking stop!!'

'Just a bit more!' Sarah gave the foot one last push and let go. 'There,' she said, turning to him, 'all done.'

'I think he's fainted.' Trish leant down to listen to his breathing, and straightened when she was satisfied he still lived. She then dug something out of her pocket, which she passed to her friend.

Sarah looked down at the Anakim pendant, glinting in the palm of her hand under the glare of her helmet's torches. It was as if the artefact didn't want to leave her, like it had a mind of its own. She ran a finger over its surface. She was tempted to launch it into the dark, to get rid of its curse once and for all, but she knew, despite its ability to attract disaster, it also represented the only way out of the black hole that had become her life.

Sarah looked up as Susan shuffled closer.

The woman, gaunt and filthy, gazed down at Jason with scared eyes.

'Its okay, Susan,' Trish said, 'he should be better when he wakes.'

Susan didn't reply; she just stood there, staring at Jason and scratching frenetically at her wrist with sharp, broken nails.

An ugly red rash had developed on the woman's skin due to the OCD-like habit and Trish grasped the girl's hand to stop her.

Susan tensed at the contact and frowned.

Trish let her go. 'It must be the stress of being down here, in the dark – alone.'

'Except she wasn't alone, was she?' Sarah said.

'Perhaps that's why she doesn't speak,' – Trish's expression turned to pity – 'she must have been terrified half to death, the poor thing.'

Sarah reached out to stroke Susan's hair. She felt for her, Trish was right; the poor woman must have suffered horribly, but her thoughts couldn't help but stray to the vision of Riley being held at gunpoint by the Terra Force colonel. Just before the carnage had begun, she'd glimpsed the Deep Reach team leader rolling away to safety. That he lived should have brought her joy, but she knew he was forever lost to her. There was no doubt in her mind that he was there to help the Special Forces track her passage through Sanctuary. *After all*, she thought, *he taught me all I know about traversing this hidden realm*; she touched the pendant in her hand, *well ... nearly all*.

That Riley knew her as the colonel had declared – a thief, a terrorist and a murderer – was also yet another nail in the coffin of their union. Not only had she betrayed his trust by stealing his multi-function card, he must have thought her responsible for the death of his friend and colleague, Cora, who'd died when touching the orb. For who else could she have killed, or been accused of killing? No one as far as she knew. *He must hate me.* The idea repulsed and dismayed her in equal measure. But such fascinations were for the past. She was stuck in the present and everything that entailed.

Sarah turned her attention back to Jason.

What with Trish's arm, his foot and this strange woman, they weren't just down the creek without a paddle, but down it without the whole damn boat. Couple that with the creature in the dark and its attraction to Susan, and it might not be long until they encountered the light again. And this time they wouldn't have the mysterious Darklight to protect them.

As Sarah's fears grew and doubts strengthened, the newest member of their company remained oblivious in silent vigil. Susan stared without blinking into the dark, watching ... waiting. The fingers on her hand twitched and a few seconds later the scratching began again.

CHAPTER EIGHTEEN

SHOUTS AND CRIES for help rang throughout the chamber as the massed ranks of Terra Force worked together to free those trapped beneath the mounds of fallen rock. Fortunately for most, the blast resulting from the Darklight missile attack had been deflected by the high escarpment on which they'd been positioned and as such, casualties had been limited to hundreds instead of thousands. But as the excavations continued, the death toll rose and along with it hope faded that any more would be found alive.

Amongst the floodlights and armoured soldiers, the teams from Sanctuary's Exploration Division assisted their Sancturian brethren in the search for survivors.

Deep Reach team leader Riley Orton struggled with a large rock before being helped by his colleague, the bearded Jefferson Church.

'There's someone under here,' Jefferson said, rolling the boulder aside with a crash.

Dust hung in the air and Riley increased the intensity of his effort as more of the man's armour was revealed.

'Can you hear me?!' Riley said, heaving off another piece of rubble.

A pair of glowing green eyes glittered to life in the dark and a powerful hand grasped Riley's shoulder.

'I can hear you, boy,' said a gravelly voice.

Riley stepped back as Colonel Samson rose from his tomb of stone. Dust and dirt cascaded down from his broad shoulders and the SFSD leader removed his helmet and breathed deep.

The colonel flexed his arms and cracked his neck before focusing his cold eyes on Jefferson and then on Riley.

'How many casualties?' Samson said.

Riley glared at him.

'You want vengeance?' Samson moved closer to him. 'You want me to apologise for putting a gun to your head?'

The memory of being moments from death flashed into Riley's mind and his hands clenched in fury.

Jefferson pulled him away. 'Perhaps a thank you for saving your life is what he wants.'

Samson laughed. 'No, I think he wants to ram a knife through my eye, isn't that so, Orton?'

An image of doing just that and more swamped Riley's mind.

'Sir,' a commando said, approaching, 'we thought you were dead.'

'No such luck,' Jefferson muttered under his breath.

'Report,' Samson said, and moved down from the pile of fallen rock.

'Over one hundred and twenty fatalities and rising, and double that number have injuries that prevent them from continuing.'

Samson rubbed a hand over his stubble. 'Morgan?

Riley tensed at the name.

'No sign of her, Colonel,' the soldier said, 'or Darklight. It's possible they escaped the fallout, but we won't know for sure till we get down there.'

'S.I.L.V.E.R.?'

'We've seen no sign of them since ...'

'Since they turned traitor and ran,' Samson told him.

'Yes, sir.'

An officer arrived on the scene and handed Samson a canister of water.

The colonel drank deeply and then wiped his mouth on the back of his arm. 'Send the order out; S.I.L.V.E.R. operatives are to be shot on sight. Finding the woman is priority. Get them ready, we move out in twenty.'

'But, sir,' the officer said, 'we need to keep looking for survivors, and the wounded—'

'Can fend for themselves until we get back,' Samson said. 'The search is over, ready the men – *now*.'

The commando saluted and disappeared back into the mayhem.

Samson gave Riley a contemptuous look and walked away without another word.

'We should have left him buried,' Jefferson said, watching him go.

Riley couldn't have agreed more as his teammate patted him on the shoulder and left him to his own devices.

Like a moth to a flame, Riley's thoughts returned to Sarah and he moved away to the newly created cliff edge and stared out into the darkness, where he hoped the woman everyone sought still lived. He removed a photo from his coveralls and gazed into the blue eyes of the person who'd stolen so much more than precious artefacts. *How can I help you, Sarah?* he thought. *Should I help you? Where are you going? Do you even want my help?* He recalled how he'd felt when he'd seen her again from afar; elated, anxious, angry. Even when the gun had been put to his head, he'd kept her in his sights. *Is there a way to slow Samson down*, he wondered, *and S.I.L.V.E.R., too? Shall I buy you time, Sarah, is that what you need?*

The sound of someone approaching failed to wrest Riley from his deliberations and they stopped by his side, the loose rock crunching underfoot. 'She's pretty,' said a familiar voice.

Riley looked round to see SED facility commander Dresden Locke staring out into the abyss beyond.

The veteran explorer sighed. 'Some men do stupid things for pretty.'

'And some men are just stupid,' Riley said.

Locke laughed. 'You're not wrong. But pretty isn't always beautiful, pretty can be twisted, mean and rotten to the core.'

'You think Sarah has a black heart?'

'No, but some women are just ... conflicted. And you have to ask the question.'

'Which is?'

'Is she worth it?' Locke turned to face him. 'Is she worth your life, your soul?'

Riley tucked the photo back into a pocket. 'The decision's out of my hands, she saw to that.'

'And yet you can't let her go.'

Riley didn't know what to say. He'd never been in such a position before, torn between equal forces. He stared down at his hands, his eyes drifting out of focus.

'He won't stop,' Locke said. 'Samson, he won't stop until he has her.'

'I know.'

'And he won't care if she, or any one of us, dies in his quest to get his hands on those artefacts.'

'No, he won't.'

'Then if we want to stay alive, and if you want to make sure she stays alive, we need to make sure we find her first.'

Riley looked up. 'We?'

Locke pointed and Riley turned round to see his twenty strong Deep Reach team, Alpha Six, geared up and ready for the off. At their head Jefferson held up his climbing equipment and grinned.

Riley's mind jumped into overdrive. 'They'll be right on our heels.'

Locke nodded.

'And if they catch up to us ...' Riley said.

'They'll be pissed.'

Jefferson approached. 'We'll need to move fast.'

'And for that ...' Locke said.

Riley attached his kit. 'We need the best explorers in Sanctuary.'

The facility commander lowered his visor and smiled. 'It's time to show these yahoos how it's really done.'

CHAPTER NINETEEN

MALCOLM JOINER STOOD at the sweeping window of the SED's command suite, an office usually frequented by the facility's commander, Dresden Locke. The GMRC Intelligence Director held his hands clasped loosely at the small of his back as he gazed down to the shuttle bay below, which continued to bustle with frenzied activity. A deep rumbling announced the arrival of another air-shuttle, the discordant sound sending vibrations through the floor at his feet. Moments later the craft hove into view, cresting the lip of the giant oval shaft that disappeared into the depths beneath.

Progress in the field had gone well; preliminary reports made by Colonel Samson's force had been beyond expectations, but still a deep sense of unease had settled upon Joiner as the days and hours passed. The other teams who'd been following the longer route to the temple had reported they'd found Sarah Morgan's trail, but it was as they'd feared, they were still many days behind.

Since his confrontation with Committee member Selene Dubois, he'd been expecting to hear word from an irate Samson on his command being usurped by Ophion and S.I.L.V.E.R., but the communication had never come. He was told later that the cabling connecting the SED substation to the colonel's transmission hub must have been severed. He allowed himself a small smile. There were a number of possibilities to account for the cessation of signals from the lead expedition; however, it wouldn't surprise him if Samson had taken measures to maintain command.

The desktop intercom buzzed as an incoming video message from Sanctuary's GMRC Command Complex appeared on the wall display. It was Grant Debden, his primary aide.

Is he in my office? Joiner thought, glimpsing a stunning coastal resort in the background behind Debden which could have only come from a 3D wallscreen.

Joiner frowned at his subordinate's transgression and touched the screen to accept the call. 'Yes?'

'Sir,' Debden said, his eyes focusing on his director, 'Ms. Dubois has requested an audience with you in Tower Central.'

Joiner suppressed a grimace. 'Did she say what it was about?'

'Her office informed me a board of evaluation had been convened. They said if you're to attend it will commence in five hours' time.'

'A board of evaluation,' – Joiner felt his chest tighten – 'you're positive that's what they said?'

'Yes, sir, although I'm not sure what it's about. Your review of directorate nominees isn't due for another month and I have no other such instances in your diary.'

Joiner knew exactly what it meant. The Committee had made his failures a priority. He'd been summoned for judgement. *If you're to attend*, he thought with bitter resentment, *they say it as if I can refuse.* If the Committee called, you answered.

'Shall I confirm your participation?' Debden said.

'Yes. Remind me when I need to leave.'

'Of course, sir, I'll arrange transport.'

Joiner cut the transmission and sat down in his chair wondering what he could do to make things right with the Committee. *Or is it as I feared*, he wondered, *have they purposefully manoeuvred me into an untenable position?* It was the not knowing that drove him to distraction, and if there was one thing Joiner hated, it was being kept in the dark.

His thoughts strayed to Professor Steiner. So far the ex-Director General had evaded the efforts of the Committee to locate him. Well, as far as Joiner knew, he had. He'd put his feelers out and found that the Pacific fleet had been tasked with his retrieval. *Or should that be assassination? As soon as they find him he'll be gunned down on sight, or interrogated and then killed when all information has been extracted on the hacker's whereabouts.*

B.I.C. – the man was relentless in his pursuit of the truth. It was something Joiner could relate to, but that's as far as his empathy extended. B.I.C.'s activities had been the cause of great consternation in the intelligence community for as long as he could remember. The man was a censor's worst nightmare, which meant he was Joiner's worst nightmare. *The Committee is right; the two of them together pose the greatest of threats to their plans. But would Steiner really jeopardise his life's work, the entire human race, to gain some sense of justice or recompense for past grievances?* Joiner put himself in his position. *No, there is no way the professor would aid the hacker,* he decided, *no way in hell.*

Joiner's mind returned to the Committee. How will they react? I'm one of their most important assets, they can't operate without me, at least not to the extent they require. Or have I, like Steiner, reached the end of my usefulness? Has my sell by date expired? If it has, I need to adapt to the changing landscape of power and that means one of three things: redefining my use to the Committee, ascending to the Committee, or perhaps the most difficult of all, destroying the Committee. How does one go about killing a hidden, multi-headed beast that operates in all corners of the globe?

A knock on the door interrupted his musings. *Perhaps I'm just about to find out,* he thought, his anticipation rising.

'Yes?' he said.

The familiar figure of Agent Myers entered the SED's command suite. The clean-cut CIA operative looked drawn, almost haggard, as though he'd aged ten years since their last encounter.

'How was the surface?' Joiner said.

'Cold and dark.'

'You're up to speed on events?'

'Debden debriefed me.'

'Good. I take it you have news?'

Myers looked around the room with anxious eyes. 'Is this office secure?'

Joiner nodded. 'I had a team do a full work up. Nothing said goes beyond these walls.'

'I hope you're right,' Myers said, 'I've found out many things ... a great many disturbing things.'

♦

Joiner pressed a button on the desk and the walls and windows to the SED office turned opaque. He leant forward and interlaced his fingers. Myers was not one to make overblown statements and Joiner all but twitched in lust for the knowledge that was about to be disclosed.

He eyed his agent over the tops of his glasses, savouring the expectation like a fine wine. More moments passed before he succumbed to his craving. 'Proceed,' he said with a flick of a finger.

Myers remained standing and dropped a thick file on the table with a thump. Flopping it open, he slid out some grainy photographs.

'These were taken from a Japanese spy satellite prior to the destruction of all four space stations. They show two Sabre transportation ships leaving for Earth moments before the explosion. Both craft are GMRC.'

'Then it's as we thought,' Joiner said.

Myers didn't reply, instead he placed a data device on the desk's induction panel and video footage appeared on the wallscreen. 'This stream was recorded by another satellite operated by the Russian military.'

Joiner watched the four space stations slowly rotating through the vacuum of space before a cluster of explosions lit up the ISS. His eyes widened as a chain reaction ripped apart the massive crafts in a choreography of perfect destruction.

After the carnage had ended, Myers paused the image. 'Since this catastrophe happened you'll know that the chaos within the GMRC's Space Programme, NASA and the other civilian space agencies is through the roof. Questions, accusations and conspiracy theories are spreading like wildfire. Multiple investigations have been launched, morale is rock bottom, and international tensions are strained to breaking point.'

Joiner knew very well about the fallout from the disaster. The Directorate had called an emergency meeting, which he'd attended by video link. What he wanted to know were the real whys and wherefores, not the well-rehearsed cover up interwoven with truth and mayhem.

Myers gestured at the screen. 'When I saw this feed, I made it my priority to find out who was on those two GMRC ships. Who knew what was to come? I managed to acquire the records from an internal contractor who logs the manifests for GMRC secure operations.

'A number of names gave me cause for concern.' Myers moved to the display and accessed a file with a tap of a finger, and a cluster of staff profiles appeared. 'These high ranking officials all have positions within the GMRC's Space Programme. On further investigation each and every one of these people has worked in close partnership with one man – a select member of the GMRC Directorate and your close associate.'

'Dagmar Sørensen,' Joiner said.

Myers nodded and touched the screen to bring up the profile of the GMRC's sallow-faced Research and Development Director. He then discarded all the other profiles except one, which he expanded to twice the size. 'Ms Sylvia Lindegaard,' Myers said, 'was the lead

GMRC delegate assigned to the United States Space Station, USSS Archimedes. As far as I can tell, she was responsible for all GMRC integration on Archimedes and liaised extensively with NASA, the U.S. military and the GMRC's R&D Division.'

'Do we have access to those communications?' Joiner said.

Myers shook his head. 'I was unable to breach their server security. Like us, they hold all records on stand-alone systems. Maybe if I was utilising our division's resources we could mount an operation to gain access without being detected, but even so it would take a lot of time and manpower and there would be no way to hide that kind of activity from prying eyes.'

Disappointed, Joiner gestured for him to continue.

'Going on from this,' Myers said, 'I also have first-hand accounts that a month prior to the incident large quantities of explosive were sourced by a department within the R&D Division, a department that works exclusively with the Space Programme. The purpose for the acquisition was unknown, but extrapolating data from the footage you've just seen, the explosive force matches the quantities sourced.'

'Confirming the sabotage came from within the GMRC itself,' Joiner said.

Myers expression remained grim.

Joiner pondered the implications before something Myers had said filtered down through his thoughts. 'First hand accounts?'

'Don't worry,' Myers said, 'I covered my tracks well; none of the GMRC intelligence community picked up on my work, including deep cover operatives and covert artificial intelligence. I ran a full diagnostic of our database to confirm – we're in the clear. If there's a leak, they'll have no idea what we're investigating.'

While he was pleased Myers had evaded the vast GMRC surveillance machine that Joiner himself directed, it was disturbing he was able to do so with such efficiency, and Myers must have picked up on his disquiet.

'You wanted off the books, no traces.'

'Yes, yes.' Joiner waved a dismissive hand. Myers knew what he was doing; it made a change for things to go right for once. Joiner couldn't afford the Committee further ammunition, especially considering his imminent *evaluation*.

'Due to Sørensen's name cropping up,' Myers continued, 'I used this information to deepen my parallel investigation into Project Ares.'

Joiner sat up straighter. He'd still to reveal to anyone what he'd uncovered on the Committee's censored videos of Sarah Morgan. As far as he knew, only S.I.L.V.E.R., the Committee themselves and those working inside Sanctuary's secret R&D laboratories knew that the pendant activated Anakim technology, and Joiner wanted to keep it that way – the fewer people who knew the better. And if that included Myers, so be it. Some things were best left unsaid.

The CIA operative accessed another folder on-screen and a familiar logo appeared.

'As we know,' Myers said, 'Ares was officially designated as an R&D Division black project. Subsequent briefings indicated it was primarily a navigational system with real world applications for underground transport and military operations, although various other uses had been mooted. My initial attempts in finding out the real purpose of Ares met with strong resistance and all outside agencies failed to provide me with the lead I desired; all, that is, except one. During my time in Europe I was able to activate an old source who works within the German Federal Intelligence Service, the BND. It seems they'd stumbled on a series of backdoor protocols inside the Internet's darker recesses which led to a complex web of computer programs created by an unlicensed artificial intelligence.'

Joiner frowned. If years of intelligence gathering had taught him anything, it was that accepting happenstance at face value was one of the biggest mistakes you could make. 'Stumbled on?' he said, his tone querulous.

Myers held up a hand. 'My thoughts exactly, and when I found out where these programs took me – which I'll get to shortly – I went back and looked into how they'd found them in the first place. It seems the coding structure that had alerted the computer technician to them matched a system he'd been working on some weeks before. As he works on all manner of projects without knowing their true purpose he was unaware of the significance of his find. In fact, at the time he never made a direct connection, he just knew he'd seen something familiar and thought it worth further investigation. When I got the BND agent to follow the chain of data back to its origin it turned out that the technician had been tasked with analysing an incident with which we are familiar. An infiltration into EUSB Deutschland using a digital signature you yourself have been chasing on a large scale op during my absence.'

Joiner's eyes narrowed. 'B.I.C.'

'Yes, the hacker Bic, or *Da Muss Ich* as he is known in parts of Europe, was the operator of the A.I. that had weaved this web of programs. A web that, on inspection, led to a host of files that the Germans couldn't make head nor tail of. They did manage, however, to decrypt certain portions of them, the odd word or phrase here and there, parts of a diagram, sections of schematics. All worthless as far as they were concerned, except that one of the phrases they deciphered was—'

'Project Ares,' Joiner said, shocked. 'Why haven't the Germans reported it to the GMRC? Why isn't it in our system?'

'They didn't know what they had.'

'But they do now.'

Myers shook his head. 'My source won't be telling anyone about anything. I've left no loose ends'

'Good,' Joiner said in distraction, 'very good.' He pondered the news he'd just been told. 'How the hell has the hacker found out about Ares?'

'This is where things get strange. I'm not sure he's found anything out about it at all. In fact, I'm sure he hasn't; only that it's something he's interested in.'

Joiner arched a brow.

'Quite,' Myers said. 'That he knows about it at all is worrying, but it appears the hacker is interested in quite a lot more than just Ares. After gaining entry to these files I managed to procure anonymous access to a GMRC mainframe in order to process what the Germans couldn't.' Myers turned back to the screen and opened another file. 'It turns out the hacker has created a vast network of computers using our own software against us.'

'Forget the technicalities,' Joiner said, growing agitated, 'get to the point.'

'Do you remember when the hacker broke into our servers some years back?'

'How could I not?'

'It seems he'd penetrated far deeper than we thought. So deep, in fact, when it came to cleaning house to prevent another such incident from occurring we failed to ensure we'd eradicated the infestation.'

Joiner stared at Myers in disbelief. 'You're telling me the hacker still has access to our servers?'

'It appears so. To what extent it's hard to tell without overhauling the entire system.'

Joiner closed his eyes as he tried to calm himself. *If the Committee finds out about this I might as well tie a noose around my neck now.* He leant back in his chair and fixed Myers with a penetrating gaze. 'What has he found? What does he know?'

'It's difficult to say—'

Joiner banged the table. 'Then guess!'

The CIA agent gave a startled blink at his director's ferocity. 'So far his activities seem limited to random communications and non-critical services,' Myers said, 'nothing that could really be used to expose the GMRC's Subterranean Programme, or any other of its classified divisions.'

'So he's found nothing?' Joiner said, his voice scathing.

'No, not nothing – in fact he's found something that helped me in my search for answers.' Myers gave the screen a double tap and a massive organisational chart appeared. 'This,' he said, gesturing at the graphic, 'is a representation of peer-to-peer networks of every mid-level to senior employee in the GMRC.'

Joiner glared at the mass of meaningless interconnecting lines.

'It might not look much,' Myer said, 'but,' – he touched the screen again to turn large portions of the lines into various colours, and then once more to isolate red, green and blue networks – 'these three colours represent a series of hidden coded messages and money transfers within the GMRC. From what I've been able to work out so far, it appears the hacker has located three distinct organisations operating within the GMRC without its knowledge.'

'Sovereign spies, corporate espionage,' Joiner said, unimpressed, 'this isn't news.'

Myers shook his head. 'No, it's more than that. The sheer scale of it is unprecedented. Whoever these groups are, they have their own agendas we know nothing about.'

Joiner had a good idea who they were and one had to be the Committee, perhaps not directly, but those that worked for them, those that would do anything for money and the lure of power.

'Using these networks and official GMRC databanks,' Myers continued, 'I was able to confirm Sylvia Lindegaard as a prominent player in at least one of these secret organisations. I was also able to track her movements in great detail. It seems Ms. Lindegaard has been far busier than just obliterating the space stations and intercept missions. Over the years she has been directly or indirectly connected with at least a quarter of all the major failures in the GMRC's Space Programme. Coincidence? I think not. With more time I believe I could connect her with many more.'

Joiner folded his arms. 'You're saying this Lindegaard could be responsible for sabotaging every mission designed to save the surface of this planet? One person?'

'Maybe not all, and no, not just her, but whoever she works for.

Whoever she gets her orders from. They want to the see the surface burn; they want the world as we know it to end. While we've been busy fighting this hacker and everyone else, we missed the enemy within. We've been deceived from the start,' Myers said in despair, 'and now it's too late.'

CHAPTER TWENTY

So, the truth is out, Joiner thought, staring at the photos on his desk. *Someone, probably the Committee, has arranged the mass extinction of every living thing on the surface of the planet, along with the destruction of humanity's greatest civilisations, or at the very least they've helped it on its way with a hefty shove.* The notion was sickening, but it didn't change his current predicament, nor would it change the fate of those left to die on the surface. He'd always accepted the billions of deaths as necessary – and perhaps unavoidable – collateral damage. What was done was done, he needed to move on and that meant securing his position with the Committee. He needed something for leverage. What he needed was more information.

'Shall I continue?' Agent Myers said, breaking the silence.

Joiner removed his glasses to polish the lenses. When he'd gathered his thoughts he gestured for his subordinate to proceed.

'Due to the secrecy surrounding the R&D Division,' Myers said, 'I realised if we ever wanted to find anything out quickly, I had to use a more direct method of data acquisition. After I'd got to grips with the hacker's activities I was able to use the networks he'd found to narrow my search for those people who actually worked on Project Ares. And what I came up with,' – Myers turned back to the wallscreen and opened up a large window – 'was this.'

A black and white picture appeared on the display. A chair had been placed in front of the infra-red camera and the muffled sound of a voice grew steadily louder.

Still off camera, someone gasped for air as if something had been removed from their mouth. 'What is the meaning of this!' said a man with a Russian accent. 'Do you know who I am?! I'm a senior scientist with the GMRC. You have no idea who you're dealing with!'

Two large men in masks dragged a struggling figure before the camera and strapped him to the chair.

The man's wide eyes searched the dark as he sought his captors. 'What do you want with me!' he said as the men left. 'People will be looking for me; you won't like it when they find you!'

A bright lamp blazed to life and the camera switched to a normal image. The man, now surrounded by shadow, blinked at the blinding light that was focused on his face. When he regained his senses he squinted into the dark behind the light, seeking, and failing, to locate whoever held him prisoner.

'Who are you?' he said, his voice shaking with poorly disguised fear. He turned his head as if hearing something to his right. 'What do you want from me?'

'We want what you know,' a voice said, a voice that Joiner recognised as that of Agent Myers.

'I don't know anything, you have the wrong man.'

'I thought you were an important person, a senior GMRC scientist?'

The man's expression turned desperate. 'I lied, I work for a private company, I—'

'Your name is Dr. Vladan Marković. You are a forty-five year old senior research scientist originally from the Ukraine and you work for the GMRC's R&D Division. You were formerly a resident of EUSB Sentinel, but you are, according to your papers, on reassignment to EUSB Superior.'

The man opened his mouth as if to say something and then closed it again.

'Now, Dr. Marković, I work for the GMRC's I.D., you know who that is, don't you?'

The doctor looked like he was going to pass out. 'Intelligence Division,' he said, his bottom lip trembling.

'Yes. Now, if you cooperate with me I'll ensure your transfer to your new base will go off without a hitch. Fail to cooperate and your dental records will be the only way the police will be able to identify your body. Do we understand each other?'

A bead of sweat trickled down the side of Marković's face.

'I SAID, DO YOU UNDERSTAND ME?!' Myers shouted.

The scientist shrank back in terror. 'YES!'

'Good,' Myers said. 'Project Ares, tell me what you know.'

'Project what?' Marković said.

A loud bang and a flash of light made the scientist scream.

'The next bullet goes in your head,' Myers said, 'I haven't got time for games. Ares, what do you know? Live or die, you decide.'

A sob escaped Marković's lips. 'They'll kill me if I tell you.'

'I'll kill you if you don't.'

'Please,' he said, 'don't make me do this.'

Something fell onto the scientist's lap, making him flinch.

'Papers, a new identity,' Myers said. 'You know who I work for, we can make you disappear. Now talk.'

Marković remained locked in his internal struggle before his shoulders slumped in defeat. 'What do you want to know?'

'Locations, personnel, goals, progress.'

'Do you know about the other race?'

'The Anakim?' Myers said. 'Yes.'

Marković nodded in acceptance, bowed his head and let out a deep sigh. 'We all come from different backgrounds, different fields,' he said, his voice still trembling. 'When it started we were all excited. We knew what we were doing was cutting edge, pushing the boundaries of science. But the more we discovered the more things started to go wrong. Some of us were scared,' – he looked up, his face full of woe – 'we should never have started, we should never have begun.'

'Begun what?'

'Anything, everything. The Anakim technology. It was far beyond anything we'd ever dreamt of. They'd harnessed the hidden dimensions. Forget the quarks and leptons, gluons and photons; they'd gone beyond, into a place we didn't understand, may never understand.'

'Where are the laboratories?'

'You know two already, EUSB Superior and EUSB Sentinel, and there is one other I know of, USSB Sanctuary. There could be more, I don't know it all.'

'Who controls the project?'

'There are many senior officials, but the whole programme is controlled by the division director.'

'Dagmar Sørensen?' Myers said.

Marković nodded. 'He oversees it personally. Every major stage goes through him, him and the generals.'

'Generals? The military help shape the project?'

'Yes,' he said, his voice growing stronger, 'but only the U.S. military; everything in Europe is purely scientific research. Had I known I'd be working for the U.S. government I would never have entered into the contract, but when I found out it was too late.'

'You have no contact with anyone else outside the programme?'

'No one, we're kept under lock and key. You're the first person I've spoken to outside the project for over a decade.'

'So what is Project Ares for?' Myers said. 'What are its goals?'

The scientist licked his lips. 'Do you know how big Ares is?' Marković shook his head. 'No, how could you. We have thousands of scientists working on Ares, thousands. EUSB Sentinel has a separate compound just for our personnel, it takes up four per cent of the entire base and the one in EUSB Superior is three times the size.'

'So you're saying you don't know?'

Marković gave another shake of his head. 'No, I know. The main goal of Ares is to break down Anakim technology into its component parts. To get it working, and understand how it works when we do.'

'So you've succeeded? You've powered up the ancient tech?'

Joiner sat forward in his chair, his interest growing with each passing moment.

'Some,' the scientist said, 'but never for long and not properly. Many think we're using the wrong power source, others think we should quit altogether.'

'Why?' Myers' voice said. 'What has you all so spooked?'

'Accidents have happened. A lot of people have died and ...' Marković stared into the camera's lens, his eyes distant.

'And what?'

'Strange things have happened.'

'Strange things?'

'Yes, we've had a lot of people go down with psychosis, hallucinations, whole teams at a time. They say it's to do with the God Device, but I think it's more—'

'The what?' Myers said.

Marković gave a blink as if remembering he was speaking to someone outside of his decade-long incarceration. 'The God Device. It's what we call the single piece of Anakim tech that actually works and keeps working.'

'I thought you'd failed to make anything work properly?'

'We had ... we have.'

'Then how—'

The scientist laughed, the sound verging on the hysterical. 'We didn't get the God Device working. It was working when they found it.'

'Already working?'

'Yes. For all we know it's been active since the Anakim still roamed the Earth.'

'What is it, this God Device? What does it do?'

Marković chuckled again. 'We don't know what it is; we don't really know what it even does to a large extent.'

'You're trying my patience, Doctor,' Myers said in warning.

The scientist sobered. 'Some think it's a way to speak to the Anakim, like a voice through history. Others say it could have been responsible for wiping the Anakim out, a doomsday device.

'What do you think it is?'

'It could be either of those things, or an advanced artificial intelligence. Or it could just be a living creation given the breath of life by the Anakim themselves.'

'It's alive?'

'Oh, yes. At least, as far as we can tell it has conscious thought. The scary thing is we don't know what it's thinking, but sometimes it seems to know what we're going to do even before we do it.'

'Hang on,' Myers said, 'this thing speaks?'

'No, not in the usual sense. It communicates through imagery. Sights, sounds, smells, feelings, sensations. It's like living plasma, it—'

The scientist jerked in his seat.

'Doctor?' Myers said.

The scientist's head snapped back and his body arched in spasm.

Myers swore and appeared on camera as the man thrashed in his restraints.

The struggle continued before the video footage stopped.

Joiner returned his focus to the room.

'Marković died a few minutes later,' Myers said. 'I did all I could to bring him back, but it seems speaking about his work triggered a device implanted in his brainstem. He was dead as soon as he opened his mouth and he didn't even know it.'

'Basic mind control,' Joiner said, 'Dagmar always was old school.'

'It's my fault,' Myers said, 'I should've had him scanned beforehand.'

Joiner removed his glasses and rubbed his eyes. 'Yes, you should have, but it's still good work. It seems Ares is much larger than we envisaged. Sørensen has done well to keep it hidden for so long; half his efforts must go on information control. Which will be who one of those networks belongs to. At least one of those hidden groups the hacker found will be the R&D Division trying to keep everything under wraps.' Joiner was impressed at the enormity of the cover up and livid his teams hadn't been wise to it. And it was only since the asteroid had hit that the veil of secrecy had begun to lift, the cracks appearing as chaos on the surface reigned. *I'll need to clean house*, he thought. *No, then they'd know I was on to them, better to keep the status quo and play them at their own game. The truth would always find its way to the light, it was inevitable.*

'So Ares centres around this God Device?' Joiner said. 'Intelligent life that knows what we're going to do before we do it.'

'Sounds like a disaster waiting to happen,' Myers said.

Joiner couldn't agree more. 'There is only ever room for one dominant species, one superior intelligence. Whatever they're playing with, it could end us all.'

'You want to destroy it?'

'It's the only course of action.'

Myers nodded and remained silent as his director digested the information he'd just provided.

After a while the CIA operative spoke again. 'I did find out one more thing about Ares.'

Joiner looked up, intrigued.

'I know which general in Sanctuary is aiding Sørensen with his work.'

Joiner's expression grew hungry. 'Tell me.'

'A man you recently became acquainted with ... General Stevens.'

CHAPTER TWENTY-ONE

'YOU'RE SURE? General Stevens? The man's a buffoon.'

Agent Myers nodded. 'As sure as I can be. That network is very specific and Stevens features on it prominently.'

Joiner knew the general worked alongside the SED to procure Anakim artefacts, so it should have come as no surprise the man was up to his neck in a project that sought to profit from the ancients' technology. That he himself had been blind to the fact was far more galling. His problems with Steadfast, Steiner, the hacker, the Morgan woman, S.I.L.V.E.R., and ultimately the Committee, had clouded his mind, compounding errors upon errors. Coupled with his other duties as GMRC and U.S. Intelligence Director, some might think it wasn't surprising, and yet in his younger days he would have taken such an onslaught in his stride. He looked at the ageing skin on his hand and looked away.

'Where is the bloated fool?' Joiner said, standing.

'I have no idea.'

Joiner pressed a button on his desk.

'Re-routing,' said a computer generated voice, 're-routing.'

An image of Joiner's primary aide popped up on-screen. 'Director?' Debden said.

'Where's Stevens?'

'The general? Isn't he at the SED with you, sir?'

Joiner scowled in realisation at his mistake. 'Have you arranged my escort to the tower?'

'Yes, sir, everything's standing by.'

Joiner nodded, switched off the transmission and then depressed another button on the desk.

'Yes, Commander – I mean, Director,' said Dresden Locke's personal assistant.

'Find me General Stevens and get him here, right now.'

'The general, sir? I'm afraid he's busy down in the shuttle bay, if you can—'

Joiner released the button and looked at Myers.

The CIA agent stormed from the room and as the doors slid closed behind him, Joiner could hear his raised voice barking out orders.

Joiner paced over to the opaque window and turned it transparent. He looked down into the shuttle bay below and it took a moment before he saw what he sought: the cigar-toting U.S. Army General, waddling around like an oversized blimp. He studied the man until a civilian rushed over to him and gestured back the way he'd come.

Stevens turned to look up at Locke's office and visibly stiffened when he saw Joiner staring back at him.

The general held Joiner's distant gaze for a moment and then puffed out a cloud of smoke before ambling into the building.

Five minutes later the oaf had finally made his way to the office.

Joiner closed the folder on his desk and minimised Myers' on-screen files, before giving his agent the go ahead to let the military man enter.

The doors to the room swished open and General Stevens wandered in, looking wary.

'You called?' Stevens said, glancing behind as Myers followed him in.

'Take a seat, General,' Joiner said.

Stevens held up the palm of his bandaged hand. 'I think I'll stand, if it's all the same with you.'

Joiner held the man's gaze and then turned away to look back out of the window. 'I hear we have a mutual friend, General.'

'I didn't think men like you had any friends,' Stevens said, his tone guarded.

Joiner chuckled. 'Come, General. Shall we not let bygones be bygones? We're all on the same side, aren't we?'

The general didn't reply.

'Dagmar Sørensen,' Joiner said, turning back round to pin Stevens under his icy glare, 'you two have been working on something I'm interested in: Project Ares.'

Stevens paled at the name and glanced in Myers' direction.

'Don't look at Agent Myers,' Joiner said, 'he won't help you. Tell me what you know and we can all get on with our day.'

'I've never heard of Ares,' Stevens said, 'and if you know what's good for you, neither have you.'

Joiner's eyes glittered with danger. 'Are you warning me, General?'

'Call it good advice,' Stevens said.

Joiner fixed the general with a stare, his expression unreadable, before he broke the silent impasse by strolling out from behind his desk.

Stevens followed his movement with suspicious eyes as Joiner reached Myers, who remained looking at the general with an uncompromising air of hostility.

Joiner walked behind the CIA operative and slid the agent's silenced sidearm from his holster.

'You're going to shoot me this time?' Stevens said, taking a step back. 'We both know there are people just as powerful as you that consider me a valuable asset.'

'Is that so?' Joiner pointed the weapon at the general.

Stevens stood up straighter in defiance. 'Shoot me and—'

Joiner whirled round to point the gun at Myers and fired.

The CIA agent's eyes widened and he looked down in shock at

the blood that had begun to seep through his white shirt, before crumpling to the floor.

Joiner walked over and stared down at him as he bled out from a gunshot wound to the stomach. He crouched down and placed the gun to Myers' forehead. 'Tell me, Agent,' he said, 'are you my leak?'

Myers stared into Joiner's eyes and opened his mouth, but no words came.

'Think it over,' Joiner said, looking down at the wound, 'you have a few minutes.'

'Are you out your mind?!' Stevens said, staring in shock at Myers on the floor.

'Quite possibly,' Joiner said. 'It seems some people can be too helpful. Now, General,' – Joiner raised his gun – 'tell me about Ares.'

♦

General Stevens eyed the man before him in shocked disbelief. He's insane, he thought, I have to tell him what I know and be damned with the consequences. Sørensen can deal with him, I have no choice.

The door to the office opened and Locke's P.A. stood in the doorway. 'I thought I heard—'

'Get out!' Joiner said, turning the gun on her.

The woman screamed and fled.

♦

'You've been keeping secrets, General,' – Joiner cocked the pistol – 'it's time to share them.'

Stevens glanced at Myers, who moved weakly on the floor, and then turned frightened eyes back on the gun. He held up his hands in supplication. 'Fine, on your head be it, but you didn't hear it from me, understand?'

Stevens moved to the wallscreen and looked to Joiner. 'I need to access some secure files.'

Joiner sat down on the edge of the desk. 'Go ahead.'

The general entered some military codes while Joiner reflected on how well his plan was going. Myers had sidestepped the leak issue when he'd arrived, diverting Joiner's attention elsewhere. The man had learned too much, too quickly. It might be that he was as faithful as he appeared to be, but Joiner had taken the opportunity to find out for sure. He looked over at the dying agent, hoping he would live long enough to either confirm he was the leak or prove his innocence. Either way, Joiner would have to decide whether to keep him alive.

Apart from exposing Myers' potential duplicity, the act of violence had also served a far more important service: convincing Stevens to fess up. Two birds with one stone was a phrase made for this moment and while Joiner tried to suppress a feeling of superiority, it was hard not to revel in his own magnificence. *It must be a rare man who could utilise such a situation to his advantage*, he thought, *it's a shame I can't share this moment; how my reputation would soar.*

'Are you watching?' Stevens said.

Joiner looked back to the wallscreen where the general had loaded three separate video recordings of Sarah Morgan conducting her illicit incursion into the military's vaults and laboratory complex; uncensored videos that Joiner wasn't supposed to have seen.

'I think you know as well as I,' Stevens said, 'that the pendant and the orb this woman stole are much more than just artefacts.'

Joiner watched the footage unfold as he had many times before. One showed Morgan activating the massive Anakim shield. In another she became incapacitated by the palm-sized orb. And in the final and perhaps most tantalising of the videos, she approached a fifty foot high pentagonal prism, which towered above her. Joiner couldn't help but be immersed in the scene once more as Morgan reached the front of the monolith to activate a large, rectangular vessel housed within. A blue glow blossomed into existence inside the transparent container until the liquid inside sparkled like a distant star.

Joiner refocused on the general. 'The pendant activates Anakim technology.'

'It does,' Stevens said, 'and Morgan is the key to everything those R&D geeks have been working on for decades.'

'What is Ares?' Joiner leaned forward. 'What is the God Device?'

'Ah, so you know more than you've let on.' Stevens' surprise turned into a knowing smile. 'Very well; we've gained many useful technologies from Ares. The camouflage suits that our elite troops possess, we reverse engineered those from Anakim tech. They tell me they combined it with what we already had and then made it ten times better. Other advanced materials have been found and used to great effect. We've already advanced our weapons programmes by nearly fifty years. Even NASA's been utilising the tech to improve their systems and spacecraft. It's a new dawn of advance and we're right on the cusp. Add to that Morgan's little trinket and we can expect to take even bigger strides forward. The sky's the limit.

'The orb is supposed to be connected to some ... thing,' the general continued. 'They call it the God Device; to me it just looks like the abomination it is. They think it's some kind of A.I., and the orbs contain readouts much like our brainwaves.'

'But you're not so sure?'

'I don't know want to think, I leave that to the science nerds and their labs.'

'What's inside the monolith?' Joiner said, returning his gaze to the video as it repeated on the wallscreen. 'What does the liquid do? What is it for? What is its purpose?'

'I don't know, even I don't have clearance for that. I was just responsible for its retrieval. Since Morgan circumvented our security it's been guarded round the clock by black ops.'

'And that's it?' Joiner said. 'That's all you know?'

'There is one other thing,' Stevens said. 'There's something your friends in the tower didn't tell you.'

Joiner's heart beat faster. *Of course Stevens knows about the Committee, how could he not?* 'And what's that?' Joiner said, staying calm.

Stevens activated another feed on-screen and a view from a Special Forces visor appeared. The soldier was accompanied by a number of heavily armed commandos and the lights from their helmets lit up a scene of bloody carnage.

'Where is that?' Joiner said.

'That was recorded a number of years back by a Terra Force unit who went searching for a missing Deep Reach team. It was east of the USSB. Ever since they found this place back in the early eighteen hundreds there's been reports of strange lights and people disappearing. Sometimes whole teams of explorers never came back. They thought it was down to climbing accidents, earthquakes and Sanctuary's general instability.'

Joiner looked at the dismembered bodies on the screen.

'But when they found this,' Stevens said, 'it changed everything.'

'What did it?'

'They don't know what it is. Only that it doesn't like company. The team of marines you're looking at never made it back alive, there were over sixty, heavily armed. It tore them apart like they weren't even there.'

'They didn't get off any shots?'

'Oh, they shot at it alright,' Stevens said, 'bullet casings were everywhere. They unloaded everything they had and it still didn't stop it. And since it takes so long to get to that area we decided to leave well enough alone, although that was after we lost another two teams. After that we sent down a tethered robot which brought back the helmet that recorded these images ... amongst other things.'

Joiner saw a shimmering light appear on the soldier's visor screen. 'What is that?'

'That's it.'

'There's no audio?' Joiner said.

Stevens touched the screen.

Sounds of gunfire erupted from the speakers and the screams of dying men filled the air. The battle, if that's what you could call it, carried on and on until the visor image suddenly ended.

'That's all the footage you have?'

'Not all.' Stevens played another file. 'The robot captured this.'

Joiner saw the same shimmering light gliding across the ground of a rock-strewn chamber. The vision slowed and then stopped before a strange, indistinct form emerged from the ether. The creature's transparent skin, if that's what it was, bulged and distorted. It looked like it might have legs, but each time a coherent shape appeared it melded back into the writhing mass. At times a protuberance, much like a head, searched this way and that, like a snake tasting the air. Moments passed until the light glowed forth once more before vanishing from view

The footage ended and Joiner considered what he'd seen.

'The scientists call it the Pharos,' Stevens said. 'Have you noticed how they always have to give something a name?'

'Like the Roman lighthouse,' Joiner murmured, 'a beacon.'

'Yeah, but rather than guide you to safety it rips you in two.'

'Perhaps Siren would be more appropriate.'

'Whatever it's called,' – Stevens sparked up his cigar, the end crackling orange as he sucked in its noxious fumes – 'when I knew it stayed in its part of Sanctuary I could sleep at night.'

Agent Myers gave a groan of pain and Joiner looked in his direction, his thoughts troubled. 'What did you just say?' he said, turning back to Stevens. '*When* it stayed in its part of Sanctuary?'

Stevens chuckled amidst his pall of smoke, his face turning sinister. 'You caught that, did you? Let's just say it won't be long until you're not the only spawn of the Devil calling this base home.'

Joiner stared at him. 'They're bringing it here?'

Stevens laughed. 'You didn't think they called in all of S.I.L.V.E.R. for just one woman, did you? They're out there to trap this Pharos and bring it back for study.'

'You can't be serious.'

'They're confident they can neutralise it. If they can't, they'll monitor and release. Personally, I'd rather see the beast dead ten times over before they even considered bringing it back, but that's Sørensen for you. The man's nothing if not determined.'

Joiner's mind was racing. 'Dresden Locke knows about this thing?'

'Of course, that's why he's always banging on about safety all the time. He knows full well what's down there. Did you see his face when you told him he'd be going? He nearly wet himself.'

'He knows why S.I.L.V.E.R. are here?'

'Locke is many things,' Stevens said, 'but stupid isn't one of them; he knows.'

The doors to the office opened and Joiner turned to see his primary aide enter the room.

'Debden?' Joiner said, frowning. 'I didn't call you here.'

'Sir,' – Debden glanced over at Myers – 'your evaluation's been brought forward.'

Joiner's grip loosened on the pistol. 'What?'

'He said it's been brought forward, Director,' Stevens said.

Joiner looked back round and something exploded against his chin. Light flashed before his eyes and he slumped to the floor unconscious.

◆

General Stevens shook out his fist and looked down at the comatose body of the intelligence director. 'Damn, that felt good.'

Debden felt for Joiner's pulse. 'You didn't have to hit him so hard.'

'He deserved it,' Stevens said, flexing his bandaged hand.

'The Committee may still require his services. Joiner is one man you don't want bearing a grudge.'

Stevens sniffed. 'I'll take my chances, as will you when he finds out you're his leak.'

'He won't be seeing me again. I'll be reassigned.'

Stevens grunted and then looked over at Myers. 'What about him?'

Debden walked over to the stricken CIA agent and crouched down next to him. He pulled open his shirt. 'Call for a medic; he hasn't got long.'

Stevens pressed a button on the wall console and while he spoke to SED emergency services, Debden stood up and returned to Joiner's side to look down at his former boss. *How many years have I had to put up with his shit?* he wondered. *Six years? It feels like twenty.* He leant down and removed Joiner's dislodged glasses, closed them and tucked them into his breast pocket. The man was a monster, but he'd been Debden's monster; he almost felt a stirring of emotion at having to part ways with him, it had been a massive part of his life. Whether it was a good part he was still trying to figure that out.

Half a minute later, two medics burst into the office to attend to the gunshot victim, while nearby the man who'd inflicted the near mortal wound remained unmoving on the floor. Grant Debden took one last look at Joiner's prone form before slipping unnoticed from the room.

He touched the implant in his ear to activate his computer phone. 'It's done,' he said.

'Your transport is waiting for you,' a woman said on the other end, 'you'll be on the first elevator out of Sanctuary. Have you decided where you'd like to be relocated?'

Debden thought for a moment. 'Somewhere hot, with lots of water, endless beaches and beautiful, sun-kissed women.'

'USSB Pelagic it is. Thank you, Grant Debden, your service has been exemplary. We wish you well in your future endeavours.'

The woman hung up and Debden continued on his way, out of the SED and into his new life, the trials and tribulations that surrounded Malcolm Joiner a rapidly fading reality, the joys of the unexpected a whole new future. He stepped out of the SED's main entrance and onto the front concourse before a screech of brakes made him turn and cry out, 'NO!'

♦

The driver's car bounced over the body of the man he'd just run down. He slid the back end out and then gunned the accelerator.

As he sped back out into the base's tunnel complex, he switched on the wiper blades to remove the blood that covered the cracked windscreen.

His car's computer bleeped and a woman's face appeared on the head-up-display.

'Is it done?' she said.

The man nodded.

'The credits will be wired to your account when we have confirmation.' The woman cut the transmission and the man continued on into the darkness, his job complete and the only thought on his mind, whether he should order out for Chinese or Indian.

CHAPTER TWENTY-TWO

Colonel Samson scanned the area with his visor and crouched down to touch the tracks on the ground. 'How long?'

'Half an hour, maybe forty minutes.'

The Terra Force Colonel dug armoured fingers into the surface. 'And no one saw them go?'

'No.'

Samson bowed his head and clenched his hand into a fist. He breathed deep as he sought to control his fury. 'And Locke's with them?'

'Yes, and the whole of Orton's Deep Reach team, Alpha Six. We think they might be trying to join up with S.I.L.V.E.R..'

Samson's brows furrowed deeper until his eyes were slits.

'We sent a squad after them,' the soldier said, 'but they were out of sight. They're moving quick.'

Samson stared into the collapsed labyrinth. 'We can move quicker.'

'Sir?'

'Ditch the supplies.' Samson pulled a shining sword from the ground, sending dust and dirt sifting down as he stood. 'Mask up, soldier,' – he held the Darklight weapon aloft and activated the blade, which reflected bright in his visor – 'it's time for war.'

CHAPTER TWENTY-THREE

Sarah Morgan sat on the hard ground watching her two friends talking in low tones twenty feet away. Nearby, the mute woman known only as Susan, lay sleeping in shallow dreams, her body trembling and twitching against an unseen ethereal threat.

After a while, Trish turned on her visor and worked her way towards Sarah over the boulder-strewn landscape.

'How is he?' Sarah said.

'Okay,' – Trish looked back at Jason – 'a bit grumpy, but alive.'

Sarah removed her helmet and switched on its torches, allowing them some relief from spectral enhancement.

Neither of them spoke for some time until Trish reached out and squeezed Sarah's hand. 'Are you okay?'

The deep concern in her friend's voice broke something within her. Sarah shook her head and fought back tears.

'Hey,' Trish said, touching her face, 'what's wrong?'

A sob escaped Sarah's lips. 'I thought I'd lost you.'

Trish drew her into a fierce embrace. 'But you didn't, did you? I'm still here.'

Sarah felt tears trickle down her face. 'No thanks to me.'

'What?' Trish leaned back so she could look into Sarah's eyes.

'I thought you were dead; it was Jason who knew you were alive, not me.'

'That doesn't matter.'

'I gave up on you. I nearly killed you and then gave up on you. What sort of person does that make me?'

'You didn't nearly kill me; you were trying to save me.'

'I led us down here to die.' Sarah's tears flowed again. 'I kept pushing us further and harder. You both said, but I didn't listen.'

'Sarah, no, Jason told me what happened. You mustn't blame yourself, do you hear me?' Trish lifted her chin. 'This is not your fault.'

Sarah wanted to believe her, but she couldn't. She knew she was right. And deep down Trish and Jason knew it, too. She'd led them into this abyss to die and there was no one else to blame but her.

Trish held her close and stroked her hair, much like Jason had not so long before, as Sarah cried silent tears into her shoulder. The sensation of being comforted reminded her of when her mum used to do the same thing when she was a little girl. Another memory flashed into her mind, a memory of stepping out into oblivion. Sarah didn't want to think about what she'd attempted. She never wanted to feel that low ever again.

A while later, when Sarah was calmer, Trish released her hold.

Sarah wiped her eyes with grubby hands. After her admission to Jason, she'd believed she'd no more tears left to give, but her guilt lay heavy on her heart and it sought to wring her dry.

More empty silence passed and Sarah felt compelled to speak. 'Do you ever feel ... wrong inside?'

'Sarah, trust me, there's nothing wrong with you, it's all in your mind.'

'That's the problem, I think you're right.'

'What do you mean?'

'I've been hearing things, like voices in my head.'

Trish tried to conceal a look of concern. 'What?'

'Sometimes it whispers to me. When there's danger it tells me things.'

'Things?'

'It tells me not to fear the dark, to embrace it. It's like death itself is calling to me.'

'Come on, Saz, you're worrying me. I've never seen you like this. You're the bravest person I know.'

'That's the thing, it's all a sham. I'm so scared, I seek out danger; I seek out thrills just to feel.'

'It's just this place.'

'No, it's more than that. Every expedition I've gone on, it's got worse. Each time I went that little bit further, that little bit higher, that little bit faster. And bit by bit I changed. People thought me fearless, courageous, but I realise now I was just afraid, afraid of standing still, afraid to face reality. A reality without my mum. A reality alone. Riley once said he felt like a fraud because he thought he'd got where he was because of who his father was. I reassured him he wasn't, but it should have been me admitting to being the fraud, the faker, pretending to be something I'm not. Everything I do turns to crap and I take even bigger risks to regain control, and it's led to this. Ever since Mum died, I feel ... lost. When I found Riley and my perfect job, I got scared because I felt so happy. Does that sound strange?'

'A bit,' Trish said.

'It's like – I don't know.' Sarah shook her head. 'It's hard to explain.'

Trish gave her hand a squeeze. 'Try.'

'It's like I want to fail.' Sarah stared into space. 'Sometimes I think I'm losing my mind.'

'You've been through a lot, what with the fire, your mum, Mark, Cora, Riley, the SED. You're trying to control everything around you, overthinking. You need to let go and relax instead of fighting all the time. When we get to the surface, everything will sort itself out, you'll see.'

Sarah knew Trish was trying to help, but she didn't understand. How could she? 'You still think we can make it?'

'Don't you?'

'We don't even know where we are.'

'We'll find a way.'

'Of course we will,' Jason said, hobbling over.

A small hand worked its way into Sarah's and she looked round to see Susan next to her. The small woman's expression didn't change, she just looked down at the ground, as timid as ever, but the gesture was there and it filled a hole in Sarah's heart.

'You shouldn't be walking on that,' Trish said, indicating Jason's foot.

Wincing, Jason looked down at his ankle. 'It's fine. Besides you can't carry me to the surface, so I'm going to have to walk on it some time.'

'Isn't it painful?' Sarah said.

'Err, yeah.' He held up a small device. 'This Darklight morphine dispenser helps, though.'

'I thought he needed it more,' Trish said to her.

'Plus these Darklight battlefield wraps are super-strong.' He held up his leg to show her. 'It's made out of nano-tubes or something; it transfers all the weight, like having bone on the outside. I can hardly feel it,' – he grimaced again – 'sort of.'

Sarah remembered something. She gently released herself from Susan's hand and delved into her coveralls to withdraw Trish's locket. 'I think this is yours.'

Trish looked amazed as she opened it up. 'I thought this was lost for good.'

'I never knew you were religious,' Sarah said, swapping looks with Jason.

Trish must have heard the accusation hidden in her words, but instead of being angry she just smiled. 'All religion isn't bad, Sarah. People like to think it is, but if there wasn't religion people would find other ways to make war, it's what they do. Besides, the fundamentals of religion are sound, it helped create our civilisation, after all. It's when people misinterpret it for their own gain that things go wrong. As to me being religious – I'm not.'

'But the cross,' Sarah said, 'the picture of Christ.'

Trish removed the gold cross and held it up to the light. 'Religion doesn't own faith,' she said. 'They like to think they do, but God – the light – is for everyone if they want it.' She held out the cross in the palm of her hand. 'My grandmother gave me this when I was six years old. She always told me it would protect me from the dark and if I ever found myself on the wrong path, all I had to do was to hold this and God would show me the way back to the light.'

Sarah looked at it with undisguised scepticism.

'Take it,' Trish said, 'I want you to have it.'

'I can't.'

'Sure you can.' Trish pressed the cross into her hand.

'Does it burn?' Jason said.

Trish gave him a withering look while Sarah turned it over in her hand, a myriad of thoughts running through her mind.

'Where are your pendants?' Trish said.

Jason adjusted his splint to increase its support. 'She doesn't want to use it anymore.'

Trish looked at Sarah in surprise. 'Why not?'

'Because it's brought us nothing but bad luck.' Sarah removed them from her pocket. 'The chain's broken, anyway.'

Trish took it from her and passed it to Jason.

Grumbling, Jason sat down to see if he could repair it.

'Well?' Trish said.

He waved Sarah over and she got up and knelt in front of him, while lifting her hair to one side.

'This will hold,' he said, 'but you won't be able to take it off again without breaking it.'

Trish took the cross back from Sarah and opened its clasp to secure it to the chain.

Sarah mustered a weak smile before positioning the pendants inside her coveralls, the gold cross bright against the grey of the pentagonal artefacts.

Sarah stood up and Trish gave her another one-armed hug.

'So,' Jason said, 'what now?'

'We look for another transportation device,' Trish said, before removing food rations from her backpack and handing them out.

They devoured the meagre fare in seconds before the waif-like figure of Susan moved closer to Trish and tugged at her arm.

'I think she's trying to tell us something,' Trish said.

Jason looked around in fear. 'Perhaps her friend is near.'

Sarah, her heart suddenly racing, put her helmet back on and activated her visor. 'I can't see anything.'

'Neither could those Darklight soldiers and look what happened to them. By the way,' – Jason lowered his voice – 'should we even be staying with her? If she attracts that thing, perhaps we should ...'

'Should what?' Trish said, turning angry. 'Leave her all on her own in the dark?'

'I'm only saying.'

'Perhaps we should just wait here,' Sarah said.

Jason avoided Trish's fierce glare and turned to Sarah. 'What? Wait here, why?'

'To let those soldiers take us back to the base,' Sarah said, 'if we stay here they'll find us eventually.'

'They'll lock you up,' Trish said, 'lock us all up.'

Jason shook his head. 'They're more likely to shoot first and ask questions later.'

Susan continued pulling at Trish's arm. 'I think she knows where to go,' she said, looking at the mute woman's earnest expression.

'Straight to that *thing*, probably,' Jason said.

'Well, we can't use the Anakim parchment,' – Trish held her ground against Susan's persistence – 'there's no point of reference. We could be anywhere.'

Susan stamped a foot and gave a squeal of anger, and Trish gave in and allowed herself to be dragged forward.

'What are you doing?' Jason said.

'Following Susan,' Trish called back.

'That's a bad idea!' He turned to Sarah for support, but she didn't know what say. Trish had told her to let go, so that's what she was going to do. Offering her shoulder to Jason for support, they followed Trish and the waif into the beyond.

CHAPTER TWENTY-FOUR

'GREAT,' Jason said, 'she's led us to a dead end.'

Sarah helped Jason over to a wall, where he propped himself up against it. The Darklight splint enabled him to put his full weight on his injured ankle without major discomfort, but there was no point damaging it any further if they could help it.

They'd been walking for hours and they'd seen no sign of the creature, but equally they'd seen no sign of any Anakim structures, either, let alone a transportation device.

'Shall we rest here?' Trish said, looking to Sarah.

'I don't know, I suppose it's as good as place as any.'

Tired, they settled down on the damp soil that made up the floor of the network of caves they now traversed.

'I'll keep watch,' Sarah said, fearing the nightmares that waited in sleep.

No one argued and Sarah soon found herself sitting on her own while Trish, Jason and Susan breathed in silent slumber.

Wondering where Susan was taking them, and then realising she no longer cared, a distant noise made Sarah start. Focusing her visor, she scanned for signs of the fearsome light. Moments passed and she relaxed. It was nothing.

More time slipped into history and Sarah found it increasingly difficult to stay awake, the sound of her friends' slow, rhythmic breathing lulling her towards sleep. Without realising it, her eyelids drooped closed and she glided into the unresisting land of dreams.

♦

A strange noise made Sarah stir awake. She could feel something digging into the palm of her hand. Releasing her grip, she realised she'd been holding onto Trish's cross. She heard the noise again and cracked open an eye. A few feet away, Susan stood staring down at Trish, her fingers, as ever, scratching at the rash on her wrist.

But where's that noise coming from? she wondered. It sounded like ... she felt her eyes drawn left and her heart rate skyrocketed as they fell upon a massive translucent form.

Stifling a scream, Sarah froze.

The beast flowed through the shadows towards Susan and the sleeping Trish. Its skin rippled and shimmered along its indistinct frame like a nightmare made real. Inside the hideous body, veins and arteries pumped black blood and lungs billowed in and out like vast bellows. Something resembling a head extended before it and, as with its body, it expanded and contracted in time with its sibilant breath. It had no eyes by which to see, and rows of jagged teeth, dripping with black mucus, appeared and disappeared as it continued to move with an abnormal gait.

Sarah found herself captivated in horror.

A shimmer of light flickered through the beast's skin and a clicking sound made the hairs on the back of her neck prickle. A sudden glow of light drew Sarah's attention back to Susan. The woman was now holding Sarah's orb aloft. The Anakim artefact glowed bright as Susan spoke into it with low tones and the wall before her trembled, sending eons of sediment crumbling to the ground.

The creature closed in on Trish while Sarah remained frozen in fear as her panic built to a crescendo. *I have to do something.* She willed herself to act. *Get up, Sarah!* Her mind screamed, *GET UP!*

The translucent body reared up over Susan and its head extended into a snake-like form that inexorably bore down on Trish.

Still unable to move, Sarah felt a scream building.

'What's that noise?' Jason said groggily. He sat up next to her and turned on his helmet's lights.

The creature shimmered into light and Jason cried out in terror. A shriek of noise broke the silence, the light vanished and Sarah scrambled to her feet.

'Trish!' Jason ran over and pushed Susan aside.

'What was that noise?!' Trish said in shock as Jason hugged her to him.

Sarah looked at Susan, whose pupils shone with an eerie glow. But as she watched, the woman's eyes faded to normal and her posture slumped as if she'd been released by whatever possessed her. The Anakim orb fell from her hands and hit the ground with a dull thud.

Sarah scanned the area for the light, but there was no sign of it.

'What the hell is going on?!' Jason said.

Trish looked scared and confused. 'What happened?'

'That thing was here, right over you.' Jason pointed at Susan. 'I told you she would lead us right to it!'

Sarah bent down and pocketed the orb, while giving Susan a wide berth. 'He's right,' Sarah said, as Trish looked to her for confirmation, 'it was here.'

Trish put a hand to her mouth and looked at Susan in shock. 'Oh my God.'

'We have to get out of here,' – Jason helped Trish to her feet – 'and away from *her*!'

Susan shied away from Jason's anger and Sarah felt a pang of sympathy for the poor girl. 'I don't think she knows what she's doing. I think it's controlling her, somehow.'

'I don't give a toss, she goes or we go!'

'But why isn't it trying to kill us, like those soldiers?' Trish said. 'Why are we still alive?'

'It wants us for something,' Jason said, 'food, who knows. I don't care. I just want to get as far away from it as possible.'

Sarah saw something glint in the dark behind them and she switched off her visor to increase the power of her helmet's torches.

'What are you doing?' Jason said, as she walked past him. 'We have to go!'

Sarah ran her hands over the wall. 'There's something here.'

'Who cares?' Jason pulled her away. 'Let's go – now!'

Sarah shrugged him off and brushed away the dirt to reveal a dark metal surface beneath. The more she unearthed, the faster she worked, while Jason ranted and argued with Trish behind.

Sarah looked up. 'It's a gate,' she murmured to herself. She glanced back. 'It's a way out!'

'To the surface?' Trish said, moving to her side.

'No, but look,' Sarah pointed up at head height, 'I think it can be opened.'

Trish reached out and touched the outline of a large indented shape. 'It's not a circle.'

'It's the right size, though.'

'I think I see something,' Jason said.

Sarah looked back and saw Susan pointing into the darkness towards a shimmer of light.

'It's coming back!' Jason took a step back, and then another.

'Open it,' Trish said.

Sarah grasped the pendant that hung at her neck and hesitated.

The light grew closer.

'What are you waiting for?!' Jason said, joining them.

Sarah remembered the promise she'd made to herself and held the pendant out to Trish. 'You do it.'

'Are you crazy?!' Jason said.

Sarah looked back to see the light was almost on them. 'This might be what it wants.'

Trish grabbed hold of the pendant and put her hand on the wall, and Jason tore off his glove and grasped her wrist.

'Sarah,' Trish said, 'nothing's happening!

The light filled her vision and Sarah placed her hand on top of Trish's.

'Time to die,' Sarah whispered.

CHAPTER TWENTY-FIVE

The ground beneath their feet rumbled and Sarah looked at the wall, waiting for a death blow that never came. She turned round to see a figure emerge from the blazing light.

The man reached up and removed his Deep Reach helmet and she felt her legs go weak.

'Hi there,' Riley said, a half smile playing across his lips, 'are you lost?'

Stunned, Sarah's hand dropped from the wall. The words echoed through her mind like a dream. *Hi there, are you lost ... are you lost?* They were the same words he'd said to her when they'd first met back at the SED, which seemed like an eternity ago. Images from the past flashed through her mind and she felt the world spin.

Powerful arms caught her and she found herself gazing up into a pair of familiar, dark brown eyes.

Riley's expression became intent. 'You're a hard woman to find, Sarah Morgan.'

They stared into each other's eyes until the earth shuddered again.

Riley glanced up and frowned. 'What the—?

Sarah regained her feet as a series of intricate symbols glowed to life across the wall. The glittering lights expanded into a pattern that spiralled out from the centre. More chunks of sediment rained down to the ground, forcing Trish and Jason to jump back as clumps of rock and earth thudded into the soil around them.

'What have you done, Morgan?!' said a powerful voice.

Sarah looked past Riley to see Dresden Locke shining a torch at the scene ahead.

With a thunderous sound of stone on stone, the whole wall ground backwards before pivoting to one side on a hidden hinge. Dirt and dust poured down from above, the shower turning to a trickle as the tremors subsided and the glowing symbols faded back to dull.

A massive entrance loomed black before them.

Locke took a step forward and Riley and Sarah followed.

On the threshold, Sarah peered into the void while her emotions lurched in turmoil at the presence of the man standing so close beside her.

'Turn off your lights,' Riley said, switching off his own, 'everyone, turn off your lights!'

The twenty men and women of Alpha Six did as their team leader ordered, the lights behind blinking out one by one. Riley reached out to Sarah's helmet and held her with a lingering look before plunging them into darkness.

As Sarah's eyes adjusted to the gloom, she realised they weren't in total darkness at all. A steady source of light emanated from the void before them, and warm, sweet-smelling air tickled her senses. Her expression changed to wonder as she realised what she was looking at. Spread out before them, a vast, misty landscape stretched down into the Earth's crust, a living world full of fluorescing plants and trees, and glistening rivers chock full of luminous algae.

Sarah took a step forward. 'So beautiful,' she whispered, captivated by the vision.

Something fluttered through the air towards her. She held out her hand as a small butterfly, its wings glowing dark red, weaved away, up over her head and out into the wasteland beyond.

Locke turned on his lights. 'You two,' – he gestured to a man and woman – 'plant a waypoint beacon.' He turned to Riley. 'We need to go back; we don't want to be here when the colonel finds us.'

'You want to go back now?' Riley said, 'after finding all this?'

Locke shepherded everyone away from the entrance. 'Morgan was our priority; we've found her. And from what we've just seen, now we know why they want her so badly. If we cut west we can work our way back to charted routes, bypass Samson and meet up with the second expedition coming from the north.'

'And will that be before or after the creature finds us?' Jason said, as everyone else switched their helmet torches back on.

Locke studied Jason for a moment and then turned to Jefferson. 'Church, give these people the once-over. We move out in two minutes.'

Jefferson nodded and moved towards Sarah.

'Wait,' Jason said, limping forward, 'didn't you hear me? Don't you know? There's something out there, and this woman,' – he looked around – 'where did she go?'

Sarah spun round to see Susan was nowhere in sight.

♦

Riley looked at the confusion – or was it fear? – on Sarah's face. He studied her appearance. Her Deep Reach coveralls were stained and torn. Dark scars blackened her jacket's sleeves and what looked like angry burns reddened her neck. Dirt clung to her hair, and her face was covered in varying layers of dust. Tracks in the grime made it look like she'd been crying. She looked exhausted and afraid and he sensed something about her had changed; that spark in her eyes had gone and defeat hung over her like a cloud. He frowned, wondering what had happened to reduce her to such a state. She caught him looking and failed to hold his gaze. This wasn't the Sarah who'd fled the base, the bold explorer; this was a timid shadow of the woman he knew.

Jefferson moved to check Sarah's kit, but Riley motioned to her two friends. 'See to them, I've got this.'

Jefferson nodded and moved away. Riley wanted to know what had happened to Sarah to bring about such a transformation. He could understand that three people travelling on their own in Sanctuary was tough, tougher than tough, but Sarah was as tough as they came, at least when it came to exploration she was. *And I should know*, he thought, *I helped train her*. He checked the front of her harness, tugging at the straps to make sure they were tight.

He removed a container of water from his backpack and handed it to her. 'Are you hurt?'

She shook her head and gulped down the water.

'How long since you've eaten?'

She shrugged and he handed her an energy bar which she consumed in seconds.

He opened a panel on her helmet. 'Your battery's low and you need a reboot.' He pulled a cord from his belt and hooked it up to the charging port. 'How did you activate that wall?'

She passed the canister back to him. 'Does it matter?'

'It does to me.' Riley looked up as Locke pulled Sarah's irate friend, Jason, to one side. 'Your pal seems stressed about something.'

Sarah followed his gaze. 'You don't know, do you?'

'Know what?' Riley said, turning back to find her looking at him.

'It's not safe down here.'

'Sanctuary's never safe for anyone.'

'No, you don't understand, there's something down here, there's—'

'Right, listen up!' Locke said. 'Time to move.' He pointed at Riley. 'Don't let her out of your sight.'

When Locke moved away, Sarah grabbed Riley's arm. 'We don't want to go that way.'

Riley disconnected the cable from her headgear and closed the panel. 'Look, I know you don't want to go back. There'll be a trial. The military will try and throw the book at you, but with good behaviour—'

'No!' She grasped the front of his harness.

He glanced round to catch some of his team looking in their direction.

'Sarah,' – he stared into her manic eyes – 'what's got you so spooked?'

Something scurried past and Riley near jumped out of his skin. He switched on his visor to see a person running away into the newly discovered habitat. 'Who the hell is that?!'

'Susan,' Sarah said, watching the woman disappear into the dense foliage.

'Where did she come from?' A distant sound echoed though the chamber and Riley looked up, startled. 'And what the hell was that?'

'Susan's friend,' Sarah said.

Riley gave her an odd look. 'Sarah, what's going on?'

'Back!' Locke said, ushering the team towards the gateway. 'Everyone back!'

Sarah left Riley's side to join her friends.

'I wish he'd make up his damn mind,' Jefferson said, jogging up to him.

Riley patted his friend on the shoulder and strode forward as Alpha Six milled around in confusion. 'Sir, what's wrong?'

'Riley, get them through that gate.' Locke glanced behind as if searching for something.

'I thought—'

'NOW!' Locke pushed past him. 'Everyone, get through that gate now, that's an order!'

Riley looked into the distance, but failed to see what had got his commander so agitated. He switched off his torches and took a step forward to flick through his visor's spectrums.

A glimmer of light drifted across the ground and his brow furrowed before someone dragged him round.

'Riley,' Sarah said, 'we need to go!'

Another shriek of sound broke through the dark, sending a shiver of fear rippling through his body.

♦

Heart pounding, Sarah ran with Riley through the massive gateway.

Fifty yards ahead, Trish helped Jason into a limping run. When they'd heard the sound they'd wanted Sarah to go with them, but she'd had to warn Riley.

'Morgan,' Locke said, grabbing her arm as she passed, 'can you close this entrance?'

'I don't know!'

Locke stared past her. 'It's too late, it's here.' He turned to everyone. 'Listen to me! If you want to stay alive you need to run, and run fast!'

'You heard the man!' Riley said, pushing those that remained forward. 'Let's go, move it, MOVE IT!'

Sarah glanced behind to see the light bearing down on them and another ear-shattering roar propelled those that weren't moving fast enough into a flat-out sprint.

CHAPTER TWENTY-SIX

SARAH'S BREATH sounded loud in her ears as she tore down the slope and into the bioluminescent ecosystem. Bright reeds slapped at her face and she held up her arms to deflect them. The sound of people in flight surrounded her.

'Faster!' Locke shouted.

Sarah glanced right to see one of Riley's team vanish from sight. Moments later two more people disappeared into the foliage, their screams cut short.

Riley guided her left.

Running flat out, they caught up with Trish and Jason and Sarah slowed as Alpha Six sped past, but Jason waved her on and pushed Trish away from him. 'Go, save yourselves!'

'I'm not leaving you!' Trish said.

Sarah went to help her friends and then Riley was there helping Jason back into flight. 'Go!' he said to her.

Sarah saw the light angle towards them before blinking out of existence.

'Where is it?' Trish said, her head swivelling this way and that.

'Keep going!' Riley said.

Seconds later the shimmering light reappeared sixty feet ahead in the middle of the fleeing Alpha Six team. Screams echoed into the air and the survey team scattered.

Half of them came running back with Locke amongst them.

The light disappeared again.

'Stop,' Locke said, raising his hands, 'everyone, stop moving!'

Sarah slowed to a halt, with Riley, Trish and Jason close behind.

'Can anyone see it?' Jason said.

Sarah heard a woman scream. She turned to see someone running off to the right. The shimmering light emerged behind her, closing fast.

A final shriek of terror lingered in the air and the beast evaporated back into the half-light.

'Sarah, what is that thing?'

She looked at Riley and gave a shake of her head. 'We don't know.'

Jason scanned the misty terrain. 'Ask your boss.'

'Where's it gone?' Jefferson said, inching towards them.

'Everyone, turn off your torches,' Riley said.

The lights on their Deep Reach helmets blinked off and the glow of the surrounding forest of plants shone brighter.

The sounds of nature crept into her perception and Sarah could hear insects buzzing and the silvery burble of flowing water. Senses on high alert, she continued to hold her breath, waiting for the inevitable return of the light.

More time passed in tense vigil before Locke spoke again. 'We need to move back to that gate and trap it in here.'

Riley left Sarah's side and approached his leader. 'How long have you known? How long have you known this thing was down here?' Riley grasped Locke's jacket. 'How long?!'

Locke grabbed Riley's wrists, his eyes fierce. 'I've always known!' He broke Riley's grip and thrust him away.

Jefferson held Riley back while Locke straightened his jacket.

'You've been sending us out for years,' Riley said, 'and said nothing!'

'Nothing? Nothing?! Without me you wouldn't have a job,' – he looked round at those left – 'none of you would. I pushed through the reforms that made the SED what it is today. They wanted to shut us down, turn it into a military operation. I made the deals that kept us going, kept us in the game – kept us safe. I did what I had to do for all of us and I'd do it again!'

Sarah moved to Riley's side. 'We need to get out of here, he's right, if we can trap it somehow ...'

A distant rumble of noise reverberated through the alien landscape. Clusters of bright insects flew into the air before the sound came again.

'Is that thunder?' Trish said.

Jason looked up.

A gust of wind ruffled the leaves around them and Jefferson pointed behind them. 'It's coming!'

Sarah turned to see a shimmering form moving at speed towards them, the plants parting before it.

'Go!' Riley shouted, helping Jason back into a run.

Behind, the green-blue light grew brighter as it arrowed towards them.

One by one people broke away, each heading off in their own direction.

But the light didn't deviate.

A river appeared before them and Sarah found herself running on her own on the opposite side to her friends.

'Sarah!'

Sarah glanced right.

Trish pointed in panic. 'It's right behind you!'

Adrenaline flooded her system and she surged forward.

Legs pumping, heart racing, mind screaming, Sarah ran from the light.

A tree loomed before her and she angled left. Cresting a rise, she tripped and fell, tumbling down a steep ravine.

After falling end over end, she regained her feet and looked back over her shoulder.

The light had slowed, but still followed. A deep penetrating growl emanated down towards her and she ran on.

A shimmer of light appeared ahead and her eyes widened in terror. There were two of them!

Her legs slipped from under her as she skidded to a stop.

The shimmering form towered over her and the beast closed in behind.

The air distorted and a man in chrome armour materialised from the ether. Leaping over her, he plunged a rod of gold into the ground.

The light ploughed towards him and then reared up as electricity engulfed it.

More chrome-clad warriors emerged from nowhere to contain the light within a circle of electrified probes.

The creature screeched in fury and Sarah scrambled to her feet and ran.

CHAPTER TWENTY-SEVEN

Ophion Nexus watched the monster struggle in its prison of crackling energy. He'd been tracking the Pharos ever since they'd picked up Morgan's trail. It was fortuitous, as the secondary objective had helped keep the primary from noticing their presence – that was until it was too late.

Ophion strode round the trap's perimeter. 'Stage two!' he said, over the noise of the thrashing beast.

On his command, S.I.L.V.E.R. deployed more devices. Wire cables lanced out to form a net that wound tight, forcing its victim to the ground.

'Shall I go after the woman?' Zhang Bai said, through the radio.

He glanced back as Morgan fled. 'When we've secured the Pharos for transport.'

As if on cue, the creature let out a roar and redoubled its efforts to escape. The cables stretched to breaking point and one snapped. Ophion ducked as it whipped past his head.

Six more cables arced out and the Pharos was forced back to the ground.

Ophion anchored his second cable and jumped back before the electricity could flow up his arms.

Zhang Bai approached and opened her visor to gaze at the shimmering form that writhed before them. 'Will it hold?'

Ophion didn't know. There were too many variables. 'Move to stage three,' he said, looking into the distance with his visor. 'Retribution draws near.'

CHAPTER TWENTY-EIGHT

SARAH MADE it to the top of a hill and looked back at the silver soldiers surrounding the light in their midst. Electricity flowed over the creature's massive form and flashes of light rippled through it, like a cuttlefish. The beast roared in pain and glimpses of translucent skin appeared as its shroud weakened.

Sarah almost felt sorry for it ... almost.

She saw one of the warriors look in her direction and she took that as her cue to run on. Reaching another ridge top, she scanned the area looking for signs of Riley and the others.

Movement to the right drew her focus and relief flooded through her. Running down through a field of fluorescing flora, Sarah waved at her friends.

'Sarah!' Trish's voice came through her helmet's speakers. 'You're alive!'

'They captured it,' Sarah said, watching as her friends and the remnants of Alpha Six changed course towards her. 'They captured the light!'

'Who captured it?'

Sarah went to reply but another clap of thunder rumbled through the chamber and a flicker of distant light lit up the land.

Riley separated himself from the group and ran up the hill towards her. Sarah ran to meet him and they shared a fierce embrace.

'Are you okay?' he said, holding her close.

She nodded, looking into his eyes.

'I thought ...' he said, searching her face.

'Those soldiers saved me.'

'Soldiers?'

'Chrome armour.'

Riley's expression hardened. 'We need to get back to the SED. As much as I hate to admit it, Locke was right, we need to—'

Something whizzed past her head.

'Get down!' He shoved her to the floor as bullets peppered the ground around them.

Sarah saw Trish and Jason take cover with Locke and Jefferson.

The barrage stopped and Riley dragged her to her feet. They looked back the way they'd come. An armoured figure stood atop a distant hilltop.

He raised a glowing sword in the air.

A swell of noise made the ground tremble and hundreds of soldiers, green eyes glowing in the shadowlight, appeared over the rise. The man held his pose before dropping the blade to point at her. A roar went up and the soldiers surged down the slope.

♦

Colonel Samson followed his men down into the valley as Morgan and Orton fled before them. Behind, his battalion continued to pour in through the massive gateway. There would be no escape. He secured the sword onto his back-plate as he ran, then picked up the pace, his heavy shod boots eating up the soft ground.

Topping another gradient, a strange vision made Samson slow. A few hundred yards to the north-west Ophion and his assassins surrounded a ... *what is that?* he thought.

Stopping, he zoomed in his visor to see something seethed and fought beneath a blanket of electricity.

One of his officers drew alongside him. 'Shall we engage S.I.L.V.E.R.?'

Samson hesitated as he stared at the beast struggling in torment. A sudden flood of emotions swamped him and visions of restraint and torture tore apart his mind. Samson staggered as pain lanced through his head.

'Colonel, what's wrong?'

Samson grasped the man's breastplate and dragged him towards him, as a vision of Malcolm Joiner swam before his eyes. *'Let him go, Colonel,'* Joiner said, *'don't forget your daughter!'*

'Sir,' another soldier said, 'there's an opening ahead, Morgan and Orton are heading for it, if they get to it ...'

'The best course of action will be for you to find this woman and return the pendant to this base,' Joiner's vision said. 'Harming Ophion will be counterproductive to your cause.'

Samson pulled the officer closer and stared into the man's visor. 'Forget S.I.L.V.E.R., I want Morgan.'

He let the man go and removed his pills from his utility belt. Opening his mask, he knocked back the whole bottle. Chewing them down, he resealed his helmet and refocused on his fleeing prey.

Samson took an unsteady step forward, followed by a stronger one and then another after that.

'Tear Sanctuary apart if you have to,' Malcolm Joiner's voice whispered in his mind, 'whatever it takes, whatever the cost, that pendant must be retrieved.'

Samson's walk turned into a jog, and the jog into a running lope.

The woman? he thought.

'Secondary,' the voice said, 'alive is better, dead will do.'

Samson switched up a gear, his mighty legs eating up the ground faster and faster. Arms and heart pumping, the thrill of the chase coursed through his veins as he overtook his men to retake the lead. All he had eyes for were the two figures in the distance and a single thought filled his mind ... *KILL SARAH MORGAN!*

CHAPTER TWENTY-NINE

Sarah looked over her shoulder at the horde of soldiers swarming over the hills towards them. Five hundred yards closer, Trish and Jason ran before them while Dresden Locke and what remained of Alpha Six angled away to the east.

Sarah slowed her pace, but Riley pushed her on. 'Keep going!'

'My friends!' Sarah said.

The whiz of stray bullets made her duck.

'They'll have to take their chances!' Riley pointed above them. 'We're nearly there, look!'

Sarah looked up as she ran. A small mountain loomed above them and at its peak a dark opening led to another chamber.

More ragged seconds passed and they reached the bottom of a huge staircase carved out of the rock. Sarah felt her adrenaline falter as she looked up at the climb and she stopped to catch her breath.

Riley mounted the first oversized step and held out his hand. 'Come on!'

She shook her head. 'I can't do this anymore.' She looked back at her struggling friends in despair.

Riley came back and grasped her by the shoulders. 'Sarah, look at me. The man leading those soldiers is out of his mind. If they catch us, he will kill us, do you hear me?'

She looked back to see a single armoured figure running ahead of the rest. 'We have nowhere to go.'

'Your pendant,' he said, as he touched the chain at her neck. 'It has power, that's how you got into Sanctuary, isn't it? That's how you planned to get out. You still can.'

'No, we need a transportation device.'

'Then we'll find it!'

She looked into his eyes with lost hope. 'We?'

He touched her face. 'I'll come with you.'

She looked at him, her heart breaking. 'After everything I've done? I betrayed you, I betrayed you all – Cora – she died because of me.'

He glanced back with anxious eyes. 'I know you didn't kill her and you did what you had to do, I get that.'

'The SED, Sanctuary, you'd leave all that for me?'

Bullets zinged off the stones around them. 'Yes, now MOVE!' Riley hauled her forward and she found herself climbing up as her mind swam.

More seconds flashed by and with each passing step Sarah felt her strength returning

They passed halfway and another glance back revealed Trish and Jason had made it to the base of the mountain, although the soldiers behind had narrowed the gap.

Riley grunted in pain and faltered.

'What's wrong?!'

'I'm okay.' He carried on climbing, but Sarah saw blood on the step behind.

She clambered up after him, the stairs getting steeper and steeper. 'You're shot!'

'It's just a scratch,' – he gestured ahead – 'look, not much further.'

She looked up to see the void above was close. Breathing hard, more moments of exertion passed before they found the steps narrowing as the staircase angled up into a vertical ladder. Steps were now rungs and Sarah felt precarious as they reached the final stone and ...

... a dead end.

The stone ladder had fallen short of its destination, the last few rungs having collapsed eons past.

Sarah gazed up in panic at the large stone slab that had recently swung down from above and the dark opening beyond. 'There's no way up!'

'I'll boost you up.' Riley braced himself against a ledge and interlaced his fingers.

She looked down to see Trish and Jason getting closer and the maniac behind bearing down on them. 'They're not going to make it!'

Riley glanced back. 'They might. But we need to get out so we can help them up.'

Sarah looked back up. 'It's too high!'

'Sarah, look at me.' He turned her chin towards him. 'Remember who you are, you're Deep Reach. You can do this!'

Sarah stared into his eyes, took a breath and placed her foot into his hands.

'On three,' he said. 'One – two – three!'

Riley forced his arms up and Sarah pushed out with her legs to propel herself up into mid-air. Reaching out a hand, the split second of weightlessness ended as her fingers grasped an outcrop above. She gritted her teeth, reached out with her other hand and found another point of purchase, before wedging herself into a vertical crack. She felt the weight of the orb slip from her coveralls. With lightning reflexes, Riley caught the artefact just as Trish and Jason rejoined them.

'They're coming!' Jason said.

Out of breath Trish waved her on. 'Sarah, GO!'

Two hundred yards down, the armoured form of the colonel tore up the steps towards them. His fearsome glowing mask locked onto Sarah.

A thrill of fear swept through her and she held out her hand.

Riley pocketed the orb and threw her a rope. Catching it, she turned and worked her way up to the chamber above. Seconds later she emerged into colder air. Clipping the rope to her harness, she turned and dropped it back down the hole, stepped back and braced herself. 'I'm ready!'

Moments later a hand appeared on the ledge; Riley hauled himself up before a scream came from below.

Riley looked at her in shock. 'Sarah—'

His hand slipped from the ledge and he disappeared from view. The rope snapped taut and Sarah was dragged across the ground. Scrabbling for grip, she skidded to the edge and jerked to a halt as she clung to a crack in the surface. She felt the force from below increase. With her hold failing, the rope went slack and Sarah released it from her harness.

She rolled away from the hole before an armoured hand appeared, clamping down onto the stone lip with a metallic clunk. Sarah scrambled back as a pair of glowing green eyes emerged from the pit like the spawn of Satan.

Gripped with terror, Sarah's feet scrabbled for traction on the dusty ground. A split second later and she was sprinting into the dark.

CHAPTER THIRTY

CONTADOR VALANTIS GLANCED round to see the massed ranks of Terra Force steaming through the fluorescing ecosystem like a herd of stampeding cattle. *Blind beasts chasing a deranged master*, he thought. *And what consideration do they have for this precious habitat, untouched for millennia?*

None, was his answer. He'd been hoping the madman would try to attack. What better way to die than to be outnumbered by a thousand to one?

Ophion Nexus signalled to him. 'Assemble the transportation sled.'

Valantis nodded to his leader while the Pharos continued to fight against its restraints. It didn't seem to realise, the harder it fought the more painful its prison became.

He crouched down and gazed into where its eyes should have been. 'Not even the gods,' he whispered to it, 'fight necessity.'

Taking one last look at the glimmering beast, Valantis moved to clear ground and released the clamps from his armour's back-plate.

As he bent down to ready the equipment for assembly, movement behind made him pause. Whirling round, he pointed his rifle into empty space. He frowned and searched the area with his scope.

A soft breeze rippled the surrounding reeds and a small insect buzzed around him before flying up past his visor and away into the night.

He relaxed while unseen behind him a massive form flowed out of the ground. Valantis tensed as he felt its presence and swung back round to see a mass of teeth plunge towards his head.

♦

Gunfire and a scream of death made Ophion reach for his weapons. Fifty feet away, Valantis hung suspended in the air before blood gushed and his severed torso fell to the ground with a sickening thud.

At the same time the Pharos in the trap fell silent and the cables holding it went slack. One moment it was there ... the next it was not.

'S.I.L.V.E.R.,' Ophion said, 'TO ME!'

The chrome warriors formed up beside their leader with weapons drawn.

The Pharos that had been trapped swirled up from the ground, its shimmering form phasing through solid matter to appear beside its mate.

'Shall we try to kill them?' Zhang Bai said.

A roar of sound to the left made them turn to see another light shimmer into being.

'No,' Ophion said, closing his visor, 'we try to live.'

CHAPTER THIRTY-ONE

'YOU CAN HIDE, Morgan, but you can't run!'

Sarah stood behind the pillar of an ancient ruin, scared eyes searching for the man that hunted her. Steeling herself, she ran to the next pillar over.

She heard the mechanical sound of a weapon being cocked.

'I see you, Morgan!'

Sarah crept back from the stone column before bullets tore into it. She dived left, rolled to her feet and ran behind a wall.

A blast of stone exploded next to her, and then another. Terrified, she ducked as another hole appeared where her head had been.

'Walls won't protect you!'

Sarah sprinted away, up some crumbling steps and into another section of the ruins. A thunderous explosion rocked the ground and a cloud of dust billowed up into the darkness. Sarah peeked around a corner and her visor revealed an army of soldiers flooding out from the ground below. Heart racing, she shut her eyes.

'I have your friends!' The colonel's voice echoed through the ruins. 'I have your lover! Surrender yourself or I'll execute them ... one by one!'

Sarah peered out from her hiding place.

Two hundred feet away, Riley, Trish and Jason were forced to their knees in the middle of a massive plaza.

'We've played this game before, Morgan! I guarantee this will have a different outcome!' The colonel strode up to Riley, drew a sidearm and shot him in the shoulder. Riley cried out in pain and toppled to the floor, while Trish sobbed in terror.

'That was a warning shot!' Samson said. 'You have three seconds! One – two—'

'Okay!' Sarah said, standing. 'Okay!'

Wiping a tear from an eye, she walked back down the steps in a daze and moved out beneath an arch with her hands raised.

The chamber's ceiling flickered with light and distant thunder rumbled.

The colonel walked forward and pressed a button on his helmet. His visor and mask retracted to reveal ice-cold eyes. 'Give me the pendant,' he said, holding out his hand.

Sarah reached to her neck just as something metallic whirred past through the air. The strange object stopped to hover above Samson's head and he looked up in surprise.

BANG!! Light exploded and smoke billowed out in clouds. More detonations and flashes erupted all around and Sarah felt someone grasp her hand to pull her back into the growing fog.

Blinded by the light, Sarah ran from shouts of fury, allowing herself to be led on until gunfire cracked out. 'Stop!' the colonel said, 'or die!'

Sarah felt her would-be saviour slow to a halt before releasing her hand. She rubbed her eyes in an attempt to clear her sight and turned to see the colonel emerge from the smoke.

♦

Samson's troops formed up behind him while he squinted with hazy vision at the shadowy figure beside Morgan.

A torch blinked on to shine into his eyes and Samson lowered his visor to block out the glare. 'Any last words, stranger?'

'I think you should leave the girl alone,' the man said.

The colonel's expression changed to one of recognition. 'You should have stayed dead.'

'And you should have stayed away.'

Samson laughed. 'You escaped me once; but this time you're one lone man,' – he raised his rifle – 'about to be one dead man.'

'Who said anything about being alone?'

A half-dozen armoured shadows shimmered into existence, rifles raised.

Samson shook his head and chuckled. 'Terra Force!'

The sound of a thousand weapons being made ready echoed through the dark, while many more soldiers continued to stream in from all sides.

'You're outnumbered,' Samson said, the glint of murder in his eyes, 'six hundred to one. As I said,' – he cocked the trigger – 'any last words?'

Purple lightning blazed across the heavens and a clap of thunder rumbled overhead.

'Just one.' Richard Goodwin stepped out of the shadows. '... DARKLIGHT!'

Samson's eyes widened as thousands more black-clad warriors shimmered into existence amongst the ruins, blue eyes glowing like an army of the gods.

He took an involuntary step back and Goodwin gave a grim smile. 'You never were any good at counting, Colonel.'

Samson bared his teeth and pulled forth his sword. 'And I told you I'd gut you like a pig.' He activated the weapon, sending its blade shining white hot.

Another crack of thunder reverberated through the chamber.

Unmoved, Goodwin looked up at the electrical storm as flashes of purple lightning lit up his dark army. 'I'm ready to die, Colonel,' – he looked back into Samson's eyes – 'the question is ... are you?'

CHAPTER THIRTY-TWO

SARAH HELD her breath as the colonel glanced in her direction. A look of doubt crept into his eyes, induced perhaps by the abnormal calm of the man beside her.

A roar of sound made Sarah glance right. A glimmer of blue-green light emerged from the ground, followed soon after by another.

The man next to her grasped her hand and a shout of warning made her look left as a third shimmering form appeared.

The beast let out a deep, menacing growl and the colonel took another step back.

Time stretched into slow motion and a break in the storm created a vacuum of silence.

Sarah felt the man's grip tighten.

Thunder rumbled again and a bolt of lightning struck the ruins. The creatures roared in defiance and Samson turned to Terra Force and raised his sword. 'KILL THEM ALL!'

CHAPTER THIRTY-THREE

GUNFIRE EXPLODED like a storm and Sarah was dragged back into the roar of chaos. Black-clad warriors surged around her with shields raised, while muzzle flashes and lightning lit up the dark like Armageddon.

An explosion rocked the ground. Sarah and her saviour staggered sideways, while debris rained down from above.

The sound of soldiers dying filled the air and Sarah glanced back to see the shimmering lights tearing into the massed ranks.

'Protect the director!' a soldier shouted. 'DEFENSIVE FORMATION!'

Darklight fell in around them to deflect a hail of bullets, while others returned fire with everything they had.

Fleeing from the mayhem, Sarah ran into the ruins beyond before the man slowed and dragged her aside as more soldiers stormed into the fray, guns blazing.

He grasped her shoulder and shone his torch into her visor. 'What's your name?!' he said over the din of war.

'Sarah!'

'Sarah, we need to get you to safety.'

'He has my friends!'

Another explosion sent ancient masonry crashing to the ground and he led her deeper into the ruins. 'I'll help you, but first we have to stay alive.'

She shook her head in wonder. 'Who are you?!'

'My name's Richard Goodwin, I'm—' He noticed Sanctuary's emblem on her arm. 'You come from the base?'

She nodded.

His gaze dropped to her neck chain and his expression changed to amazement. He reached out shaky fingers and touched her golden cross.

On instinct, she reached for her pendants, but his other hand grasped her wrist.

He looked at her with haunted eyes. 'Sarah, do you believe in fate?'

She opened her mouth to reply, but the intensity of his expression made the words catch in her throat.

He released her arm and held up her Anakim pendant to study with spellbound reverence.

Another detonation brought him out of his trance; he grasped her hand and they were running again, but back towards the carnage.

Sarah resisted, but his iron grip wouldn't be denied and she found herself dodging past black-clad warriors along the fringes of a war zone.

'I thought you were taking me to safety?!' she said.

Bullets and explosions filled the air as the fighting intensified.

'I will. I am ... trust me!' Moments later he dragged her back into the ruins, through a series of arches and on into open air.

'Director!' someone shouted from behind.

Goodwin kept running and Sarah glanced back to see a unit of Darklight soldiers following.

'Director, STOP!'

Goodwin gave a growl of frustration and slowed Sarah to a halt.

The black-clad mercenaries fanned out around them to cover their flank while a Darklight officer approached.

'Captain Winter,' Goodwin said.

The soldier raised his visor. 'Sir, what are you doing?'

'Incoming!' someone shouted.

Everyone ducked and a massive blast set Sarah's ears ringing.

Goodwin pulled her behind a crumbling wall, out of harm's way, before leaning in to Winter to shout something to him.

The captain shook his head.

Goodwin said something else and pointed at her.

Winter glanced at Sarah's pendant while Goodwin continued to shout into his ear.

The man's expression changed to one of scepticism.

'Are you with me?' Goodwin said to him as Sarah's hearing returned.

Winter hesitated and then looked to one of his team. 'Sergeant, secure our eastern border. Tell Major Offiah they're trying to outflank us.'

'Sir,' the man said, looking confused, 'where are you going?'

Winter glanced at Goodwin and lowered his visor. 'To the gates of hell.'

CHAPTER THIRTY-FOUR

SARAH RAN through the dark amongst crumbling ruins, led on by the mysterious Richard Goodwin, while behind ten Darklight soldiers shadowed their every move. The sounds of terror and gunfire from the battle faded to a dull roar and Sarah could hear Captain Winter speaking into his radio as thunder rumbled overhead.

A minute later another Darklight unit came jogging out of the gloom. They slowed to a stop and one of them passed Goodwin one of two transparent helmets while another soldier held out a plastic bodysuit to Sarah.

Uncertain, she looked at Goodwin, her expression questioning.

'Put it on,' he said, 'you're going to need it.'

Not knowing what else to do, Sarah accepted the garment, removed her backpack and, with a soldier's help, struggled into the suit. The elasticated hems pulled tight around the skin on her wrists and ankles, while the rest fitted loosely over her coveralls, jacket and climbing harness. It had a metal ring around the neckline, an in-built mask and lightweight air canisters. She realised it was a decontamination suit and matched the one Goodwin already wore.

She pulled the front zipper up over halfway and put her backpack back on, then the small party set off again at a jog while the new arrivals fell in behind.

'What news from camp?' Goodwin said to Winter as he drew Sarah alongside.

The captain slowed his pace. 'No sign of the lights. It seems they've decided to stop hiding and fight.'

'Kara?'

'Dr. Vandervoort's gathered the civilians to help with triage.'

'Do we know how they found us?'

'No idea.' Winter glanced at Sarah. 'Perhaps your new friend can tell us.'

Sarah remained silent as Goodwin looked at her. She had no idea who these people were. That they were Darklight meant they had to be connected to Commander Hilt, and by association, to Susan, too. Whether their aims were aligned with hers was another matter entirely. Goodwin had already shown a disturbing interest in her pendant, which meant he was a threat to their escape to the surface. *That's if Riley, Trish and Jason are even alive.* She thrust the horrific thought away. *They're alive*, she told herself, *they have to be.*

But Riley's shot! The image of the colonel shooting Riley in the shoulder flashed before her mind's eye and she stumbled.

♦

Goodwin caught the woman's arm as she almost fell, and he slowed their jog to a striding walk as they left the ruins behind to pick their way over uneven ground. Releasing her hand for a moment, he pulled on his diving helmet and activated its torches and image intensifier. With his sight improved he was able to study the newcomer. She was English, by the sound of her accent, and inside her suit the woman's harness softly jangled with climbing gear. The emblems and wording he'd seen adorning her jacket told him she worked for USSB

Sanctuary's Exploration Division, and was a member of one of their elite Deep Reach teams, alluded to some weeks before by the late Corporal Walker.

Lightning continued to flicker across the heavens and Goodwin saw her look up, perhaps marvelling at the size of the immense chamber she now traversed. He wasn't surprised; at sixteen thousand feet high and boasting the surface area of a small country anyone could be forgiven for thinking they were on the surface instead of deep underground.

His eyes drifted back to the pendants at her neck.

It was almost too much for him to bear. His sanity had been returning since he'd escaped from the lake hours before – at least he'd thought it had. Now this woman had stirred everything back to the surface, sending his emotions and thoughts swirling around his mind like a seething whirlwind.

He scratched at the rash on his wrist. *But the signs are clear,* he told himself. *The golden cross and the pendant ...*

'Stand to!' Winter said, raising his rifle and pushing Goodwin and Sarah behind him.

♦

The Darklight soldiers prepared for an attack and Sarah turned to see lights appear out of the ruins to the north.

'Get down!' Goodwin said, pulling her into a crouch.

'On my signal—' Winter said to his troops, as he trained his rifle.

Sarah focused her visor and saw two familiar figures. 'Stop, don't shoot!'

She shrugged off Goodwin's hold and rushed past Winter, who made a belated grab for her.

Running and stumbling over hidden obstacles, Sarah flew into the arms of her friends.

She hugged Trish and Jason to her in a fierce embrace.

'We didn't think we'd be able to find you,' Trish said, refusing to let her go.

'What's with the suit?' Jason said.

Sarah glanced down at her new attire. 'I'm not quite sure. Where's Riley,' she said, searching their faces.

Jason smiled and stepped aside.

Sarah looked past him to see the tall, Deep Reach team leader walking towards her. She stood transfixed as he drew closer, unsure if he was a figment of her wishful imagination, or whether he'd changed his mind about leaving the SED for the surface in their short time apart.

'Miss me?' Riley said, stopping before her.

She found herself smiling in relief as he reached out and dropped something heavy into her hand. She glanced down at the orb's ridged surface before quickly slipping it inside her new suit and into her coveralls. He gave her a wink and then she noticed the blood on his jacket. 'Your shoulder …' she said in concern, reaching out to him.

He grimaced and flexed his arm. 'This one's a bit more than a scratch.'

'He'll heal,' a man said, in a rumbling baritone, 'he was lucky I was there to patch him up.' Jefferson Church gave Sarah a small nod as he emerged from the dark.

'How did you escape?' Sarah said.

Dresden Locke appeared alongside his colleague. 'When the fighting broke out the marines were distracted.' He held up a large serrated knife. 'It didn't take much to take out the few left behind.'

Riley's expression hardened at the sight of his superior. 'We tied them up,' he said, touching Sarah's cheek. 'We're not killers.'

'But we are.' Captain Winter stalked out of the dark, his rifle raised and his unit flanking him on either side. 'Who are you and what are you doing here?'

Riley went to speak, but Locke stepped past him. 'My name's Dresden Locke, I'm the commander of Sanctuary's Exploration Division, and it should be me asking you what you're doing here. This land is United States territory, *restricted* United States territory, and you're here without authorisation,' – he pointed towards the gunfire and explosions that continued to set the subterranean skies ablaze – 'and your hostilities are an act of war!'

'And yet your soldiers are led by a man who's a traitor to his own country,' Richard Goodwin said, moving past Winter. 'A man who murdered innocent civilians and led an unlawful coup against the Director General of the GMRC himself.'

'Who's that?' Trish whispered to Sarah.

'He saved my life,' Sarah said, looking at Goodwin, 'he saved us all. His name is Richard—'

'Goodwin,' Locke said, 'I know who you are, Director, but this isn't Steadfast. You have no jurisdiction here and like it or not you entered Sanctuary without clearance, which is a federal offence. Tell your mercenaries to stand down and stop this insanity.'

'Stand down.' Goodwin gave a chilling laugh, the sound muffled by his transparent helmet. 'Have Samson arrested and then we'll talk about standing down. Tell me who rules in USSB Sanctuary? Who would put a madman in charge?'

Locke shifted uneasily and a look of realisation stole over Goodwin's face.

'The USSB is a military run installation, is it not?' Goodwin said. 'Let me guess, have you heard the name Joiner?'

'Intelligence Director Malcolm Joiner?' Riley said. 'How did you know?'

Goodwin shook his head in disbelief. 'Of course Joiner is involved. Which leaves the question, where's Professor Steiner?' He looked from Locke to Riley.

'Isn't Steiner the man from the induction video?' Jason murmured to Sarah.

Goodwin grew angry. 'What's happened to Steadfast? Tell me what you know!'

'I don't know what you're talking about,' Locke said, 'the Director General was taken ill. I don't know anything about Steadfa—'

'Ill?' Goodwin grasped Locke's jacket. 'And you believed that?!'

Winter moved to intervene. 'Sir, we need to secure these civilians and return to camp.'

Goodwin looked at the Darklight officer. 'What?'

'Sir, I just received a communication from Dr. Vandervoort, she told me to escort you to camp. She was quite clear; you're not to enter the lake under any circumstances.'

Goodwin looked shocked. 'Even after I convinced her and the major to come north? Without me they'd never have known Terra Force were here. They wouldn't have been ready.'

'I'm sorry, Director, perhaps when this is over they'll reinstall you to lead, but—'

'You told her, didn't you?' Goodwin pushed the man's arm away and gestured to the storm clouds above. 'Don't you see what's happening, Captain?' He strode forward and pointed beyond the fighting. 'Look, look at the tower!'

Sarah turned to look into the distance and her eyes widened as she gazed upon a massive city with towers soaring to the heavens.

'The spires,' Trish said, 'it's what we saw in the parchment.'

More lightning flickered over the Anakim metropolis before a surge of purple energy engulfed the tallest peak in a dazzle of energy.

'Can't you see? I have to go back.' Goodwin grasped Sarah's arm and pulled her forward. 'Look at her pendant. It's a sign, a pentagon!'

Sarah could see Captain Winter wasn't convinced and she saw the same look of fervour in the director's eyes she'd glimpsed before.

'A pentagon,' Goodwin said again, as if that explained everything, 'it matches the map that led me to the lake,' – he released her arm and pointed at the emblem of USSB Sanctuary on their Deep Reach uniforms – 'the same shape that's hidden inside Sanctuary's badge. The same shape that lies at the heart of the pentagram on the map and under the lake!' He turned and looked to the sky. 'How could I have let myself be distracted so easily?'

Sarah swapped a look with Riley. 'We need to get out of here,' he said under his breath.

Sarah nodded as she eyed the Darklight soldiers. *But how?* was the unspoken question.

'The land, through which we have gone to spy it out,' Goodwin said, raising his arms as he launched into oratory, 'is a land that devours its inhabitants, and all the people that we saw in it are of great height. And there we saw the Nephilim, and we seemed to ourselves like grasshoppers, and so we seemed to them.' He pointed at Sarah and then to the city. 'The people are greater and taller than we. The cities are great and fortified up to heaven. And besides, we have seen the sons of the Anakim there.'

'He's lost the plot,' Jason said.

Sarah frowned at the references. She'd heard them before. Anyone that hunted for traces of giants had scoured the biblical passages, and she was no different. She glanced back to the city.

'Sir,' – Captain Winter grasped Goodwin's arm – 'we need to go.'

Goodwin shook him off. 'And the angels who did not stay within their own position of authority, but left their proper dwelling, he has kept in eternal chains under gloomy darkness until the judgement of the great day—'

'The great day has come and gone, Director,' Locke said, sounding amused, 'and we're still here.'

Goodwin turned his gaze on the SED commander. 'Has it?' He turned to look at each of them in turn. 'None of you know, do you? You all think we've survived the fall, you all think AG5 was the end.' He moved back to Sarah and held up her cross. 'God has spoken and I've seen through the Devil's deception.' He pulled Sarah over to a worried Captain Winter. 'Look at the pentagon; it has the same constellation as those in the Sphinx – the same as the carvings in the city.'

Winter peered at the pendant and Sarah looked down at her artefact. 'Libra,' she said in realisation.

'Yes,' Goodwin said, 'yes! The three statues with the frieze, the Anakim women, they each wore a pendant the same as this.'

'Sphinx?' Sarah said.

Goodwin focused on her and then gave a knowing smile. 'The Temple of the Gods.'

'Temple?' Trish looked at Sarah.

'Did it have a device with a large indented circle on?' Jason said, using his hands to act out the size.

Goodwin stared at them and then smiled before turning to the Darklight captain. 'Do you see now? They can help us; they can help bring back Rebecca.'

Sarah stepped forward and held up her pendant. 'You've seen this symbol elsewhere?'

'Many times,' Goodwin said.

Sarah ran her finger over the metal surface. 'But it only appeared recently.'

'Exactly. You were brought here, like I was, like we all were.'

'Brought here for what?'

Goodwin's expression turned unsure.

'And by whom?' Trish said.

'It's obvious, isn't it?' Jason said. 'Those damn creatures.'

'The Pharos,' Locke murmured.

Sarah glanced at him as the thunder rumbled overhead and the sound of gunfire drew nearer.

'Sir, we have to go,' Winter said to Goodwin.

Jason pointed into the distance. 'What's that?'

Sarah followed his gaze. 'It looks like water.'

'It's the lake,' Goodwin said.

Jason shook his head. 'No, further along.'

Sarah zoomed in her visor to see a strange ethereal glow reflecting off rippling liquid and Trish gave her a worried look. 'Is it one of those things?'

'No,' Sarah said, 'it's something else.'

Riley touched her arm. 'Sarah, you think this temple could take us to the surface?'

She tore her gaze away from the strange phenomena. 'Not the temple, but an Anakim device, yes.'

'A way to the surface,' – Goodwin's face was a mask of inner torment – 'it was there all along ... I was so close.'

'You can take us to this place, this temple?' Riley asked Goodwin.

Winter waved his unit forward. 'He's taking you nowhere; you're all coming with me.'

'I can take you there,' Goodwin said, ignoring the soldiers that moved to encircle them, 'if you help me free Rebecca.'

'Free her,' Sarah said, 'from what?'

Goodwin was about to reply when the sound of fighting increased in volume and Captain Winter grasped his arm. 'Time to go, Director.'

'I think there's someone out there,' Jason said, still looking at the strange light, 'it looks like ... a woman.'

Sarah returned her attention to the glowing vision and adjusted her visor to see a figure moving before a small obelisk. 'It's Susan.'

'What did you just say?' Goodwin shrugged off Winter's grip. 'Susan?'

'Short woman,' Jason said, holding out a hand, 'yay high, doesn't say much – monsters for friends.'

Goodwin's expression froze as he looked at Winter.

Lightning blazed across the heavens and the crack of thunder boomed loud.

The captain shook his head. 'Sir, no—'

Goodwin leapt forward to knock aside one of the soldiers before sprinting off into the darkness.

Winter swore and Locke and Jefferson launched into action, fists swinging.

Riley grabbed Sarah's hand. 'Let's go!'

CHAPTER THIRTY-FIVE

Sarah and Riley ran after Goodwin, who sped away like a man possessed.

Locke and Jefferson followed behind them, with Captain Winter and his unit in hot pursuit.

An explosion made Sarah glance back to see the battle erupting from the ruins in a mass of gunfire. Stray bullets whizzed overhead and she ducked.

Captain Winter's unit slowed as they turned to face the threat while Trish and Jason, who'd been lagging behind, veered around them to carry on after Sarah.

Ahead, Goodwin closed in on the glowing light while Sarah ploughed on, her eyes fixed on the man that held the key to their survival.

Riley began to lag and Sarah dropped back beside him.

'Go,' he said, 'we can't lose him!'

Sarah stretched out her legs as adrenaline surged through her.

A hundred yards away, a bolt of purple lightning struck the obelisk, followed by another and then another.

Silhouetted against the blazing light, Goodwin raised his hands to ward off its intensity.

The lake's edge neared and the electrical storm sent down a wave of scything strikes that flowed out across misty waters.

Seconds later Sarah reached the stone protrusion. The glowing runes that encrusted its surface faded back to black and she looked around for her quarry.

Goodwin ran down a shallow slope to the lake's edge and Sarah followed.

Reaching the shore, she skidded to halt on the stony beach to gawp at the sight before her. Goodwin had carried on, and even as she watched, he walked across the water's surface like the Son of God himself.

'Where is he?' Riley said, wheezing to a stop beside her.

Still gazing at the spectacle, she raised her arm to point and his expression turned to amazement.

Locke and Jefferson arrived, and soon after so did Captain Winter.

'Director!' the Darklight officer called out. 'Come back!'

Goodwin glanced round. 'I'm not entering the lake, I'm on it!'

'He's not wrong,' Jefferson said.

Locke adjusted his visor and squinted. 'How's he doing that?'

'There's a causeway.' Winter turned on his rifle's torch and moved out onto the inky surface.

Jason and Trish, who'd been struggling to catch up, appeared over the rise behind them, while Winter's Darklight unit was a further hundred yards back fighting a rearguard action.

Sarah glanced round at her friends to make sure they were still with her and then followed the captain onto the water.

♦

Colonel Samson swung his sword left and right, cutting down Darklight soldiers in a spray of blood and bone. The images of his torture stung his mind. Each cut – each THRUST – eased his torment, each death vicious payback against those that had sought to crush his spirit. He gripped the handle tighter and cleaved another man in two.

A rocket whooshed past his visor. He turned to bury his blade into an enemy's chest and let go of the weapon to produce his rifle in one smooth motion and fired.

A single shot whistled through the air and a distant soldier with a rocket launcher toppled to the ground, dead.

Movement to the right made Samson raise his rifle. Bullets ricocheted off the weapon and a glowing light sliced towards his head. He swayed back and dropped his gun. Spinning on his heel, he avoided a second strike and slid his sword from its human sheath to parry a killing thrust. The weapon fired again, but Samson's blade flicked out to slice his attacker's pistol in two.

The Darklight officer discarded his crippled gun and retreated before circling back towards him, thermal sword in hand.

Samson eyed the glowing weapon that mirrored his own, and glanced at his opponent's chest armour. 'Major Offiah – I hear you're the leader of this rabble.'

The Darklight officer didn't respond.

Samson dropped his guard and Offiah struck.

Their swords rang as they met – once – twice – three times before Samson feinted right. Offiah ducked and Samson delivered a crunching left hook that sent the Darklight man sprawling.

He swung his sword, but the blade bit into stone as the major rolled aside and regained his feet.

Samson drew a knife to complement the sword in his other hand. 'Is that all you've got?' he said, advancing.

Offiah aimed a strike at his head, but Samson blocked the blow and punched his knife into the major's arm before pulling him into a vicious head butt, shattering his visor.

Offiah stumbled back and Samson launched into a series of overhead blows that forced the mercenary down onto one knee.

With a final strike, Samson powered his sword through Offiah's defence and down through his arm.

The Darklight officer screamed in agony as his severed limb gushed blood.

Slapping aside a despairing thrust, Samson rammed his knife into the man's visor, crunching it through glass and bone and on into his brain. He gritted his teeth and drove the blade deeper, twisted it for maximum damage, and then kicked the twitching body to the floor.

A rush of exhilaration coursed through Samson's veins as he savoured the sight. He'd never enjoyed killing in the past. He'd enjoyed the sense of power at vanquishing a foe, but he'd never lusted to kill – to feel pleasure at the thought ... to savour the moment his enemy died by his hand. He wondered why when the feeling was this good.

The fighting around him continued east and Samson sheathed his knife before picking up the dead major's blade. He held it up beside his own, the two glowing swords shining in the dark.

He glanced round. The strange lights that had decimated hundreds of his men had vanished back into the night, leaving bloody carnage in their wake.

Movement to the left made him zoom in his visor. Beyond the fighting, running figures disappeared into the distant gloom. He switched off his thermal blades and his eyes narrowed. 'Goodwin,' he said, before switching his gaze to the figure giving chase. His voice dropped to a growl. 'Morgan.'

Samson sheathed his swords and broke into a run.

CHAPTER THIRTY-SIX

OUT ON THE NARROW CAUSEWAY, Sarah picked her way through shallow water while closing in on Captain Winter, who in turn had caught up with his single-minded director. As she drew closer she could hear the two men arguing as they edged further out onto the misty lake.

'What did you tell me before, Captain? You told me you believed in me, you told me to believe in myself!'

'I didn't mean this!' Winter looked down at his feet. 'And how did the causeway get here? Something's not right.'

'I don't know how it got here!' Goodwin said in frustration. 'Perhaps it was Susan.'

'I don't like it. Why is she out here at all? Where did all this mist come from?' Winter shone his torches back to shore. 'We should at least wait for my unit.'

'Rebecca's waited long enough,' Goodwin said.

A splash of water made Sarah glance right to see a large, scaly fin break the surface. She stepped back and then slipped. Her arms flailed before an armoured hand grasped her arm.

'Trust me,' Winter said, helping her regain her footing, 'you don't want to fall in.'

Sarah nodded and then turned as Riley came up behind her, closely followed by Trish, Jason, Jefferson and Locke.

She looked back at the dark waters where more black shadows glided past. 'Be careful,' she said, pointing.

Riley gave a nod before a flash of lightning lanced into the lake. Thunder cracked and the chamber's heavens rumbled and flickered.

'Have you seen anything like this in Sanctuary before?' Sarah said.

Riley shook his head as another rumbling boom echoed out. 'Never!'

The chamber's skies continued to simmer with light and Sarah glimpsed an island through the fog bank that hung thick over the lake's centre. Movement through the cloud-like shroud caught her eye. 'I think I see someone,' she said.

Goodwin looked over his shoulder. 'It's Susan!'

The director increased his pace as more lightning cascaded down.

The causeway beneath their feet shuddered and Trish screamed.

'Keep moving!' Locke said.

Waves lapped at Sarah's feet as their walk turned into a teetering jog.

Precarious moments passed and then they made it to dry land and relative safety, but before Sarah had time to catch her breath Goodwin was off again, heading towards a gaping hole in the ground.

'Sir, wait,' – the Darklight captain grasped his arm – 'my unit's at the causeway.' The sound of muffled gunfire came from the shoreline and a garbled message came through his radio.

Winter pressed a button on his helmet, listening. 'Sergeant, hold the beach!' he said, before pausing. 'Do you copy?' He waited for another response. 'Say again ... who?'

Goodwin took the opportunity to slip from Winter's grasp and he disappeared from view.

'Wait! DIRECTOR?!' Letting out another curse the Darklight captain followed Goodwin down into the pitch-black.

Hot on their heels, Sarah stepped onto a narrow slope that spiralled down round the edge of a wide, circular shaft. A deep drop yawned on the left and Riley shouted a warning to those behind.

Sarah moved with care over wet stone, but on the opposite side of the shaft the light from Goodwin's transparent helmet moved down at speed, with Captain Winter in close attendance. She picked up the pace; they couldn't afford to lose them now.

A number of spirals later they reached the bottom of the giant shaft. Ahead, Goodwin's light vanished into thin air, as did Winter's seconds after.

Sarah rushed forward to pass into a dark entrance surrounded by crumbling stonework. Uneven ground made her trip and stumble, but she managed to keep her feet to scramble over loose rock.

As she emerged from the opening, a stone staircase appeared through the gloom and lightning lit up the foreground of a vast hall shrouded in mist. Sarah gazed up to see ethereal forms through the haze, their gargantuan bulk revealed by the flickering storm like titanic gods of myth.

Captain Winter stood twenty feet away. He turned and signalled for her to stop. A few yards ahead of him Goodwin crept towards a distant figure.

Susan's shadowy form stood stock still a hundred yards in front of them, staring back at the approaching Goodwin. Sarah felt a shiver of unease spread through her as the small woman was lit up like a ghoul in the night.

Thunder cracked and Susan was off and running once more, disappearing into the mists.

Goodwin and Winter leapt forward and Sarah followed, Riley by her side.

A strong wind swirled through the hall and an avenue of enormous statues emerged through the parting fog. Goodwin vanished into the dark between the two rows of towering sculptures and a spine chilling howl cut through the air. Sarah looked up into the snarling face of an Anakim warrior. Purple lightning blazed across the chamber and the statue's massive eyes glowed bright with the same dazzling hue.

Sarah quailed at the sight, but carried on as the figures' howling grew louder and the winds gusted more fiercely.

'What is this place?' Riley said, over the noise.

Sarah glanced up with fear at the gruesome spectres that appeared like demons in the clouds. 'It's Tartarus!'

'Tartarus?'

Sarah looked into his eyes. 'Hell!'

'There she is!' Goodwin pointed to the small figure of Susan running ahead of them, passing beneath a winged monstrosity that spanned the hall's end.

Sarah splashed through a pool of water, dodged round a spine-chilling statue of an Anakim woman being dragged to her doom, and ran on.

♦

Colonel Samson fired his rifle into the Darklight soldiers, his mask lit up with the flash of gunfire. More Terra Force arrived from the south and ploughed into the retreating mercenaries.

A flash of lightning lit up the nearby lake and Samson spied a hidden path leading out into the mists and a Darklight unit moving across it. He unclipped a device from his armour and launched it into the fighting masses. The cluster grenade exploded, severing limb and bone on both sides.

Samson leapt forward and several carnage-filled moments later reached the shore. Scanning the water, he located the causeway and worked his way out onto the lake.

A hundred feet out, he glanced back through the mists to see Ophion and four of his team emerge on the shoreline to cut a swathe through the Darklight ranks. S.I.L.V.E.R.'s leader was a blur as he leapt and spiralled through the air, killing and maiming with unholy precision. Samson took aim at the assassin's visor, tracing his every move. Ophion somersaulted over two soldiers and landed on one knee beyond them, arms outstretched. The two men keeled over dead and Samson fired.

Ophion's arm came up and the bullet deflected off his armour. S.I.L.V.E.R.'s leader turned his chrome mask in the colonel's direction and gave a slow shake of his head.

Samson unleashed a barrage of shots sending Ophion into evasive action before his armour shimmered and the assassin vanished from view.

The rest of S.I.L.V.E.R. drifted into invisibility as they headed towards the causeway and, with a snarl, Samson secured his rifle to his back and moved into a run.

CHAPTER THIRTY-SEVEN

CHASED BY THE HOWLING WINDS, Sarah entered a twisting tunnel full of horrific carvings and surfaces that oozed with foul-smelling, black oil. She glanced back to see Locke and Jefferson following, but Trish and Jason were nowhere in sight.

Knowing her friends would catch up, she kept up the pace and Riley grasped her hand as the running figures of Goodwin, and then Captain Winter, disappeared round a final bend and into the thickening mist.

Sarah splashed through another puddle of water and felt a deep chill as they entered the white wall of vapour. Behind, the howling statues continued to wail and Sarah gripped Riley's hand tighter as flashing thunder solidified the surrounding fog. They slowed their flight to a walk and Riley squeezed her hand in reassurance.

'Susan!' someone ahead shouted. 'It's Richard, where are you?!'

Sarah fiddled with her visor, which had failed to auto-adjust to the dense cloud, but try as she might the technology refused to penetrate it.

A dark figure emerged from the gloom before them.

Captain Winter held up his hand as they approached and put a finger to his lips. His rifle was raised and he scanned the way ahead with his scope.

Sarah's anxiety spiked. What has he seen? One of the lights?

As the fog cleared a little, Sarah saw Goodwin looking this way and that into a dark expanse.

He turned around in anguish as they approached. 'I can't find her.'

Captain Winter moved past him to scan the area as Jefferson and Locke arrived behind, but as yet there was still no sign of Trish and Jason.

Sarah let go of Riley's hand and turned to go back.

'What's that?' Riley pointed into the distance.

'Fire,' Locke said.

Sarah paused and zoomed her visor in to where an orange glow spread and grew higher. Lightning continued to flicker high above and she realised they must be in some vast basin inside the lake, although the standing water and wet surfaces made her wonder if it was always thus. She looked down at pale weeds lying limp between stone cracks before noticing vast pools of slimy, black tar which lurked all around.

'The fog's clearing,' Riley said.

A powerful wind rippled her coveralls before dying away, and Sarah turned to see the vapour behind thinning. Soon after, Trish and a limping Jason emerged from the tunnel.

Sarah felt a hand slip into hers and she looked round to see Riley by her side, still staring into the beyond.

Jefferson stepped past him to look in the same direction.

The ground trembled and Sarah took a step back as small stones tumbled past.

The tremors built before, with a loud roar, fires exploded upwards all around them. Sarah stumbled back in shock. Napalm-like clumps rained down and everyone took evasive action. Sarah dodged and weaved as more pools of tar burst into flame to light up massive, stone monoliths that towered through the mists.

Forced back by the heat, Sarah gazed in astonishment at the

weathered standing stones, which stretched out to either side in a great arc.

'Is everyone okay?!' Winter said as the fires died back to lower levels.

If anyone replied Sarah didn't hear them as the storm bellowed through the heavens and lightning lanced down onto the megaliths. The winds returned, and with the way ahead revealed, Goodwin moved towards an arch in the stones.

'Director, please ... wait!' Winter went to follow, but gunfire behind made him pause and look back the way they'd come.

'I have to go,' Goodwin said, 'Susan and Rebecca need me.'

Winter looked back at him, his expression torn. 'It's not safe!'

'It's not safe here!' Goodwin gestured towards the sounds of more fighting. 'It's not safe anywhere, that's the problem. It's time for us to leave Sanctuary, Captain, and this is our way out.'

Goodwin turned and passed beneath the ancient stones and disappeared into the glowing mists.

More lightning blazed down and the fires multiplied.

Gunfire echoed again and Sarah looked back through the building flames to see Winter's Darklight unit emerge from the tunnel as its walls ignited into flame. The soldiers walked backwards in tactical formation while continuing to fire back into hell.

Sarah suddenly realised the fires had cut her off from everyone else and she ran back towards the tunnel as Trish and Jason passed her going the other way. They slowed and she waved them on. 'Keep going, I'll catch you up!'

'Everyone, go!' Winter ushered Trish and Jason through the stones. Locke went next, and Riley helped Jefferson brush off flames that clung to his back as they followed behind.

Sarah doubled back round the growing pools of burning pitch and sprinted back.

The storm overhead sent more bolts hammering into the ground and, on either side of the stones, two trails of flame closed in on the entrance.

Bullets whizzed past and Riley called out, 'Sarah, hurry!'

She neared the stones and Winter waved her past as he remained on sentry. Feet away from her friends, the ring of fire completed and Sarah slid to a stop and raised her hands against the heat.

Beyond, Riley moved back in shock, not realising what was happening until it was too late.

Sarah retreated and looked through the shimmering flames into Riley's eyes.

More gunfire made everyone duck and Captain Winter stepped forward and raised his weapon, searching for a target. 'Darklight,' Winter said through his radio, 'I have your six.'

One of the men turned to acknowledge their leader. 'Copy that, sir, reinforcements are en route.'

Sarah crouched down as the Darklight unit spread out to wait for the unseen enemy.

Muffled gunshots echoed from beyond and the sky continued to flicker before thunder cracked loudly.

A figure burst from the black, guns blazing. Colonel Samson dived forward as Darklight unleashed their weapons.

The colonel raised a black shield to deflect the bullets, while firing at five shadowy forms that were chasing him.

Sarah's expression turned to horror as the chrome-clad assassins spun into being and tore into the Darklight unit.

Seconds later, more black-clad soldiers surged from the tunnel; their battle cries making the assassins re-camouflage as they turned to face the new threat.

'Sarah,' Riley called out, 'come on!'

She looked round to see Riley had removed his jacket to create a narrow bridge through the flames.

Sarah stood up and moved closer, but the heat was too great. 'It's too hot!'

She retreated again and looked back to see the colonel cutting a path towards her on the left. One man went down, and then another. Her friends called out to her from behind, but Sarah remained rooted to the spot in detached fascination as Samson smashed aside another Darklight soldier.

Captain Winter leapt to meet him, but Samson deflected his onslaught and heaved him into the flames. Terror seized her as the killer loomed large. Sarah wanted to run but her legs wouldn't move, and she stumbled backwards to the ground.

And then Riley and Jefferson were there, rushing past her only to be knocked aside by the unstoppable colonel's brutal blows.

Sarah scrambled away, knowing she couldn't escape, knowing that she wanted to live – so desperately wanted to live. She looked at Riley in despairing horror. *I don't want to die!* Her mind screamed inside. *NOT NOW!* A whimper of fear escaped her lips as Samson bore down on her.

'There's nowhere left for you to hide, Morgan.' The colonel raised his sword aloft and its shining blade reflected in Sarah's terror-stricken eyes

Riley shouted and Trish screamed. Time slowed as the glowing weapon plunged towards her head ...

... and shuddered to a stop with a resounding CLANG and a shower of sparks.

A tear rolled down Sarah's cheek as she stared at the pulsating blade an inch from her face.

With a screech of metal on metal, the sword was knocked aside and Samson was catapulted backwards.

A hulking figure emerged from the ether, glowing sword in hand. The formidable mask turned towards her, its eyes burning like a demon.

'Go,' it said, its voice deep with power, 'I'll handle this.'

Sarah shook her head. 'I saw you die.'

Commander Hilt raised his visor as Riley and Jefferson helped her away. 'Things,' Hilt said as he turned back to face Samson, 'are not always as they seem.'

CHAPTER THIRTY-EIGHT

COLONEL SAMSON SHOOK his head and climbed to his feet. The powerful figure of the Darklight leader turned towards him, visor raised and Samson flexed his arm and picked up his sword. 'Still alive, Darklight?'

'I'm a hard man to kill.'

Samson gave a quick glance round to see S.I.L.V.E.R. holding their own against overwhelming odds. He turned back to Hilt, who slid his large rucksack to the ground. The man's black armour was dented and scarred as though a building had fallen on him.

'It's about time you stopped running,' Samson said, retracting his helmet's face-plate and moving away from the stones for more room. 'You fled Steadfast like a coward, leaving better men to fight.'

Hilt followed, his black armour reflecting the pools of flame between them. 'And you massacred them with no offer of surrender.'

'Surrender is for the weak.'

Hilt loosened his sword arm with three cutting sweeps of his blade. 'And the sane.'

Samson's grip tightened on his sword and his armoured glove creaked under the strain. He withdrew his second blade and activated the thermal device. The weapon glowed white hot and he held it up to Hilt. 'I got this off your Major. He fought badly. He died ... badly.'

Hilt's eyes narrowed as he removed his shield from his back-plate and lowered his visor. 'Tell me, *mad man*,' he said, 'what's it like in hell?'

Samson bared his teeth and closed his face-plate. 'I don't know,' – he surged forward as Hilt leapt to meet him – 'TELL ME!'

CHAPTER THIRTY-NINE

SARAH JUMPED over smouldering jackets before the fires flashed over them in a pall of smoke and flame.

Glancing back at the Darklight leader, Sarah felt a rough hand turn her face.

Riley kissed her. 'I thought I'd lost you.'

Sarah stared into his eyes before looking down at her feet.

He raised her chin with a finger and kissed her again.

'Err, guys,' Jason said, 'we've got a problem.'

Reeling from the heights of terror to giddy love, Sarah gave Riley a shy smile before turning to see a network of paths leading through pools of bubbling tar, many of which had already caught alight.

The flames spread and black smoke merged with the fog to create a toxic cauldron.

'Deploy your masks,' Locke said.

Sarah pressed a button on her helmet and the breathing apparatus slid over her face to produce an airtight seal.

'There's no way we can get through that,' Jefferson said as the heat built, 'it's a furnace.'

But as they watched, the oozing fluid sank into the ground, sucked down by gravity into unseen voids. In its wake, gaping holes revealed the paths were in fact a lattice of narrow bridges that spanned the flaming tar pit beneath.

The inferno decreased in intensity, but the fires persisted as the burning pitch clung to the walkways' sides.

Trish pointed at some of the bridges. 'It's too dangerous, look; some of them are ready to collapse.'

'She's right,' Sarah said, over the noise of the storm, 'it's too risky.'

'We can't go back,' Riley said. 'And we can't stay here.'

Locke strode forward. 'Then we move.'

Riley stayed where he was and Locke looked back. 'You may not like my methods, Riley, but when has my judgement in the field ever let you down? I take care of my own, you know that.'

Riley held his superior's gaze before relenting and, one by one, they followed the SED commander out onto the fiery lattice.

But as Sarah reached the first path, the heat made her recoil.

'What's wrong?' Riley said from behind.

Sarah shook her head. The vision of flame and smoke captivated her soul, dredging up scenes from nightmares past.

'Sarah,' Trish said, waving her forward, 'come on!'

Stepping out onto the first span, Sarah flinched as the flames licked at her feet. Steeling herself, she moved with haste towards the next junction where respite from the fires beckoned.

Safely past the first obstacle, the six explorers, bedecked in their Deep Reach gear, pressed on, working their way deeper into the infernal pit as they sought the man ahead and fled from those behind.

CHAPTER FORTY

HILT RAISED his shield as the strikes rained in. Deflecting a scything blow, he spun sideways, ducked another killing thrust and advanced. Powering forward, he drove Samson back with blow upon blow. The ring of steel on steel sang out, the glowing blades weaving arcs of light through the air as the two men clashed and clashed again.

Samson rallied and it was Hilt's turn to defend against a ferocious onslaught that forced him towards a deep pit of boiling tar.

Wheeling away, Hilt parried a cutting slice and sent a riposte whistling past Samson's visor.

The colonel retreated and opened his mask as they circled one another.

'Your men are dying,' Samson said.

Hilt glanced past him to where his team struggled to contain the chrome-clad assassins. 'And you'll be joining them,' Hilt said, 'sooner than you think.'

Samson laughed as lightning lit up the skies. 'You can't kill me, Darklight, I'm already dead.'

Hilt gazed into the man's insanity and adjusted his grip on sword and shield.

'Do you know who I saw in Hell?' Samson said, advancing.

Hilt sidestepped a pool of fire as he let Samson stalk him.

The colonel smiled. 'Your beloved professor, the all-powerful director general. He'd been scheduled for termination by lethal injection.'

Hilt continued to back away, drawing the madman on.

'The old man's already six foot under. And do you know who put him there?' Samson's smile broadened into exultation. 'ME!' The colonel closed his helmet and launched forward.

Hilt blocked a series of strikes before Samson connected with a jarring kick that sent him tumbling back through a wall of flame.

Rolling to his feet beyond the standing stones, Hilt glimpsed Morgan and her team disappearing into the fiery mists. He inched out onto a narrow bridge and Samson's wavering form appeared through the searing flames like an avenging spirit, mask and swords aglow.

'Had enough, Darklight?' Samson said.

Hilt brought his sword and shield together to signal his defiance and Samson leapt forward once more.

♦

The sound of distant fighting made Sarah glance back through the thickening smog to see the Darklight commander still locked in single combat with the fearsome colonel. Praying for Hilt's victory, she turned back to the path ahead. Trish and Jason had already made it to a position of relative safety on the next intersection, but as the storm's winds increased, the crackling flames grew higher.

'We need to go back!' Jefferson said, bringing up the rear.

Locke shook his head. 'No, we go on.'

'Look out!' Riley dragged Sarah forwards as a sudden gust of wind whipped up waves of burning tar.

Fire roared over the bridge and Jefferson jumped back. The bearded archaeologist cupped his hands and shouted, 'I'll find another way round!'

Riley called out a confirmation as Sarah felt the heat flood over her.

Trapped with Riley and Locke between rising flames, Sarah's panic tightened its grip.

Locke shielded himself from the fire and held something up in his hand.

Through his visor, Sarah saw Riley's expression turn to shock. 'No!' he said.

'We have no choice!' Locke pointed at the flames. 'We go forward or back, either way we have to extinguish the fire.' He turned and threw the device onto the bridge before them.

Riley pulled her into a crouch as an explosion ripped through the air. The ground shuddered and stone debris rained down around them.

The heat in front reduced and Sarah opened her eyes. The walkway that Trish and Jason had already navigated was now a gaping chasm into the scorching abyss beyond.

'Why did you do that?!' Sarah said, looking at the massive barrier between them and safety.

'So, I can do this.' Locke produced a grappling gun and fired a bolt into the crumbling stone near Trish's feet. Connecting the cable to his harness, the SED commander swung out over burning tar. His feet skimmed the flames mid-flight and he twisted round to shoot another anchor back from whence he came. The bolt slammed home and the second cable slowed his momentum as it unwound from his gun. An instant later Locke reached out to cling to the bridge support halfway between the boiling tar and the walkway above. With an agility that belied his age, Locke scaled the crumbling stone and rejoined Trish and Jason, where he disconnected the cable and threw it back to Sarah.

'You go first.' Riley pulled down the zip on her decontamination suit and clipped the cable to her harness beneath, then handed her his grappling gun.

Sarah eyed the jump and the black ooze that wept from the newly exposed stone below Locke's feet. As she watched, the fires took hold and crept up the face of the destabilised bridge. She gazed down into the pit. Visions of Trish aflame and falling to her death spun through her mind like quicksilver. Over and over again Sarah's own screams of anguish repeated like an omen from the past. *Love you*, Trish's voice said as she slipped from Sarah's grasp. *Love you*.

'Sarah,' Riley said, looking at the fire behind. 'You need to go.'

She looked at him and shook her head. 'I can't do it.'

'Of course you can. You have to, you don't have a choice.'

Sarah glanced back to where Jefferson disappeared back the way they'd come. 'Look,' she said, pointing, 'the flames are dying down; in a few minutes we can go back and find another way round.'

'In a few minutes Goodwin might have gone. In a few minutes the colonel or those assassins will be on us.' He frowned and grasped her arms. 'Sarah, you've made jumps far harder than this. Remember the SED when we jumped to the atrium wall – remember your training!'

'That had no smoke! No fire!'

'And no cable,' he said, giving her harness a jiggle, 'this is safer, you must see that.'

Sarah looked back to where the fire spread and pointed. 'It's too late ... the flames.'

Riley grew angry. 'Sarah—' He winced as he lowered his arm.

She looked at him and realisation dawned. 'You were going back anyway, weren't you?' she said in accusation.

'I can't make the climb,' he said, 'my shoulder's too bad. If I get the chance I'll go around and catch up to Jefferson.'

She made a decision and unclipped the largest of the Anakim pendants from the chain at her neck.

'Jason!' she said, waving her friend forward.

'Sarah,' Riley said, 'what are you doing?'

She glanced at him. 'Where you go, I go.'

Jason moved past Trish and Locke on the far side of the chasm.

She held up the five sided disc. 'We'll find another way round. Find Goodwin and the transportation device and I'll meet you there,' – she wound back her arm – 'catch!'

She threw the ancient artefact into the air and Jason's eyes grew wide as the pendant sailed towards him.

Horrified, Sarah's heart skipped a beat as her throw went wayward, but Jason sank down onto one knee and snatched the metallic pendant from its flight into ruination.

Trish stepped forward as the flames swept higher. 'What are you doing?!'

'I'll meet you there!' Sarah waved her on. 'GO!'

Trish hesitated, her expression a mixture of confusion and fear.

'Don't worry, the flames are clearing,' – Sarah gestured behind – 'we'll find another way, but we can't afford to lose Richard Goodwin, we need that transportation device!'

Jason tugged on Trish's arm as the flames licked at their feet.

'Go!' Sarah said, shooing them on.

Trish gave her one last look of despair and turned to follow Jason into the smoking fires.

'Another minute,' Riley said, his voice muffled by his breathing mask, 'and we go through.'

Sarah nodded as her friends disappeared into the fog while behind them, Locke hung back to make sure she and Riley made it to safety.

Heat-filled seconds passed and, as the flames crept lower, they prepared to make their move.

'This bridge is unstable,' Riley said. 'You need to unclip now.'

As Sarah went to detach herself from Locke's cable the narrow bridge beneath their feet lurched sideways. Sarah let out a shout and Riley wrapped his arms around her. 'Hang on!' he said.

The stone bridge collapsed, Sarah screamed and they plummeted into freefall.

The cable connected to her harness whipped taut and they arced down into the steaming pit before slamming into the other side. Riley grunted as he took the impact and the fires seethed around them. 'Climb!' he said.

Sarah fought her way up through smoke and fire. Black tar stuck to her hands and feet and the temperature gauge on her visor soared. Seconds of torment came and went and Sarah heaved herself onto the walkway above.

Brushing the flames from her body, she threw herself down and plunged her arm back into the smoking fires. 'Grab my hand!'

Riley reached out and grasped her wrist.

Sarah tried to pull him up, but his weight was too great. She braced her feet either side of the walkway and gripped his harness with her other hand.

'You need to climb!' she said, gritting her teeth.

The flames blackened Riley's coveralls and he sagged against the wall. 'I can't,' he said, panicking, 'my shoulder's not strong enough!'

Sarah gazed down at him as the fire spread to her arms. 'I'm not going to let you die!'

He shook his head. 'Sarah, it's no use, let go!'

The image of Trish falling into nothing seared into her mind. She locked her eyes to his and her grip tightened. 'NO!' She sucked in air through her mask. 'Now PULL!'

Mustering every ounce of strength she had, Sarah's muscles surged with adrenaline as she stretched every sinew in her body, every atom of her being. Riley cried out in agony as he forced his shoulder to work. The flames grew and the heat seared and Riley inched higher. Bit by bit, their combined willpower brought Riley to the brink and then – finally – over into blessed salvation.

Patting down the flames that sought to cook them alive, they collapsed to their knees in a fierce embrace.

She retracted her visor and breathing mask and he did likewise. Stained with soot and sweat, they shared a lingering kiss.

He leaned back to look into her eyes and smiled. 'That was close.'

A laugh of joyous relief escaped her lips and she kissed him.

'I thought you were going to let me go,' he said, pulling away again to hold her gaze.

'I'm never letting you go.' She turned serious. 'Don't you remember? Where you go, I go.'

He grinned and then his expression changed to one of confused shock.

Riley looked down at his chest and Sarah followed his gaze. A patch of dark red soaked through his uniform and the glint of steel cut through the fabric.

'Sarah?' he said in fear, as blood trickled from his mouth.

Riley toppled into her arms and Sarah saw Dresden Locke standing behind him, a large knife in his hand, its long blade dripping with blood.

Sarah's shock turned to an anguished scream. 'NO!'

Riley grasped her jacket as he battled for breath and she lowered him to her lap.

Locke opened his helmet and knelt down next to them. 'I'm sorry, Riley,' he said, his eyes full of genuine sorrow. 'I couldn't let you get to the surface, I hope you can see that.'

Sarah didn't know what was happening. Riley coughed as he tried to speak and more blood spilled out of his mouth. Sarah pulled him higher and pushed her hand against his chest in a vain attempt to try and stem the flow of vital fluid.

'Wh – why?' Riley said, between gasps.

Locke sighed and hung his head. 'I've told you before,' he said, looking up at Sarah and then back to Riley, 'I look after my own. If Sanctuary is exposed, my life's work was for nothing, but more than that – much more than that – the lives of the thousands of men and women who've worked in the SED for over two hundred years will have all been in vain. Sanctuary will become embroiled in a war between us and those on the surface. Some secrets are worth dying for, and this is one of them.'

Riley shook his head. 'You know – I wouldn't – let – that happen.'

'I couldn't take that chance. If you had time to reflect, you'd understand I had no other option. And you'd realise – like I have –

that the SED must go on. I'm sorry it had to end like this,' – Locke laid a hand on Riley's shoulder – 'you were like a son to me.'

Riley opened his mouth to try and speak, but nothing came out. After a moment he managed to say, 'I have – a father, and you ... you were – never – him.'

Locke nodded. 'You're right, a father gives, and sadly it's left for me to take.'

Riley struggled in Sarah's arms. 'Go ... to hell.'

Locke looked behind them into the fiery mists. 'Maybe I will, but I've still got one more thing to take.'

Riley shook his head.

'I don't have the pendant,' Sarah said, her voice sounding like it belonged to another person.

Locke didn't seem to hear her; he looked back at his dying colleague. 'I'm sorry, Riley,' – he stood up, knife in hand – 'she knows too much, they all do.'

Riley tried to rise, but he dropped back down and looked up into Sarah's eyes in despair.

Sarah looked at Locke, her mind numb.

Locke thrust the knife at her heart, but Riley's hand came up to grasp the blade.

The SED commander's look of shock turned to anger as he tried to pull the knife free. Riley's grip tightened, blood flowed and Sarah put her hand behind his to stop the blade's advance.

Locke gave a growl of frustration and pushed his fingers into Riley's chest wound.

Riley groaned, his grip loosened and Sarah felt the blade slide into her palm and she gasped in pain. Blood welled between her fingers and she used her other hand to grasp Locke's wrist to force him back.

The SED commander stared into her eyes and leaned into the knife.

Riley clenched his teeth in desperation as the blade bit deeper into his hand, severing tendon and crunching through bone.

The ground shook and Sarah's visor flashed up a host of warning symbols. Locke swayed to the edge and wrenched the knife clear.

The ancient walkway shuddered again and Locke stood for a moment, torn between killing Sarah and saving his own skin. The tremors continued and the latter won out as he retreated to safety, and with a final look back, he turned to disappear into acrid smoke.

CHAPTER FORTY-ONE

SARAH MOVED Riley away from the flames and laid him down as the ground continued to shake. She removed his helmet and her own before opening his jacket to reveal the wound. Pressing down with trembling hands she tried to stem the bleeding, but try as she might the deep gash refused to heal.

Riley groaned in pain.

'I'll get help,' she murmured, and looked round in a daze.

But only fire and smoke remained. Sarah's nightmares had come true, re-imagined from the old to the new.

No one could help them now.

She daubed at the blood with his jacket, revealing a tattoo of a crucifix beneath. She stared at the symbol, wondering why she'd paid it no heed before. *Why had Trish's affiliation to the Vatican felt like a betrayal when Riley's had not? Because I was too busy enjoying the sins of his body to care.*

Riley grasped her hand and tried to speak.

She leant closer.

'Leave me,' he whispered, 'get to the surface.'

She shook her head as tears rolled down her cheeks. 'I'm never letting you go.'

'You ... must.'

She held back a sob. 'I've only just found you.'

He reached up and touched her cheek to wipe away a tear. 'You're pretty ... when you cry.'

Sarah stroked his face as his breathing eased and his eyes closed.

The ancient walkway still shook and his eyes fluttered back open. 'Sarah,' he said, his voice full of fear, 'where are you?'

'I'm here,' – she leant over him – 'I'm right here.'

He grasped her hand tighter. 'You must ... go.'

She stroked his cheek with her thumb. 'I don't want to go on without you.'

He gave a weak shake of his head before his gaze drifted down to her neck and his expression changed to hope. He tried to raise his other hand and his breathing grew ragged. Sarah helped his effort and he guided trembling fingertips to brush the golden cross that hung down from her chain.

His eyes grew distant. 'I see it,' he said, weak fingers reaching to nowhere, 'so beautiful, so—'

'No!' Sarah grasped his face. 'Riley, don't leave me, don't leave me here alone!'

He frowned and his focus returned to her face. 'I'll always ... be with you ... Sarah,' – his voice grew fainter – 'have faith ... there's always light ... in the dark.' He looked into her eyes as his grip went loose. 'I ... love ... y—'

Sarah saw the light fade from Riley's eyes and his chest ceased to move from the rhythm of his breath.

She stared down through shimmering tears at the man who'd stolen her heart and caressed his face with shaking hands. 'I love you, Riley,' – Sarah pressed her lips to his – 'I love you too.'

CHAPTER FORTY-TWO

THE FIRES of hell continued to simmer and burn, and black smoke coiled into misty skies like the pyres of the damned. Sarah held Riley to her as her tears ran dry from the searing heat. The precarious bridge on which she sat shuddered and the words she'd spoken before echoed in her mind. *Where you go, I go.* She looked over the edge of the narrow walkway and down into the abyss, where the orange flames of burning tar created strange forms in the wind. The storm rumbled overhead like the death knell of her soul and she hugged Riley tighter as the ground shook again.

All I have to do is wait, she thought, wait for the end to come and I can be with him again.

Pain in her hand made her look down to see white knuckles gripped around her cross. She released her hold to stare at the golden keepsake ... Trish's golden keepsake. A vision of Dresden Locke sprang to mind, along with his words. *I'm sorry, Riley; she knows too much, they all do.*

A shock of realisation wrenched Sarah from the chains of grief. *Locke is going after Trish and Jason.* She stumbled to her feet, pulled on her Deep Reach helmet and pressed the button for two-way communication, but all she could hear was static.

'Trish, Jason, if you can hear me, Locke ... Locke killed Riley. He wants to stop us getting to the surface. Be careful, I'm on my way.'

She turned back to her dead lover as lightning flickered above, reflecting in his eyes that stared fixed into the nothing of beyond. Sarah reached out a hand and breathed deep before closing his eyelids with a featherlike touch.

'I have to go,' she whispered, kissing Riley goodbye, 'he's going to kill my friends.' She stood to face the seething furnace as a powerful wind sent flames curling around her like the Devil's breath. Sarah's brows furrowed deep with cold fury. 'But not if I kill him first.'

CHAPTER FORTY-THREE

SARAH RAN FORWARD through smoke and flame. *Trish and Jason think Locke's on their side* – she leapt over a fissure as her senses switched sharp – *they won't stand a chance!*

Visor warnings spun over her display in all directions, but she ran on, trusting instinct over technology.

The ground shook and the flames roared higher. She glimpsed movement on a bridge to her left.

Jefferson Church emerged through the shimmering heat. 'Sarah!' he said, calling out. 'Where are the others, where's Riley?'

She slowed and glanced round to where she'd just been. 'He's gone!' She looked back as a gust of wind revealed the way ahead. Sixty feet away, the figure of Dresden Locke moved through the flames.

Sarah's heart raced faster and she closed her mask and ran on through fire.

'Sarah, wait!' Jefferson stared after her before turning to look back the way she'd come. 'Gone where?'

♦

Searing heat filled Sarah's lungs, but it only served to fuel her anger. Vaulting a fallen column, she closed the gap on Locke.

The noxious mists cleared a little and a black mass loomed out of the darkness. Sarah gazed up at the colossal form of a winged sphinx wreathed in cloud, its enormous Anakim face and sweeping headdress lit up by sporadic flashes of purple light from the storm above.

She looked down to see Locke turn in her direction. Their eyes met across the expanse and his surprise at seeing her changed to determination, and he upped his pace. The chase was on.

Sarah felt a surge of rage and she leapt forward.

Second by second, Sarah's long legs ate up the ground between them, her youth and skill a match for the ageing SED leader fleeing before her.

He glanced back to see her closing and pulled something from his utility belt and threw it in her direction. A huge explosion sent shockwaves through the network of crumbling bridges. A large section disappeared in a pall of dust and flame and Sarah skidded to a halt at the edge of shattered stone.

Warning messages bombarded her head-up-display and she pressed a helmet button to switch off her visor. The dark of Sanctuary descended, but the fires and storm lit up the scene with enough light to see by. Sarah saw movement in the distance. She could just make out the tiny outlines of Trish and Jason pass through the towering entrance built into the sphinx's chest. Locke had seen them, too, and he angled his route towards the staircase between the beast's pair of giant claws. Her gaze dropped back to the chasm before her. Some of the walkways hadn't collapsed. Enough remained that she could see a way across. If she'd had the time she would have gone around, but if she wanted to save Trish and Jason it was this way or nothing.

With no more time to think, Sarah took four long strides back the way she'd come and sucked in a deep breath. 'You can do this, Sarah,' she said as fear sought to cripple her, 'remember your training.

Remember who you are.' She closed her eyes. 'I'm Deep Reach,' she whispered, 'I'm Deep Reach.'

Her eyes snapped open and she powered forward. Arms pumping, legs straining, Sarah leapt out over the abyss.

◆

Dresden Locke raised his arms against the roaring flames and took a step back. He'd seen Morgan's accomplices entering the colossal sphinx moments before. He was amazed to have seen Sarah still alive; he'd been certain the stone walkway was about to collapse. He cursed his impatience. If he'd had a little more resolve she'd no longer be a problem. *Although*, he thought, glancing back, *there's no way she can catch me before I reach her friends. She'll have to go back and find another way round, and by then I'll have the pendant and be waiting for her.*

He touched the knife at his belt and felt a twinge of regret for killing Riley. *I had no choice*, he told himself, *he left me no choice.*

Waiting for the wind to die back down – and with it the flames – Locke stared in disbelief at a figure crossing the expanse behind. He zoomed in his visor to see Sarah leap across an impossible gap, haul herself up an inverted overhang and then scale a sliver of rock as it collapsed behind her. The Englishwoman's slim figure disappeared in a cloud of debris ... only to emerge seconds later onto another section of walkway. With only half of the collapse left to traverse, he realised she might make it across. Urgency seized him and Locke threw himself forward through the fires. Rolling to the ground, he jumped up to extinguish the flames that clung to his jacket and ran towards the sphinx. Moments later he was leaping onto the first step of the oversized staircase. Scaling it as fast as he could, his breathing grew laboured and passing halfway he paused to look back. There was no sign of Morgan, but his hopes of her demise were dashed as a hand appeared over the final ledge. Unable to believe what he was seeing, his fingers sought his utility belt for another explosive charge, but he was all out. He turned back to the Anakim monument to resume his ascent, his efforts redoubled.

♦

Sarah rolled away from scorched stone and clambered to her feet. She activated her visor and saw Locke high above, disappearing up the ancient stairway. Jumping forward through dying flames, she ate up the distance to the first step and launched herself upwards. Higher and higher she climbed, her movement settling into a rhythm. Step – step – climb. Breathe. Step – step – climb. Breathe.

Seconds ticked by and her exertion continued, heart and lungs working in unison to power her on until, finally, she reached the mist-veiled summit and the entrance beyond.

Locke had long since gone inside and Sarah prayed Trish and Jason were okay. She tried the coms button on her helmet again. The message, '*No Signal*', flashed up on her visor. The only benefit of her not being able to reach them was that neither could Locke.

Removing a small pocket knife from her belt, she prised the blade out and moved into the dark.

CHAPTER FORTY-FOUR

SARAH CREPT forward through the giant Anakim Sphinx, her ears straining against the quiet while the sound of the storm faded away. Her footsteps sounded loud to her ears as they echoed through the enormous structure. Her visor adjusted to the interior light, or lack thereof, and she double-checked her helmet's torches remained in the off position. The worst thing she could do now would be to advertise her location. With her knife held before her, she advanced through an avenue of enormous statues. The dynamic sculptures struck powerful poses above her, the eyes of man, woman and beast from eons past appraising her from lofty heights. The whole place glistened with the sheen of water and the drip drop of falling liquid intensified the damp hush that closed in around her.

Locke was nowhere to be seen and if he lurked in the shadows he could already be behind her. But she didn't have time for caution. Trish and Jason were all that mattered. With this in mind she realised her idea of remaining hidden was erroneous, at least in part.

She cupped her hands to her mouth. 'Trish, Jason!' she said, her voice booming into the dark. 'Don't trust Locke!'

A moment later, the sound of her voice echoed back towards her. 'Don't trust Locke ... Locke ... Locke.'

She shouted again. 'He killed Riley!'

'Riley ... iley ... iley.' The echo died once more and silence returned.

Did they hear me? she wondered. Locke must have done. What will he do now? Wait for me, or press ahead for Trish and Jason?

Either way she had to keep moving, as even if her warning had got through, her friends were still in grave danger. A distant sound alerted her to the need for haste and Sarah struck out to her left and into another section of the sphinx and a forest of soaring columns shrouded in mist.

CHAPTER FORTY-FIVE

Darklight leader, Commander Hilt, leapt over a gaping chasm and landed with a jolt on the other side. Chunks of stone tumbled into the fiery abyss and he turned as Samson took two strides and jumped across after him. Hilt raised his sword to deflect the incoming strike and Samson's blade scraped across stone in a shower of sparks. Kicking away the colonel's legs, Hilt rolled to his feet and powered his blade down at Samson's neck. The colonel blocked the strike and thrust his other sword into Hilt's shield, forcing him back.

'Tiring, Darklight?' Samson said, getting to his feet.

Breathing hard, Hilt didn't respond. Samson was human, and just like him, was feeling the pace.

Hilt moved back onto firmer ground and glanced left to see one more intersection remained before the lattice of bridges ended near the feet of the Anakim Sphinx.

His visor warned him his armour was overheating and he made a run for it. Flames roared around him and ten strides later Hilt burst through into the clarity of clean air. Opening his mask, he breathed deep and turned to see Samson following.

The Terra Force leader slowed to a walk as he emerged from the flames and allowed a twenty foot gap to open up between them. He also retracted his face-plate and then wiped the sweat from his face with an armoured wrist.

Hilt stared into Samson's cold eyes as each studied the other. He knew the colonel would like nothing more than to relieve Goodwin of his head, but that was something Hilt could not, and would not, allow. He also knew Goodwin and Susan must be close, for as far as he could tell the immense sphinx was the focal point of the surrounding complex. If they were anywhere, it was inside the ancient structure. He edged towards the stairway to block off Samson's route inside.

'What's with the Englishwoman, Morgan?' Hilt said, buying himself more time to recuperate.

Samson didn't reply. Instead, the Terra Force officer dropped to one knee to rest while keeping his eyes fixed firmly on Hilt.

'Do you even know why they want her?'

'She has something she shouldn't,' Samson said.

'The pendant?'

Samson glared at him and said no more.

As Hilt prepared for the resumption of hostilities, he noticed a large figure emerge from the lattice of bridges to the left. From the look of his uniform he was a Deep Reach explorer and he carried the limp body of one of his team in his arms. Hilt recognised the dead man as the person Samson had threatened with death should Morgan not give him the very thing he'd just mentioned, the mysterious pendant.

The man moved away from the toxic fumes and his breathing apparatus slid back to reveal a bearded face. He paused as he saw the two soldiers before him.

Hilt stood aside to let him pass.

The man adjusted his grip on his grim burden and moved up onto the Anakim steps to begin a crippling ascent.

With the moment gone, Hilt closed his face-plate before moving back to face his opponent, who stood in response.

'Ready to die, Darklight?' Samson said.

Hilt sliced the air twice with his glowing sword to leave a cross of light fading in the dark. 'As ready as you, Terra Force.'

Samson showed his teeth in something approaching a grin and sealed his face back inside his helmet.

Hilt surged forward, catching the colonel by surprise and laid into him with everything he had, sword and shield against sword and sword.

The ring of clashing steel sung out over howling winds as the battle ebbed and flowed. First Hilt gained the advantage, only for Samson to come storming back in a snarling rage.

Hilt sensed an opening and sent Samson spinning to the ground, but the colonel surged to his feet and unleashed a relentless barrage that drove Hilt back – and back again.

Ducking a vicious slice, Hilt anticipated a feint and slammed his shield down, sending one of the colonel's swords clattering to the ground. Samson altered the direction of his counter-strike and snapped Hilt's head back with a brutal uppercut, before backhanding the shield from his grasp.

Hilt seized Samson's arm and brought his sword down with all his force.

The blade stopped a whisker from the colonel's visor.

Inch by inch, Samson forced Hilt's sword back with his own before Hilt halted the advance.

The two men stood locked under tension, glowing masks inches apart and shining swords sparking with heat. Their arms shook as the battle of strength continued.

Moments turned to seconds and Hilt, ever so slowly, forced the blade back towards Samson's head. With a sudden snarl, Samson pushed himself away and reached down for his other sword while on the move.

Gunfire cracked out and Samson's weapon skittered beyond his grasp.

Hilt turned to see three chrome-clad warriors shimmer forth from invisibility and stride towards them.

♦

Glancing at Hilt, Samson moved away to face his nemesis.

Ophion Nexus raised his mirrored visor and pointed his gun at Samson's chest. 'Judgement has come for you, Colonel.'

Samson reached for his rifle, but realised his only remaining weapon was in his hand, his thermal sword. He surveyed those arrayed against him. *I can take them*, he thought, *I can kill them all*. But another voice, a smaller, feebler voice spoke of caution, spoke of family – spoke of Brett.

'Judgement?' Samson opened his mask and sneered in contempt. 'Judgement?! Who are you to judge me?'

'Not I,' – Ophion gestured to the figure next to him – 'her.'

Zhang Bai stepped past her leader and raised her rifle.

Samson tensed for the killing shot that never came. 'What are you waiting for? DO IT!'

Zhang attached her rifle to her back-plate and removed her helmet. 'I will kill you, Colonel, slow and painfully, so my sister will have her vengeance. But,' she said, drawing an ornate sword from her armour, 'it will be as the gods demand, skill against skill, piece by piece.'

Samson grinned in victory; the bitch was as good as dead. 'Come on then, little girl,' – he resealed his helmet – 'show me what you've got.'

♦

Hilt edged away from Samson and towards the Anakim Sphinx. He knew three against one at the best of times was testing, against

S.I.L.V.E.R. operatives it was a forgone conclusion. The colonel was a dead man.

S.I.L.V.E.R.'s leader noticed Hilt's movement and placed a hand on Zhang's shoulder, staying her attack on Samson.

'Commander,' Ophion said, 'I cannot let you leave.'

Hilt eyed Ophion and the third assassin, who moved to his leader's side.

So much for three against one, Hilt thought, and he stopped his retreat, while noticing his discarded shield lay on the ground to his right. 'I have no quarrel with S.I.L.V.E.R..'

The third assassin adjusted his grip on his rifle. 'You should have told your men that before they attacked us.'

'It is a pity you didn't accept our offer all those years ago,' Ophion said. 'The benefits of S.I.L.V.E.R. are beyond anything Darklight can provide.'

'I don't live to kill,' Hilt said.

'We all kill, Commander.'

'Indeed, but I do it to protect the weak; you kill to protect the strong, there's a difference.'

Ophion shook his head. 'And that is where you are wrong.' He glanced at the man at his side and then to Zhang. 'Take them.'

Zhang leapt towards Samson while Hilt dived to his right as the other assassin opened fire.

Bullets ricocheted off his armour and Hilt grabbed his shield and deflected another barrage before Ophion's man was on him. A blade lanced towards his visor. Hilt twisted and the sword scraped down the side of his helmet. With a heave he thrust the man back as they both shimmered out of sight. Hilt scrolled through his visor's spectrums, trying to locate the man's ever-changing visual signature. Movement left made him duck as an explosion threw him from his feet. He landed on his back, dazed – his sword gone.

The chrome-clad figure emerged from the dark and stood over him, rifle in hand. 'I expected more.'

Hilt glimpsed the glint of steel lying on the ground a few feet away and he raised his shield and rolled towards it as the rifle discharged. Hilt scooped up Samson's deactivated sword and launched it at the assassin's head. The blade sliced through the air to plunge through the man's visor and out the back of his helmet with a sickening crunch.

The S.I.L.V.E.R. operative toppled to the ground, dead, and Hilt got to his feet and pulled the sword free. He turned back to Ophion as Zhang stalked Samson in the background.

'That was well done,' Ophion said, approaching, 'but lucky.'

Hilt picked up his own sword, reactivated both blades, and opened his helmet's face-plate. 'Luck should never be underestimated.'

Ophion nodded and drew forth a sword of his own, its long blade also glowing white with heat.

The storm intensified and S.I.L.V.E.R.'s leader looked up to the heavens. 'A student can only learn from a master.' He produced another sword, but this blade shimmered dark, like its sibling's ghost.

Hilt lowered his visor. 'And which one are you?'

Thunder rumbled and Ophion sealed his own helmet before looking back at him. 'I am your death.'

CHAPTER FORTY-SIX

THE VISOR on Sarah's helmet blurred, its digital image distorting against the dark. She rapped her knuckles against it and the picture cleared. She touched the wall before her, its surface slick with water. She'd taken a wrong turn.

I'm lost, she thought in despair.

A vision of Locke killing her friends flared in premonition. She turned and ran back the way she'd come, dodging through a sea of towering columns, unsure which way was where and which side was which. Mist hung in patches, thin and thick, and her helmet wasn't tracing her path as it should.

A message flashed on her visor:

Signal Acquired
Deep Reach Verification
TEAM: ALPHA SIX

And then another replaced it:

Designation: Team Leader
Riley 'Ace' Orton

Sarah slowed as her helmet's speaker system crackled from an incoming communication.

'Sa – is – I can't—'

She pressed a button on her helmet to boost the signal, but it had gone.

'Riley?' she whispered. *How can it be?* Her visor plotted a rough course to the source of the signal and she was running again, weaving through columns with the pain of hope in her heart.

As she ran, the message appeared again, but slightly different:

Signal Acquired
Deep Reach Verification
EXPIRED

Followed by another:

Designation: Team Leader
Dresden 'Torch' Locke

Sarah slowed as her visor showed a new source marker, and saw it was heading straight for the first. She gripped her knife and surged forward. Statues, tombs and columns flashed past and then she saw a light in the dark. She headed towards it before it blinked out and both signals on her visor vanished.

Skidding to a stop, she scanned through different visual spectrums and saw the faint heat signature of a man through the mist, close to where the light had been. As she approached, the haze cleared and the image intensified. She switched back to the previous setting to see a person kneeling on the ground, their head bowed.

Looking all around, she crept closer and the man looked up.

'Sarah,' Jefferson said, 'is that you?'

'Jefferson?' she said, confused. 'I saw Riley's signal.'

He gestured at a shape before him. 'My helmet's radio was damaged by the heat; I tried using Riley's instead.'

Sarah stared down at the body and she felt her legs go weak. She dropped to her knees and reached out a hand to touch Riley's face.

'I couldn't leave him there alone,' Jefferson said, his voice choking with emotion, 'not like that.'

Sarah's world collapsed around her as reality returned with crushing finality.

'Sarah,' – Jefferson touched her hand – 'what happened? Who did this?'

'Locke,' Sarah said, remembering the second signal. She turned round and stood up to scan the pitch-black.

'Dresden?' Jefferson said. 'Dresden Locke did this?'

'He doesn't want anyone getting to the surface,' she said, distracted. 'We know too much.'

Jefferson shook his head in disbelief. 'But Riley was his favourite, his golden boy.'

'Is it so hard to believe?' She took a couple of steps into the dark, still searching for signs of the SED leader. 'He was willing to put everyone at risk for years, he knew about those things – the lights – and said nothing. He says he's protecting everyone, but all he's protecting is his job – his legacy.'

A noise to her left made her turn in its direction. She stared into the dark, eyes straining to see what might be there. Walking forwards, another sound made her spin back round. Thirty feet away, Trish and Jason emerged through the mists.

Sarah felt relief sweep through her and she lowered her knife.

'Sarah, thank God,' Trish said, 'we lost Goodwin in the mist.' Her friend slowed and gasped when she saw Riley's body.

Jason knelt down to feel for a pulse. 'Sarah, what happened?'

'Locke killed him.' Jefferson got to his feet and switched on his helmet's torches.

'The SED must go on,' Sarah said, her voice bitter.

'And go on it shall,' said a voice from behind.

Sarah spun round, but Locke smacked the knife from her hand and pressed his own blade to her throat.

'Turn,' he said, 'slowly.'

Sarah refused his command and glared into his hateful eyes with defiance.

He grasped her shoulder and spun her round to face the others. 'Give me the pendant,' he said to Jason.

Jason's hand strayed to his coveralls, but Sarah shook her head. 'Don't give it to him.'

Locke grabbed the back of her neck and switched the position of the knife against her throat. 'Give it to me,' he said, drawing blood, 'and I promise I won't hurt her.'

Jason withdrew the Anakim artefact. He looked at Trish and then back to Sarah.

'Don't listen to him,' Sarah said, raising her chin as the blade cut deeper. 'He has to kill us to make sure no one knows what he did.'

Jason looked down at the pendant before launching it at Locke's head.

The SED commander moved on instinct and Sarah rammed her elbow into his midriff and slipped from his grasp as the pendant flew into the dark.

Jefferson gave a roar of fury and ran at Locke, lifted him from his feet and smashed him into a stone column. Both men tumbled to the ground in a flail of arms and legs. A moment later Jefferson was on top and raining down blows with his massive fists.

A flash of steel sliced through the air and Jefferson fell back, clutching his arm. Locke got to his feet and lashed out again with his blade, and Jefferson retreated.

Sarah held out her hand to Jason. 'Give me a knife!'

'Say it,' Jefferson said to Locke, 'say you killed Riley.'

Locke wiped blood from his face. 'If you want someone to blame,' – he gestured at Sarah – 'blame her, she left me no choice.'

Sarah searched around for her knife while Jason hunted in his backpack.

Locke lunged forward and Jefferson parried the thrust with his forearm and landed a ferocious punch that sent Locke flying to the ground. The bloodied blade clattered onto stone and Jefferson bent to pick it up. Dazed, Locke struggled to his feet while the bearded archaeologist looked at Sarah, who gave him the nod of approval for what had to come next. Jefferson's grip tightened on the knife and he grasped Locke's harness and raised the blade in preparation for the killing blow.

Sarah saw a shimmer of light emerge from the dark behind him and Trish screamed a warning. Jefferson spun round, but it was too late. The creature lifted him from his feet in a spray of blood. Locke scrambled away and Jefferson fell to the floor in a bloody mess.

'Look out!' Jason said.

Another flash of light whooshed past and Sarah was thrown to the floor. Thirty feet away, Jefferson stared at her through the mist, his eyes full of terror, before he was dragged screaming into the dark.

The other light vanished into the gloom, while a small figure emerged further back amongst the columns. It was Susan. The small woman stooped down and picked up something from the floor. Sarah switched on her helmet's lights and the object glinted metallic in the dark.

'The pendant,' Trish said.

Sarah turned as Locke stumbled away into swirling mists, and when she looked back Susan had gone, and along with her, their way out of Sanctuary.

CHAPTER FORTY-SEVEN

'JESUS WEPT,' Jason said, unable to take his eyes off the gruesome blood trail that disappeared into the dark.

Trish backed towards them. 'Have they gone? Can anyone see them?'

Still sitting where she'd fallen, Sarah looked around, but there was no further sign of the lights, Susan, or Dresden Locke.

'What do we do now?' Jason said.

Sarah climbed to her feet and walked over to where a discarded Deep Reach helmet lay on the ground. She bent down and picked it up.

'Is that Riley's?' Trish said.

Jason turned to look and then frowned. 'Where's his body?'

'They took it,' Sarah said, feeling sick at the realisation.

'What?' Trish sounded hysterical. 'Why? What do they want?'

Sarah ran her finger over the white lettering which read: *R. Orton* and then looked up at her friends. 'I don't know, but I intend to find out. And Locke's out there, somewhere, and he needs to pay for what he's done.'

'You really want to keep going,' Jason said, 'after what's just happened?'

'What choice do we have?'

'I'd rather go up against bullets than face those ... things,' Trish said.

Sarah saw the glint of metal on the floor, walked over and picked up her knife. 'Then I'll go alone.'

Jason shook his head and looked at Trish. 'We've come this far, we're not splitting up now.'

Trish gave a tremulous nod.

'Then let's go,' Sarah said, and she moved off into the dark.

CHAPTER FORTY-EIGHT

Colonel Samson sliced through the air once, twice, a thousand times, but every time he struck, the female assassin whirled away out of reach. Growing tired, he waited for her to come to him.

As Zhang Bai circled back, Samson could see Hilt and Ophion fighting high above on the sphinx's giant stairway. *If I can get rid of this assassin,* he thought, returning his attention to Zhang, *nothing will stand between me and the pendant.*

The thought was all the motivation he needed and he gripped his sword tighter and waited for his chance.

Zhang leapt to the attack and Samson raised his sword to parry as the blows rained in. The woman danced and weaved around him and her blade spun through the air faster and faster. He struck and missed, struck again, and then felt something pierce his side; he staggered back and looked up to see Zhang raise her visor. She smiled, victorious, and held up her sword, the blade glinting red with blood.

Visions of torture filled Samson's mind. He roared in rage and surged forward.

Zhang deflected the initial barrage with ease, but her defence turned to desperation as Samson's onslaught continued. She retreated, and he powered strikes down, again and again and again.

Harder and harder he hacked, until her sword shattered in an explosion of sparks. She somersaulted away, but Samson anticipated the move and spun round with his sword extended. The thermal blade sliced through Zhang's armour, leaving a gaping wound in her side. The assassin staggered, but didn't fall; instead she managed to enter into a run towards the sphinx and Samson followed.

Zhang discarded her broken blade and produced her rifle.

Samson ducked as bullets whizzed past before her ammo ran dry and he was on her. Grasping her throat, he lifted her off her feet and plunged his sword through her chest. The assassin shuddered and the gun fell from her grasp.

Samson stared into her visor. 'Where's your vengeance now, girl?'

Zhang Bai raised her hand and Samson saw a grenade pin dangling from her index finger.

A blast of energy exploded in a flash of light.

Flung apart, Zhang slammed into the stairs and Samson arced into the air, before weightlessness passed and he crunched into the ground. Electricity flickered over his armour and he let out a groan.

Trying to rise, Samson's strength faded and he dropped back down as darkness took him.

◆

Hilt ducked and parried as Ophion's blades whirred through the air in a dazzle of light and shadow, but no matter how hard he tried, he was unable to breach the man's defence and, step by inexorable step, he was driven back. As they passed the halfway point on the sphinx's giant staircase, Ophion halted his attack and opened his visor. 'You fight well for an uninitiated. It would have been interesting to see how you fared once fully trained.'

Hilt didn't respond, his armoured chest heaving from exertion.

A detonation from below made Ophion take a step back. The

assassin turned his head to look down at the distant forms of Samson and Zhang lying on the ground at the bottom of the stairway. He stayed thus for a moment and Hilt prepared to attack, but Ophion raised one of his swords and looked back at him. The assassin's face hardened and he leapt forward.

Their swords clashed as Ophion pressed ahead with renewed vigour. Hilt retreated as the speed of the assassin's blades increased and increased again. Ophion feinted left and sent one of Hilt's swords spinning into the dark. And moments later, a cutting thrust sent Hilt's second blade clattering to the steps.

Hilt swayed back as Ophion's sword cut a molten gash across his chest armour. An instant later, two blades came to a rest at his neck and Hilt gazed into the assassin's ice cool eyes.

'And so it ends,' Ophion said

Hilt's face remained impassive as he waited for the killing thrust.

'It is good you do not fear death,' Ophion said, 'we all must die with honour.'

Hilt made to raise his hand, but Ophion increased his force and the blades melted into armoured panels.

Heat seared Hilt's skin and Ophion smiled. 'You still seek to win?' The assassin relieved some of the pressure. 'Go ahead, show me ... slowly.'

With care, Hilt opened his hand.

'Pretty,' Ophion said, 'and yet not an explosive. A gift perhaps?'

'Perhaps,' Hilt said, holding the shining blue crystal aloft, 'but not for you.'

A shimmering light appeared behind Ophion and a menacing growl changed the assassin's expression to shock.

The beast moved closer and Ophion's eyes narrowed as he closed his visor. 'So,' he said, turning to face the creature, 'we meet again.'

With a deafening roar the Pharos leapt, Ophion vanished and Hilt ran.

CHAPTER FORTY-NINE

SARAH WALKED through the dense mist inside the Anakim Sphinx. Towering pillars emerged through the dark, and Trish and Jason followed behind in silence.

Five minutes had passed since Locke's attack and there was still no sign of the SED commander or of the elusive Susan. Whatever was controlling the strange, mute woman, it had a plan, but what that was Sarah couldn't guess. When the question had been posed to Goodwin he'd become uncertain as to why they'd been brought to this place, if indeed that was the case at all.

Sarah felt the weight of the orb in her coveralls, which were concealed beneath the decontamination suit given to her by Goodwin. She reached down to press her hand against the artefact in reassurance. Goodwin had suggested the symbol on her pendant indicated she'd been brought to this place much like he had, drawn in by an unseen power that manipulated those under its thrall, a power far older than anything they could comprehend. *Did these creatures – what had Locke called them? Pharos? – did these Pharos really lead us here? Have they been shepherding us through Sanctuary from the beginning?* It was hard to believe, although, Sarah had seen Susan speaking to the orb as if it were alive and could hear her words.

Sarah looked at her palm. *Have I been under its control ever since I first touched it back at the USSB's military laboratories?* A memory came to mind of silver symbols transferring from the orb's surface to leach into her skin and she slowed to a stop.

'Sarah?' Trish said in concern.

Sarah turned to her friend. 'I think Goodwin was right.'

'What do you mean?'

Sarah held up her chain to examine her remaining pendant and not for the first time wished it had the same power as its larger cousin. 'The orb altered the pendant's surface to show a symbol.'

'The Libra constellation?' Jason said.

Sarah nodded. 'Yes, but why did it alter it? Goodwin said he'd seen this symbol many times before. It can't be a coincidence. When Susan was holding the orb, she was speaking to it as if it could hear her, as if it was alive. What if ... what if it activated something in the pendant so that the creature, the Pharos, could find us?'

'Even if that were true,' Trish said, 'what would be the point?'

Sarah looked around them. 'This place – to bring us here.'

Jason and Trish eyed the mist with nervous eyes.

'We were so close to a way out of Sanctuary,' Sarah said, 'not once, but twice. On two occasions we've been near temples that held transportation devices, yet both times the creature was there, chasing us on, forcing us into risks, moving us away from our goal. If it wasn't for the Pharos we'd be on the surface by now. And it could have killed us ten times over, but we're still here.'

Her friends didn't say anything, but Sarah knew she was right, it felt ... right. And she also knew the Pharos were as much to blame for Riley's death as Locke. She pulled down the zipper on her decontamination suit, reached into her coverall pocket and withdrew the orb. The twelve sided object throbbed inside its protective cloth, almost as if talking about it had awoken it.

'What are you doing?' Trish said. 'It's dangerous.'

Can it hear what we're saying? Sarah wondered. She stared at the artefact's concealed form. The idea was disturbing. *But even if it can, it wouldn't be able to understand our language. Unless*, she thought, *it's learning as we speak*. She gazed at the orb and felt a powerful compulsion to touch it, and an image of her holding it flashed into her mind's eye.

Sarah looked up at her friends. 'We need to find out what it wants. What it does.'

'It might not do anything,' Jason said, 'except kill or knock you unconscious.'

The sound of a distant explosion penetrated the mist and Sarah peeled back the orb's cloth.

'Wait,' Trish said, grabbing her wrist, 'it could attract the lights.'

Sarah looked at her friend. 'Some risks are worth taking.' She grasped the Anakim artefact and its surface grew warm.

CHAPTER FIFTY

SARAH HELD the orb in her hands and a familiar tingle ran down her spine. The hairs on her neck bristled and the orb grew light. Sarah knew what was coming next and she gripped the artefact tighter. The metallic surface vibrated and turned smooth. Her hands shook, pain seared through her head and she cried out as she fell to her knees.

Someone called her name, but she clung on, trying to remain conscious. The top of the orb glowed and slid back. The rest of its pentagonal sides pulsed white, and the agony increased. An Anakim face flashed before her eyes and she gasped and collapsed to the floor, her body convulsing.

♦

'Sarah!' Trish shook her friend's shoulders, but there was no response.

Jason crouched down and tried to prise the orb from her hands. 'It's stuck fast.'

'What do we do?' Trish said as Sarah's body continued to twitch in spasm.

'There's nothing we can do. We wait.'

Trish glanced around at the icy mist that surrounded them and withdrew her small pocket knife to stand guard over her friend.

♦

Visions flashed before Sarah's eyes and a spark of electricity washed over her brain like a storm. She saw strange lands and stranger peoples. A procession of Anakim priests and priestesses walked across a causeway. The flames from their torches glowed orange in the dark and flickered in the breeze. Sarah looked up through their eyes and saw the great Anakim Sphinx, glinting silver against a ring of fire. And then she was inside, looking at a bloodstained altar amidst a sea of black, and flanked by strange walls that glowed from within. Beyond this curiosity, Sarah floated towards another wall and a sculptural relief that glittered like stars in the night. It showed the heavens and the Earth, and all manner of constellations decorated its great width. Amongst these images, five objects shone like diamonds. Each was too large to be a distant star, but far too small to be the moon. A glimmer of remembrance formed before a crushing pain surged through her mind and darkness closed in.

♦

Sarah opened her eyes and looked up to see Trish and Jason looking down at her.

'Are you okay,' Trish said, helping her into a sitting position.

Sarah nodded and breathed deeply.

'It's still glowing,' Jason said.

Sarah looked down to see she still held the Anakim orb, which shone from its activation. There was no pain, just a tingle that tickled her palms. As they watched, the topmost pentagonal side reappeared, before tendrils of electricity flickered over its surface. The orb dulled and then its whole shape changed, its sides sliding over one another like some kind of spherical Rubik's cube.

'What's it doing?' Trish said.

The orb's sides rearranged themselves until it flattened into a saucer-sized pentagonal disc, and Jason reached out to touch it. 'It's like a bigger version of your pendant.'

'Which helps us how?' Trish said.

Sarah ran her fingers over the disc's smooth surface. 'I think it's trying to tell me something.'

Trish frowned. 'Like what?'

'I don't know. I saw images, like ... like it was trying to speak to me.'

'Did it tell you how to get out of here?' Jason said.

'Maybe, I—'

A flicker of light made Sarah look up.

Beyond the gloom, a deep growl emanated from the mist and a Pharos shimmered forth, its rows of razor-sharp teeth disappearing and reappearing through its alien glow.

'Sarah, get up,' Jason said, as he and Trish backed away.

The beast followed their movement, ignoring Sarah as she struggled to her feet.

Jason moved in front of Trish as the Pharos bore down on them and Sarah grasped the disc, unclipped a shackle from her harness and threw it in the vicinity of the creature's back to distract it.

The object bounced harmlessly from its hidden bulk and the Pharos continued backing Trish and Jason up.

'Hey!' Sarah waved her arms and aimed a kick at the creature's trailing light. Her boot rebounded from something hard and the Pharos swung round and bared its teeth.

Sarah backed away as it turned towards her. A strange clicking sound emanated from within and she went to move towards her friends, but the Pharos darted the same way, cutting off her escape.

'Sarah!' Trish called out.

'Go,' she said and held the flattened orb before her, 'it won't hurt me!'

The beast opened its gaping maw and roared, and Sarah's sense of security evaporated.

She backed away as it stalked her and felt something press against her back. She'd walked into a stone column. The Pharos let out a predatory growl as it prepared to strike.

Sarah dived right as the light surged forward and caught her with a glancing blow. She was thrown from her feet and the disc slipped from her grasp.

'Sarah,' Jason said, 'RUN!'

Heartbeat pounding, Sarah scrambled to her feet and sprinted into the dark.

CHAPTER FIFTY-ONE

SARAH RAN through the sphinx's endless halls and glanced back to see the Pharos chasing her down. She veered left and then right, but a bellow of fury told her the beast was closing fast. Her manic flight thrust her headlong into thickening mist and a column loomed before her; she dodged left and stumbled, but kept up her speed, driven on by terror.

Careering past statues and tombs, she glanced back again. The light from the Pharos had gone and when it failed to re-materialise on a second inspection, she slowed as silent darkness surrounded her.

No sound from the creature reached her ears and she wondered if it approached unseen. She strained her ears, listening, but all she could hear was her own breathing, which sounded muffled by the thick vapour.

An icy chill permeated her bones and Sarah pressed a button on her helmet. 'Trish,' she whispered, 'I'm okay, can you hear me ... Jason?'

A crackle of static washed through her helmet's speakers before a faint voice replied.

'Sarah,' Trish said, her voice sounding distorted, 'where are you?'

She was about to reply before a rough hand clamped over her mouth and she was dragged back into the dark.

She tried to speak, but whoever held her tightened their grip.

'Shhh,' a voice whispered in her ear, 'they're close.'

Sarah recognised who it was and she turned her head to see Richard Goodwin staring over her shoulder into the darkness. She followed his gaze and her visor adjusted to show a massive plaza shrouded in thinning wisps of mist. At its furthest edge, Susan moved in a shuffling walk towards a steep slope.

Goodwin let go of Sarah's mouth and pointed to the right, where the shimmering form of a Pharos glided across the ground. Every so often the two unlikely companions stopped and moved closer together, before carrying on their slow procession.

'Locke called it a Pharos,' Sarah said, keeping her voice hushed.

Goodwin gave a nod.

She frowned. 'What are they doing?'

'I don't know, but I know where they're going.' Goodwin moved back behind the column and Sarah followed.

'I need to find my friends,' she said.

He gestured behind her. 'I think they've found you.'

She turned to see Trish and Jason approach out of the mist.

Sarah moved towards them and put a finger to her lips to signal for quiet.

'We thought we'd lost you,' Trish said while Goodwin returned to his vantage point to spy on the Pharos.

Jason held up the orb-turned-disc and passed it to her. 'So much for the light not wanting to hurt us.'

'We're still alive, aren't we?' she said, tucking the artefact into her coveralls.

'For now.' Trish reached out and touched a jagged gash on Sarah's chest. 'But we have to get out of here, our luck's running out.'

Sarah looked down at the bleeding wound. The Pharos had got closer than she'd thought. She felt her neck and face where a host of other lacerations had resulted from her close shave with the creature. She hadn't felt any of them; not even the deep cut on her palm dealt by Locke's knife back outside the sphinx. 'Susan's close,' she said, ignoring the pain that belatedly kicked in.

Jason pointed behind her. 'Where's he going?'

Sarah turned to see Goodwin disappear into the mist. She swore and waved them on. 'Let's go, we can't afford to lose him again.'

The three friends pursued Goodwin across the plaza, Sarah leading, Trish following and Jason bringing up the rear.

Further ahead, the shimmering light of the Pharos disappeared from view and they slowed their approach.

Goodwin, oblivious to their presence, reached the slope, crept up it and vanished into a dense bank of fog.

Sarah grasped Trish's hand, who repeated the process with Jason and, linked together, the three friends inched forward, fearing what was ahead as much as what lay behind.

Sarah's visor fuzzed as she entered the freezing cloud. The vapour clung to her like an apparition and blocked out all vision. If she'd put a hand in front of her face she wouldn't have been able to see it. She felt Trish tighten her grip.

Seconds later the way ahead cleared a little and Sarah saw Goodwin crouched down in a shallow trough next to a towering wall encrusted with ice. A hundred feet away the light from the Pharos shone through slow, swirling mists. If it had spotted them it didn't show it, and Susan was nowhere to be seen.

Sarah dropped down onto one knee behind Goodwin. She glanced left to see a deep alcove sunk into the wall. The tall, coffin-like aperture looked like a gateway to another world as its deep interior was wreathed in an icy miasma. Two hundred feet on their right, and in mirror image to the one next to them, another frost-encrusted wall could just be glimpsed soaring into the dark. Between them and it, a massive silver statue towered over them. Half shrouded in cloud, the figure sat upon a golden throne and Sarah felt her gaze drawn upwards to its beautiful, feminine face. It reminded her of a larger version of the Ageless King she'd seen in Sanctuary's military vaults. Either side of it, two massive sculptures of Anakim sphinxes lurked in the dark, their forms exact replicas of the monument in which they now found themselves trapped.

As she looked back down, something caught her eye. Two bodies had been laid out in offering before the god-like silver statue. Their static forms peeked out through the mist laden ground, and the sight of one of the two made her feel dizzy with grief. Riley lay in unmoving death beside his friend and teammate, the late Jefferson Church. Both men had been arranged in the shape of a star and Sarah felt all reason leave her. She stood up, meaning to go to him, but Trish grasped her arm and pulled her back down.

'Sarah,' Trish said, her expression full of sympathy, 'you can't help him now.'

Sarah stared at the lifeless form before Goodwin whispered something to her.

She looked back in a daze to see him pointing beyond to where the Pharos lurked. 'Your way out of Sanctuary is through there,' he said.

He crawled forward and Sarah, her mind in turmoil, glanced back at Riley before following.

'What's he doing?' Jason said.

After ten more feet Goodwin stopped at a second alcove in the wall, and Trish leant past Sarah and touched his shoulder. 'We need Susan, she has the pendant.'

He looked startled by the news, nodded, and then turned to face the wall. He ran his hand over the frost to uncover a transparent surface beneath. Where the first alcove had been deep, this one was shallow, as if it had been back-filled.

With care, Goodwin stood up and wiped away more of the icy coating. After the shock of seeing Riley, Sarah felt her attention returning and she kept her eye on the Pharos in case it decided to move. When it failed to do so, she looked up to see a figure inside the crystalline structure. It was a woman. *This must be Rebecca*, she thought, *the person Goodwin said he wanted to free.*

Goodwin placed a hand against the crystal and Sarah was shocked as the woman's eyes moved inside her solid prison. At least she thought they'd moved. Goodwin meanwhile slid his hand over the surface as if looking for some way to release Rebecca from her bonds.

Sarah could see another person trapped inside the transparent wall behind the first. Much like the woman, the man looked to have been frozen mid-pose. On a hunch, Sarah pressed her ear to the cold surface. Concentrating, she could hear the steady rhythm of the woman's heartbeat and as she listened a second beat could be heard, fainter and erratic, but it was there.

'They're alive,' Sarah said.

Goodwin crouched back down beside her. 'No – only Rebecca.'

Sarah shook her head. 'I heard two heartbeats.'

Goodwin gave her a sharp look before pressing his ear to the wall. His eyes widened as he heard what she had.

'It's impossible,' he whispered, 'Joseph died.' He looked up at the man and his expression turned to astonishment. 'His wounds are healing.'

Sarah saw gunshot holes riddled the man's clothing. Within these, the flesh was red and laced with blood vessels, but the wounds were shallow, not deep penetrations like a bullet would make.

Sarah gazed into the wall, counting the number of bullets that must have torn into the man's chest. 'You saw him shot?' Sarah said.

Goodwin didn't reply.

Sarah yanked him round. 'Did you see him get shot?' she said, her eyes intense.

He stared at her through his transparent helmet and gave a nod.

Sarah looked back into the wall before the ground trembled and a glow of light blossomed into being alongside the Pharos.

'Susan,' Goodwin said, turning.

The ground shook and the Pharos moved towards them.

Trish grasped Sarah's arm. The creature let out a shriek and sped past them into swirling mists, and they breathed a collective sigh of relief.

Meanwhile the ethereal light shone brighter to reveal Susan's shadowy outline next to an altar much like Sarah had seen in her vision.

Sarah turned her attention back to the wall which now glowed from within, and looked past Goodwin to see more alcoves lining its crystalline structure at regular intervals.

'Can you get them out?' she said.

Goodwin gave her a look of despair. 'I don't know, I think the altar controls it somehow.'

Sarah looked back towards the light. 'And Susan controls the altar.'

She took one more look at the alcove and then ran towards Riley.

'What are you doing?!' Trish said, standing.

Sarah reached Riley's body, grasped his climbing harness and dragged him towards the nearest alcove. 'I can bring him back.'

'What?'

'I can bring him back!'

Jason tried to stop her, but she pushed him away, her look ferocious.

'Help me!' Sarah said to Trish.

Her friend looked at her, uncomprehending, and Sarah continued to drag Riley's corpse across the ground.

Reaching the alcove, she heaved his body inside its icy mist and waited for something to happen.

'Sarah, he's gone,' Trish said. 'You have to let him go.'

'NO! I can heal him.' She crouched down and touched his face. 'I can heal you.'

CHAPTER FIFTY-TWO

SARAH KISSED Riley's cold lips and turned away from the alcove to look for Goodwin.

'Sarah,' Jason said, grasping her shoulders, 'Riley's dead, you can't heal him.' The distant roar of a Pharos echoed through the sphinx. 'We need to get out of here.'

Sarah pushed Jason aside and joined Goodwin, who stood facing the strange glow that permeated the misty air a hundred feet away. She made to move towards it, but Goodwin grasped her arm.

'Wait,' he said, 'something's not right.'

A faint light spread through the mist-shrouded ground and a strange vibration rippled up through their feet. They retreated, but seconds later the sensation ceased and the illumination faded. The vapour that covered the ground cleared to reveal a massive, circular crater, two hundred feet across and twenty feet deep. Whether this feature was newly formed or had been concealed by the mist all along, Sarah didn't know, but the concave depression bridged the gap between one iced wall and the other; both of which pulsed with the faintest light. Her visor fuzzed and adjusted to the changing range to reveal a massive, metallic pentagram resting at the bottom of the crater. In its centre, steps led up to a raised, circular dais on which stood the altar, and standing next to this was the small figure of Susan. The woman was looking straight at them with bloodshot eyes. It was as if she was waiting for them to approach. Sarah zoomed in her visor to see she held the pendant clutched in one hand.

Something moved in the dark and Sarah's eyes grew wide as Dresden Locke appeared through the mist and grabbed Susan from behind. A second later he'd wrested the pendant from her and sent her tumbling down the steps.

'You're too late, Morgan,' Locke said, holding up the pendant, 'you're never getting back to the surface!'

Rage swamped Sarah's senses like nothing she'd ever felt before, and she went to jump down into the crater, but Jason hauled her back.

'Get off me!' she said, writhing in his grasp.

'Sarah, no,' Trish said, 'look!'

A dark liquid gushed up from the bottom of the depression to cover the giant metal pentagram, which lurched into a clockwise rotation. Locke saw his escape route disappearing before his eyes, while Susan had already made it to the far side and scrambled up the slope to safety.

Locke jumped down onto the moving pentagram, intending to follow her, but seconds later he was wading waist deep in viscous oil. He looked around him as the level reached his chest, then cried out and clutched his head in pain. Unable to make it out, he staggered back to the steps and up towards the altar, his face contorted in agony. By then he was covered in black ooze and he fell to his knees to writhe in torment. With a sudden screech, he reared up and dug his fingers into his face, tearing into his flesh with his nails. He screamed and screamed again before gouging his knife into his cheek and down into his neck.

Trish gasped and averted her gaze as the blood flowed. The oil surged higher, and in a moment of lucidity Locke managed to drag his grappling gun clear and fire it towards them. The bolt whistled past their heads and punched into the glowing wall, but the discharge from the device ignited the oil. Flames licked up his arm and over his body. An instant later Locke had turned into a human torch as the fires raged and spread. With a final bloodcurdling shriek of terror, the SED facility commander plunged the blade into his own chest, once – twice – three times. The knife fell from his grasp and Dresden Locke slumped onto the steps and slid down into the black fluid to vanish beneath its burning surface.

Sarah stared in shock at the fiery lake that now encircled the central platform. Locke was gone, and with him her chance to save Riley.

'My God,' Jason said, 'what is that stuff?'

'It's a neurotoxin,' Goodwin said, 'or a hallucinogen, or both. It's everywhere down here. I had to swim through it to get here the first time. It nearly killed me. I think it's used as some kind of test.'

'Test?' Jason said.

Goodwin looked past him to Sarah. 'A test of faith.'

Sarah held his gaze for a moment before looking back to the central dais through the waves of heat and noticed something glinting in the oil near the altar's base. She zoomed in her visor to see the edge of something metallic. It was the pendant.

She looked at Goodwin. 'What did you just say?'

'It's a test of faith.'

'No, before that; you said you swam through it?'

He nodded. 'I used this.' He indicated his helmet and baggy decontamination suit. 'It doubles as a diving suit.'

Sarah looked down at her own suit and back to the pendant, then reached up to remove her Deep Reach helmet, which she held out to Goodwin.

He considered her for a moment and a sense of shared understanding passed between them. They would each do anything for the ones they loved. Goodwin twisted his transparent helmet from its locked position and they swapped headgear.

Trish grasped her arm. 'What are you doing?'

'I'm going to get the pendant.' Sarah secured her suit's breathing mask over her face, then pulled on Goodwin's helmet, locked it in place against her collar's mechanism, and switched on its head-up-display.

'It's gone,' Jason said, 'we're done.'

'No, it's there, I can see it.' Sarah pointed in its direction and Jason turned to look.

'It doesn't matter if it's there or not,' Trish said, 'you just saw what happened to Locke.'

'And you heard what Goodwin told us,' Sarah said, 'it's a test and without the pendant we can't activate the Anakim tech and we'll be stuck down here forever.'

'I worked the megalith without your pendant,' Goodwin said, 'you just need the blue crystals.'

Trish gestured to him. 'See, we might not need it!'

'Although,' – Goodwin looked at the frozen form of Rebecca – 'it controlled me more than I did it ... and someone died.'

Sarah stared into the burning oil that flowed round in a spiral from the crater's centre out, its speed increasing into a slow, hypnotic whirlpool of flame.

'I'm not sure if the suit will withstand the heat,' Goodwin said, following her gaze. 'The longer it burns, the hotter it'll get.'

The roar of a Pharos echoed through the sphinx, sounding closer than before, and Sarah pulled up the zipper on her suit. 'Then I better get moving.'

'No.' Trish moved in front of her. 'It could kill you!'

Sarah glanced back at Riley's alcove through the clearing mists. The vivid memory of his look of shock as the knife pierced his heart replayed over and over in her mind. 'I have to try. I have to try and bring him back.'

The speed of the fiery whirlpool increased and the flames grew higher.

'You can't go in there,' Jason said, as they backed away from the heat, 'it's too dangerous.'

'I have no choice.' Sarah hugged him. 'Find the transportation device; if I don't make it, you may still be able to get to the surface with Goodwin's help.'

Goodwin shook her hand. 'Call me Richard.'

She gave him a tired smile. 'With Richard's help.'

Goodwin stepped in to check her breathing apparatus. 'The oil will enter the helmet,' he said, 'and as soon as it touches your skin the hallucinations will start. You'll need to focus your mind, or you won't come back.'

'If I can get the altar to work,' she said, 'I'll do my best to free your friends.'

Goodwin gave her a grim nod. 'Good luck.'

'Sarah,' Jason said, 'please don't do this.'

She touched his cheek before Trish dragged her into a fierce embrace.

Sarah held her friend tight, the agony of separation unbearable. She made to pull away, but Trish wouldn't let go.

'I have to go,' Sarah said.

Trish shook her head and mouthed '*no*' as a tear ran down her face.

Sarah prised herself away and moved towards the flames, but her friend held onto her hand. Sarah gave Trish a fond smile and squeezed her fingers in a final farewell before turning to face the sinister crater, her expression hardening into determination.

CHAPTER FIFTY-THREE

ALONE AND BEREFT, Sarah approached the inferno, which swirled past with ever-increasing speed. She double-checked that her helmet was sealed and dropped into a crouch. She could just make out the metal pentagram at the crater's centre as the oil was thrown out from its rotation. The metallic structure spun faster around the dais, which remained static, and Sarah fought back her fear of the terrifying flames.

The heat built and she knew she couldn't afford to wait any longer. She rocked back on her heels, took a deep breath and leapt into the swirling cauldron.

Fire roared around her before she plunged into the oil and darkness swallowed her like the blackest night. Swept sideways, she sank to the bottom, where the oil cooled and thickened. A flash of terror tore through her mind and she gasped in shock as horrific thoughts and images bombarded her like the strobe from hell. Fighting back a scream, she bowed her head and crawled forward against the flow. Sparks of electricity flashed before her eyes as the oil poured into her helmet. The internal display flickered dead and the hot, viscous liquid crept higher.

Blinded, Sarah felt the oil seep into her mask and she coughed and choked as noxious fumes made her eyes water and throat burn. Strange, ethereal lights flickered around her and the visions intensified. Panic swelled as pain seared her body and oil flowed into her mouth and up her nose.

Swept up by the whirlpool, she floated in semi-conscious freefall along the bottom of the crater. Her helmet clonked and scraped across its surface before shattering into pieces. Oil flooded into her lungs and Sarah spun into the pitch-black, out of control ... and out of time.

CHAPTER FIFTY-FOUR

SARAH GROANED and opened her eyes. A strange object moved in front of her. It flickered with a dull orange light and spun on its axis like a giant spinning top. Pain filled her chest and she coughed and retched as she choked for air. Rolling onto her front, she vomited up a gallon of black oil and sucked in a shuddering breath. The shock of reality returned and she saw the thing she'd been looking at wasn't moving at all, she was. *I'm on the pentagram*, she thought. The steps of the dais that led up to the altar were thirty feet away and it was that which she'd seen moving round and round.

She glanced back to see a wall of black oil forced out by the pentagram's speeding rotation. Five feet above, on the surface, the fires still raged and she clung on as the centrifugal force tried to cast her back into the seething flow. *The metal pentagram must have risen ten feet*, she realised, *and the faster it spins, the higher it gets*. As if on cue, the pentagram's speed increased again and the structure inched higher, while buffeting winds caused her oil-damp hair to flutter in its wake.

Sarah shuffled forward on all fours, but almost slipped from the pentagram's edge and into one of its voids. Flinging out a hand, she halted her momentum at the point of no return. She stared down into a darkness that rippled like liquid metal. Through this strange effect she could see another pentagram spinning beneath the first, although every now and then she glimpsed something different, something that enticed her into its depths – an incomplete image of somewhere ... else.

Black oil still coated her from head to toe and before she could make sense of what she was seeing, chilling sounds attacked her senses. The hairs on the back of her neck bristled and a sense of fear washed over her like a plague. The assault on her mind returned with a vengeance and she grasped her head in agony. A familiar voice echoed through the ether. *Why do you fear me? ... you fear me ... fear me?* Her gaze was drawn to the void and its dull flicker of light. *Am I not what you desire? ... you desire ... desire?*

Sarah felt an overwhelming compulsion to let herself be dragged into the shimmering surface – to let it take her into its dark embrace. She toppled towards the void as the suction pulled her down, down into its depths. Something glinted in the shadows' light ... something gold. Sarah reached out shaky fingers and grasped her cross that hung down on its chain. The air continued to rush past as she stared, entranced, into the abyss. The wind howled and ghost-like fingers brushed her skin. She shut her eyes against the horror that consumed her and grasped the cross tighter. A vision of fire and smoke billowed into being. She felt her lungs choke and skin burn. Pain seared through her body and her hand clenched into a fist. Blood welled as the cross bit into flesh. A flash of light broke the dark and she willed herself back to safer ground.

Holding the golden keepsake before her like a shield, Sarah crawled forward, her hand bleeding, her mind a sea of pain. Time slowed and terrifying noises and wraith-like shrieks made her flinch in fear. Ghostly apparitions flew at her through the dark, their hideous forms tearing at her mind with raking claws. Terror seized tight and she gasped for air as her throat constricted before she saw something crawling under the skin of her hand. Her whole body rippled with parasites. She felt like her flesh was being eaten from the inside. The desire to tear them out, to rid her body of its torment, to stop the excruciating pain, was unbearable! She screamed and squeezed her eyes tight and the cross tighter still. Her body contorted in seizure before the flicker of fire fought back the dark and she saw the dais within reach.

Panic-stricken, she relinquished her blood-soaked grip on the cross to lurch onto stone steps. Thrust sideways by the mismatch in motion, Sarah found herself tumbling back towards the spinning pentagram. She scrabbled for purchase as she fell and halted her slide into oblivion by a hair's breadth. The metal pentagram whooshed past below and she collapsed back onto the circular stairway in exhaustion.

Time continued to pass before she recalled her mission. Mustering an inner reserve, she got to her hands and knees and hauled herself up towards the altar.

The whirlpool of flame beyond the pentagram made the darkness flicker and writhe, and with no helmet display by which to see, Sarah reached out to search for the Anakim pendant with her hands.

Something rough, like fingers, skittered from her touch.

She stifled a scream and snatched back her hand.

'It's all in your head,' she whispered, 'it's not real; it's all in your head.'

She continued searching for the artefact, terrified by the thought of what she might encounter next.

Seconds of dread ticked by before she felt the cold of metal. Relieved, she coiled her fingers around her pendant and staggered to her feet, holding onto the altar. Her mind slowly cleared after its ordeal and she clipped the pentagonal disc to her chain.

She glanced up to see the distorted forms of her friends watching her through the flames and to their left, she could just make out Riley's alcove and his mist-wreathed form within.

Sarah looked back down at the metallic altar and its deep runic carvings. All she had to do now was to figure out how to turn it on.

CHAPTER FIFTY-FIVE

SARAH STARED at the five-sided altar, trying to find something that looked familiar. There was no circular indent, but she knew this didn't mean it couldn't be activated. She ran her hands over its surface and around its rim, before pressing them down in its centre. An icy chill permeated her skin, but nothing happened. She noticed a circle of symbols arranged around the altar's edge. One in particular caught her eye, the constellation of Libra. She touched it. Again nothing happened, but she noticed the faintest flicker of light where she'd placed her hands before. She leaned down to inspect it, but it had disappeared. Wondering if her mind was still playing tricks on her, she saw the imprint of fingers on the surface – an imprint in blood.

She held up her hand, the palm stained red where the cross had cut into her skin, and then remembered part of the vision induced by the orb: a bloodstained altar amidst a sea of black, and flanked by strange, glowing walls.

She looked beyond her friends to the faint light pulsing inside the crystalline structure and realised the orb had been showing her where to go. *Has it been trying to help me save Riley?* Her eyes drifted to the alcove where she'd laid him to rest. *Has it been telling me more than just the destination? What if it has given me the key to the altar's activation itself?*

There was only one way to find out.

Sarah put her hand back to her cross and squeezed hard. Blood dripped down through her fingers and onto the altar. She leaned in to see tiny tendrils of electricity crackling over its surface.

Her blood was the key!

She held out her other hand and cried out in pain as she reopened the wound given her by Locke's knife. More blood flowed and she placed her hands back on the altar and the pendant grew warm.

♦

Goodwin held his breath as the spinning pentagram rose higher and a faint glow of light from the altar penetrated through the flames. He glanced at the crystal wall where its glow intensified, before the sound of stone grinding on stone made him look up.

High above, a crack of light appeared in the ceiling. Second by second the opening grew wider and longer, stretching down the sphinx's entire length as the roof retracted to reveal the flickering storm clouds in the chamber beyond. Thunder rumbled and a cold wind swept down into the hall like the hand of Zeus. The roaring flames bent and fluttered and the pervasive mists curled into a swirling mix.

A sparkle of light tore Goodwin's attention back down to ground level, where an armoured figure holding a glowing sword jogged towards them.

Goodwin could have wept with joy at the sight of the Darklight commander's approach. It seemed like months since Hilt had departed on his mission to bring back Susan and locate the USSB, and by the look of the small figure that dogged the man's steps, he'd lived up to at least half of his promise.

'Sorry I'm late, sir,' Hilt said over the growing storm, before glancing back at Susan, whose eyes were no longer bloodshot. 'We need to get you both out of here.'

Goodwin gestured towards the giant silver statue. 'I think that might be a bit of problem.'

Either side of the golden throne, cloaked in mist, the indistinct lights of two Pharos had appeared to hover in silent sentry.

♦

Sarah's pendant continued to pulse with heat against her chest. Her bloody palms tingled against the altar and tiny fingers of purple electricity licked at her skin. She looked up as the ceiling retracted and storm clouds gathered. Thunder rumbled and lightning flickered through the sky before a spike of pain shot through her hands. The first symbol on the altar's circular pattern lit up with an electrical glow, while either side of her hands the metal surface turned liquid and drained away to reveal two large handles.

Removing her hands from the altar, its centre distorted and melted down into a pentagonal indent. The size and shape was unmistakable: it matched the newly transformed orb. She withdrew the discus-sized artefact from her coveralls and gazed at its strange surface. *Should I be doing this?* The thought came unbidden. *Isn't this too convenient? If the orb has brought us here for a purpose, why would that purpose be ours? Why would it be mine? I could just be a pawn in its plan.*

'Sarah,' a voice said, 'can you hear me?'

The communication system built into the bottom rim of her smashed helmet sparked and crackled beneath a layer of oil.

'Jason,' – Sarah peered through the flames – 'is that you?'

'Yes. Are you okay?'

'I'm fine. The orb did bring us here. It all fits, the visions, everything.'

'Then you're doing what it wants.' Jason sounded scared. 'You have the pendant, come back to us.'

'I know—' An image of Riley flashed into Sarah's mind and her reasoning faltered. *I have to save him.* She gauged the speed of the rotating pentagram; she couldn't go back now even if she wanted to. She reached out and held the artefact over the altar before hesitating again. *What is its real agenda? What do the Pharos want?* An overwhelming compulsion to place the disc into the aperture forced her hands down and before she knew what was happening the disc snapped into position with a metallic clunk. A mechanism in the altar released and the handles rotated round and up to present themselves for Sarah to hold.

'Sarah,' Jason said, 'can you hear me? Sarah?!'

What had Goodwin said? Sarah thought, as Jason's calls fell on deaf ears. The oil was a test of faith. And I passed that. Now all I have to do is take the final leap ...

Driven on by the heartache of grief, her doubts forgotten, she reached out to grasp the metal handles.

A sharp tingle swept up her arms and the altar twisted on its dais. More symbols on the altar flickered alight as the electricity continued to spread around its circumference. Sarah saw the alcove two along from Rebecca's glow brighter as the altar turned towards it, the metal device forced on by an unseen mechanism. With a grunt of effort, she helped it round until Rebecca's alcove lit up. The pendant around her neck grew hotter and she squinted through the wavering heat of the flames to see if the crystal was dissipating, but before she could tell if it was working, the altar resumed its leftward creep. She tried forcing it back, but her feet slipped and skidded on the slick surface and the altar continued its motion until Riley's alcove glowed bright. She gripped the handles tight and managed to wedge her foot into a crack to halt its rotation.

Pinpricks of light glittered before her eyes before a flash from the void dragged her vision down. Strange shadows moved in the beyond, flashing in and out of reality in time with the spinning blur of the pentagram's star. Sarah felt a sense of dread descend over her and two more symbols at the edge of the altar lit up – and then another ... and another after that – each one adding to an arc of light that would become a circle. The altar jerked left and the light behind Riley's alcove died. She tried twisting it into reverse, but an unseen force held it fast. She let out a scream of fury. The sinews on her neck stood out as she strained every muscle, and the altar inched back.

♦

Goodwin could tell Sarah was struggling. He'd seen Rebecca's alcove brighten momentarily, but the crystal remained intact. Everything told him the Englishwoman needed his help, but the burning oil and spinning pentagram at its centre blocked off any route through. He felt helpless, but found himself moving towards the fires to join Sarah's two friends, who continued to watch in similar impotence.

A mighty hand closed on his arm and he looked up into the face of Darklight's leader.

'She's beyond our help,' Hilt said, before gesturing towards an alcove. 'And so is he.'

Goodwin looked at the body of the man Sarah wanted to save. 'His name's Riley.'

'Sir,' – Hilt grasped his shoulder – 'we need to find another way out.'

Goodwin snapped out of his reverie and shook his head. He pointed at the other alcove where Joseph and Rebecca remained imprisoned. 'I'm not leaving without them, not again.'

Susan, seeing her carer immersed in crystal, approached the wall to touch it with tentative hands.

Hilt raised his thermal sword. 'Have you tried heat?'

Goodwin's hope rose and he shook his head.

'Stay here,' Hilt said, and Susan stood aside to give him room as he strode to the alcove and placed his glowing blade against the face of the crystal.

The Darklight commander pushed his sword into the surface and then drew the weapon down inch by agonising inch.

At such a rate Goodwin realised it would take hours to cut Rebecca and Joseph free. He glanced back at the two creatures that remained lurking a hundred feet away and knew that time was something they didn't have.

Goodwin felt his frustration rise and he searched around for something, anything, he could do to save those he held dear. His eyes drifted beyond the crater to the distant frieze, its night sky filled with constellations. He frowned and gazed back at the spinning pentagram in the middle of the burning whirlpool of oil. The rotation increased and he glimpsed something in its interior that shimmered translucent.

'It's a void,' he said, and a sense of déjà vu struck him. He racked his mind and looked back into the flickering oil as the storm built overhead. Something silver and gold reflected across its silken surface. He glanced right to the giant silver statue ensconced on its golden throne. He then looked back to see the beautiful face of the Anakim god reflected in the pentagram's void of metal and light.

'And the Spirit of God was hovering over the face of the waters,' he murmured and the spark of remembrance grew. He looked back to the frieze and its depiction of the heavens and the earth.

'Genesis,' he whispered and looked up at the sky, 'Genesis, of course!'

He tried to use the Deep Reach helmet Sarah had given him, but he couldn't activate it. He dropped the headgear and waved to Sarah to gain her attention and pointed at the statue. He cupped his hands to his mouth and shouted, 'GENESIS!'

Sarah's friends looked in his direction.

'It's Genesis,' he said to them, 'tell her to face the Anakim God, the statue!'

They looked at him, uncomprehending.

Goodwin let out a growl of frustration and ran to the frost-laden wall and drew his fingers across the surface to create a note for Sarah to read. He thought he saw her glance in his direction beyond the flames and he gestured to his message and then pointed at the statue and mouthed: *'The other way! Face the other way!'*

The wind from the storm continued to increase and the flames died down before the oil in the crater dropped lower. A small figure moved to the edge of the rapidly disappearing lake as the fires extinguished. Goodwin saw Susan look back at him. She held a large, blue crystal in her hand and she gave him a look of sorrow before jumping down into the oil.

'No!' Goodwin leapt after her and moments later he was splashing knee deep in the hot, viscous fluid. Shocking images flashed through his mind as the black oil's hallucinations attacked him, but he managed to grab Susan round the waist and drag her back. The glowing rock fell from her hand and vanished into the disappearing ooze.

'Susan,' Goodwin said, as she fought him, 'stop!' He stared into her eyes expecting them to be bloodshot, but her whites were clear. In his moment of hesitation she plunged her teeth into his hand.

He cried out and let go.

The crater's last drops of oil drained away to reveal the crystal, now glowing beneath a covering of black fluid. Susan dived for it and Goodwin leapt after her.

♦

Sarah gritted her teeth as she struggled with the altar's handles to keep Riley's alcove lit, but as she fought to bring him back from death she felt something enter her mind, something that controlled her thoughts, her actions, her life. Her hands shook as she sought to wrest back control and the light from Riley's alcove died again as the altar moved left. The pendant burned hotter and another light lit up on the altar. A voice spoke in her mind. *Let go ... give in ... it will feel so gooood ... let go.* Sarah felt her resolve weakening, the feeling of surrendering so wonderful, so easy ... so right ... so pleasurable. Another part of her mind screamed '*NO!*' and her eyes inched from the pentagram's spinning void and back to Riley. '*I can save him!*'

The flames had died out and the metal pentagram sank down and turned into a blur. The ground at Sarah's feet shifted and a large ring of glittering metal twisted up from the floor around her. A curved section rose up a couple of feet on crystalline rods from the bottom of the ring's interior surround, creating a platform which contained two circular indents positioned side by side. The altar split down the middle and shifted forward to connect to the bottom of the ring.

The speakers in her broken helmet crackled again. 'Sarah,' Trish said, 'don't get on it, you don't know what it'll do!'

'I can't ...' – Sarah clenched her teeth as she felt compelled to step forward onto the device – 'stop myself ... it's controlling me!'

Her left leg moved against her will and she found herself mounting the platform. The altar's handles shifted onto the interior of the ring, spreading her arms wide. She wanted to release her hold, but the entity inside her mind had other ideas. Her palms remained clenched against cold metal and clamps closed around her wrists, before two more encircled her ankles. The metal circle rose up and she felt herself lifted from the floor to hang suspended inside the vertical ring, her limbs forced out into the shape of a star like the Vitruvian Man.

She tried to fight back against the thing that controlled her, summoning every ounce of willpower to save Riley. The handles twisted and the metal ring turned towards his alcove before a surge of energy sent a rush of pleasure flooding through her body. She gasped in rapture. More voices whispered to her, telling her to relax, to enjoy – to be. Her eyes filled with the spinning pentagram and she felt an ache in her chest spreading through her skin. The ecstasy grew, but so did the pain. Her head felt too heavy to hold up and her chin dropped to her chest.

Another symbol on the altar lit up.

She could feel the energy draining from her body, her soul torn from its home.

She was the sacrifice for the thing unknown.

The void flared with light and Sarah felt the darkness taking her.

♦

'Let me go!' Trish dug her fingernails into Jason's arm. 'It's killing her!'

Jason clung to Trish as he watched Sarah die; there was nothing they could do.

♦

Sarah's vision drifted lost and images from her life flared real.

She was a child chasing a butterfly across a field ... sharing her first kiss with the boy next door ... accepting her diploma at graduation ...

The pendant throbbed against her chest with excruciating pain and the altar's circle of symbols neared completion.

'This is SED Command. We are a go for shuttle launch in T minus thirty seconds.'

'Sit down, Miss Morgan,' a man said, folding his arms, 'my name is Dresden Locke.'

Pain exploded in her face. 'I told you,' Mark said, standing over her with madness in his eyes, 'you're not going anywhere.'

Sarah's eyes flickered closed and the spinning pentagram whirred faster, its pitch increasing.

'This is SED Command. We are a go for shuttle launch in T minus ten seconds.'

'The blinds,' – her eyes widened as Riley pleasured her – 'people ... are watching.'

Sarah held the ancient skull in her hands; it was proof positive of the existence of Homo gigantis!

He kissed her deeply. 'Let them watch.'

Dresden Locke held her gaze. 'I employ the best, so I expect the best.'

Riley smiled. 'Did you miss me?'

'Where you ... go,' she murmured. Fire blossomed into being and smoke choked her lungs.

'Why do you fear me?' a sibilant voice whispered.

Sarah gazed into the mirror. 'Am I not what you desire?'

'One thing is for certain,' Jason said, 'you don't deserve to die.'

'Let go ... give in ... it will feel so gooood.'

Riley gazed into her eyes. 'You're a hard woman to find, Sarah Morgan.'

'It's all my fault,' Sarah clung to Jason and cried. 'I killed her. I killed Trish and I've killed you too!'

'Sarah, are you okay?' Trish's face loomed before her.

'I killed my mother. I deserve to die, I have to die. I want to die!'

'Only you're crying.'

A tear rolled down her cheek.

Jason placed his hand against her heart. 'You decide who you are and if you don't like what you are, you damn well fight back!'

'Let go ... give in ... surrender.'

'Never give in, as at the end of the day, when there's nothing else left—'

'Let go ... give in.'

'That's all we have—'

'Let go ...'

'—that's who we are.'

Sarah's heartbeat stuttered slow.

'This is SED Command. We are a go for shuttle launch.'

'Why do you fear me?'

'In T minus three—'

'One thing is for certain.'

'—two—'

'Give in.'

'You don't deserve to die.'

'Let go.'

'—one—'

'Am I not what you desire?'

A strobe of images flickered through her mind.

'—launch!'

Sarah's heart pulsed its final beat and a white brilliance emerged from the void.

'I'll always ... be with you ... Sarah.' Riley's voice echoed through time.

The altar's final symbol lit up.

'—have faith ... there's always light ... in the dark.'

Through a sea of black, a blue glimmer blazed bright. Susan shrugged Goodwin aside and slammed down the glowing crystal, shattering it over the spinning pentagram. Electricity enveloped the altar and Sarah's eyes flew open as power surged through her. The pendant blazed beneath her coveralls, the void opened into a swirling portal and winds shrieked as the storm funnelled down. Riley's alcove crystallised and a star of light formed around her. A black patch appeared on her chest as cloth smouldered and peeled back, aflame. Her cross glowed orange and beneath it the Anakim pendant shone white hot.

Sarah cried out in agony as metal seared into flesh.

The power kept increasing, growing stronger, bigger, faster, filling her body with agonising pain. Darkness streamed out of the portal and Sarah's eyes drifted to Goodwin's sign.

Genesis
The light
FACE GOD!

Sarah gritted her teeth against the onslaught of power, her body shaking. The gold cross melted through its chain and merged with the Anakim pendant.

Electricity coalesced on the pentagram and crackled round in a massive spiral of energy towards the altar.

Sarah knew she was going to die and the force that held her vanished.

Blood seeped from her palms, metal fused to bone and tears streamed down her face. She looked at Riley's frozen form with bloodshot eyes. 'Where you … go,' – she wrenched the device round toward the statue – 'I … GO!'

The portal vanished in a whoosh of air and a vacuum of sound. The Anakim pendant sank into her chest. Sarah screamed and a blast of energy shot into the silver statue and on into the sphinx's head. The ground shook, Sarah's scream stretched on, and a massive beam of light powered into the Anakim city.

CHAPTER FIFTY-SIX

Blinding, white light roared from the sphinx's eyes, blazing through the underground chamber like a galactic gamma ray. Miles distant, Anakim towers flared bright as the energy slammed into their translucent structures like a supernova.

The earth shook. Goodwin covered his ears and closed his eyes. Wind tore at his clothing. Thunder rumbled and lightning flashed.

The barrage of noise continued. Light seared bright and Goodwin squeezed his eyes tighter, praying for an end.

The noise reached an unbearable crescendo. Pain lanced through his ears and then ... moments later ... it was gone.

The white brilliance vanished, the gale dropped to a breeze, and Goodwin cracked open an eye as the storm dissipated to cloud. The pentagram continued to rotate, but the altar's symbols dimmed and the glow inside the crystal wall died along with them.

Outside the sphinx, on the chamber's horizon, the Anakim spires shone bright with the charge of power, and those who could see it were transfixed by the sight.

Back inside the ancient monument, Goodwin was equally awestruck by the glowing statue of the Anakim god, before someone's scream broke the silence.

♦

Jason and Trish rushed forward and leapt onto the metal pentagram as it slowed. Their helmet torches revealed a gruesome scene in the darkness. Sarah hung in limp suspension from the metal ring. Her clothing smoked with heat and her chest was bloodied and charred. Blood dripped from her palms and the soles of her boots had melted. The strange mechanism released the clamps holding her wrists and ankles, and Sarah's body slumped onto the altar.

Crying, Trish turned her over.

Jason pulled back his friend's eyelid. Her pupil was fixed and dilated and her iris shone with a purple sheen.

'Sarah!' Trish shook her friend. 'SARAH!'

Jason felt for a pulse then pushed Trish aside to begin CPR, but no sooner had he placed his hands on Sarah's chest than a jolt of electricity shot through his hands. He yelped in pain.

'What's wrong?' Trish said.

Jason tried again. Light sparked and another shock zapped through him. He swore and looked at his singed fingers.

Trish touched Sarah's scarred chest and snatched her hand back in pain. She looked at Jason in anguish. 'Do something!'

Jason saw the glint of metal beneath the congealed blood on Sarah's chest. The pendant had sunk into her breastbone. He tilted her head back and breathed into her mouth.

Trish held Sarah's hand as tears rolled down her cheeks.

'I'm not giving up on you, Sarah!' Jason made a fist and delivered a precordial thump to her chest. Electricity flashed and pain lanced through his hand. 'Do you hear me?! I won't,' – he thumped her again – 'give up,' – his fist fell again – 'ON YOU!'

He brought his fist down a fourth time and Trish grasped his arm.

'Stop! STOP!' She pressed two fingers to Sarah's wrist. 'I think I feel something.'

Jason felt Sarah's carotid artery and waited for a sign of life.

None came, but as he gazed at his friend's gruesome wounds a wave of energy flowed out from her chest. Trish shouted a warning and Jason leapt back.

After the electricity had faded, he reached out a tentative hand and pulled back her eyelid once more. The pupil contracted under the glare of his helmet's torches and the purple iris faded back to blue. Seconds later her chest expanded and settled into the rise and fall of shallow breath.

He looked down in amazed, joyous relief. 'She's breathing!'

'Her pulse is weak,' Trish said, 'very weak.'

'What do we do?'

Trish squeezed Sarah's hand. 'I don't know. We need help.'

'What do you need?' said a voice.

They looked up to see Goodwin standing close by, with Susan at his side and Commander Hilt just behind.

'A doctor,' Trish said, 'and fast.'

The ground trembled and Jason realised the altar was sinking.

A flood of transparent fluid bubbled up from beneath the metal pentagram.

'Move!' Goodwin said.

Jason picked Sarah up then cried out in pain. 'My ankle!'

Hilt rushed forward and scooped Sarah into his arms, and they ran from the crater.

CHAPTER FIFTY-SEVEN

Colonel Samson opened his eyes and let out a groan of pain. The last thing he remembered was plunging his sword into the chest of the S.I.L.V.E.R. assassin – Zhang Bai. He raised his armoured hand to see it blackened and charred. Pain throbbed through his body and he turned his head towards the staircase which led up to the colossal Anakim Sphinx.

At the bottom of the steps, forty feet away, the still form of the chrome-clad assassin lay sprawled on the ground in a pool of her own blood.

The mirrored visor on Zhang's helmet slid up. Blood trickled from her mouth and her eyelids fluttered as her vision faded. Her arm was extended in his direction and her fingers unfurled to release a large sphere, which slid to the ground with a clunk. Samson watched in fascination as the object rolled towards him.

Zhang Bai focused on him. 'For ... my ... sister.' Her hand dropped loose and her lungs exhaled their last shuddering breath.

Samson looked at the metallic ball as it came to a stop near his head. A small display lit up on one side and his mind cleared, enabling him to figure out what he was looking at: digits counting down. His eyes widened in realisation. *S.I.L.V.E.R. operatives always have redundancy!*

Samson reared up and scrambled for the high yield bomb. Grasping the device, he spun round to see the lattice of burning bridges spread out before him.

He glimpsed the timer as he wound back his arm.

FIVE SECONDS!

Samson launched the device into the air.

The bomb arrowed out into the dark, cleared the flames and disappeared into the abyss beyond. Seconds ticked by before a distant detonation shook the ground. A sudden rush of light erupted upward and Samson staggered back.

A deep rumbling sound grew louder and stronger. Cracks criss-crossed through the stone beneath his feet and up onto the sphinx's stairway.

A terrifying sight reflected in Samson's visor as the earthquake struck. The fiery walkways collapsed in every direction, and beyond them the standing stones toppled as water seethed into the basin.

There was no escape!

He turned and sprinted up the splintering steps towards the sphinx's entrance. But as he ran his visor showed structural warnings in all directions. The cracks extended up onto the sphinx's body and widened.

He ran faster.

The stairs flashed past and Samson saw the entrance ahead.

Great rents appeared in the sphinx's face and chunks of masonry thumped down around him. Samson glanced up as the giant Anakim head sheared free and plummeted towards him. He snarled in defiance as death approached, and dived forward. The monument smashed down through the stone staircase, obliterating everything in its path. A cloud of dust billowed up and the shaking increased.

CHAPTER FIFTY-EIGHT

GOODWIN WADED THROUGH TRANSPARENT FLUID, up out of the crater and onto solid ground. Hilt emerged alongside him, carrying Sarah's limp form, while the Englishwoman's two friends, with Susan in tow, joined them moments later. Behind them, the pentagram and altar had long since been immersed in the rising tide, leaving a rippling covering that slowly solidified. The Pharos were nowhere to be seen, but the calm didn't last for long as a distant tremor set the ground vibrating. Goodwin turned on his torch to see debris and dust sifting down from above.

'What's happening?' Jason said.

Goodwin wasn't sure. He stood frozen in place, listening.

The silver statue, still glowing with the residue of energy, rocked on its golden throne. Cracks appeared in the crystal wall and then the ground lurched violently.

'Earthquake!' Goodwin grabbed Susan's hand and made for the exit, but through the mists he could see pillars toppling to the ground in all directions. Skidding to a stop, he ran back the other way.

'Where are you going?!' Jason said.

'This way.' Goodwin waved them on. 'The whole place is coming down!'

Goodwin ran past Rebecca's frozen alcove and the fracturing crystal, and on up a slope.

Massive statues toppled to the ground, exploding in showers of shattered stone. Someone screamed, but Goodwin kept running.

Seconds later three statues loomed through the dark, their Anakim forms still kneeling before a pewter frieze.

Goodwin hauled Susan down onto shadowy, oversized stairs. Steps flew by and Goodwin ran on. They reached a tunnel and splashed through shallow water. The ground continued to tremble. The beam from his flashlight rose and fell, and a crack appeared in the ceiling and raced ahead like a runaway train. The stone floor groaned and sagged. Goodwin jumped over a growing fissure, with Susan following.

He glanced back. Sarah's friends followed, and close behind them ran Hilt with Sarah in his arms.

Ploughing on, Goodwin saw light ahead. Another Anakim staircase loomed and they dashed up into a growing blue radiance.

As they burst out into fresh air, the ground buckled and broke. Susan stumbled and Goodwin fell towards a wall of flame.

♦

Jason ran for his life as the earthquake gained momentum. A gaping hole appeared before him. Unable to avoid it, he leapt out into mid-air. An instant later he landed, but his ankle buckled and he slammed into the ground. Lava spewed forth from behind and the ground tilted up. He scrabbled forward, but the incline increased, forcing him towards molten rock.

'Jason!'

He looked round to see a hand appear through the steam. He reached out and grabbed it and Trish hauled him to safety and then helped him into a run.

Susan and Goodwin reappeared alongside and the Steadfast director pointed towards the blue glow. 'Keep going, the transportation device is close!'

Jason didn't need telling twice, and they ran on with Hilt hot on their heels.

Soon after, they passed between two standing stones and moved down into a basin lined with shining, blue crystal. Rattling down translucent steps, they reached the bottom which was filled with mounds of compacted soil.

Goodwin ran over to an oblong megalith wreathed in symbols and pointed at a circle indented in its surface. 'Your Anakim device.'

Jason rushed to examine it, but his elation was short lived as he looked around, frantic. 'Where's the platform?!'

'What?' Goodwin said.

'This isn't a transport device, there's no platform!'

'There must be!' Trish said and ran round the bowl-shaped depression, searching.

♦

With care, Hilt lay Sarah down on the ground while Goodwin looked around in confusion. Hilt's back ached and his soul was weary. He'd lost too many people, far too many; Major Offiah, Rebecca, Joseph, hundreds of operatives under his command. He wondered if Darklight had ever witnessed a darker hour.

While the earth shook around them and Sarah's friends dug for God knows what in the dirt, something touched his hand. He looked down to see Sarah's arm drop back to the ground and he crouched down beside her.

She said something and he leant closer.

'Ri – ley?' she whispered.

He held her hand and shook his head.

'I'm sorry ... about Rebecca, I—' Sarah fought for breath. 'I wasn't able ... to ... save her.'

'I know,' he said as her eyes fluttered closed, 'try to rest.' He looked round as the crystal stairs fractured and collapsed. 'It'll all be over soon.'

CHAPTER FIFTY-NINE

JASON STARED at Goodwin in despair. 'You said it was here, you said there was a transportation device!' He lashed out with a foot, sending a clump of earth flying.

'I thought there was,' Goodwin said, looking equally dismayed.

The ground's shuddering intensified and a nearby mound of sediment vibrated down to reveal more of a large, bronze globe positioned in the centre of the basin.

'What's that?' Trish said, pointing at it.

Jason saw something glinting beneath the sediment at its base and he scrambled forward to dig away at the dirt with his hands. Trish joined him and they'd soon revealed Goodwin's promise: a large, ceramic platform.

Jason gestured for Hilt to bring Sarah over. 'Put her here,' he said as the Darklight leader picked her up.

The earth lurched again and giant standing stones crashed down into the basin. Crystal exploded and blue shrapnel lanced out.

Jason snatched up a glowing shard and moved towards the circle device before looking at Trish. 'Get on the platform.'

'I'm not leaving you!'

'Get on the damn platform!'

'No!' Trish picked up another piece of crystal and lunged for the megalith.

Jason leapt forward and dragged her kicking and screaming to Sarah's side.

The whole world shook and Trish kept fighting.

'Let me go,' he said, 'or we'll all die!'

Breaking her hold, he turned to see Goodwin standing by the Anakim device.

The Steadfast director picked up a large chunk of crystal. 'Tell Sarah ... tell her goodbye.'

Dumbfounded, Jason nodded as Trish pulled him back to the platform.

'Sir,' Hilt said, 'what are you doing?'

'Get Susan on the device, Commander,' Goodwin said. 'You as well, that's an order.'

Hilt guided Susan over to Trish before moving back to his director's side.

Goodwin held the Darklight leader's gaze. The man's loyalty knew no bounds. He gave Hilt a nod before muttering, 'I hope this works.'

Goodwin placed his hand on the stone circle and a swirl of energy swept around his arm. Strange visions flashed before his eyes of Anakim worlds shifting through time. Pain throbbed through his head and white radiance flared. The globe shuddered and inched into rotation with a shriek of metal on metal. Eon's worth of compacted earth tumbled to the ground and the transportation platform rose up half a foot.

Four more platforms emerged from the dirt floor around the globe as soil vibrated from their long hidden surfaces, but the slab beneath their feet stayed dull.

'It's not working!' Trish said.

The bronze globe spun faster and turned translucent, and Jason saw a static circle shimmering beneath its rippling surface. His grip tightened on the crystal still in his possession and he reached out his other hand through liquid metal.

♦

Goodwin's hand released from the megalith as the transport device continued its activation. A shining blue light lit up around the platform's edge, growing brighter and stronger as the globe whizzed round.

One side of the crystal basin sagged down into seething lava and a crack opened up in the ground. Susan slipped from Trish's grasp and leapt over the widening fissure to return to Goodwin's side. The split in the earth grew bigger, cutting off any route back to the platform.

Sarah's friends gazed back at them through the haze of shimmering heat, knowing as well as Goodwin that his fate, like Susan's and Hilt's, was sealed.

Lava oozed from the ground and searing flames roared high. The ground shifted and rocked. A whoosh of steam forced Goodwin back, and Sarah and her friends momentarily disappeared from view.

Goodwin remembered something. 'Wait!' he called out, but it was too late, they couldn't hear him.

He stared at them through raging fire. 'The surface,' Goodwin said, holding Susan close as the lava closed in, 'it's not safe.' He looked round to see the entire front of the sphinx collapse in a pall of dust and flame. 'The apocalypse is coming.'

CHAPTER SIXTY

THE GIANT GLOBE continued to spin with light, but Sarah and her friends remained on the platform.

'Why isn't it working?' Goodwin murmured.

More of the basin collapsed behind him to reveal a thin strip of land that disappeared into laval heat.

Hilt saw the opportunity and grabbed Goodwin's arm. 'Let's go!'

The Darklight leader scooped up Susan and ran for it, and Goodwin gave one last despairing look at Sarah and followed Hilt into the inferno.

♦

Jason watched Goodwin go before looking down at the glowing shard in his hand. He could feel power rising up from the crystal, through his arm and into the spinning globe.

'We don't know where it'll take us!' Trish said.

Huge rents shattered the basin in all directions.

'Anywhere's better than here!' Jason looked down to see the platform's centre remained dull. 'We need more power.'

Trish placed her hand on his, but nothing changed.

Sarah's eyes fluttered open and she raised her hand to them.

'It will kill you!' Trish said.

The ground collapsed all around as the quake hit. Heat flooded over them and Sarah raised her hand higher.

Jason stared into her eyes, a tear rolled down his cheek and he dropped his crystal.

'NO!' Trish screamed.

Jason grasped Sarah's hand. The platform they stood on swirled bright, as did the next, and the next, until all five shone like stars. The pendant in Sarah's chest glowed white and a high-pitched whine built to a crescendo. The globe turned colour, spinning so fast it looked static. It was planet Earth. The power whined louder. Trish cried out. Energy surged and Jason felt himself propelled upwards through blazing light.

CHAPTER SIXTY-ONE

Sarah and her friends vanished in a flash of brilliance. Their platform's glow faded, and an instant later two more platforms flashed, then dulled in quick succession. The earth gave a final groan and the Anakim device shattered and broke, consumed by the cataclysm.

♦

Goodwin ran after Hilt as the ground rocked and rolled beneath their feet. A sea of lava surrounded them and sweat poured down their foreheads as the unbearable heat increased. The escape route petered out and Hilt slowed his advance to a stop.

Goodwin glanced behind to see the Anakim Sphinx disappearing into the depths.

A hundred yards closer a dazzle of light shot skyward, leaving a glowing trail in its wake.

Goodwin gazed after it as it vanished into the flickering clouds. 'Godspeed, Sarah,' he whispered.

Fires roared on both sides and Hilt wrapped his arms around Susan to protect her from the heat. The Darklight leader withdrew his knife and looked at Goodwin with anguish in his eyes.

Goodwin knew what he intended, better for Susan to die quickly than to suffer the agony of being burnt alive. Goodwin's eyes filled with the orange glow of flame and he braced himself for their final moments. His lungs burned and his clothing caught alight. Hilt placed his knife to the base of Susan's skull ready to deliver the killing blow, but before he could do so the ground reared up beneath them. The lava fell away and a massive wall of water rushed in. Steam exploded upwards as cold met hot and the flames were extinguished. The lake was reclaiming its domain and flooded into the abyss at its centre.

The cascade of water roared loudly, and with the heat gone, so had the light. Hilt sheathed his knife and turned on his torches, enabling them to see their bridge of land continued into the lake. But it was far from safe. The ground beneath them dropped away and they leapt forward as gushing waves sought to sweep them away. Somehow they managed to stay upright and Goodwin blinked droplets from his eyes to see the lake's waters rushing past on either side.

Hilt put Susan down and led the way over slick rock, his powerful frame acting like a human shield against the roaring flow. Goodwin grasped Susan's hand and followed close behind as the earthquake continued unabated. He glanced back to see their narrow strip of land disappearing into the seething tide. 'Hurry up!' he said.

Hilt upped the pace and Goodwin feared the worst as he found himself waist deep before the Darklight leader helped Susan, and then Goodwin, up onto more solid ground. The shaking subsided to tremors as the water continued to speed past. A hundred yards on the natural causeway of rock ended short of the beach, but as Goodwin watched that same shoreline drew closer and closer as the lake's level fell. Soon the waters had receded far enough for them to drop down to the newly exposed bedrock.

With Susan by his side, Goodwin waded through pools of weed

and mud before reaching what had been the lake's edge. The roar of the water faded behind and he collapsed to the ground in exhausted relief.

He closed his eyes and breathed deeply while Susan sat down cross-legged beside him.

But hardly a moment had passed before Hilt redrew his sword and activated its blade. 'Someone's coming.'

Can't I ever get any rest? Goodwin wondered. With a groan, he sat up to see a host of torch lights approaching from the south. 'Are they friendlies?

Hilt pressed some buttons on his helmet. 'I don't know my system's down.'

'We could make a run for it.'

Hilt shook his head. 'If they're Terra Force they'll have long range weapons.'

'Then we wait.' Goodwin squinted at the torches before transferring his gaze to the distant city, which shone like a colossal beacon of light.

The Anakim towers pulsed with power, and energy crackled up their soaring spires to arc across wide avenues like electrified coils. Susan seemed equally captivated by the scene and Goodwin knew the power released by Sarah inside the sphinx must have been responsible. *Where else could such a power go?* He frowned. *But was I wrong about Genesis?* he thought. *Everything had made sense at the time, but now ...*

Storm clouds built over the city and the winds that had died down picked up again as the torch lights drew ever closer.

A short while later Captain Winter came jogging out of the dark with a unit of Darklight mercenaries at his back. 'Director, thank God, I'd feared the worst.'

'Captain,' Goodwin said, getting to his feet.

Captain Winter drew to a halt and saluted his commanding officer. 'Sir!'

'At ease, soldier.' Hilt deactivated his sword. 'Report.'

'The Terra Force commandos are in full retreat,' Winter said. 'Once their leader abandoned them they lost cohesion.'

'And what *of* Colonel Samson?' Goodwin said.

Winter looked at him. 'No sign, if he didn't follow you out, then he didn't make it.'

Goodwin nodded, his face grim.

'S.I.L.V.E.R.?' Hilt said.

'The assassins haven't been seen since we engaged them at the standing stones,' Winter said. 'When we fell back to shore, we held the causeway. No one came back out.'

Hilt removed his helmet and ran his hand over his head. 'The lights?'

The captain shook his head. 'Nothing, yet. We're still on full alert, if they return, we'll be ready.'

Hilt appeared satisfied with the news. He turned to Goodwin. 'I'm sorry, sir ... about Rebecca and Joseph. If I'd had more time—'

Goodwin waved away his apology. 'You lived up to half your promise, Commander.' He placed his hand on Susan's shoulder and she looked up at him with innocent eyes. 'You brought Susan home.'

'You're right,' Hilt said, 'but not in the way you think.'

Goodwin gave him an odd look. 'What do you mean?'

'I did live up to half my promise.' Hilt held up his malfunctioning headgear. 'When I first encountered Sarah Morgan, we were able to download the files from her Deep Reach helmet. We have their maps and a route through to the USSB.'

Goodwin gave a sigh. 'That's good news, but after recent events any entry into the base would be met with fierce resistance.'

'For Darklight, maybe,' Hilt said, 'but the civilians—'

'Not an option,' Goodwin said, 'I'm not leaving you down here to rot. Darklight are as much under my care as everyone else.'

Captain Winter gave a nervous cough. 'Don't you mean Dr. Vandervoort's care, Director?'

Hilt frowned and looked at Goodwin.

'It seems my actions led them to believe I was unfit for command,' Goodwin said. 'Kara runs the camp now.'

The Darklight leader arched a brow, his expression questioning.

'The director has been ... troubled,' Captain Winter told Hilt.

'Troubled, how?'

'They thought me insane,' Goodwin said, 'my actions a danger to others.'

'And are you?' Hilt said.

'What?'

'Insane?'

Goodwin hesitated and looked at his wrist. The red rash from the crystal bracelet had faded. Does that mean I'm free of whatever was controlling me? Or was it all in my mind all along? The answers remained as elusive as ever. But I was right about the lake, he reminded himself, and there was a way to the surface.

'Sir?' Hilt said in concern.

'I wasn't myself,' Goodwin said, 'I put people's lives at risk, and ...' – he looked at Captain Winter – 'people died.'

'They weren't the first,' Hilt said, 'and they won't be the last. Leadership comes with many burdens, you know that – we *both* know that.'

'But what if my actions weren't my own?'

Hilt considered him with impassive eyes.

The silence dragged on and Goodwin felt compelled to speak. 'Joseph was being controlled by the lights, the entity. He attacked me and then Rebecca. The blue crystals didn't attract the lights, the lights – the Pharos – used the crystals to control us, to control Joseph, Susan ... me.'

'You?' Hilt said.

'Maybe.' Goodwin shook his head. 'I don't know, perhaps. I saw things, visions, things that couldn't be explained. Coincidences, amazing coincidences.' Goodwin wanted to tell Hilt about the things he'd seen in the Anakim Sphinx, about the biblical passages that linked this most ancient of races with one of humanity's most precious texts, the Judeo-Christian Bible. But even as he thought it, his crippling doubts returned. *Have I imagined it all? Have I lost my mind? Am I still me?*

'He was quoting scripture,' said a woman's voice.

They all turned round to see Dr. Kara Vandervoort moving through the Darklight ranks with a number of civilians in tow.

Goodwin looked at Kara. She looked as beautiful as ever, relaxed even, the weight of command taken in her stride.

She walked forward and stopped in front of him.

Their last meeting had been intense, with harsh words spoken and trust lost on both sides. He still loved her, of course – he couldn't turn off such emotions easily – but his thoughts turned to Rebecca and he knew his heart had been divided. Kara had known it, too, perhaps before Goodwin himself. And yet while Rebecca was gone, the problem remained.

He gazed into Kara's eyes, searching for that lost connection, wondering if their union could – or should – be resurrected.

'Rebecca and Joseph,' Kara said in her South African drawl, 'did they ...?'

Goodwin shook his head, the heartbreak hitting home anew.

'Oh, Richard,' – she touched his cheek – 'you've been so lost.' She pulled him to her.

He held her in a lingering embrace and the tension between them melted away.

When the moment had passed, Kara pulled away and bent down to speak in low soothing tones to Susan. She called a medic to her and they tried to lead the mentally-handicapped woman away, but Susan refused to leave Goodwin's side.

'You were quoting scripture?' Hilt said, keeping his tone neutral.

Goodwin couldn't tell what the Darklight leader was thinking, but he could hazard a guess.

'I heard what you said to Sarah's friends,' Hilt continued, when Goodwin failed to answer. 'I saw your message. Genesis; what does it mean?'

Goodwin held Hilt's gaze for a moment before turning to Kara. 'Do you know how long it is since the tower last activated?'

'I'm not sure,' she said. 'Monitors at the camp said over the last twenty-four hours it was discharging energy every thirty minutes.

Goodwin nodded. 'It won't be long then.'

'For what?'

'To see if I was right.'

'Right about what?'

'About the Pharos – the lights – what they wanted.'

'You figured it out?' Kara said, shocked. 'How?'

Goodwin looked towards the city. 'Does it matter?'

'Of course it matters!'

'You'd think; but if I'm right, none of it matters anymore. I thought I'd found a way back to the surface – for all of us – but it wasn't what I thought it was. But when I saw it ... I knew.'

'Richard,' Kara said, exasperated, 'knew what? What did you see?'

'You'll think I'm crazy.'

'You won't know until you tell us,' Captain Winter said.

Goodwin looked at Hilt, who gave him a nod of encouragement.

'There was another frieze in the sphinx,' Goodwin said, relenting, 'similar to the one we found in the city. It showed the night sky, full of constellations. And beneath that was the Earth.' He paused to gather his thoughts. When he looked at it now, afresh, the links seemed more tenuous.

'Go on,' Kara said.

'It was an image of the heavens and earth. But when Sarah activated the Anakim device—'

'The woman from the base?' Kara said.

'Yes, when she activated it, I could see something at its centre ... a void.'

Hilt nodded. 'I saw it, too.'

'It was like molten metal, shimmering like water, and I could see the Anakim's silver statue, their God, reflecting in its surface.'

A rumble of thunder echoed through the chamber and everyone turned to the city, which still glowed bright with power.

The winds grew stronger and rippled their clothing with invisible fingers, and lightning flickered over the city's central, and tallest, spire. Clouds gathered, forming into a giant storm cell that circled the Anakim metropolis.

'It's happening,' Goodwin said.

'What's happening?' Kara looked at him. 'What have you seen, Richard? Tell us.'

'Genesis,' Goodwin said, as a build-up of purple energy swirled around the tower's base. 'Chapter one, verse one. "In the beginning, God created the heavens and the earth."'

Bolts of lightning hammered down into the city.

'Verse two,' Goodwin said, raising his voice as the tempest increased in volume. '"The earth was without form and void, and darkness was over the face of the deep—"'

Goodwin moved forward into roaring winds and pointed towards the city. A swirl of energy spiralled up the tallest tower and a single orb of pure, radiant light appeared at its peak and floated through the air towards the chamber's highest vaults. The sphere of energy disappeared into the clouds before it impacted the ceiling and flowed outwards like a sea of sparkling jewels.

'"And the Spirit of God was hovering over the face of the waters!"' Goodwin said.

The air in the chamber was sucked into the city with a great whoosh of noise. The ground shook beneath their feet and more lightning lanced down.

'Verse three!' Goodwin raised his hands to the heavens. '"AND GOD SAID!!"'

A shockwave exploded from the city and an endless blast of power erupted up from every spire. The stored energy roared forth, igniting the ceiling with a mass of seething electricity. With a tremendous flash, Sanctuary's dormant ceiling blazed into life. Light streamed out and a wall of energy swept through the chamber and down into the tunnels beneath. Down and down the electricity spread, increasing in speed as it flooded the pitch-black depths with a blazing radiance. Ancient monuments and buildings, hidden for untold millennia, emerged from the gloom beneath the racing brilliance.

Darklight and Terra Force soldiers alike paused to gaze up as the phenomenon streaked past like the essence of life. Tunnels, chambers and long forgotten caves, none were immune to the ceiling's power. Light filled Sanctuary's endless halls like time immemorial in an unstoppable, expanding wave.

Goodwin shielded his eyes as the city flared brighter before the towers' luminance faded and the final stream of energy released into the heavens.

Hilt and Captain Winter moved to his side to look up at the storm of electricity that continued to unfold above. Thunder rumbled and the howling gale died back to a strong breeze as dark clouds flowed out into a white blanket.

Goodwin couldn't quite believe his eyes. He'd been proven right once more. And yet, he thought, did I really figure out the entity's motive, its end game, or did it implant the idea in my mind, leaving clues for me to find?

As he struggled with the concept, Kara came to stand by his side and her fingers slid between his as they clasped hands.

He looked down at her before looking back at the chamber's ceiling and the clearing clouds. Blue skies peeked out through the haze and the glare of a yellow sphere bathed them in its warm, shimmering glow.

'Genesis,' Kara said, awestruck.

Goodwin couldn't prevent a smile from breaking through his depressive mask. '"And God said",' he whispered, drinking in the sight of the Anakim sun, '"let there ... be light."'

CHAPTER SIXTY-TWO

BLINDING light and the rush of air died away to a pitch-black calm. The silence was deafening, but out of the quiet the sound of dripping water could be heard plip-plopping with an audible echo through a concealed space.

Sarah opened her eyes and groaned. The heat from her pendant faded to a dull ache and she reached out a hand in search of her friends. Pain-filled moments passed, but her fingers found nothing except a cold, flat surface.

Time had no meaning in the dark and Sarah's consciousness slipped in ... and then out ... of existence. In with pain ... and then back out with relief.

In this twilight state, strange images returned to haunt her and she drifted inside the clutches of delirium.

♦

The sound of drip ... drip ... dripping water told Sarah she'd returned to her waking dream. She opened her sand-dry mouth to speak, but she could only manage to emit a faint croak of noise. *I'm alive*, was the first thought that worked its way into her battered psyche. By all rights, she shouldn't have been. Before they'd activated the transportation device she'd been knocking, perhaps hammering, at death's door. If even a hint of her body's bioelectricity had been removed she would have died. *So how, then*, she thought, *did I survive?*

Perhaps you didn't, said another voice inside her head. Perhaps you're dead.

Sarah closed her eyes against the all-consuming dark. *How can I be dead? I'm in too much pain.*

Perhaps you're in hell, said the voice, perhaps you're destined to live an eternity alone in endless suffering.

The thought sent a shock of panic racing through her mind.

Where am I? The thought echoed through her head. *WHERE AM I?!*

The trickle of falling water continued to conduct its monotonous rhythm and Sarah felt herself slipping back into darkness.

CHAPTER SIXTY-THREE

'TRISH!' Jason said. 'Sarah! Where are you!?'

'Where are you?' said the distant echo. 'Are you ... you ... you ... you ... ou ... ou?'

Moving his head, Jason angled the torches on his Deep Reach helmet around the cave system he now occupied. He glanced back down at the stone platform on which he'd been deposited by the Anakim transportation device.

That the rectangular stone was not ceramic told him something was different. And that Sarah and Trish were nowhere to be seen, told him something had gone very, very wrong.

You're alive, aren't you? he asked himself. Surely that's better than where you were? His response was swift: Not if I'm alone and trapped!

Bombarded by unwanted thoughts, Jason adjusted the visor on his helmet and approached the edge of the large square structure on which the platform sat. It was ten feet to the ground, so he lowered himself over the edge to hang down and let go.

He landed on his injured ankle and cried out in pain as he collapsed to the floor. In agony, he rolled onto his back and stared up at the cave's gloomy ceiling. 'FUCK!'

'Fuck ... fuck ... uck ... uck ... ck,' said the echo.

'Jason?' a voice said.

He peered up from his prone position to see the upside down figure of Trish emerge from the dark.

He sat up and turned towards her in relief.

She rushed to his side and embraced him. 'Where's Sarah?' she said, anxious.

'She wasn't with you?'

Trish shook her head. 'I woke up on a stone plinth a hundred yards that way.' She pointed back the way she'd come.

Neither voiced their deepest fear that Sarah might not have survived the journey.

'The device must have separated us for some reason,' Jason said. 'If we're both here, she must be close. Come on.' He struggled up and hobbled forward to go in search of their lost companion.

After a few minutes of walking they rounded another bend in the rock formation to enter a narrow passage. Up ahead the ceiling had collapsed, but a small opening at the top of a steep mound of dusty earth gave them the opportunity to keep moving forward. Jason scrambled up and wormed his way through. He slid down the other side and Trish joined him moments later.

A metallic dampness permeated the air and Jason licked his dry lips as they surveyed the scene by the light of their helmet torches.

Trish pointed to the left. 'There!' she said, and sprinted forward.

Jason chased after her as best he could and soon found himself kneeling down beside a glistening ceramic platform and its single occupant.

Sarah lay on the pale surface of the transportation device, unmoving. Her chest remained scarred with congealed blood and her palms were a bloody mess.

Trish leaned in to listen for a sign of life.

'Is she ...' Jason felt his stomach clench tight and he reached out to feel for a pulse, 'alive?'

♦

Sarah opened her eyes to blinding light. She blinked against the glare. The intensity of the radiance shimmered and pulsed like an ethereal being. Gradually the outline of a blurred figure emerged from the white and she reached out to it.

'Mother,' she whispered.

'Sarah, can you hear me?'

The voice sparked recollection and Sarah fought for clarity. 'Trish?' she said, through cracked lips.

Her eyesight cleared and she focused on her friend.

'Yes, it's us,' Trish said, and Sarah felt water touch her lips.

She coughed and swallowed as the glorious fluid flooded her mouth.

'Can you sit?' Trish said.

Sarah felt her strength returning and gave a tremulous nod.

Jason helped her into a sitting position and Trish fed her more water from a small canister to quench her thirst and soothe her parched throat.

Able to sit up on her own, Sarah looked into her friends' concerned faces. 'Did we ... did we make it?'

'Yes.' Trish touched her cheek. 'We made it, thanks to you.'

Sarah looked round to see the form of a crumbling statue a few feet away from the platform on which she sat. Its shape seemed familiar, but she couldn't quite place it.

She looked down at the wound on her chest and remembered the agony when the pendant had seared through flesh and into bone. Horrified by the sight, she brushed the area with the tips of her fingers.

'I don't understand,' Jason said, 'she's stronger now than when we left.'

Trish glanced at him. 'We don't have to understand it, just be thankful.'

He gave a nod and squeezed Sarah's hand. 'Can you walk?'

Sarah sipped some more water and pondered the question. 'I don't know.' She struggled to rise before dropping back, out of breath.

Trish turned to assess their surroundings. 'It doesn't matter if she can, there's no way through.'

'You didn't see any other way out before you found me?' Jason said.

Trish shook her head. 'No, we're trapped here, wherever "here" is.'

He pulled off his rucksack and delved into its contents to produce a circular case. 'Then it's just as well someone came prepared.'

'What's that,' Trish said.

Another flash of recollection entered Sarah's mind, a recollection of a structure made of glass and steel: Sanctuary's Exploration Division. 'It's a shaped charge,' she said.

Trish shook her head in amazement. 'I thought you'd lost that days ago.'

'Give me some credit; I'm not a total idiot.'

Trish leaned in and kissed him on the cheek. 'I know that.'

Bemused, Jason opened the case to read the instructions. 'This says we should be at least one hundred feet away before detonation.'

'That's if we're close enough to the surface for it to work,' Trish said.

Jason stood up and moved to the far side of the dark cave, where a mass of old tree roots hung down from the ceiling. 'Trees don't grow underground,' he said, giving them a tug.

'Unless we're still in Sanctuary,' Sarah said.

'No, those were dead, these are alive.'

'There's only one way to find out.' Trish looked at Sarah before gesturing to him. 'Do it.'

He nodded and secured the device to the ceiling of the cave, entered a code into a digital display on the reverse, and then snapped shut the case and rejoined them.

'This doesn't look like one hundred feet away,' Trish said.

'It's as far as we can get from it in this part of the cave,' – Jason pointed to the steep mound of dirt where they'd entered – 'or we manhandle Sarah up that incline.'

'We could wait until she's got the strength,' Trish said.

Jason gave her a meaningful look, his expression grave.

Sarah knew they were worried about her condition. She was, as well, but Jason obviously thought her life was still in immediate danger.

'I'm fine.' She tried getting up again and dizziness swamped her.

Trish grasped her shoulder to keep her upright. 'We'll stay here,' she said, giving Jason a nod of approval.

They carefully moved Sarah as far back as they could to gain a few more precious feet of room between them and the shaped charge. Jason then discarded the shattered helmet given to Sarah by Goodwin and swapped it with his Deep Reach headgear. When Trish and Sarah had deployed their breathing masks, Jason dialled another code into the case, which doubled as the wireless detonator. A red light appeared on top and a transparent cover slid back to reveal a red button.

The light switched to green and Jason looked at them. 'Ready?'

'No,' Sarah said. 'You two go, there's no point all three of us being this close.'

'Not a chance,' Trish said, and positioned herself over Sarah to create a protective shield with her body.

Jason did the same, linking arms with Trish to form a joint barrier against the blast.

Sarah looked up into the faces of her friends as they huddled over her and felt an upswell of love for them.

Trish smiled at her and Jason gave her a wink before holding out the detonator.

Sarah lowered her visor and raised a shaky hand. 'Here goes nothing,' she said, and depressed the button.

CHAPTER SIXTY-FOUR

A MASSIVE BLAST thundered through the cave. The ground shook and a dense cloud of dust enveloped the three friends. Small stones ricocheted around them before the air cleared and the aftershocks dissipated.

Jason shook the debris from his hair and retrieved his helmet from Sarah so he could survey the damage.

'Well?' Trish said.

Chunks of rock continued to thud to the floor of the cave, but eventually the area stabilised, allowing Jason to take a closer look.

The section of shattered rock appeared to be quite small in size, dashing Sarah's hopes that their endeavour had been successful.

'It's gone higher than I thought it would,' Jason said, peering up, 'and I can feel warm air.'

'But can you see a way out?' Trish said.

'I'm not sure; there's a hole, but if it's the surface it's night time as I can't see any light.'

'What about the dust cloud?' Trish said.

Jason muttered a curse. 'I forgot about that.'

He returned to Sarah's side and with Trish's assistance, helped her up.

'Does that look like a sphinx to you?' Sarah said, gesturing to the statue she'd noticed before.

'A little,' Trish said.

'That was amazing wasn't it,' she said, her speech slurring.

Trish shot Jason a look of concern.

'What was?' Jason said, as they moved towards the newly formed hole.

'The sphinx, the standing stones, everything ... it was like a dream.'

'I'll go up first,' Trish said, propelled by a sense of urgency and she left Jason propping up Sarah.

Trish climbed up through the hole and a moment later she dropped a short rope back down to them.

'Can you see anything?' he called up.

'It looks like the inside of an Anakim building.'

'We're still in Sanctuary?' Sarah said in dismay.

'Let's get her up,' Jason said to Trish.

He secured the rope to Sarah's harness, and with great difficulty, they wrestled her through the crumbling opening.

When they reached the top Sarah felt a strange sense of light-headedness, almost as if she was floating beyond her body.

They rested her against a wall and Jason shone his helmet's torches around the building. 'There's an opening,' he said to Trish, 'help me.'

Sarah squinted through the dark. A curtain of dead branches blocked a half-collapsed entrance and Jason and Trish hacked and pulled at it in a frenzy.

When they'd cleared it, they returned to Sarah and carried her through the gap.

As they squeezed through the tight space, Sarah reached out a hand and touched the carvings on the wall. 'May—' she said, finding it hard to speak, 'may—'

'I don't think she's got long,' Trish said, on the edge of tears.

'Keep going,' Jason said.

Sarah felt herself slipping back into the dark. Her vision narrowed and she grasped Jason's arm.

'Hang on, Sarah,' he said.

She reached out as they entered a narrow passageway and her hand brushed against more carvings.

Trish glanced down at her. 'Oh, God, she's bleeding from her eyes.'

Sarah swallowed and cleared her throat.

'Jason,' Trish said, 'stop – STOP!'

'We need to get help!' he said, sounding desperate.

'There is no help, we're still trapped underground!' Trish looked down at Sarah. 'What is it, sweetheart? What are you trying to say?'

Sarah summoned her last ounce of strength and pointed a shaky finger at the wall. 'May ... may ... Mayan.'

♦

Jason looked at Trish in shock.

'She's right;' Trish said, 'these inscriptions aren't Anakim, they're Mayan!'

'We're on the surface?' Jason said.

Trish got them moving again. 'There's an opening.'

Moments later they rounded a corner and emerged out into fresh air.

Jason stared out at the dark scene before him in disbelief.

'It's the Copán ruins,' Trish said, 'we're back in Honduras.'

They stumbled down a set of stone steps before Jason halted their advance. A strange flickering light had appeared two hundred yards away and it glided across the ground towards them at high speed.

A second later the shimmering vision veered left and Trish let go of Sarah and sprinted into the dark to intercept it.

'What are you doing?!' Jason said, but Trish had already disappeared into a grove of trees.

He lowered Sarah to the ground as the strange light continued its course and Jason realised he wasn't looking at the horror of a Pharos, but a set of headlights. It was a car!

'It's okay, Sarah,' he said, looking down at his dying friend, 'help's coming.'

♦

Light flared and the sound of an engine roared loud. Doors banged shut and raised voices drew near. A babble of activity engulfed Sarah's senses and she was lifted from the ground.

'How far is the nearest hospital?' someone said.

'El hospital, ¡¿hasta dónde?!'

Another voice responded in a rush of words before doors slammed and wheels spun.

'They're taking us to the airport,' Trish said.

Sarah's head rolled sideways as they bounced over uneven terrain.

'What!' Jason said. 'Why?'

'The nearest hospital's a hundred kilometres away.'

Sarah felt Trish take her hand.

'Oh, Jas, we're not going to make it.'

Sarah drifted into the dark and a moment later she opened bleary eyes to see she was being carried across a floodlit field of grass. Blood trickled down her cheeks like tears and her chest rose and fell in ragged bursts.

The person who held her adjusted their grip.

'Keep fighting, Sarah,' Jason said, 'keep fighting.'

Sarah wanted to do as he asked, but she had no more energy left to give.

Moments later the whir of a helicopter sent vibrations pounding through her head and they were airborne. Sarah managed to open her eyes again, and she could feel the end draw near. Another light emerged from the dark, its yellow glow appearing before her eyes like the spirit of God. The blinding brilliance blazed so bright that she could feel its warmth beating down upon her skin.

'Sarah, look,' Jason said, pointing, 'we made it to the surface. Look, it's the Sun, the dust cloud is clearing.'

Sarah gazed out of a window into the glory of a breaking dawn. Below, swirling mists parted before a light breeze, and shining blue rivers glistened and shimmered in the morning light. A flock of exotic birds flew up from the canopy of the forests below, where vibrant greens fought back the withered limbs of an embattled ecosystem.

The dust cloud still encircled the planet, but gaps were appearing in its thinning shroud.

For now the darkness was in full retreat and Sarah smiled a small smile as the beauty of life gifted her one of its greatest sights. Her friends were safe at last. And she knew, somewhere ... out there, beyond the black, her mother and Riley would be waiting for her on the other side.

Finally at peace, Sarah's eyes fluttered closed and her consciousness passed into the wonder of a dreamless light.

CHAPTER SIXTY-FIVE

'What do you make of it?'

The man coughed into a handkerchief and wiped away a string of blood-laced spittle. 'Fascinating,' he said, his voice rasping and breathing laboured, 'our attempts at replicating the design always met with failure.'

'It doesn't look much different to the dome.'

'To the casual observer I can see why that would be the case, but believe me,' – he paused for breath – 'when I say this is a marvel beyond measure.'

General Stevens scratched his bulging stomach and glanced at the man next to him. Dagmar Sørensen, the director of the GMRC's secretive and highly classified Research and Development Division, was a sallow-faced individual with pockmarked, sunken cheeks and an expression that had probably never felt the touch of a smile, let alone a grin. With the majority of people, it was easy to incorrectly stereotype personality based on looks; however, in this case, the initial presumption of the man's internal nature – by any outside observer save the blind – would have been correct. The man looked ... wrong – evil even – and it wasn't just his features or manner, but something in his eyes, those dead, bulging, unblinking eyes. And from what Stevens had heard about the R&D director's experiments, such a label was fully justified.

Perhaps it's because I know what he's capable of, Stevens thought. *Would he creep me out so much if I hadn't heard the stories?* Dagmar turned his gaze toward him and Stevens looked away, unnerved. *Yes*, he decided, suppressing a shudder, *he would*. Trying to dispel the gnawing unease at being in such close proximity to the sickly R&D director, he concentrated on the vision before him.

High up in Tower Central, USSB Sanctuary's soaring Anakim edifice, the lush greens of the New Park district of the subterranean base's uppermost tier – the Dome level – lay sprawled out far below like a patchwork quilt. Above this scene of beauty, the great dome itself blocked out the rest of his view as the tower intersected its convex twenty mile wide expanse.

In front of and above General Stevens' position, massive supporting cables tethered the immense weight of the dome below to the ceiling of the even larger chamber that housed it. And it was this sight that was unusual. While the dome created simulated skies, sunlight and weather for the many millions of people living out their days as productive Sancturians, it didn't shed its illumination outwards, thus the exterior was always shrouded in darkness that was, until recently. The last twenty-four hours had seen a catastrophic failure throughout the USSB's power grid after a strange wave of energy had swept through the entire chamber and the human construct nestled within. Plunged into the pitch-black, the whole base had been in turmoil ever since, with engineers rushing to reboot the dome's mass of systems.

Those with a keen mind would ask, if the illumination in the base had gone out, then how could the level below be bathed in such a radiant light? Stevens gazed up at the chamber's ceiling which shone bright with clear, blue skies. The answer was astounding, unbelievable, and one he was still having trouble accepting. The ancient ceiling, which must have been nearly a million years old, had somehow reactivated and even through the glass window before him, he could feel the power of its rays warming his skin.

'And you say it's operational beyond this chamber?' Stevens said.

Dagmar gave a slow nod of his head. 'We already have ... teams analysing its output. If we can find the source of its power we might be able to harness it.' The R&D director cleared his throat and took a rattling breath. 'Failing that, we can attempt to simulate its energy signature.'

'To activate the Anakim tech?'

'I hear concern in your voice, General,' Dagmar said, 'Are you afraid of our research?'

Stevens glanced behind him and the empty corridor beyond. No one was within earshot, but he knew their conversation was being recorded. The Committee sought leverage like it was going out of fashion; he'd learnt that lesson to his cost. *Now I'm theirs*, he thought, *and I'm up to my neck in it. No, it's worse than that, much worse, I'm ten foot under and treading water*. There was no one else, no other organisation with as much power and reach as the Committee, they had people everywhere. No one could match their scale of operation and neither could anyone match their thirst for control and power, save perhaps one man, a man they now sought to bring to heel. Stevens knew they needed Malcolm Joiner, but how badly? That was the question. He was the conduit through which their eyes and ears were inextricably linked. And yet it was the GMRC's Intelligence Division itself they craved. As far as Stevens knew, they'd had designs on Joiner's vast operation for years, but without the intelligence director's unique talents they would find it increasingly difficult to maintain the groundwork Joiner had worked his whole life to create. Stevens had been well aware of the intelligence director's methods and reputation prior to their meeting; he'd been given a dossier to read. What he hadn't been prepared for was the man's ferocious intensity and how far he was willing to go to get what he wanted. The profile the Committee had drawn up on Joiner needed to be updated, of that there was no doubt.

Stevens wasn't stupid, at least he liked to think he wasn't, and that he was alive today was testament to that fact. But he'd underestimated Joiner's resolve on more than one occasion and he wouldn't make the same mistake again. And until the Committee had him fully under their control he would seek to distance himself from the man as far as was humanly possible. He remembered the satisfaction he'd felt when he'd knocked Joiner out cold; he felt it still. His fist couldn't have connected with the man's chin any sweeter and while it was a memory to savour it was still regrettable. The late Grant Debden, Joiner's primary aide, had warned him Joiner would bear a grudge, and Stevens didn't doubt it, which was why he'd pushed hard for the intelligence director's expulsion from Sanctuary, although it seemed Joiner's fate was well beyond his power to control. If he was lucky the Committee would see fit to end the intelligence director's miserable life.

'General?'

Stevens could see Dagmar peering at him, but he remained looking straight ahead.

'You didn't answer my question,' Dagmar said, 'are you having doubts ... about our course of action?'

'I don't know what you mean.'

'I think you do.'

Stevens adjusted the collar of his uniform, which suddenly felt itchy and restrictive. 'The less I know about your little experiments, the better.'

'They're not little, General, you should know that better than anyone.'

'I told you, I want nothing to do with it.'

'And I believe you.' Dagmar placed a gnarled hand on his arm and Stevens felt a ripple of revulsion spread through his body. 'But we need more subjects, the trials ... they've taken their toll.'

'How many?' Stevens said.

'More than twenty ... less than fifty.'

'Fifty!?'

'Less than.'

'And I suppose you want them the same as before?'

'Young adults, yes. The more athletic the better, they need ... to have endurance.'

Stevens closed his eyes. The thought of what Dagmar was doing to those poor people didn't bear thinking about, and so he decided not to. 'I'll get them to you within the week.'

Dagmar removed his hand and Stevens felt instant relief.

He opened his eyes to resume his scrutiny of the Anakim simulation and the electrical storm forming in the distance. 'They say the lightning might damage the dome's integrity.'

'It might,' Dagmar said.

'Do you think it's permanent?'

'There's no way of knowing.'

'But if it is, it makes the dome redundant, doesn't it?

Dagmar remained silent.

'Do you know of Joiner's fate?' Stevens said.

'I have been privy to some of the Committee's deliberations.'

'That's a "no" then.'

'The evaluation is about to begin. I have just facilitated its undertaking.'

Stevens looked at him. 'Facilitated?'

'It's one of my ... little hobbies,' – Dagmar Sørensen turned to hold his gaze before a gruesome smile spread across his face like a sack of writhing maggots – 'and I always aim to please.'

CHAPTER SIXTY-SIX

Malcolm Joiner opened his eyes and stifled a groan. He reached up and touched his jaw, which felt swollen and tender. The back of his head ached with a dull, persistent throb while his mouth tasted of a strange, unpleasant chemical.

Sitting up, he saw he was on a bed in a plain white room. He glanced down at the medical gown that clung to his tall frame. He felt a sense of panic rising before a rush of fury squashed it like a bug.

He tried to recall the events that had led him to this humiliation. An image of an army uniform worked its way into his mind and his eyes narrowed. 'Stevens.'

Before he had time to collect his thoughts any further, the door to the room swung open and a woman entered. She wore the plain blue clothing of a nurse and an expression of detached concentration. She moved to the end of his bed to check a transparent digital chart full of live data and streaming graphs.

Joiner reached up to his head to find a small, round patch stuck to his temple.

'How are you feeling, Director?' the nurse said, looking up at him.

Joiner peeled off the device and threw it to the floor. 'Where am I?'

She removed the chart from the end of the bed and typed something onto its screen before approaching. 'You're being well cared for.' She slipped the chart into a large pocket in her apron. 'Can you lie back, please? I need to conduct a physical exam.'

Joiner didn't move.

The nurse sighed. 'Do you have a headache or feel nauseous?'

He remained silent.

'Can you tell me your name?' she said.

'I'll tell you nothing until you tell me where I am.'

She removed a torch from her pocket, turned it on and reached out to him.

Joiner's hand snaked out to grasp her wrist.

She glanced down at his whitening knuckles. 'I need to check your eyes for any sign of concussion.'

His fingers squeezed tighter and a look of pain stole across her face.

'You're hurting me, Director.' She reached out and laid her other hand on his, making him flinch at the touch.

'Get,' he said between clenched teeth, 'your hands off me.'

The woman leaned in close and whispered, 'You still have friends.' She removed her hand and flicked her eyes down at the digital chart, which she raised from its place of concealment in her apron.

Joiner focused on the words written on its screen:

THEY'RE WATCHING!
DO AS I SAY!!

Startled, Joiner suppressed the urge to react.

He released his hold and she dropped the device back into her pocket and reached out and lifted up his left eyelid before half-blinding him with the torch.

Apparently satisfied with the left, she moved onto the right while Joiner's mind shifted into overdrive.

'Move closer, please,' she said.

He leaned towards her and realised she was trying to conceal any interaction between them, so he whispered, 'Who?'

'The Committee.' She dropped something into his lap, a tiny, white pill, which he scooped up. 'Swallow it,' she said, 'it will help.'

'With what?'

'Keeping your mind your own.' She switched off the torch, held up her hand and raised her voice back to a normal level. 'Follow my finger, please.'

Joiner did as he was told while the tips of his fingers investigated the small capsule clasped in the palm of his hand.

The nurse moved away and poured him a glass of water from a nearby sink. She held it out to him. 'Would you like a drink of water?'

I have no idea who this person is working for, he thought, I have no idea what this pill might do. For all I know she might be working for the Committee. Another part of his mind screamed at him: Never put your trust in blind faith!

He hesitated and the nurse flicked her eyes to where she knew he held the pill. 'Dehydration leads to cognitive deficiency,' she said, 'and you need to keep your fluids up; I believe you have an important appointment scheduled.'

A knock on the door made them both look round.

It opened and an armed soldier entered. His purple armour glittered under the lights and he bore no visible signs of allegiance except for the emblem of USSB Sanctuary on his shoulder. He looked from Joiner to the nurse. 'Is he ready?'

She nodded and he disappeared back outside.

Left alone once more she placed the glass down on his bedside table. 'You need to get dressed, Director, they're waiting for you.'

'They?'

'Ms. Dubois and her business partners. It's best if you don't keep them waiting.' She moved to the door. 'I think they like to adhere to a strict schedule and my advice, like theirs, is in your best interest.'

'So you say.'

She glanced at the glass of water before giving him a meaningful look. 'Sometimes we just have to trust our instincts.'

The nurse left the room, leaving Joiner to mull over his decision. *Take a pill from a stranger who works for someone aligned against the Committee, or keep the status quo and rely on the Committee not to manipulate me by devious means.* The choice was not an appealing one, as either way his action would lead to a complete loss of control. *My life lies in the hands of another.* The thought of not being master of his own destiny shook him to the core. But there was no third option he could see, he had to make a choice, for good or for bad.

He swung his legs from the bed to place bare feet on a cold floor.

His suit, shirt and undergarments hung from a hanger on the back of the door. Ignoring the glass of water, he stood up and walked over to slip the pill into his jacket pocket before going about the chore of dressing himself. When he'd finished tying his shoes, he looked into a full length mirror and breathed a sigh of relief. Adjusting his collar, he removed his spectacles from his top pocket and slid them on. Satisfied with his appearance, he manoeuvred the capsule back into his hand and approached the bedside table.

He stared down at the glass of water. Should I take this pill or not? he thought. That is the question. The structure of words brought a famous paraphrase to mind: 'It is not in the stars to hold our destiny, but in ourselves.'

And better to put my hands in the unknown than the Committee's, even more so considering our recent clashes. He simulated a cough and slipped the pill into his mouth before sipping the water to let the fluid carry the small object off his tongue and down his throat.

A sense of anxiety made his stomach tense. There was no turning back now.

Committed to his course, Joiner grasped the door handle and emerged into a massive, crystalline hallway. He realised where he was: Tower Central, the Anakim creation positioned at the heart of the subterranean base.

'Director?'

Joiner looked round to where the female nurse waited for him, accompanied by two soldiers clad in purple armour.

One of the armed men stood aside and gestured Joiner through. 'If you'd care to follow us, sir.'

Joiner glared at them. 'I'd *care* to know what's going on. Where's Debden?'

'Your aide?' said the nurse.

'Yes, my aide, where is he?'

'I'm sorry to break this to you, sir, Grant Debden is dead, an unfortunate car accident.'

'Accident?'

'Yes, sir. I believe it happened outside the SED.'

Joiner stared at them and reached for his personal computer. When his hand closed on nothing he checked his other pockets.

'Have you lost something, sir?' the nurse said.

'Where's my computer?'

'If you'd come this way, Director.' The soldier's hand strayed towards his sidearm.

Joiner's mood darkened further. He wondered where Agent Myers was when he needed him and then he remembered what he'd done. Myers' look of shock when Joiner had shot him in the stomach replayed through his mind. *I'd do the same thing again*, he thought, *I had to know. I had to know if he was the leak and, more importantly, I had to find out what Stevens knew about Ares, about everything.*

The soldier moved further aside and Joiner held his ground before letting out a snort of derision. He strode past them and on down the hallway. The further he walked, the greater his pace became until he'd stretched out his stride to its full extension, which forced both the nurse and his armed chaperones to scamper along in order to keep up.

As they neared the end of the hall, first the nurse, and then the soldiers, ceased their pursuit and Joiner turned a corner and walked alone into a huge, multi-sided atrium.

He paused in the quiet, waiting for someone to greet him. When no such occurrence came, he moved forward across polished tiles to approach the central feature: a twenty foot wide circular emblem wrought from precious metals; the great seal of Sanctuary.

Disorientated, he gazed around at semi-translucent walls wreathed in subtle carvings. He'd always thought it apt that the architects had decided to build humanity's greatest structure with an Anakim tower at its centre, but due to the timeless grandeur and sheer enormity of the interior Joiner experienced a familiar sense of irrelevance, a sense that his very existence was as of much consequence as a flea to a dog.

When he'd last been summoned to experience the rarefied air of this most exclusive of inner sanctums, it was to be informed of the mission to come, a mission to secure an Anakim artefact capable of activating long-dormant technology. How that mission fared he didn't know. Communication links with Samson's expedition had been severed. For all he knew Sarah Morgan had been captured and the pendant device secured, although considering his recent run of luck, he realised such an assumption was just a desperate attempt by his mind to cling to some faint hope of redemption. The thought soured his mood even further, if that were possible, and he stood staring up at the internal aspect of the tower's spire, which soared into blue skies above.

He frowned. *Blue skies?*

Before he had a chance to pursue that thought, a whisper of sound drew his attention to a pair of dark, red doors that swung open on the far side of the antechamber, their gleaming, metallic sheen reflecting the radiance from above in a glittering cascade.

Joiner waited for someone to appear, but the entrance remained absent of movement.

As he wondered whether he should go through, the sound of footsteps approaching from behind made him turn to see the tall figure of a woman emerging from one of the many hallways that converged on the atrium.

The clip-clop of heel strikes echoed closer and Selene Dubois, the Committee member who'd been the source of all his problems, swept past without a hint of acknowledgement.

'This way, *Intelligence Director*,' she said over her shoulder as she continued walking.

Joiner noted the condescending tone she directed at his title and he stifled a cutting retort before following her toward the double doors.

Selene Dubois glided into the room beyond and Joiner increased his pace as the doors inched closed behind her. A moment later the entrance sealed shut with an audible boom, leaving the atrium empty once more save for the glimmering light of the Anakim skies above.

CHAPTER SIXTY-SEVEN

JOINER STARED in trepidation at the immense hall laid out before him. On the furthest wall a magnificent frieze constructed of a weathered, pewter-like metal dominated the backdrop, its three-dimensional figures and strange design attesting to its non-human creators. Overhead, the internal aspect of the Anakim tower soared into infinity, its great spire angling to a distant point. Joiner couldn't help but notice once again the strange vision of natural skies beyond its translucent gleam.

He continued walking forward, his vision drawn back down to the horizontal, the hall and the individuals seated within. Eight people – six men and two women – considered him from their position at a large, semi-circular table located on a raised dais at the centre of an otherwise empty expanse.

As he approached this daunting vision, Joiner realised he'd never seen so many Committee members in one place and when Selene finally joined their number, taking her seat at one end, eight became nine and he knew he was facing the power elite, the top echelon of the secretive organisation known only as the Committee.

Joiner moved to face the select panel, ensconced as they were in their position of elevation. Each wore plain, identical attire, the women, tailored white gowns, and the men, jet-black suits, red shirts and white ties.

One of the men got to his feet. 'Malcolm Joiner,' he said, 'you have been a valuable asset to the Committee over many years, your service exemplary, and yet you find yourself here today under evaluation.' He gestured with his hand. 'Please, be seated and we shall begin.'

Still smarting, physically and mentally, from the knockout blow delivered by General Stevens, Joiner glanced round to see a single chair and took his position as directed. *How long was I out?* he wondered. *Minutes, hours ... days?* His mind felt foggy and slow, as if he'd been drugged, and his vision blurred out of focus. *What was in that pill?!* He shifted in his seat in discomfort and concentrated on the people before him. *Now is not the time for weakness*, he told himself, *or has my incapacitation been engineered to induce just that?*

The man who'd spoken sat back down and flicked through a paper document. 'Tell us, Intelligence Director,' he said, glancing up at Joiner, 'in your own words, how is it that Professor Steiner still lives?'

Joiner suppressed the temptation to remove his glasses and rub his eyes; instead he sat up straighter and focused his attention on the speaker. 'My—' his voice broke and he cleared his throat. 'My team had the matter well in hand before an outside intervention derailed its efforts.'

'You refer to the cyber terrorist?' a woman said. 'The one known as "*Because I Can*"?'

Joiner nodded. 'Yes, the hacker B.I.C., *Da Muss Ich*.'

'So,' the man continued, 'one man *derailed* the efforts of the GMRC's entire Intelligence Division, a multi-trillion dollar organisation with near limitless resources?'

Joiner could see how this was going to play out. He'd long since mastered the art of dragging subordinates over hot coals and more often than not he'd left them there to burn. Such a review could go one of three ways. One, an admission of responsibility and full capitulation, also known as falling on your own sword. Two, a robust and unending defence resulting in humiliation and a loss of control; or three, the high risk strategy of an uncompromising, full blooded attack.

Of course, Joiner thought, *there is always a fourth option, an amalgamation of all of the above*. 'Regardless of the size of an organisation and its relative resources,' he said, 'unexpected events will always occur. I react as required. If you'd have given me more time—'

'More time?' The woman shook her head in disbelief. 'Time was something you had plenty of, Director, along with ample opportunity.'

'Forgive me,' Joiner said, 'I don't know your name ...'

The woman frowned at his tone and stared at him over the tops of her glasses.

'You must have been well aware of the situation,' Joiner said, unfazed. 'Steiner was the Director General of the GMRC's most powerful division and a singular force on the Directorate.'

'Your point being?' the woman said.

'My point being he was also secured in a maximum security prison awaiting the death penalty. If you wanted him out of the way so badly, perhaps you should have utilised your own resources to hasten the process.'

'If you refer to S.I.L.V.E.R.,' she said, 'they were engaged in other tasks. If we'd have known you intended to wait for the Director General to succumb to the natural course we would have intervened. But you forget yourself, Director; it is not our performance that is under review.'

Joiner felt his mind clearing as Selene Dubois raised her hand to beckon someone forward.

A man dressed in a plain grey suit approached her position. He passed her a portable screen and they exchanged a few words before he left her side and walked over to where Joiner sat.

'Could you hold out your left arm, please, Director.'

Joiner studied the man before looking at Selene Dubois with suspicion.

'Dr. Laurent is here to facilitate your evaluation,' she said. 'He was also responsible for your care during your ... incapacity.'

'You are in good physical health,' the doctor said. 'Now we need to know if you're of sound mind.'

Joiner knew he had little option, so he raised his arm to enable the doctor to carry out his work.

Dr. Laurent tugged the sleeve of Joiner's jacket up his arm, undid the cuff, and rolled back his shirtsleeve, before attaching a long flexible metal collar around his forearm. He then withdrew a wire from the instrument and secured it to a round patch, which he placed on Joiner's left temple, a patch similar to the one Joiner had removed back in his place of enforced convalescence.

When he'd finished, the doctor fixed the apparatus to the arm of Joiner's chair and activated a small screen on the metal device before retreating to one side.

Joiner looked down at the display to see a number of oscillating figures and a set of bars that rose and fell, much like a graphic equaliser on an audio system.

'Don't be alarmed, Director,' the man on the Committee said, 'we just need to be sure of your continued mental health, and that also means we need to know where your allegiance lies if you are to continue to be of use to us.'

Joiner's pulse quickened. 'I thought you said it was to determine mental acuity?'

'That as well,' Selene said, 'that as well.'

Joiner thought he glimpsed a glimmer of satisfaction on her face and he recalled what the nurse had told him about the pill. *It will help keep your mind your own.*

Perhaps this device does more than find the truth in my words, he thought, *perhaps it's designed to make the Committee's desires my own.*

The notion that they might be trying to rewrite his mind, to control his very being and sense of self, made him want to wrench the contraption from his wrist, but he fought down the desire with an iron will. *You have contingencies for this,* he told himself, *relax. If they do manage to insert something into your subconscious, Debden and Myers are trained to notice the signs. Except Debden is dead and Myers is ... I don't even know if he lives,* he realised. *In any case, I can never rely on him again. Who else could conclude I'd become a security breach?* He wasn't due another psychological review for months; Debden had rearranged his schedule and asked if the mandatory tests could be pushed back due to his heavy workload. Something connected in his mind. Two and two became four and Joiner realised why Debden was dead. *He was my leak! And they killed him for it. He'd served his purpose and that was his reward.* Joiner had seen it happen before, and on occasion he'd even been the one to implement it on the Committee's behalf.

'So,' Selene said, 'let's start again, shall we? Tell us, Intelligence Director,' – she pressed a button on her screen – 'in your own words, how is it that Professor Steiner still lives?'

Joiner glanced down at the readout on his wrist and realised the first question was a control to test his baselines. Now came the real test.

'As I said before, my team had the matter in hand before the hacker intervened.'

'So the failure was not due to any desire on your part to see the professor live?'

'No.'

'And you are not working with Professor Steiner?' the man said.

'No, of course not.'

'And your goals are aligned with the Committee's?'

'Of course.'

The graphics on the device inched higher, turning from blue to red.

'Answer yes or no, Director,' Selene said.

'Yes.' Joiner felt the device on his arm tighten and a tingle of pain bit into his temple.

Selene exchanged hushed words with the member next to her, while Joiner began to fear the worst. Even if the pill ensured his will was his own, it didn't seem to be able to trick the device into believing he was telling the truth.

The device on his arm eased and the fluctuating bars on its display dropped back down to their previous levels.

'On a scale of one to ten,' Selene said, 'where ten is very high and one is very low, how optimistic are you that the expeditions will locate Ms. Morgan and retrieve the stolen Anakim artefacts?'

Joiner tensed as the graphics on the device crept higher.

'Answer the question, please, Director,' one of the men said.

Joiner switched his gaze back to the Committee. 'The communication link with Colonel Samson's force was lost; we have no way of knowing the outcome of their efforts until the second expedition reinitiate contact.'

'If you seek to evade every question, Director,' Selene said, 'we are all going to be here for a very long time. We require a one word answer, is that so difficult to understand? I repeat, on a scale of one to ten, where ten is very high and one is very low, how optimistic are you that the expeditions will locate Sarah Morgan and retrieve the stolen Anakim artefacts?'

'On a scale of one to ten? I would say ... seven.'

Miniature motors whirred to life. The device on his arm squeezed tight and another tingle of pain lanced into his temple.

'Would you care to answer again?' Selene said.

'If S.I.L.V.E.R. were in charge, then I'd downgrade that to four.'

The metal band constricted further and Joiner suppressed a gasp of pain.

Selene raised an eyebrow. 'Director?'

Joiner gritted his teeth. 'Three if Samson leads, two if Nexus does.'

The pressure reduced and Selene noted something down on her screen.

'I'd point out,' Joiner said, 'that I voiced my concerns over the success of the mission at the outset, and installing Samson ahead of Nexus was only done to ensure the best possible outcome for all involved.'

No one on the Committee responded and Joiner felt his anger swell.

'Malcolm Joiner,' said one of the men who'd not previously

spoken, 'can you tell us why you saw fit to shoot one of your intelligence agents at near point-blank range?'

Joiner pondered the question, desperately seeking a way to answer truthfully, while at the same time not revealing the real reason for his actions. 'Agent Myers was a potential threat to GMRC security; when I disarmed him I was forced to act in order to prevent further conflict.'

Joiner waited for the device to react, but it stayed as it was with the display showing blue across the board.

The man who'd spoken looked to Selene, who gave a shake of her head.

'And there was no other reason?' the man said, facing him again.

'No.'

The device clamped tight.

'Are you sure?'

'Yes.' The pain increased and Joiner clenched his fist as he fought to maintain an impression of calm.

'The machine doesn't appear to agree with you, Director.' Selene pressed a button on her portable screen. 'Would you care to reconsider your position?'

The metal sheath twisted tighter still and Joiner gasped in agony and clutched at his arm.

'The pain will only get worse,' she said. 'I've been told it has the power to break a man's arm clean in two.'

'Turn it off,' Joiner said, 'TURN IT OFF!'

The agony decreased and Joiner's eyes blazed with fury as he met Selene's unyielding gaze.

'The reason for the shooting, Director,' said the man, 'if you please.'

Joiner's chest rose and fell with the rapid breath of duress. He wiped the back of his hand across his mouth and switched his hate-filled eyes onto the man who'd spoken. Thoughts, desperate thoughts, rushed through his mind, like a rabid dog seeking a way out from an inescapable maze. Every route was met with a dead end and he finally realised as the silence dragged on, that the truth or a broken arm were the only options. And he knew they wouldn't stop at his arm. They'd keep going until they had what they wanted.

'Stevens needed to be persuaded,' Joiner said. 'He had information I required and shooting Myers provided a powerful motive for him to comply with my demands.'

'What else?' Selene said.

Joiner gave a shake of his head in defeat. 'I also believed Myers might have been responsible for an internal breach within the Intelligence Division. Leaving him mortally wounded ensured he would give me the truth in order to live.'

'And if he died?'

'Then it would have been one less person under suspicion.'

'A ruthless decision,' Selene said. 'How did that work out for you?'

Joiner glared at her with unconcealed loathing.

The woman with the glasses leaned forward. 'And who did you think this leak was reporting to?'

Joiner ran his gaze over the nine people before him. 'The Committee.'

'And why would this disturb you, Director,' the woman said, 'if our objectives are aligned?'

And there it is, Joiner thought, the answer they crave, my duplicity laid bare. Is it what they'd been after all along, a confirmation of guilt?

The woman removed her glasses. 'Let me rephrase the question. How do your objectives differ from those of the Committee?'

Joiner remained silent and he glanced at the device on his arm.

'You will learn to obey,' – Selene's finger hovered over the control panel – 'and you *will* answer. One way or another, you will give up your secrets.'

Joiner considered the people arrayed before him, his mind racing and hands clenched. Now more than ever he wanted to bring the Committee low, to expose their hidden workings and to wring the life from their self-righteous necks. He knew they plotted with Dagmar Sørensen on Project Ares and toyed with things that endangered the entire species of man. *The God Device has to be destroyed. It's an abomination; something that can predict the future?* The mere thought terrified him. And then there was the issue of the Committee's role in sabotaging the GMRC Space Programme, effectively condemning the surface and every living thing on it to an eternal death. Joiner came to a sudden conclusion. *They have to be stopped and be damned with my ambition. If I'm to rule it will be at the head of the GMRC, not of the Committee. And if anyone deserves to lead, to govern, it's me.*

A tingle of discomfort at his temple interrupted his thoughts.

The woman who'd asked the question replaced her glasses, her expression hardening. 'How do your objectives differ from those of the Committee?'

The metal shroud on his arm constricted once more.

I can't tell them the truth! Joiner felt panic rising as the pain increased.

One of the men leaned forward. 'How do they differ, Director?'

Metal bit into flesh and Joiner grasped the arm of the chair.

'Tell us, Director,' Selene said, 'tell us and the pain will stop.'

'They don't differ! Our objectives are the same!'

'A lie!'

The pressure increased again and Joiner cried out in agony.

'This is your last chance, Malcolm Joiner,' Selene said. 'Listen to my voice, you will obey me, how do your objectives differ from the Committee's?'

Through a sea of pain Joiner looked down at his arm. The device inched into a curl, blood dripped to the floor and he knew what he had to do. *I have to make it real.*

Selene stood up. 'How do they differ?!'

He shut his eyes. 'THEY DON'T!'

The graphics on the device peaked, its motors whined. Joiner screamed and his forearm snapped.

CHAPTER SIXTY-EIGHT

Malcolm Joiner, the director of one of the most feared and powerful organisations in the world, sat slumped, alone and semi-conscious in his chair. His broken arm lay limp and motionless while his lifeblood pooled on the floor at his feet, the steady drip drip of blood feeding its spreading mass.

'Can you hear me, Director? Say something if you can hear me.'

Joiner opened his eyes and looked up into the face of a man.

'I'm going to remove the device now, hold still.' Dr. Laurent unclipped the restraints and Joiner felt the weight lifted away before a shadow fell over him.

'Attach it to his right arm,' Selene said.

'Ms. Dubois, with respect, I'm not sure he can take any more.'

'He can and he will.'

Dr. Laurent reached out to probe the wound. 'At least let me stop the bleeding.'

Selene grasped his wrist. 'Dagmar said the device can be used multiple times and on all different body parts. Was he lying?'

Dr. Laurent shook his head.

'Then do as I say, Doctor, or you'll find yourself testing your device,' – she gauged the size of his neck with her hand – 'on somewhere entirely more vital.'

Dr. Laurent paled and went about securing the machine to Joiner's other arm.

Moments later Selene leaned down to peer into Joiner's eyes. 'We can do this all day, Director. And don't think a lack of blood or the good doctor here will save you. If you pass out we'll have you patched up and brought back again, and again,' – she grasped his chin – 'and again.'

Joiner shook off her hold and, despite the pain, managed to sit up straighter.

'Good,' she said. 'I feared you'd lost your resolve.' She gave a nod to Dr. Laurent. 'Fire it up.'

Joiner heard a faint whir of motors and the metallic sheath resumed its vice-like grip.

Selene walked back to her seat and the evaluation resumed.

'We'll start again with the same question, Director,' said one of men, 'how do your objectives differ from the Committee's?'

Joiner cleared his throat. 'They don't.'

Red bars elevated, motors whined and the pain came again.

Joiner clenched his teeth as the agony increased. 'Enough!' he said. 'Enough.'

The pressure subsided.

'You have something to say?' Selene said.

Joiner breathed deeply against the pain and nodded. 'I know why S.I.L.V.E.R. are here; it's not just for the pendant, it's for the thing, the light in the deep.'

'The Pharos?' Selene said.

Joiner gave another nod. 'Yes. I know you want it brought back for analysis. I can't—' He winced as he moved his broken arm.

'Can't what, Director?' Selene said, her finger hovering over the device's control panel.

'I can't let that happen. It's too dangerous.'

'How did you plan to stop us?' said the woman with the glasses.

'I would have found a way.'

Selene tilted her head to one side as her colleague whispered into her ear. She nodded and returned her attention to Joiner. 'What else?' she said. 'What else are you hiding from us?'

Joiner glanced at the horror of his crippled arm. 'I've seen what General Stevens retrieved from Sanctuary, the giant monolith, the one Morgan activated with her pendant.'

Selene frowned. 'What do you know of it?'

'That it contains some type of fluid, but apart from that … nothing.'

The device on his arm remained unmoving.

'Go on,' Selene said, accepting his words as the truth they were.

'But I've seen what the pendant can do,' he said, 'I've seen its power.'

'And let me guess, you wanted it for yourself?'

Joiner hesitated. 'Is that such a crime? Have none of you wanted more control, *taken* more, seized and wielded it?'

The Committee failed to respond; they just sat there, staring at him.

Joiner sagged back into his chair and tried to will away the intense pain that throbbed from his arm and up into his body, but the attempt failed and he remained locked in his earthly prison while those without feeling remained watching in silence.

Did my deception work? he wondered. *Are they convinced?* Sacrificing his arm had been a difficult decision, but it was one that may well have saved his life. If he'd revealed his secrets too early they would have sought more, they would have dug deeper until they found out about his desire to destroy their *God Device* and the Committee itself. And if that had happened, he'd already be dead, of that there was no doubt. But disclosing lesser truths – his lust for the pendant and his fear of the Pharos – may have been enough to convince them that while they had their differences, they were not insurmountable. At least that was his theory, his hope, the only way out of an otherwise impossible situation. Whether it had worked or not, he had yet to find out.

After more moments dragged by, the nine Committee members

rose as one and moved away towards the Anakim frieze, where they formed a circle to discuss Joiner's fate. At least that's what he assumed. *Either that*, he thought, *or they're deciding whether to continue my so-called evaluation*.

A minute passed, and then five minutes turned to ten, before the tall figures of the Committee returned to their seats; all except for Selene, who moved to stand before him.

'It seems our goals have diverged, Director,' Selene said, and she gestured for the doctor to return to her side. 'And that degree of separation has become too great to reconcile.'

The doctor produced a syringe, inserted it into a vial full of a bright green liquid and pulled back the plunger.

'Wait!' Joiner said, his eyes fixed on the long, metal needle.

'For what?' Selene accepted the primed hypodermic from Dr. Laurent.

'I can tell you more.'

'More?'

'I know the Committee engineered the destruction of the intercept missions. You've worked for years to ensure the GMRC's Space Programme failed.'

'And why would we do that?'

'I don't know!'

Selene gave a nod to someone behind him and a powerful arm, clad in purple armour, clamped down over his chest.

Joiner struggled against the soldier's iron grip before a similarly armoured hand pulled his head to one side to expose his jugular.

Selene moved closer and the sight of the syringe filled Joiner's vision.

'It seems we cannot control you, *Intelligence Director*,' she said, 'and if we cannot control you it leaves us with only one choice.'

'Wait, WAIT!' The needle moved closer and Joiner's eyes grew wide with fear. 'Bic is still inside the system!'

Selene paused and looked into eyes. 'The hacker?'

'Yes. He has access to the GMRC's servers.'

'All of them?'

'No, low level arrays.'

Selene studied him for a moment before resuming her task and Joiner felt the needle prick his skin and then – ever so slowly – slide into muscle and sinew.

'I'm sorry, Director,' Selene said, her thumb poised over the plunger, 'but you can consider your evaluation ... failed.'

Her thumb depressed and the piston glided through the syringe's transparent barrel. Green fluid was forced into his neck and a second later the needle was removed and Joiner released.

A warm sensation spread through his body before a sudden flash of clarity pierced his awareness. A circle of causation was complete. It was Samson who'd first been held down and injected at Joiner's instigation; now it was him. And likewise, Steiner and Samson still lived when it was *they* who should have died by lethal injection, *not* him. *NOT ME!* He couldn't believe the injustice. *Such injustice.* His eyes slipped closed, the bitter irony carrying him down into bleak, empty nothingness while the Committee – arranged in detached fascination – looked on in silent vigil.

CHAPTER SIXTY-NINE

DEEP beneath the landscape of the ancient lands of Mesoamerica, Richard Goodwin no longer battled against the oppressive pitch-black of Sanctuary's underworld. Instead, he sat bathed in the purity of daylight.

Eyes closed, Goodwin breathed deeply and appreciated the warmth of the Anakim sun as it reinvigorated his mind, body and soul. It had been fourteen hours since the chamber's ceiling had activated and he'd savoured every minute, every second of the glorious transformation. He expelled the air from his lungs with a slow release and another layer of tension departed tired muscles. *How many months have I been in the dark?* he wondered. *Eight, ten, more? Too long*, he decided, *far too long. No one should be immersed in darkness ... no one.* Thinking about the unending blackness interrupted his meditative state and his thoughts inevitably returned to Rebecca and Joseph, which filled his heart with pain.

Goodwin heard someone approach across the pebbly beach and he opened his eyes.

Kara Vandervoort walked towards him and sat down by his side to gaze out across the lake and the strange barren landscape of the massive three mile high chamber that had become their world.

Neither of them spoke for a while, each absorbed in the contemplation of their own thoughts, until Kara decided to break the silence.

'It's strange, don't you think?'

'What is?'

'All this.' She gestured towards the blue skies and the dazzling light. 'It's very similar to our sunlight generators back at Steadfast.'

'It's better than Steadfast's systems, much better. It almost looks like the real thing.' He thought for a moment longer. 'And why is that strange, anyway?'

She gave him an odd look. 'Because this could be a million years old, that's why.'

'Perhaps it's the optimal design. Isn't there a case where two completely different species turned out looking like the same thing, a hedgehog and something else?'

'An echidna, yes. There are many more examples, too. The process is called convergence, or convergent evolution. It's where life comes up with the same environmental solution from different start points.'

'So if evolution can produce two animals with similar, or near identical, traits over millions, even billions of years, surely two closely related species, Humans and Anakim, can come up with the same solution to the same problem?'

'Maybe,' Kara said.

'What other explanation is there?'

'The one that's staring us in the face.'

'Which is?'

'What if our versions come from theirs?'

'You think we reverse engineered them from Anakim technology?'

'Why not?'

Goodwin looked up at the sky again. It was an interesting theory.

In the distance a rumble of thunder echoed through the chamber and the haze of rain could be seen falling from a smattering of clouds.

'It's beautiful, though, isn't it?' she said, looking up.

'Magnificent, I only wish ... all of us, could have been here to see it.'

Kara placed her hand on his. 'You can't save everyone.'

'I can't stop wondering ...'

'What?' She glanced at him.

'Did they suffer when they died? Or did the crystal shield them from any pain?'

'Don't torment yourself. You did what you could, no one could ask more.'

Goodwin stared at the lake, its cold waters turned blue in reflection of the artificial skies above. Did I do what I could? he asked himself. Did I do enough? Could I have done more? I should never have involved Rebecca. That was my first mistake ... the first of many.

The buzz of insects interrupted the flow of his thoughts and he paused to watch the tiny winged creatures dance across the ground like a miniature aerobatic display. It was odd to think such an innocuous sight had become so enchanting because of its absence. Life in Sanctuary's depths, with the exclusion of the lake itself, was – or should that be, *had been* – a rare commodity indeed.

'Your theory that Sanctuary's atmosphere was created by a large ecosystem turned out to be true,' Goodwin said.

'It's ironic.' She sighed. 'It was right under our noses all along and we didn't even know.'

Goodwin nodded. 'Captain Winter said there's a whole other world down there. It must have been sealed for thousands of years, maybe hundreds of thousands.'

'Do they know how big it is?'

'Hilt's already sent two recon teams down to take a look. They're also keeping an eye on Terra Force as they retreat back to their base.'

'Has he mentioned the lights?'

Goodwin gestured at three figures approaching from the south. 'You can ask him yourself.'

Kara turned to look, her expression full of mixed emotion. 'The Commander,' she said, hesitating, 'Hilt ... has requested that you be reinstated as camp leader.'

Goodwin refrained from saying anything at first. He knew she was proud of how she'd been coping with the tribulations of being in charge and he felt no ill will toward her that she'd seen fit to dethrone him during his struggles. With hindsight he'd have probably done the same thing. *I was out of control, I can see that now. Although*, he thought, *sometimes extreme circumstances called for extreme action*.

'What did you say?' he said, keeping his tone neutral.

'I said it was a good idea.'

'You did?'

'Now that things have calmed down and we're not looking over our shoulders to see what's lurking in the dark, it's for the best. I think your mood has already lifted and that whatever else was going on has run its course.'

Goodwin grunted in response and Kara gave him a questioning look as they got to their feet.

Hilt and Captain Winter came to a halt in front of them.

'Commander,' Goodwin said, 'Captain.' He peered round Hilt's armoured form to spy Susan hiding in the Darklight leader's shadow. He gave her a wave and she ducked out of sight.

'She's taken quite a shine to you, Commander,' Kara said, her expression wary.

Hilt glanced behind him. 'It appears so.'

'Her carer,' – Kara moved to keep Susan in her sights – 'Julie, is worried she might still be dangerous.'

'She has never been dangerous,' Hilt said. 'The creature that was attracted to her was.'

'But you can see her point,' Kara said, frowning.

Hilt said nothing. What could he say? No one knew what would happen next and they couldn't just abandon the poor girl because some *thing* had formed an attachment to her.

Goodwin saw an altercation brewing and he attempted to avert it. 'Has there been any sign of the Pharos?'

'None so far,' Captain Winter said, 'although now we have light they might be harder to spot.'

'Can we track them?'

'This is their domain,' Hilt told him. 'They'll only be found if they want to be found.'

'But there's still a strong possibility they all died in the lake,' – Kara looked from Goodwin to Hilt and back again – 'isn't there?'

Goodwin swapped looks with the Darklight commander. 'It's possible—'

'But unlikely,' Hilt said. 'There are three of these entities, these Pharos, that we know of. Even if they perished in the lake, there could be others.'

Goodwin gazed at the water, which suddenly seemed more ominous than before. 'They could still be alive down there,' he said, 'watching.'

Kara shuddered.

Captain Winter put a hand to his Darklight helmet and his eyes went distant as he listened to an incoming message. 'Ma'am,' he said, looking at Kara, 'you're needed back at camp, something about burial pits.'

Kara's face grew grim and she made to leave. 'Gentleman,' she said to the two black-garbed soldiers. She turned to Goodwin. 'I'll see you later?'

'Sure.'

She flashed him a tired smile and then strode away.

'Escort the doctor back,' Hilt said to Winter as they watched her go, 'there're roving patrols, but let's not take any chances.'

The captain saluted his commander, gave Goodwin a nod, and then jogged off in pursuit.

Goodwin waited until Kara and her chaperone were out of sight before turning back to Hilt. 'Do we have many injured?'

'We do, casualties were high on both sides. The bigger problem is what we do with the enemy injured.'

'Terra Force aren't our enemy,' Goodwin said, 'nor are those in the base, perhaps with the exception of Malcolm Joiner and those under his control.'

'Do I need to point out the contradiction in that statement?' Hilt said.

'You know what I mean; those soldiers are just following orders. It's the people at the top who are the real threat.'

'If someone shoots at me, they're my enemy,' Hilt said, 'until they prove otherwise.'

Goodwin didn't argue. Hilt sometimes saw things in black and white. And perhaps that's how it needs to be for a man who shoulders the burden of both protecting and taking life. In war, hesitation would get you killed ten times over. His mind wandered and he recalled something the Darklight leader had said previously.

'I've been meaning to ask you,' Goodwin said, 'what did you mean before when you said you lived up to half your promise, but not in the way I thought?'

Hilt held his gaze, his expression as enigmatic as usual.

'You secured the Deep Reach maps,' Goodwin said, 'and you returned Susan to us.'

'Did I?' Hilt said.

'Yes, you said it yourself, you got the maps to the base from Sarah's Deep Reach helmet,' – Goodwin looked at Susan, who sat on the ground playing with pebbles – 'and unless she's a figment of my imagination, you found Susan and brought her safely back, too.'

'Except Susan was already here by the time I arrived,' Hilt said.

'But you found her, didn't you?'

'We found something.'

Goodwin felt a tingle of unease spread up his spine. 'She's not something; she's right there, flesh and bone. It's Susan. Look.'

The small woman looked up at the mention of her name before going back to her game of stones.

'From what I've heard and seen,' Hilt said, 'I'm not certain of anything anymore.'

'I know that look,' Goodwin said, 'there's something you're not telling me, isn't there? Something happened while you were down there, something you've kept to yourself.'

Hilt stayed silent for a moment as he gathered his thoughts. 'We tracked the creature for many days,' he said, staring out at the lake's idle waters, 'and it wasn't until the sixth that we caught our first sight of Susan.'

'Go on,' Goodwin said when Hilt paused.

'Before that time,' the commander continued, 'I feared she was already long dead and that the mission was a seek and kill. As far as I was concerned stopping the creature was my priority. I couldn't allow it to get back to camp under any circumstances.'

'But you changed your mind?'

'When we saw Susan with the entity, yes. Knowing she was alive changed everything, but when some of my team started to experience vivid dreams – powerful, mind-altering dreams – I began to suspect they were linked to her, somehow. Every time she showed up the more we were affected.'

'Linked?' Goodwin frowned. 'Their nightmares, were linked to Susan?'

'Night terrors would be more accurate, violent night terrors.'

'And you experienced these terrors?'

'To a degree, but mine were nothing compared to others.'

'What happened?'

'One night we caught Susan amongst us when we were asleep,' Hilt said. 'She was touching people's temples. When someone sounded the alarm she turned rabid, like an animal. At the same time the creature probed our defences, drawing our attention elsewhere, and she made her escape. The same night, the man she'd touched last shot himself in the head.'

'What?' Goodwin said, horrified.

'Quite, but that was after he'd scrawled a message in the ground for us to read.'

'What did it say?'

Hilt detached a screen device from his armour, unfurled it and held it out to him.

Goodwin looked at the image and saw five words inscribed in dark earth, soaked in blood:

Goodwin studied the photo, trying to make sense of the senseless. 'What does it mean?'

'Scroll to the next image,' Hilt said. 'We found this scratched into a wall the next morning.'

Goodwin did as he was bid, and found a second message, which read:

Goodwin's disquiet deepened. 'Who knows who's where?'

Hilt retrieved the screen to study the message again.

'Is the "*we're*" us?' Goodwin said. 'And the "*here*" Sanctuary?'

'It seems the logical conclusion.'

'Then who is the "*they*"?'

Hilt looked at him. 'That's the million dollar question.'

'Does it mean the Pharos?'

'Perhaps.'

'Or Terra Force, S.I.L.V.E.R. ... Joiner even?'

Hilt's expression showed his doubt at such reasoning.

'If not them,' Goodwin said, 'then who?'

'Whoever, or whatever, "*they*" may be, the first part of the first message is perhaps the most troubling.'

'It's too late?'

'Indeed.'

'Too late,' Goodwin murmured, 'too late to hide?' A recollection of Rebecca quoting the Bible drifted up from the past. And the angels who did not stay within their own position of authority, but left their proper dwelling, he has kept in eternal chains under gloomy darkness until the judgment of the great day. 'Jude, chapter one,' he said, 'verse six.'

'Sir?' Hilt said, confused.

Goodwin gave a shake of his head. 'It's nothing.' But is it? he wondered, is it nothing? The 'great day' must mean the Apocalypse. And the next wave of meteors due to impact the surface in less than a year couldn't be viewed as anything else.

Goodwin knew Hilt wouldn't shy away from any biblical fervour; the Darklight Commander would supersede any personal judgement with an open mind and a deliberate logic. And yet Goodwin didn't want to risk damaging the man's trust in him. After all, he hasn't seen me at my worst. But the question remained: is the passage from the Bible a prophecy from the past, a truth hidden in plain sight, or just a fanciful reach conjured forth by my own desire for answers? The latter seems the most likely. Except, he thought, the message left for Hilt said otherwise. What if it wasn't the Pharos that 'knew they were here', but the beings I saw in the Anakim frieze, the Nephilim? He recalled something else Rebecca had said when they'd first been investigating his theories. The Nephilim were one of four things: the children of fallen angels and human women, fallen angels who possessed men, the descendents of Adam who followed false gods, or ordinary men who rejected God and chose to be wicked.

The second definition in the list jumped out at him: *Fallen angels who possessed men*. If Joseph and Susan hadn't been possessed, he didn't know what was. And even though he'd kept his sanity, however tenuously, he accepted he may well have been a victim of a more insidious type of possession. *Which means the Pharos could be the Nephilim.* He shook his head. *Only they don't match the beings depicted in the Anakim friezes.* He squeezed his eyes shut and grimaced. *You're going round in circles, Richard!*

'Are you alright?' Hilt said.

'Yes, I'm fine, just a headache.' Goodwin looked round at the small mentally-handicapped woman as Hilt's previous words returned to haunt him. 'So, you think Susan isn't Susan anymore?'

'She's still her,' Hilt said, 'she's still in there, but so is something else; at least we have no reason to believe whatever was controlling her has gone.'

'The rash on her arm,' Goodwin said, 'from the blue crystal bracelet, it's faded.'

'And that proves what?'

Goodwin looked down at his own wrist where his skin healed from a similar inflammation.

'That the visual indicator has gone,' Hilt said, 'doesn't mean the cause has. How many viruses stay in the body and show no symptoms? I can think of a handful without any effort.'

'You think it's dormant inside her?' Goodwin touched his wrist and looked at Hilt. 'Then that means—'

The Darklight officer held his gaze.

'That's why you were reluctant to tell me, isn't it?' Goodwin said. 'After I told you about Joseph and what happened to me you think it's still in me too.'

'It's a possibility.'

Goodwin felt dizzy and he moved away from Hilt to gather his thoughts. That he'd rather have not known about the latent entity that might be residing in his mind was an understatement. *But equally*, he reasoned, *forewarned is forearmed*. A part of him had known, anyway, that whatever had disturbed his mind might still be there, he just hadn't wanted to accept the reality of it. Except now he felt like a noose hung round his neck and that any moment the trap-door could be opened.

Goodwin heard the crunch of stones underfoot as the Darklight leader returned to his side.

'You saw how Dr. Vandervoort viewed Susan,' Hilt said, stopping next to him, 'and she didn't even have the whole picture. Would you want her viewing you with the same hostility, the same distrust?'

Goodwin had already experienced such a scenario, but it would be nothing to how people would view him if they knew the full truth. 'And you want me back in charge?'

'From what you've told me, this thing wasn't able to control you as comprehensively as it did Susan and Joseph, which gives us an advantage. A window into how it thinks. If it happens again, we'll have the opportunity to anticipate its next move. As to being in charge, I'll leave that up to you. Do you think you're still capable?'

Goodwin considered his options. Hilt obviously still trusts me. God knows why. And I do feel better. Kara was right; my mood has lifted since the ceiling activated. So what do I do? Take control of my destiny once more, or sit back and wait for things to take their course? Deep down, Goodwin knew he was fit enough to lead, at least, for now. 'I do,' he said, 'I am, but as soon as I show any sign of ...'

'Losing it?' Hilt said.

'Yes, we'll revert back to Kara taking the lead.'

'Agreed.'

Goodwin stood in silence, watching while Susan continued to rummage in the pebbles close by, and then he thought of something. 'Do you think the Pharos chose Susan and Joseph because of their learning difficulties?'

'Maybe.'

'Then what about me?'

'What do you mean?'

'If that's the case why choose me? Do you think it sensed my depression as a weakness, making me easier to control?'

'It's possible.'

Goodwin cursed inwardly. Hilt could be a frustrating man to talk to at times. 'Unless I was chosen by chance. Although, you said the Pharos would only be found if they wanted to be found, and you're probably right. Which means it revealed itself to me and Kara first, on purpose. It selected me on purpose.'

'Why not?' Hilt said. 'It makes sense if it knew you were our leader.'

'We say "*it*",' – Goodwin picked up a handful of pebbles – 'but there was more than one of them.' He launched a stone into the lake in frustration. 'We know nothing about them; we're as lost as we were before.'

'Only now we have light,' Hilt said. 'It changes everything.'

'Does it though – really? We're still trapped down here; the surface is beyond our reach. You've located USSB Sanctuary, but it'll be more hostile than ever. Everything is different, but we remain – cut off from the rest of humanity.'

'For now,' Hilt said, 'but now we have a living ecosystem that could sustain us, and light to live by. Our position has improved beyond measure. Maybe not in the way we foresaw, but it's in the right direction. And it's all down to Susan.'

'Don't you mean the thing that was controlling her?'

'Maybe, except after she'd stolen the crystal from my armour she appeared to be her old self. When we'd seen her before, under the creature's thrall, her eyes were bloodshot and her movement was ... abnormal.'

'She got the blue crystal from you?'

Hilt nodded. 'When I was trying to free Rebecca from the wall.'

'How did she know you had it?'

'A sixth sense from whatever's inside her? I don't know.'

'So Susan saved Sarah?'

'It appears so.'

'Or there's still the possibility she was being controlled,' Goodwin said, 'and the thing inside her just wanted to activate the device.'

'Yes.'

'So basically we have no way of knowing what really happened, or why. We may have light, but we're still very much in the dark.'

Hilt tapped the Darklight emblem on his chest. 'Then it seems I've come to the right place.'

Goodwin managed a smile before looking up at the ceiling. 'Will this last, do you think, now that it's activated?'

'We'll have to wait and see, but if these Pharos wanted the ceiling operational, I doubt they would have gone to so much effort for just a few hours, or days, of light.'

Goodwin threw another stone into the lake and studied the concentric rings that rippled out across its surface. 'I hope you're right,' he said. 'I don't think I could have gone on much longer the way we were.'

'You'd be surprised, the human spirit can shine unbreakably bright,' Hilt looked at Susan. 'Where strong men and women would have broken, a fragile child in an adult's body survived.'

Goodwin flicked a pebble to the ground. Hilt's right; I could have gone on, but I would have been existing, not living, and what life is that? Life is still life, his other voice said, and where there's life there's hope ... beautiful hope.

'So the question remains,' Hilt said, 'what was it all for?'

Goodwin sighed. 'What do you mean?'

'We're always falling into the same trap; we get blinded by events and the one question we need to ask, we don't. We know these creatures, the Pharos as you call them, are highly intelligent. They've proven again and again that they can manipulate and control us, if not directly then indirectly, although it seems, if they have the mind, even the sanctity of our inner reasoning, even our dreams, can be influenced. They can outthink us, pre-empt us and devise a complex web of unconnected events that will further their plans.'

'What are you getting at, Commander? As you're not inspiring confidence.'

Hilt looked out at the city as the Anakim sun dipped below the chamber's horizon. 'The Pharos led Sarah Morgan to us, or us to Morgan. It was waiting for her, like it knew she was coming. She was crucial to its plan, as Susan was, as Joseph was ... as *you* were. The central spire was activated well in advance, in preparation for the final act. It conspired across hundreds of miles of underground terrain with exact precision. To me, that smacks of a higher power ... of a controlling, singular force.'

Goodwin watched as a simulated dusk took hold. It was an awe inspiring sight and yet he felt the oppressive weight of the dark returning.

'The ceiling's activation helps us, but the question is who – or *what* – else does it help?' Hilt pointed at some of the distant spires, which had retained the faint glow of energy, the vision only now revealed by the fading light. 'And why,' he said, 'did it want Sanctuary's power turned back on?'

Goodwin stared at the gleaming towers of the city, unable to answer the Darklight leader's questions.

The flicker of purple lightning preceded a rumble of thunder before the pitter patter of rain drops could be heard falling from the skies above.

Water trickled down Goodwin's face and neck, but the uncomfortable sensation couldn't distract his mind from what Hilt had just said. Why has light returned to Sanctuary? What do the Pharos want? Is there something guiding their actions, and who – or what – knew they were here?

A fluorescent shimmer caught Goodwin's eye, momentarily distracting him from his deliberations. A beautiful butterfly fluttered through the air towards him as it sought shelter from the cloudburst. He held out his hand and the creature landed on his palm while it's tiny red and blue wings vibrated and shook from the impact of the continuing fall of rain. Goodwin considered the tiny creature for a moment before moving his other hand to shield it from the growing storm.

As the ceiling's lightshow finally ended, Goodwin looked up through the clouds to see starlight constellations twinkling high above on the chamber's ceiling. And in the distance, hovering over the abandoned city, the white glow of an artificial moon hung in suspended animation. The long dead Anakim architects had designed Sanctuary not only to stand the test of time, but to replicate the surface above in all its splendour.

'And God said, "*Let there be light*", and there was light,' Goodwin murmured.

'And God saw that the light was good,' Hilt said. 'Revelations, chapter one, verse four.'

Goodwin looked up at the Darklight leader, who was watching Susan as she held her arms aloft while a small host of luminous butterflies swarmed above her head.

The certainty with which Hilt had quoted the scripture and its location was a revelation in itself. Goodwin was surprised, shocked even. He wondered how much more of the text the Darklight man knew.

'And God separated the light from the darkness,' Goodwin said, 'God called the light Day—'

'—and the darkness he called Night.' Hilt looked at him, his expression full of shared understanding.

'And there was evening and there was morning,' Goodwin said, his heart lifting, 'the first day.'

'And tomorrow will be our first day,' Hilt said, 'the first of many.'

'They know we're down here, now,' Goodwin said. 'Sanctuary's generals, Terra Force ... Joiner. Whatever else, we know that much, *they* really do know we're here.'

Hilt nodded. 'As do the Pharos.'

'And they'll be back.' Goodwin felt his spirit falter as the rain eased. 'They might *all* be back.'

'They might, and if they do return ...' – Hilt's face darkened – 'we'll be waiting.' He reached out to remove Goodwin's hand from its protective duty and the butterfly he'd been sheltering flew up into clearing skies.

The beautiful, glowing insect flitted away to join its siblings as they headed towards the distant gleam of the Anakim city. And as Goodwin stood there gazing out at the fantastical vision of the underground world, he wondered what they should do next. He wondered how he could continue to protect those under his care and how he could answer the confounding riddles posed by circumstance and the immense structure that continued to hold them hostage within its endless halls.

The greatest wonder the world had ever seen was thrust into illumination once more, as it had been when the mighty Anakim had once strode the Earth, eons past. At least part of their ancient realm had been resurrected and regardless of what happened next, Goodwin knew the darkness may have been vanquished for now, but the days ahead were still fraught with peril.

The questions remained. Was Goodwin's mind still his own? What did the Pharos want? Why had the light returned? No one knew, but one thing was for certain, Sanctuary, the once eternal domain of darkness, the most majestic of ancient structures on Earth, would never be the same again.

CHAPTER SEVENTY

AS THE STORM retreated into the distance two lone men, the deposed Director of USSB Steadfast, Richard Goodwin, and the indomitable figure of the Darklight leader, Commander Hilt, made their way back to camp. But as they reached a rise, they paused and looked back the way they'd come.

'Susan,' Goodwin said, 'Susan, come on, this way!'

Further down the beach, the small woman remained deep in concentration as she placed down a final stone before rising and running to catch up.

Left on the ground behind her, positioned in near perfect formation, was the outline of a symbol made out of pebbles, a symbol of forgotten origins and one – had Goodwin seen it – that would have sent a shiver of warning coursing down his spine. Comprising a five pointed star and a surrounding circle, it was a symbol loaded with both human and Anakim meaning ... the symbol of an inverted pentagram.

SYMBOL

CHAPTER SEVENTY-ONE

'SIR, the second expedition should be two days' hike away from our location. Shall we rest up and rendezvous with them here?'

The Terra Force commando, Major Delph Armstrong, turned to his lieutenant before looking up at the twinkling stars on the ceiling of the cave system they now traversed. 'No, we wait for daybreak and then head back to base.'

'Daybreak?'

Armstrong gestured towards the roof of the cave. 'We've had a sunrise and sunset on the last two days; do you think it's going to change now?'

The lieutenant peered up at the strange, but welcome, phenomena. 'It's not really the sun though, is it, Major? More like a brightening light.'

'I don't care what it's *like*, all I know is it's better than the pitch-black.' Armstrong stowed his weapon on his back-plate and looked behind. A few thousand Special Forces soldiers wound their way through a long system of tunnels as they retraced their steps to USSB Sanctuary. Ever since their encounter with the Darklight mercenaries and the three lights – the things the assassins had referred to as Pharos – the mission had imploded. They hadn't been expecting a war, no one had. They were there for one thing and one thing only: the capture of Sarah Morgan and the retrieval of the stolen artefacts. And even though they were trained to expect the unexpected, the three phantom lights had struck fear into the hearts of all but the stupid or psychopathic.

Armstrong signalled a halt and the column of soldiers slowed their forced march to a stop. 'Send out the scouts, I want the way ahead secured. I don't want any more surprises.'

'The Pharos?' The lieutenant grasped his rifle tighter. 'Sir, what are they? Some are saying they're some kind of guardians of Sanctuary.'

Armstrong stared into a dark tunnel where the ceiling had failed to activate. Its sinister blackness seemed worse now that the rest of the area sparkled with simulated stars. 'I don't know what they are,' he said, 'I just never want to see one again.' A memory of screaming, dying men flashed into his mind before a whisper of movement made him reach for his weapon.

'I'm afraid, Major,' said a chilling voice that made Armstrong freeze in place, 'on that score, you're going to be disappointed.'

♦

The tall figure of Ophion Nexus emerged from the darkness. The camouflage on his armour shimmered back to gleaming chrome and the Terra Force commandos relaxed their guard a fraction.

'I thought you were all dead,' Armstrong said, gesturing for his lieutenant to lower his rifle.

Ophion raised his visor. 'The weak always doubt the strong.'

'And the arrogant are the first to die,' Armstrong said, riled.

Ophion glanced down at his left side where his armour had been breached. 'I came close to glory,' he said, 'but death still eludes my skill.'

'Shouldn't that be the other way round?' said Armstrong's lieutenant.

Ophion turned his measured gaze upon the man who'd spoken before returning it to Armstrong. 'Get your men back up, Major, our objectives are unmet.'

'What are you talking about? The mission's a bust, or haven't you realised? The rest of your team is gone, a third of our force is dead, captured or injured, and Sarah Morgan is under a thousand feet of water. If you think we're going anywhere but back to base you need your head read.'

Ophion moved closer. 'Your assessment is flawed. You will do as I say, or I will replace you with someone that will.'

Armstrong tensed at the threat before ten more assassins materialised from the gloom. He looked at the formidable array of weaponry on show and realised that discretion was the better part of valour. 'I thought you said they were two days' hike away,' Armstrong said to his lieutenant who looked suitably sheepish.

'The rest of your force is,' Ophion said, 'but S.I.L.V.E.R. are not Terra Force.' He turned his back on them to address his team. 'The target is close, last sighting three miles south, south west.'

'Do we proceed as planned?' said one of the assassins.

'Nothing has changed,' Ophion said, 'except our numbers will need replenishing when we return to the surface. The coordinates have been sent to your systems. Stay in contact, the beast will seek to isolate you.'

Without another word, the assassins melted back into the darkness as they moved to enact their leader's command.

'They told me you were trying to capture it,' Armstrong said, 'I didn't believe them.'

Ophion turned back to fix the major with his ice cool gaze. 'The Pharos are formidable opponents, but they are not without weakness. We will locate, subdue and return it to USSB Sanctuary, as ordered.'

Armstrong shook his head. 'This is madness; I want no part of it. Do you hear me? No part!'

'Insanity is a perspective of thought by which you are chained.'

Ophion reached for his sword and swung it through the air with a cutting swipe. 'Your resignation is accepted.'

Armstrong's eyes grew wide in shock and a red line of blood appeared around his neck. With a strangled sigh, the major's head slid from his body as he collapsed to the ground in a bloody heap.

The Terra Force lieutenant looked down at his decapitated superior in horror.

Ophion resealed his mirrored visor. 'You've just been promoted, soldier.' He pressed a button on his helmet and his armoured panels shimmered into the background. 'Ready your men, the hunt has only just begun.'

CHAPTER SEVENTY-TWO

SELENE DUBOIS, Deputy Governor of USSB Sanctuary's Central Bank and high ranking member of the clandestine Committee, stood to one side as Dr. Laurent inspected Malcolm Joiner's body.

'Well?' she said.

The doctor removed his fingers from the intelligence director's throat and gave a nod.

She pursed her lips. 'How long until he wakes?'

'Twenty minutes, thirty at the most.'

'Good. And the device worked? His mind has been – how did Dagmar put it – rewired?'

Dr. Laurent handed her a display screen full of data. 'Only time will tell the extent of the transformation, but yes, it appears he will be more susceptible to your control.'

'And no one else's?'

Laurent nodded. 'Yes, only to you and the other Committee members present at the time of his ordeal. The greater the pain, the stronger the bond between subject and controller and he experienced great pain. According to those readouts,' – he gestured at the device he'd given her – 'his personality will be more submissive and obedient. Parts of him will resist, but more often than not he will seek the path of least resistance.

'It is quite astounding,' the doctor continued. 'Director Sørensen's mind control techniques are cutting edge. It used to take months of intensive work to manipulate a person's mind; he's compressed that into minutes using pain as a gateway to permanently rewrite a person's psyche. It's amazing, don't you think?'

Selene murmured her agreement before handing back the screen. 'See to his arm.'

Dr. Laurent bobbed his head and moved to carry out the command.

'And yet the rest of his personality remains,' a man said. 'He will not forget this.'

Selene turned round to see two members of the Committee standing close by.

The man who had spoken waited for Selene to respond while his associate, a woman with glasses, gazed down at Joiner with calculating eyes.

'We had to find out what he knew,' Selene said, 'it was agreed.'

'And what he knows,' said the man, 'is too much. We have underestimated his resolve.'

The woman adjusted her glasses. 'And yet he still held back, even when faced with death.'

'Which is as it should be,' Selene said. 'If he is to become one of us such strength of mind is necessary.'

'His blood work is ... unexpected,' the man said.

Selene glanced at the unconscious intelligence director. 'I had my suspicions.'

'And you said nothing?'

'It was irrelevant.'

'His characteristics are very subtle,' the woman said, 'except for the obvious.'

The man nodded. 'And yet the results speak for themselves.'

The woman turned to him. 'Do you think he knows?'

'How could he?'

'Even with his ... *alterations*,' Selene said, 'if we are to keep him in check, we have to keep him close.'

'Then we are in agreement?' the man said.

The woman considered him for a moment. 'Yes.'

'We are,' Selene said, and held out her hand, palm up.

The man placed his hand on hers and said, 'From the past.'

'In the present,' the woman said, and repeated his action.

Selene bowed her head to each of them. 'To the future.'

The three members of the Committee turned to look at Malcolm Joiner's unmoving form. 'Throughout time,' they said in unison.

CHAPTER SEVENTY-THREE

A BUZZ of sound penetrated his unconscious stupor until it roused his mind into thought. *What is that?* he wondered. *What is that infernal sound?*

Malcolm Joiner opened his eyes to see Dr. Laurent wrapping a nano-cast around his broken arm using a piece of medical apparatus. Each time the buzzing device circumnavigated his forearm another layer of fibrous wrap was applied and it was this that had awoken him.

Dr. Laurent glanced up at him. 'Ah, good, you're awake, I was beginning to worry.'

Joiner frowned, his mind a hurricane of emotion. *I'm alive*, was his first thought. *Why?* was his second. He flexed his hand.

'You shouldn't experience any long-term effects from the break,' Dr. Laurent said, as he worked. 'You've been out for nearly forty minutes. I've been able to set the bone and stitch the wound. You're lucky; I've become quite proficient at such procedures.'

'Lucky?' Joiner felt like gouging the man's eyes out with a fork.

Dr. Laurent gave a nervous laugh before he glanced up to see Joiner's expression and his mirth switched to fear.

'Don't blame the poor doctor,' said a familiar voice.

Joiner swivelled his head to see Selene Dubois watching him with hooded eyes.

She walked round to stand in front of him, her heel strikes echoing throughout the grand Anakim hall. 'You're probably wondering why you're still in the land of the living.'

'It had crossed my mind.'

Selene waited as Dr. Laurent placed Joiner's arm in a sling and then, after a quick bow in her direction, he took his leave.

'We have decided,' Selene said, 'that your position and past duty requires an acknowledgement.'

Joiner flexed his arm inside its sling. 'Acknowledgement?'

'Yes, you have earned the right to ascend to the next caste within the Committee.'

'The *next* caste? I wasn't aware I was in the first.'

'You weren't,' Selene said, 'you were a fourth tier member. However, recent events have ensured your ascension to the fifth caste has been approved by the Committee.'

Joiner wondered if the injection had fried his brain as he couldn't quite believe what he was hearing. 'But before that happened, you wanted to conduct your evaluation to find out what I knew. You never had any intention of failing me.'

'Oh, we would have failed you, Director, had your answers not been forthcoming, and you would have suffered as a result before being ... disposed of. The Committee does not suffer duplicity within its ranks.'

Joiner's brow furrowed. 'I find that hard to believe.'

'Believe what you will, our actions against those beyond our walls are not indicative of the bonds within. This, in time, you will learn.'

'How many of these *castes* are there?'

'There are a variety of avenues you may take, but they all converge on the thirteenth step.'

'Thirteen? And I suppose you're on that *step*.'

'I am of the tenth caste. Only nine may hold the uppermost position.'

Joiner had heard of these exalted nine before; their number

alluded to by another Committee member. Joiner had assumed, wrongly, that the nine people at his evaluation had been they. He didn't know what was more galling, that he'd not warranted the attention of the upper echelons, or that he'd had no idea – no inkling at all – that he was already part of the Committee's order. *Be thankful you're still alive*, he thought, *the game has just swung in your favour*.

Joiner shifted in his seat. 'Do you submit all your members to torture?'

'You may hold ill will against me,' Selene said, 'understandably, but that well of emotion must be channelled elsewhere if you are to continue to rise within our ranks.'

'And if I refuse your offer?'

'And yet you will not,' Selene said, '*will you*, Director?'

The tone of her voice, and a widening intensity to her eyes as she'd spoken, made Joiner pause. *Does she really think I'll just do as she says because she's spared my life?* A memory of his torture returned and with it the voice of Selene commanding him to give up his secrets. '*You will learn to obey*,' she'd told him. '*Listen to my voice, you will obey me.*'

Joiner then recalled the white pill the nurse had given him previously and her words or warning. '*It will help*,' she'd said, '*keeping your mind your own.*'

So, he thought, *the pill really did work*. At least as far as he could tell, it had. He still felt the same in every way, his mind was no more another's than his thoughts were now. Of course, only a series of rigorous tests could find out for sure, but if it turned out he was free of their control, it meant he had the upper hand in a big way.

'Director,' Selene said, 'you don't want to refuse, do you? This is a limited time offer.'

He gave a shake of his head as if confused. 'No, of course not,' he said, playing along, 'but I'd still like to know what would happen if I declined the offer.'

'You'd remain outside of our confidence.'

Which means what? Joiner thought before his mind supplied the answer. A sudden, unexpected death when I reach the end of my usefulness.

Although, he knew this might happen regardless. At least inside I can learn more, increase my reach, understand how the Committee operates and with whom.

'If I accept,' Joiner said, 'when do I find out more? I know you seek direct control over the Subterranean Programme, but to what purpose? And what of Project Ares?'

'The time for such answers is not yet at hand.'

Joiner suppressed a surge of frustration. 'Then why admit me?'

'I understand. As Intelligence Director, and an incumbent on the GMRC's Directorate, you are used to complete control, your power is absolute. But as a member of the Committee your external position counts for nothing. You need to earn your right to ascension and the knowledge that brings, and that right will not come easily.'

Joiner tried to get his head round his newly acquired status as a self-aware member of the Committee, but after his recent ordeal he was having trouble processing his abrupt change in fortune, not least because those who'd been responsible for his mental and physical torment were now purporting to be his sworn kin.

'You must also accept,' Selene continued, 'that our goals are now aligned. We must work in harmony, not discord, or the Committee, and subsequently its members, will suffer. Commit yourself to this ethic and you will find all your problems will fade away.'

She held out her hand and helped him to his feet. 'Come, she said, 'walk with me.'

Without another word she moved towards the exit and its double doors, which swung open at her approach. Joiner weighed up his options before deciding to follow.

A moment later he'd caught up with her and they walked back through the grand atrium and into an equally immense adjoining corridor. Behind them, two armoured soldiers emerged from the shadows to accompany them at a discreet distance.

At the end of the long passage Selene stopped before a massive panel of glass that had been installed into an opening in the side of the Anakim edifice.

Joiner gazed out at a puzzling sight. Blue skies and blazing light stretched into the distance, while below the curvature of the twenty mile wide dome of USSB Sanctuary could be seen suspended beneath the immense ceiling of the chamber above. Where darkness should have reigned only the purest of lights remained and the vision made him question if what he was experiencing was actually real.

'It is curious, don't you think,' Selene said, 'that such a wonder happens now, when the world above awaits its fate in darkness?'

'I don't understand,' Joiner said, 'how is this possible?'

Selene glanced at him. 'Sanctuary has awoken, its power returned.'

'But how?'

'We don't know. Twenty-six hours ago a wave of energy was recorded passing through the chamber and the tunnels beyond. The base has been experiencing power failures ever since. Recent reports from the SED indicate the ceiling has activated throughout Sanctuary.'

'Throughout?' Joiner said in disbelief.

Selene took a step forward and pressed her hand against the glass as if trying to bring herself closer to the vista's magnificence. 'From the past,' she murmured.

Joiner frowned. The Committee member suddenly seemed human, a flash of weakness in an otherwise ironclad façade. She was exposed – vulnerable. He glanced behind at the two armed guards who watched his every move. When he turned back it was to see Selene studying him.

'It is time to decide, Director,' she said. 'We are moving through pivotal times, a new age is dawning and you can help us shape its future – *if* – you join us.'

'What changes if I agree?'

'You will be called to attend scheduled meetings and to report on the tasks allocated.'

'Tasks?'

'Think of them as ad hoc projects.'

'Like the Steadfast deception?'

'Yes, exactly,' Selene said. 'But since you facilitated USSB Steadfast's destruction, that issue has been solved and we now require a more ... *cerebral* application of your skills.'

'Such as?' he said, remaining wary.

'You mentioned the hacker was inside the GMRC's servers, we will need a full report on your findings.'

Joiner nodded. *That I can do*, he thought. 'What else?'

'This *event*,' – Selene gestured at the radiant Anakim ceiling – 'we need to know how the technology was activated and its implications for this base and those residing within.'

'I will need to maintain control of the SED.'

'Yes,' she said, 'and you will also need to liaise with Dagmar Sørensen.'

Joiner looked down at his injured arm. Sørensen, he thought, the man responsible for creating the torture device. And the man behind Project Ares, he reminded himself.

'Will that be a problem?' Selene said.

'No.' Joiner looked her in the eye. 'Not at all.'

'Good – very good. Then all that remains is that you pledge yourself to the Committee and your ascension is complete.'

'Pledge?'

Selene held out her hand palm up and reached out to take his hand and placed it atop hers, palm down.

'Repeat after me,' Selene said, 'I, Malcolm Joiner, pledge my life, heart and mind to the Committee.'

Joiner searched her face to see if she spoke in jest, but her expression was deadly serious. 'I, Malcolm Joiner,' he said, 'pledge my life, heart and mind to the Committee.'

'And I will uphold and protect the Committee's ideals, laws and tradition until the end of days.'

'And I will uphold and protect the Committee's ideals, laws and tradition until the end of days.'

'And if my pledge is broken and my word is false I will endure endless torment.'

Joiner hesitated, his eyes locked to hers. 'And if my pledge is broken and my word is false I will endure endless torment.'

'So say I,' she said.

'So say I.'

'There is no going back now, Director,' Selene said, 'your life is ours, and ours, yours. Welcome, Malcolm Joiner,' – she enclosed his hand within hers – 'to the Committee.'

CHAPTER SEVENTY-FOUR

Malcolm Joiner walked back through the halls of Tower Central as a newly pledged member of the Committee. His thoughts, understandably, were many, and after parting ways with Selene Dubois, he was led back to the atrium where the familiar figures of two men waited – much as he had – for an audience inside the great hall.

Neither man had noticed his approach, immersed as they were in conversation and facing the other way.

Joiner signalled for his armed escort to stop and the soldier, clad in his lustrous purple armour, did so without question. Joiner gave an inward smile at his new-found power and approached his prey.

'Gentleman,' he said.

Dagmar Sørensen glanced round, while the other man visibly tensed at the sound of Joiner's voice.

General Stevens turned to face him and Joiner revelled at the exquisite sight of the man's suppressed horror, which spread across his cretinous mug.

'Intelligence Director,' Dagmar said in greeting, 'how are you feeling?'

Joiner held Stevens' gaze for a moment longer, eking out the man's discomfort like fingernails down a chalkboard. He then switched his attention to the R&D director, who couldn't stop his eyes from flicking down to Joiner's sling and his injured arm within.

Joiner felt a sudden surge of fury at the unspoken recognition of his wound, but he kept his emotions ice cool. The age old adage was very true and he was a past master in refining its deliverance, and so he knew – when it came – the dish would be freezing and his revenge sublime. 'Dagmar,' he said, 'what brings you to Sanctuary?'

Sørensen raised a handkerchief to his mouth and produced a racking cough. 'I was called in to inspect the anomaly,' – he wiped away a fleck of blood – 'it was quite unexpected.'

'You mean the chamber's ceiling?'

'You've seen it?'

'Of course.' Joiner glanced up through the tower's transparent spire at the blue skies beyond. 'It's impressive.'

'These are exciting times for us all,' Dagmar said, 'isn't that so, General?'

Stevens grunted something unintelligible.

'You're probably wondering how my evaluation went.' Joiner touched his broken arm. 'The initial exchanges were quite heated, but the outcome was amicable, beneficial even.'

The hint of a smile creased Dagmar's features. 'It's good to be part of something bigger, to have your burdens released. Why fight the mind when you can just give in and obey?'

'It's funny,' Joiner said, realising the man thought he was under the thrall of his mind-altering machine, 'I feel like a great weight has been lifted; it's intoxicating.'

'I'm sure that feeling will only continue,' Dagmar said. 'The mind is a beautiful thing, analysing it is one of my greatest pleasures.'

I bet it is, Joiner thought, you pasty-faced fuck.

The towering red doors to the Anakim hall swung open and Joiner beckoned the soldier to rejoin him, a motion not lost on Stevens, who frowned.

'The Committee awaits,' Dagmar said. 'Until we meet again, Director.'

Joiner gave him the faintest of nods before looking to Stevens. 'I hope you enjoy speaking to my associates, General. Selene said she'll be with you shortly.'

'Associates?' Stevens said.

'Didn't they tell you?' Joiner smiled a malevolent smile.

'Tell me what?'

'That I'm now a fully-fledged member of the Committee.'

General Stevens' face dropped a mile while Joiner's euphoria soared.

'I'll also be operating out of the SED for the foreseeable future,' Joiner said, his expression hardening into murderous intent, 'so I expect we'll cross paths again ... very soon.' He let that information sink in as far as it would go and then waited some more before he broke the spell by walking away with his armed guard in tow.

♦

Dumbstruck, General Stevens watched until Malcolm Joiner had disappeared from sight. And there the army officer remained, his exterior frozen in shock while his interior broiled in a sea of dread.

A distant sound brought Stevens out of his trance and he glanced round to see Dagmar disappearing into the adjoining hall.

With a final look back at the empty corridor into which Joiner had previously entered, General Stevens turned and followed the R&D director into the Committee's conclave, his mind furiously seeking a way out of the prison that had become his life.

♦

Malcolm Joiner breathed a deep sigh of satisfaction as he slowed his pace to a measured stroll. *That couldn't have been more enjoyable if I'd planned it*, he thought. He touched his jaw; it still smarted from the General's sucker punch. *I'll make the bloated oaf rue the day he ever crossed me.*

Walking on through the undulating halls of the Anakim tower's crystalline interior, Joiner finally reached the human installation that would take him back down to the base's Dome level far below. Two other people waited at the elevator, an armed guard and the nurse who'd warned him about the Committee's plan to brainwash him.

A couple of minutes passed before the lift arrived and Joiner boarded, while his guide remained behind to guard the entrance alongside his armed colleague. The nurse, however – without showing any sign of recognition – joined him on the platform and a moment later they descended the tower together, safely ensconced within their glass clad transport.

A minute of silence ensued before the nurse spoke.

'I hear they've managed to get the base's power grids back up.'

Joiner glanced in her direction, but the woman remained staring out at the spectacle beyond. He followed her gaze and the interior of the great dome glided by as they continued their descent.

'The dome is still down, though,' she continued. 'It's said it might take another day to get it working again.'

Joiner despised small talk; however this woman was responsible for helping him and he couldn't help but wonder why. And that she was with him now defied the odds of chance. *Is she trying to communicate something to me? If she is*, he thought, *this is neither the time nor the place. The Committee's surveillance will be listening.*

The elevator slowed to a stop and with it so did his chance at attempting to breach the invisible divide between them. The doors slid back and Joiner moved forward, but as he did so the nurse brushed past him in a rush.

Joiner felt something heavy drop into his pocket and his hand reached in to close around his personal computer. The woman walked away down a floodlit path towards the nearest transport hub, while a retinue of black-suited intelligence agents fell into step alongside him.

'Sir,' the lead agent said, glancing at his director's injured arm, 'are you okay?'

'Why wouldn't I be, agent?' Joiner held out his hand and the man passed him a set of snap-on shades, which he attached to his spectacles.

'We lost contact with you at the SED. Agent Myers was shot and Grant Debden was found dead soon after. We had the entire office out searching for you when the whole power grid went down. We feared it was some kind of terrorist attack.'

'Your inability to locate my whereabouts will be reviewed,' Joiner said, 'but for now just take me back to my office. I've had a stressful couple of weeks.'

The agent opened the door to a blacked out SUV. Joiner climbed in and eased himself into comfort. The door closed behind him with a soft thud and seconds later the five-strong motorcade was speeding through the streets of USSB Sanctuary towards the GMRC Command Complex.

Joiner settled into his seat and allowed his head to sink back onto the headrest. He was back in his world, surrounded by armed agents and shielded within a bulletproof cage of steel and glass. He closed his eyes and realised it was good to be home. *It's good to be me.*

The soft scent of the leather interior caressed his senses while the directionless motion induced by the car lulled him towards sleep. But before the hands of slumber could enclose him in its welcome embrace, a subtle pain made itself known at the base of his skull. The throbbing annoyance grew stronger as he concentrated on it and then he remembered his personal computer. No doubt he would have a thousand messages waiting to be read. And since Debden had selfishly died, it would be up to him to vet his replacement. He heaved a sigh and reached down to extract the device.

He frowned and raised his shades. The display screen was already unlocked; the complex web of biometrics, passwords and inbuilt artificial intelligence having somehow been breached. He accessed the security guardian and a digitised, metallic face appeared on-screen.

'Hello, Director,' the A.I. said in a bland voice, 'how can I be of assistance?'

'This device has been hacked. Why are there no warnings?'

The simulated face feigned a look of surprise before it disappeared to be replaced by a flashing message:

SYSTEM DIAGNOSTIC
<SCANNING>

A moment later the face reappeared. 'You are correct, Director. This device was breached three hours, twenty-seven minutes and three seconds ago. Preliminary scans indicate high level decryption software was utilised.'

'Source?'

'Unknown. Although I have determined the attack originated from a large scale quantum array.'

'What's been accessed?'

'Your schedules, files and correspondence are all secure. No data has been downloaded or accessed.'

'None at all?'

The A.I.'s expression became confused. 'No, Director, none.'

'Then what was the target of the attack – software?'

'On further analysis there appears to be only one abnormality detected.'

'And what's that?'

'A line of code has been inserted into the operating system shell. It has been designed to activate at a specific set of coordinates located in USSB Sanctuary.'

Joiner leaned forward in concern. 'Show me.'

A three dimensional map of the base appeared and the view zoomed in to a series of interconnecting roads.

'Overlay our location.'

A moving red dot appeared on-screen showing the motorcade heading straight for the coordinates. Joiner's eyes widened and he looked up to see an intersection looming large.

He slammed down the intercom. 'STOP THE CAR!'

But it was too late; his computer beeped and the first SUV exploded into the air. The second SUV barrelled into the falling wreck and Joiner's vision filled with the fireball. His driver swerved. Men shouted, brakes screeched, and they went airborne.

CHAPTER SEVENTY-FIVE

MALCOLM JOINER'S SUV spiralled through the air before slamming down on its side. Glass exploded, safety foam deployed and the vehicle ploughed into an oncoming lorry. The front end disappeared in twisted steel and they were thrust backwards in a shower of sparks and flame. An instant later the motion ceased and Joiner tried to clear his disorientation with a shake of the head. He was upside down, and he rolled onto his front as smoke filled the cabin. He saw a way out through the smashed rear window and crawled forward to escape the building heat, and emerged into fresh air. The sound of the car's electric engine whined loudly while its wheels spun without traction. Joiner leaned against the rear bumper as his head swam.

The first two SUV's continued to burn, while the two that had been following Joiner's had skidded to a stop behind. Intelligence agents swarmed out, guns raised, and shouted commands as they ran towards him.

'Sir,' one said, grabbing his arm, 'this way!'

Joiner was dragged towards the nearest vehicle before automatic gunfire exploded all around and the man who'd been guiding him dropped to the ground, dead.

Joiner staggered towards the open door of the SUV as his agents were gunned down all around. He turned back to see armoured Terra Force soldiers bearing down on him.

Realising there was no escape; Joiner stood his ground as the lead man approached, and two Humvees skidded to a halt behind.

'Malcolm Joiner.' The soldier grasped his arm. 'Get in.'

Joiner was forced into the back of one of the vehicles while the military squad piled in around him. Wheels spun and the two Humvees sped off into the night.

The front passenger removed his helmet and pointed to the driver. 'Down there!'

'Who sent you?' Joiner said. 'General Stevens, the Committee?'

The man glanced round. 'Jesus Christ, cover his head!'

A rough sack was pulled down over Joiner's eyes and the man spoke again.

'He's fucking seen me now, you idiot!'

'Don't worry,' another man said, 'he'll never remember what you look like.'

'He's the goddamn Intelligence Director; of course he'll fucking remember! Check him for devices.'

Rough hands searched him. They removed his computer and multi-function card, then ran a device over his body. 'He's clean.'

'Good,' said the man in the passenger seat, 'let's get this done.'

Joiner remained quiet, listening, but the conversation failed to continue and he had to endure an ominous silence for a further twenty minutes before they drew to stop and he was forced out and down some steps. Doors opened and closed, more steps came and went and the air grew cool. Armoured hands guided him to a chair, where his cloth mask was removed.

Joiner blinked in the half-light. He sat at a table inside a dingy refrigeration room stacked high with plastic crates. Before him, a single Terra Force soldier stood in silent sentry, while another entered the room from behind.

The newcomer sat down in the chair opposite and Joiner noticed both he and his comrade had removed the identifying marks on their armour. *If General Stevens is behind this*, he thought, *he's covering his tracks*.

The soldier opened the lower half of his helmet's mask and dialled a number into a military handset, which he then held to his ear. Joiner recognised him as the man he'd glimpsed inside the Humvee.

'Yes, it's done,' the soldier said, 'it was as you said, they were easy pickings.'

He paused as the person on the other end spoke.

'How long until extraction?' he said, and waited again before nodding.

He slid the device across to Joiner and stood up and – along with the other soldier – left the room, the latter leaving the door ajar.

Joiner glanced around. He was alone and unrestrained. The door was left open and he was unhurt. *What is going on?*

He looked down at the handset and reached out to put it to his ear. No sound came from the other end, but Joiner knew the difference between an absence of noise and the faint whisper of static.

'Who is this?' he said.

'Malcolm Joiner?' said a deep, distorted voice.

'I said, who is this?'

'Who I am is irrelevant, Director. What I know is not.'

'If you know who I am,' Joiner said, 'then you also know I can bring the might of the entire GMRC down on your head. There is nowhere – *nowhere* – you can hide from me.'

'There is and I will. You will not find me or those I work for. But we can find you and it is down to us that you are still of sound mind.'

Joiner's thoughts returned to the nurse and the magic pill she'd provided. 'Explain.'

'The woman you met in Tower Central, she gave you something before your evaluation. Did you take it?'

Joiner didn't reply. It was a leading question. If he revealed what it was he'd taken, then he'd just given them the answer. 'Something?'

'The pill, a small white capsule designed to protect your mind from those that sought to control it.'

'What if I did?'

'Then you are still your own man. Listen well, Director, what I am about to tell you is going to change your life.'

CHAPTER SEVENTY-SIX

MALCOLM JOINER STOOD UP, walked to the open door and peered through. 'Change my life?' he said into the handset. 'There is nothing you can possibly say to me,' – he moved out into a deserted corridor – 'that will change my life.'

'Is that so, Director?' said the disguised voice. 'What if I tell you that I am able to converse directly with the Committee any time I like? What if I was to tell them that you evaded their attempts to control you?'

'Then I'd say, what was the point in helping me in the first place?'

'The Committee still fears you, Director. They fear and need you in equal measure, which is why they have gone to such lengths to manipulate you to their cause. But if you think you are one of their number, think again. Your induction into their ranks means nothing until you reach the higher echelons; only then will you be beyond their duplicity.'

'Says the person who just had me abducted.'

'Believe what you will, Director. Just know that we can reveal your own duplicity whenever we feel like it. You will do as we say when we say it, or your secrets will come out.'

Joiner gripped the handset tighter. Do they think me some naïve agent fresh out of training? Don't they know who I am?! 'Secrets? What secrets?'

'You seek power for yourself, you always have. You want the Anakim device for yourself. You don't want to help the Committee, you want to stop them. You want to destroy their work; you want to destroy the key to Project Ares.'

Joiner moved up a flight of steps. Whoever he was talking to knew more than he'd expected; he needed to trace their signal as soon as possible. He increased the speed of his ascent. 'Who are you to know what I do and don't want?'

'We have been watching you for many years, Director. You seek to destroy the God Device. How do you think the Committee would react to seeing a video of you discussing such action with your right hand man, Agent Myers?'

Joiner opened another door and moved through an abandoned office. 'I would say you're grasping at straws.'

'Would you?' The deep voice gave a chuckle. 'You know I speak the truth. But if you want further assurance that I'm not bluffing, perhaps you would like to know where these incriminating recordings came from.'

'Fabricated, most likely,' Joiner said, emerging into fresh air. He looked around and saw he was in the industrial sector. 'The Committee will never believe a fake.'

'The recordings can be verified genuine if the proper device is used, you know that, Director. And you also know the Committee has the resources to interpret such data.'

'And where have these mysterious recordings come from?' Joiner said. The sound of a high-speed monotube could be heard in the distance and he headed in its direction.

'It may come as a surprise if I tell you your primary aide was a man of many masters.'

Joiner felt a knot of anxiety tighten his chest. 'Grant Debden is dead.'

'That he is, but before the Committee killed him he wired us the recordings of which I speak.'

Joiner reached a fork in the road and saw an information point glowing in the dark, half a mile ahead.

He had to trace this call. They'd backed him into a corner and there was only one way out: to fight. He broke into a jog.

'You know as well as I, Director, you have nowhere left to hide. Controlling others has been your stock-in-trade for decades, now the tables have turned. Your only way out is to find and kill us, but unfortunately for you that task will prove futile.'

'Then tell them,' Joiner said, 'tell the Committee! I know who their GMRC operatives are, I will eradicate them, root and branch.'

'And if you do, they will act.'

'And I will destroy them, as I will their abomination.'

'Not if you're dead, Director.'

Joiner reached the information point, put down the handset and tapped in nine one one.

A woman appeared on-screen. 'Nine one one operator, what is your emergency?'

'GMRC alert code level alpha,' Joiner said, catching his breath, 'niner five eight eight two kilo whiskey zulu, code in.'

'I'm sorry caller, that code is not recognised, what is your emergency?'

'Check again, Directorate override, GMRC alert code level alpha,' Joiner said, 'niner five eight eight two kilo whiskey zulu, code in.'

'I'm sorry, caller, our systems are down; what is your emergency?'

The sound of laughter could be heard coming from the military handset.

Joiner swore and put the device back to his ear and the voice spoke again. 'Are you there, Director?'

'So you're going to kill me if I don't play ball?' Joiner said. 'I think not. Alive, I still have potential; dead, and that promise of power has gone. I'll take my chances with the Committee and then I'll come for you.'

'You misunderstand, Director, we're not going to kill you, at least not directly.'

Joiner removed his arm from its sling and tapped a button on the information point to hang up the operator. He then accessed a messaging system to contact the GMRC switchboard.

'How are you feeling?' the voice said. 'How are the headaches?'

Joiner stopped typing. The back of his head still throbbed with a dull ache and it was the same pain he'd experienced before the car crash.

'Have you not wondered why you woke up in a hospital gown, Director?'

Joiner's heart beat faster. 'I was knocked unconscious; they kept me in for observation.'

'The device they used on your arm and mind wasn't the Committee's only play; they had a failsafe if things didn't go to plan.'

'Tell me.'

'You are partially right; you were under observation, but not for concussion. Dagmar Sørensen and Dr. Laurent conducted a delicate ... *procedure* on you during your enforced sleep.'

Joiner's grip tightened on the handset. 'Procedure?'

'Yes, they call it a Kill Switch, a small capsule placed—'

'—at the base of the skull,' Joiner said, his heart sinking. He recalled the man Agent Myers had interrogated about Project Ares and the seizure that had claimed his life. 'How is it rigged?'

'We're uncertain, but activation due to information dissemination is unlikely, given your occupation. They couldn't have you drop dead by accident. The most likely alternative is a simple explosive charge set off by a roaming signal.'

Joiner reached up a reluctant hand and touched the back of his neck. After a tentative search he found a stitched incision on the nape of his neck. He closed his eyes in despair. 'Sørensen always was old school,' he murmured.

'The Committee may have the power to end your life,' the voice said, 'but we have the power to control it. Your fate now rests in our hands. Do as we say and you get to live. Cross us, and the Committee will see fit to end your life faster than you can blink.

'What do you want?'

'What do we want? We want you to infiltrate the Committee, to feed us with information.'

'To what end?'

'To the end we desire,' said the voice. 'The life as you knew it is over, Director, you belong to us now.'

The receiver went dead and Joiner was left listening to the monotone hiss of a terminated call.

A powerful gust of wind made him look up. A drone hovered overhead and a powerful searchlight illuminated him in blazing light.

'This information point is the source of an unverified emergency call,' said a computerised voice, 'remain where you are and await the relevant authorities.'

Joiner stared unseeing at the light above while a wave of dizzy reality tore through his mind like a storm. Thoughts and long laid plans collapsed to dust and memories of forgotten impotence surged forth from a distant past.

His grip loosened and the handset slipped, clattering to the ground. The control and power had gone, but Joiner knew – perhaps better than any other – that his nightmare had only just begun.

CHAPTER SEVENTY-SEVEN

THE TIME WAS fifteen minutes later than it was before, and ten seconds before she'd question it again. The wait was unbearable! 'How long did they say, again?' Trish said. 'An hour and a half?'

Jason nodded.

'How long's it been now?'

'Just over four.'

Trish stood and paced the waiting room's white-tiled floor before walking back over to the nurses' station. '*¡¿Cuánto tiempo más?!*'

'*No mucho ahora , señorita.*'

'What did they say?' Jason said when Trish returned to his side.

'The same as the last ten times, not much longer.' She slumped forward in her seat with her head in her hands.

Jason put his arm around her shoulders and she leant into his chest for comfort, but just as they'd resigned themselves to more hours of endless worrying, a set of double doors banged open and a surgeon emerged.

Full of anxiety, Trish and Jason jumped to their feet.

The doctor said a few words to one of the nurses and then turned towards them. '*Ah, bueno*, you're still here.'

She removed her face mask and surgical gloves, dropping them into a clinical waste bin before walking towards the two friends; Trish couldn't help but notice the gloves had glistened with the sheen of blood.

She gripped Jason's arm as they waited for the news, good or bad, but the woman merely looked at them with suspicion and remained silent.

'Well?!' Trish said.

The woman blinked. 'There were complications,' she said in a rich Honduran accent. '*Su compañera* – your friend – was suffering from serious haemorrhaging throughout her body, including an intracranial bleed.'

Trish put a hand to her mouth in dismay.

'The slurring speech you mentioned was probably a sign of a stroke. We had to carry out an emergency operation after she was stabilised.'

'But she's okay now?' Jason said. 'Sarah's okay?'

The surgeon's expression remained deadpan. 'We've had to put her into an induced coma; it will be hours, maybe days, before we know if our intervention has been successful. I suggest you let us see to your wound, *señorita*,' – the surgeon gestured to Trish's bandaged arm – 'you experienced an open fracture, we will need to operate.'

Trish shook her head. 'I'm fine.'

'The anaesthetic we gave you will wear off. The wound needs to be cleaned and the bone set; if we do not do this, you risk serious complications.'

'You should do as she says.' Jason inspected his palms, which had been stitched and wrapped in gauze. 'They did a good job on my hands and ankle.'

Trish looked down at the strapping that encased his foot and lower leg. 'You didn't need surgery, though; I want to be here when she wakes up.'

'Listen to your friend,' the surgeon said, 'let us help you. Then you can get some rest and return tomorrow.'

Trish shook her head. 'We're not leaving her here alone.'

Jason nodded his agreement.

'Can we see her?' Trish said.

'No. She is in UCI, intensive care; visiting restarts in eight hours.'

'Eight hours,' Jason said, 'that's ridiculous!'

'Those are the rules, *señor*.'

'Let us see her and I'll let you operate,' Trish said.

The doctor considered her offer, glanced back at the clock and then exchanged a flurry of words with one of the nurses. She sighed and waved them forward. '*Vamos*,' she said, and moved towards the doors she'd just come through.

Relieved and anxious in equal measure, Trish and Jason followed as they were led through a series of corridors.

'Be prepared,' the surgeon said. 'You may find her condition distressing.' She stopped outside a glass wall and gestured inside.

Trish looked through the window to see a large room housing three beds and a host of medical apparatus. On the far wall, a large wallscreen displayed tables full of fluctuating numbers for each patient, along with various charts and graphs that plotted in real-time. The two beds to the left held male occupants and Trish's gaze turned to the bed directly in front, where two nurses blocked the view beyond. A moment later they moved and Sarah's stricken form emerged from the surrounding distraction. A myriad of cables and tubes fed into her body and her chest rose and fell in time with a nearby ventilator. White bandages encased the top of her head and her chest, and her hands and feet had been similarly treated.

'She looks so pale.' Trish said, holding Jason close.

'We've made her as comfortable as we can,' the surgeon said. 'She feels no pain.'

Jason reached out to touch the glass. 'And she's stable?'

'Yes, stable, but critical.'

Trish wiped away a tear. 'Can we go in?'

The surgeon shook her head and Trish went back to studying her friend as a sense of helplessness sought to overwhelm her.

'We have left the foreign object alone until she recovers consciousness and strength,' the surgeon said, 'then we will operate again.'

'Foreign object?' Jason looked confused.

'*Sí.*' The woman pointed to the right hand side of the room where a number of X-rays had been clipped to a light box.

Trish looked at the images which showed the pentagonal outline of the Anakim artefact positioned squarely on Sarah's breastbone.

'Yes, the pendant.' Jason massaged his eyes. 'Of course.'

'And you say lightning did this, *relámpago*?'

Trish nodded.

'Why?' Jason said. 'Don't you believe us?'

'Anything you can tell us, no matter how small, may help us help your friend. What you say to us, the lightning ... the necklace and melted shoes are unusual, yes. And this degree of haemorrhaging is also ... I've never heard of such an extreme case. But the cuts to her palms ... and then there is also ...'

The surgeon failed to continue, her expression uncertain.

'Also what?' Trish said.

'She has high toxicity levels, like she's been poisoned. Her immune system is attacking itself and we don't know why.'

'Poisoned,' Jason said, 'poisoned by what?'

'We don't know. The results came back inconclusive. I was hoping you might be able to tell us more.'

They shook their heads. What could they say? The truth was liable to get them taken away by men in white coats.

The surgeon reached out and touched Trish's jacket. 'Deep Reach,' she said, 'USSB Sanctuary. What are these? Your friend had the same uniform.'

Trish looked down at the emblems, then back up. She opened her mouth to speak, but nothing came out.

'It's a potholing club,' Jason said, 'united submerged subterranean ...'

'Bandits,' Trish said.

'*Potholing*, I don't know this word.'

'Caving, spelunking,' Jason said, giving Trish a look of reproach. 'We explore deep holes in the ground.'

The surgeon frowned, her expression telling them they'd failed to convince, but the uncomfortable silence ended when a nurse called her away.

'Bandits?' Jason said.

Trish turned back to look at Sarah. 'It's all I could think of.'

'She doesn't believe anything we say.'

'Would you?'

Jason murmured, 'No,' and they remained in silent vigil for a few minutes until a nurse approached them with a wheelchair.

'You better get that arm sorted,' Jason said. 'I don't think they're going to take no for an answer this time.'

'Stay here with her,' Trish said, 'I don't want her on her own.'

'What about you?'

Trish got into the wheelchair. 'I'll be fine. Promise me you'll stay here?'

He bent down and kissed her cheek. 'I promise.'

The nurse wheeled Trish away and she glanced back to see Jason watching her go, and she held his gaze until he was out of sight.

A thousand thoughts bombarded Trish's mind as she travelled through the network of corridors, but as she continued to worry about Sarah a troubling sight broke her abstraction. A couple of police officers walked towards them and one of them carried two familiar objects: hers and Jason's Deep Reach helmets. She tried recalling where she'd last seen them. *We must have left them in the foyer*, she realised, and she covered her face with her hand as the officers strode past. One of the men gave her a cursory glance, but they didn't stop. Trish made to get up, but the nurse was already pushing her through double doors. A host of medical staff bustled around her and she was forced to submit to their care. *Jason will know what to say*, she told herself as she was guided into the operating theatre, *won't he?*

CHAPTER SEVENTY-EIGHT

HOSPITAL DEL VALLE, San Pedro Sula, Honduras

Six days had passed since Trish's operation and her initial fears about the police had proved unfounded. They'd asked Jason some searching questions about the events leading up to their hospital visit, but his answers had satisfied them and they'd returned their Deep Reach helmets and left. Jason had theorised they had more important things to worry about than three injured foreigners, and Trish had decided he was probably right, especially considering the civil unrest that continued to blight the country's streets.

As soon as she'd been able, Trish had rejoined Jason and they waited together for Sarah's condition to improve. Sadly, any progress had been minimal which was why Trish found herself kneeling down inside the hospital's chapel and praying for the miracle that might never come. A numb silence hung over the small place of worship, its whitewashed walls dull in the low light that filtered through a stained glass window above. Trish was amazed any light came through at all, but during their time back in civilisation they'd learned that the dust cloud had thinned the world over.

She thanked God again for bringing them out of the dark and then sent another prayer for Sarah's recovery fluttering into the ether. So far her pleas had gone unanswered, but she took strength from Jason's encouragement. When she'd told him of her trips to the chapel she'd thought his scepticism would show through, but all he'd said was, 'I'd take a bit of divine intervention right about now.'

The muffled sound of the chapel door opening broke the cocoon of peace and Trish glanced round to see a woman enter. Small in stature, she wore the traditional garb of a Catholic nun.

Trish turned back to face the large crucifix that hung on the wall while the woman's footsteps echoed closer. The bench to her left creaked as the religious sister eased her burden. Trish closed her eyes in an attempt to regain a semblance of spiritual connection, but before she could elicit such an awakening the woman spoke.

'You pray for your friend, *señorita*?'

Trish looked round. It was unusual to be interrupted in prayer, especially by someone who should have known better. 'This is your chapel?' she said.

'*Sí*.' The woman nodded and smiled, but said no more.

Trish got to her feet; her meditative state had gone. *I'll come back later*, she thought, and left the woman to it.

She had just stepped out of the chapel when the nun slipped through the door behind her and blocked her way.

'You should leave,' she said, her eyes fervent, 'it is not safe for you here.'

Trish looked at her in confusion. 'What?'

'It is not safe, *señorita*.' She grasped Trish's hands. 'You must leave. All three of you must leave!'

'We can't leave, Sarah's in a coma in UCI.'

The woman shook her head and released her hold as a large group of people approached. Some dabbed their eyes with handkerchiefs, others cried openly, and Trish gathered from their words they had lost someone dear.

'Your friend is awake,' the nun said, then stepped back to allow the grieving family to pass between them.

'What?' Trish felt the shock of the woman's words, but she was unable to continue the conversation as the people filing into the chapel blocked the nun from view.

Seconds dragged on and when the final mourner walked past, Trish dodged round them to find that the woman had disappeared. She ducked her head inside the chapel, but the dark room offered up no sign of the religious emissary.

She frowned before remembering what the woman had said. *Sarah is awake!*

Trish set off at a run, dodging round disapproving medical staff as she made her way back to the ward.

When she got there she stopped and stared in stunned amazement at the sight before her. Sarah was sitting propped up in bed and Jason sat next to her, holding her hand.

A nurse waved her inside with a smile and Trish walked forward as if in a dream.

Jason looked up as she entered and Sarah turned her head and mustered a tired smile, and it was then that Trish knew that whatever else happened, everything was going to be okay.

CHAPTER SEVENTY-NINE

SARAH ACCEPTED a glass of water and sipped at it as Jason helped hold it to her mouth. The refreshing liquid trickled down her parched throat like a heavenly elixir, and when she'd finished, she rested her head back on her pillow in satisfied relief.

She glanced over at the bed next to her and the poor man still fighting for his life, then looked down at her own sorry state. Bandaged hands, chest and feet. *A bit more*, she thought, *and I'd look like an Egyptian mummy*. She reached up and scratched at the bandages covering her head before a nurse pulled her hand away and gave her a disapproving look. Sarah did as she was told, even though the itching on her scalp sought to drive her mad.

The nurse bustled around her seeing to this that and the other, adjusted the intravenous drip and then moved away to annoy someone else.

Sarah owed these people her life, but just lying there like the invalid she was made her want to scream. And then there was the smell, a persistent stench of disinfectant mixed with a host of other unpleasant aromas, some of which she suspected were naturally produced. *And even worse*, she thought, *some of them probably come from me*. She sighed. 'I can't stand hospitals.'

'You should count yourself lucky.' Jason yawned and then stretched. 'You've been asleep through most of it.'

'I just want to get out of here.'

'That's a good sign,' Trish said, 'and Jas is right, you should count yourself lucky. Things could have been a lot worse, they expected you to have neurological problems. And they say all your vitals are normalising too, we couldn't have hoped for better.'

'They haven't told us why the sudden change, though,' Jason said, 'even after they did all those tests and scans.'

'I don't think they know.' Trish glanced over at the nurses' station. 'Haven't you seen them, the confused looks and hushed discussions. They're surprised, I think, at how well she's doing.'

'So am I,' Jason said, and then looked at Sarah. 'You've been getting better by the hour. Give it a few days and I reckon you'll be up and about.'

Sarah shifted in her bed. She wasn't sure about a few days, she'd been conscious for half that and her body still ached all over, although she felt strangely elated. They told her it was probably the result of the morphine she'd been getting, but even so, apart from the general agony, she felt pretty great considering she'd had major surgery a week earlier. She still couldn't believe she was alive. Everything told her she should be dead, but somehow here she was. She didn't know how to explain it and perhaps she never would. Jason just told her to accept it and be thankful and she'd decided, for now, it would take too much effort to do otherwise.

When she'd first woken, recent memories had tried to assemble themselves into chronological order, but her time before the hospital remained jumbled in a blur of pain and suffering, and any thoughts of her experience underground had been locked in a fortress of self-imposed ignorance. She didn't want to process any of it, not yet ... not ever ... and so she concentrated on what mattered most – her friends, who resumed a conversation they'd been having on and off for the last twenty-four hours.

'And she said it wasn't safe?' Jason said. 'You're sure?'

'Yes,' said Trish, in exasperation, 'how many more times? She said it wasn't safe and that we should leave; that's when she told me Sarah was awake.'

'And she didn't say why?'

'No. But she meant it; you could see the fear in her eyes.'

'But no one knows we're here,' Jason said. 'Unless she meant no foreigner is safe.'

A flash of recollection made Sarah frown. 'Perhaps someone does know we're here.'

'The people that were after us, you mean?' Trish glanced round to make sure no one would overhear. 'Terra Force?'

'They're inside a base that has GMRC influence,' Jason said. 'Perhaps the GMRC are looking for us on the surface, too?'

Trish moved her chair closer. 'But how would they know we got out?'

Jason shrugged. 'Perhaps that Goodwin fella told them – if he survived.'

A memory of fire and blood sent pain lancing through Sarah's head. She grimaced and pressed the heel of her hand against her eye.

'You okay?' Jason said.

Trish reached out and touched her shoulder in concern. 'Sarah?'

The sensation subsided and Sarah gave a nod. 'I'm fine.'

'I can get the nurse,' Jason said.

Sarah shook her head. 'No, I'm okay, honestly.'

Trish sat back and gave Sarah a final look of appraisal before turning back to Jason. 'Even if Goodwin did tell them, they'd have no idea where we went.'

'Richard wouldn't rat us out,' Sarah said, 'he's not that type.'

Jason made a face. 'You hardly know him.'

'You don't have to know someone to *know* someone,' Trish said.

'Eh?'

'It's called intuition.' Sarah paused for breath as she fought to suppress the past. 'And anyway I don't mean anyone from ... down *there*.'

'Then who? Trish said.

'The militia at Copán.'

A look of realisation stole over Trish's face. 'The monument you defaced before we found Sanctuary, of course!'

'Shhh,' Jason said, as one of the nurses looked over at them, 'keep your voice down.'

Trish leaned forward in her chair. 'How could they know, though? Do you think the driver of the pick-up told them?'

'Or the helicopter pilot,' Jason said, 'who knows? It makes sense, though. We only just got away from them last time. If they've found out we're back ...'

'That was a year ago,' Trish said. 'Do you really think they'd remember?'

Jason gave her a look, a 'what do *you* think?' kind of look.

'Oh my God.' Trish put her hand to her mouth. 'The explosion, the shaped charge we used to get out. We caused loads more damage. If they were angry before, they'll be apoplectic now.'

'Then that must be it,' Jason said, 'your nun meant the militia, which means we're in trouble. They control this whole region. The police won't get in their way, no one will; if they want us, they'll just come in and haul us out.'

'Even with Sarah in recovery?' Trish said, alarmed.

'They won't care, if they want to string us up, it just makes their job easier. We're all in one place, easy pickings.'

'Then we need to think about getting Sarah out of here.'

Jason frowned. 'I know I said she could be up and about soon, but she's had brain surgery, she needs proper care. We can't drag her out on some kind of mission.'

'I'll be okay.' Sarah tried to sit up, felt dizzy and slumped back onto her pillow.

'See,' he said, gesturing at her.

'Then one of us should keep watch,' Trish said, 'while the other stays with Sarah at all times.'

'We need to find that nun,' Jason said, 'that's what we need to do.'

'You're right.' Trish stood up and moved to the door. 'Don't go anywhere,' she said, and she slipped out into the corridor and disappeared through a pair of doors.

Jason reached out and gave Sarah's hand a squeeze. 'We'll look after you.'

Sarah didn't respond. All she wanted to do was to go home and rest. *Home*, she thought, *where is that now? England, London, my flat with Mark ... Sanctuary?*

Does it matter? she wondered. Wherever that place of familiar safety might be, she knew the fickle finger of fate would have other ideas. *Doesn't it always?* she thought, as her eyelids drooped closed. It certainly seemed that way.

CHAPTER EIGHTY

'WHAT DO YOU MEAN, they don't have a nun?' Jason said. 'You spoke to her.'

Trish sat down. 'I know, but that's what they said and I asked about ten different people, from doctors to the janitor. They all said the same thing; the chapel is run by a priest who comes in at weekends.'

'Then who the hell did you speak to?'

Trish shrugged.

'And you're sure you didn't dream it?' Jason said.

Trish glared at him.

'Then she could be anyone.' Sarah looked from one of her friends to the other.

'She could have been on a flying visit,' Trish said.

'A flying nun?' Jason said with a straight face, before puffing out his cheeks. 'But she told you she ran the chapel.'

'Look I don't know what to say, that's what they said.'

'Then what do we do now?' Sarah said.

No one spoke as the nurse, who'd been seeing to the other patients in the room, walked over to check Sarah's charts.

'*Permiso*,' she said to them, 'forgive me, the *monja*, the nun you speak of, I have seen her.'

'You have?' Jason said, shocked.

'*Sí, señor*.' The nurse gave him a shy smile and then looked at Sarah. 'She left something for you, *señorita*.'

'For me?'

'*Sí*, she told me to give it to you when you were feeling better. Shall I get it for you?'

Sarah nodded and the nurse left the room while the three friends waited for her return in confused anticipation.

The nurse came back and placed a small padded envelope on the bed.

'And she said nothing else?' Sarah said.

The nurse shook her head and moved away.

'*¡Gracias!*' Jason called out, making the woman blush.

'Open it, then,' Trish said.

Sarah picked up the package and tore it open, then upended it onto the bed.

A small black rectangle fell out and Sarah, feeling tired after her brief exertion, just stared at it.

'It's a car key,' Jason said, picking it up, 'and an old one by the look of it.'

Trish reached out to look inside the envelope. 'There's a message.' She pulled out a piece of folded paper and offered it to Sarah.

'You read it,' Sarah said.

Trish opened it out. 'It's in Spanish,' she said, concentrating. 'Follow the map and for ... I'm not sure what this means ... follow the map for – no – *to find* safe haven.'

'Safe haven,' Jason said, 'what else does it say?'

Trish turned the paper over. 'That's it.'

'What?'

'What map?' Sarah said, confused.

'Perhaps it's in the car.' Trish passed the paper to Jason.

'If there's a car,' Sarah said.

'My turn.' Jason got up and made to leave.

'Where are you going?' Trish said.

'To look for the vehicle that goes with this key. That woman, nun, or whoever she is, would have left it close by if she wanted us to find it.'

Before Sarah or Trish could voice their concerns Jason was out the door and giving them a parting wave through the glass partition before disappearing from view.

'Idiot,' Trish said. 'It could be a trap for all he knows.'

'Who'd want to trap us?' Sarah said. 'No one knows we're here.'

'Someone would trap us for that thing in your chest.'

Sarah looked down at the bandage masking the offending object and reached down to touch it.

'And apparently the militia know we're here,' Trish continued, 'and sooner or later we're going to have to accept the GMRC or whoever wants that pendant will come after us again, unless we can stay off their radar, which, all things considered, will be pretty difficult, if not impossible.'

'Not if we stay in central or southern America,' Sarah said, 'or China, maybe.'

Trish didn't look convinced, perhaps because civil wars still raged in the south and to get to China without detection would be a mission in itself.

Thoughts of what they needed to do next circled Sarah's mind and she willed them away. It was still too soon. Everything was too soon. She closed her eyes again to clear her mind and before she knew it she'd drifted back into the arms of sleep.

♦

Sarah awoke the next day to find Trish and Jason discussing something that lay on her bed. She looked around at an unfamiliar room. 'Where are we?'

Trish looked up and gave her a smile. 'Morning, sleepy head.'

'The doctor had you moved to this recovery room,' Jason said. 'They needed the space in UCI for someone else.'

'We thought you'd wake up when they moved your bed, but you obviously needed the sleep.' Trish held up a map. 'Jason found something.'

'It was in a beat up old car parked in a side street next to the hospital,' he said. 'It works, too. The car, I mean, I gave it a quick run round.'

Sarah sat up and saw a tray laden with food on a trolley next to her. She'd never felt so ravenous. She pulled it onto her lap and attacked it with a vengeance.

'There's a route marked on it,' Trish said, showing her the map as she ate. 'It directs us to a house on the outskirts of a small village in southern Honduras. It looks remote, so it might be beyond militia and GMRC control.'

'You think we should go?' Sarah said, between mouthfuls.

'What other choices do we have? We don't have our passports, money, or anything else for that matter.'

'We do have money,' Jason said, 'I forgot to say; I found this in the door pocket.' He held up a wadge of well-used notes.

Trish gave him a stern look of disapproval and held out her hand. He passed her the cash and gave Sarah a wink.

'There's quite a bit here,' Trish said, counting out the money, 'enough to see us good for a few months.'

'So this mysterious nun really is looking out for us?' Jason said.

'Looks that way.'

'So do we follow the map or not?'

Trish looked at Sarah. 'What do you think?'

She gave a shrug and continued eating as her friends discussed what to do.

After much debate and a few arguments, it was eventually decided that following the map was a bad idea. Who knew what awaited them at the other end? They had money now and their destiny was their own and, until Sarah had been released from hospital, they would take it in turns to watch the building's entrance for signs of any militia activity.

And so that's what they did. The days came and went, Sarah's strength returned, and there were no signs of armed men swarming into the building. The warning from God's vanishing messenger had been false, although there was always a nagging doubt at the backs of their minds that maybe it wasn't the militia they should be worried about. And that reservation grew bigger and stronger until they reached the tenth day, a day before Sarah was due to have an operation to remove the pendant from her chest.

It was lunchtime and Sarah was watching TV and enjoying her last meal before she was nil by mouth. Jason had just returned from his stint as lookout down in the lobby and stirred Trish awake from a deep sleep.

'Your turn,' he said, shaking her shoulder.

Trish groaned and opened her eyes. 'So soon?'

'I can go back down if you want?'

Trish rubbed her face and sighed. 'No, it's okay, I'll do it.'

Sarah offered Trish a drink of water before turning her attention back to the ancient television that hung on the wall and the Honduran news channel that streamed on it. She broke off another piece of bread and popped it in her mouth before almost choking on it.

She pointed at the TV in horror.

There on-screen, as plain as day, was a reporter speaking into the camera outside a familiar set of Mayan ruins.

Seeing the source of Sarah's reaction, Trish stood and turned up the sound.

The reporter spoke in Spanish, but Sarah got the gist of the broadcast and the images told them all they needed to know. In the bottom right corner was the caption:

DESTRUCCIÓN
EN COPÁN RUINAS!

'What are they saying?' Jason said, anxious.

'They say the site has been vandalised,' Trish said, 'desecrated by outsiders.'

An image of the area where they'd blasted the hole was shown.

'They're saying they think it's the same people who destroyed another monument last year.' Trish sat down on Sarah's bed as crude photofits of three people appeared.

'Is that meant to be us?' Jason said.

They all looked round as the door to the room opened and a nurse walked in.

Jason jumped up and switched off the screen.

The nurse didn't seem to notice their discomfort; instead she swapped out Sarah's empty water jug for a full one, checked the monitoring equipment and a nearby chart and then felt Sarah's pulse. Satisfied, she mentioned something in Spanish about the doctor coming by later and then left without another word.

Jason turned the TV back on and amazingly, or perhaps worryingly, the same story was still being broadcast. Their photofits remained on display, but shrunk to quarter size, and the reporter interviewed a man who stood in front of a small aeroplane.

'Is that who I think it is?' Trish said.

'If you think it's the helicopter pilot who brought us here,' Jason said, 'then yes, that's exactly who it is.'

A new picture came up on-screen, an image that made Sarah feel sick. It was a picture of a hospital. 'Is that this building?'

Trish nodded and Jason wiped his hand across his face. 'Jesus, I hate it when we're right.'

'Do you think you're up to leaving?' Trish said.

'I don't know; I think so.' Sarah looked at her bandages and the drip attached to her arm. 'Would I prefer to have the artefact removed? Yes. Do I want to be hung from a tree or worse? Not really.'

'Jason,' Trish said.

He didn't respond, he just stared at the screen, transfixed.

'Jason!'

He looked round.

'Are the supplies ready?' she said.

'Yep, and I put the parchments, helmets and the Mayan tablet in, too.' He pulled out their Deep Reach rucksacks from underneath Sarah's bed. 'We just need food and water.'

'Okay, go get that and I'll get Sarah ready.'

He nodded and left the room.

Trish looked at Sarah and pulled off her bedcovers. 'They said your wounds are healing well. We'll leave the bandages on and dress them again when we have more time.' Trish reached out and laid a hand on her shoulder. 'Now, are you sure you're up to this?'

Sarah looked down at the IV line inserted into the vein on her arm. Pulling off the tape, she slid the needle free and then grasped the cannula that protruded from her skin. She looked up at Trish and then at the TV where their images remained. Their choices had gone. They had to go. Taking a breath, she tensed her face and yanked the device free.

♦

Fifteen minutes later Jason returned laden with food and a five gallon bottle of water.

'Did anyone see you?' Trish said.

He shook his head. 'Turns out I'm a pretty good thief. And it's still technically the nightshift, the nurses are spread thin and the kitchen was empty. I feel bad, though, most of this stuff is for the patients.'

'Don't worry' Trish said, 'they'll have more where that came from.'

Jason dumped the keg of water on the floor and stuffed the stolen food into the bags. 'I thought you said you'd get her ready.'

Sarah looked down at her hospital issue pyjamas.

'They cut her coveralls off when she was admitted,' Trish said, and manoeuvred a wheelchair round for Sarah to get into.

'Is your arm okay to push me?' Sarah said, draping her Deep Reach jacket over her legs. 'Walking doesn't make me as dizzy as it did.'

'As long as it's not uphill it'll be fine.' Trish looked at Jason. 'You ready?'

'Hang on.' He rolled the large bottle of water over to Sarah's chair and placed it on a rack located underneath. He then picked up the bags and held open the door, but before they could leave a nurse appeared in the doorway.

She looked at Sarah in concerned confusion. '*¿Qué está haciendo?*' she said, '*¿por qué no es ella en la cama?*'

'We're taking her for a walk,' Trish said, and wheeled Sarah into the hallway.

The nurse shook her head and grasped the back of the wheelchair. 'No – no outside.'

'We asked the doctor,' Trish said, 'they said it would be okay. *Le pregunté al médico.*'

'*¿Eh?*' The nurse glanced back down the corridor.

'Go and ask her. *Ir y preguntarle.*'

The nurse hesitated, reluctant to leave Sarah's side.

'We'll wait here for you,' Trish said.

Jason nodded and smiled, and the woman let go of Sarah's chair and walked away while glancing back every now and then to make sure they were still there.

'We'll be right here!' Trish called after her.

As soon as the nurse had gone round the corner, Trish moved into action and Sarah found herself being rolled down the corridor towards the nearest elevator.

Jason trotted alongside and kept glancing back to see if they were being followed.

A minute later they were exiting the building into the hospital's car park.

'Which way?' Trish said.

Jason looked around and then pointed left. 'There, I parked it at the back.'

They moved forward again and Sarah looked up at the hazy light from the sun, which penetrated the thinning dust cloud. It looked like a perpetual dawn.

'That's it?' Trish said. 'That's not a car; it's a lawnmower on wheels!'

'Who cares, get in.' Jason dumped the rucksacks and water in the boot and then helped Trish get Sarah into the passenger seat.

A shout from behind made them look round. The nurse they'd spoken to before ran towards them, with two security guards in close attendance.

Jason slammed Sarah's door. 'Get in!' he said, and ran round to jump in the driver's seat.

Trish didn't need telling twice; she leapt into the back seat as Jason revved up the gasoline engine and then floored the accelerator. The car lurched forward and the nurse jumped out of the way as they sped out into the city streets and the freedom beyond.

CHAPTER EIGHTY-ONE

WASHINGTON D.C., USA

Over a year had passed since the asteroid AG5 impacted the Earth off the South African coastline and yet in that time, as human civilisation and the global ecosystem hovered on the brink of collapse, the impact winter's lifespan had fallen short of predictions. Even now the sun's rays beat down through hazy skies, penetrating the remnants of the once dense veil of particulates that had engulfed the planet and, not for the first time, Malcolm Joiner cursed the essence of time. The GMRC Intelligence Director gazed down at Capitol Hill and the fluttering banners of the Stars and Stripes as his black helicopter flew over the country's seat of power. Before and behind, similar twin-rotor aircraft shadowed their route while a host of military gunships patrolled their flight path's borders with unerring precision. With the world returning to a semblance of normality Joiner knew transition to the underground bases would prove more difficult. Under the cover of perpetual darkness, the final protocols would have been harder to detect by those left on the surface, but as it was, light had a tendency to expose that which the Global Meteor Response Council sought to conceal, an unfortunate trend Joiner could attest to during his many years in power. He pushed such thoughts from his mind. The GMRC would continue to execute its directives with or without his input. He had bigger problems to attend to – far bigger problems.

It had been two months since his ascension to the post of self-aware Committee member and it was also two months since he'd learned of the device in his head, primed to kill at a moment's notice. So far he'd heard nothing from the disembodied voice that had promised to make his life a misery, which was both as surprising as it was ominous. Strangely, Joiner had grown used to having his life hang in the balance. At first he'd been unable to sleep. Night after night he'd lain awake fretting over the possibility his life could be snuffed out at the whim of his enemies, but gradually he'd grown used to the prospect. He had even begun to use it to his advantage, harnessing the sense of urgency to focus his mind, and step by step, day by day, he'd mastered his suffering.

Apart from his woes, life in Sanctuary had returned to normal once the dome's sunlight generators had resumed function. Weather patterns had been reformed and the only problem now was that the dome was considered obsolete, as outside the massive structure the Anakim chamber and its incredible ceiling remained in a continual cycle of night and day. And added to this marvel of ancient design was the presence of weather systems that eclipsed those created inside the USSB. Great storms and tranquil calms flooded through Sanctuary's ancient halls, and many engineers and scientists questioned the dome's relevance in this new era of underground survival. Some even suggested dismantling the human structure in favour of the Anakim. Even Joiner had to admit, despite his continued distractions, that those people had a point. But the powers that be, which meant the military fraternity and their hidden puppet masters, the Committee, decided that it was still too soon to defer to a technology over which they had no control, and so the status quo remained.

As to the Committee itself, Joiner didn't class himself as a bona fide member. The voice had been right about his supposed newfound brethren; the meetings he'd attended were second-rate wastes of his time. No power was to be gained by his attendance and no information he didn't already know had been divulged.

He glanced to his right where six bodyguards sat in silent sentry, guns primed and grey armour glinting. No longer did he rely on his reputation and exalted position to keep him safe; everywhere he went, they went. They were the best of the best, handpicked elite operatives from within the enormous wealth of human resource that the Intelligence Division could draw upon. And it didn't stop at a half dozen men, his vast retinue now made the U.S. President's look like amateur hour. Joiner was not about to let lightning strike a third time. That someone had even dared attempt to abduct him had been bad enough, that it had happened twice and with such ease was beyond the pale. And while one of the perpetrators, the Committee, had not shied away from disclosing its identity, the other had not been so forthcoming. What was more, that hidden threat continued to evade his attempts at hunting them down. It was as if they'd never existed.

So far the Committee remained interested in, but strangely unconcerned about, the whole affair. At first Joiner had wondered if they'd had a hand in the attack on his motorcade, a double bluff worthy of the name. But as much as he wanted to find an answer, he knew that possibility was slim to none. He'd decided, however, that there was no way they'd compromise their own position of superiority, unless, of course, it was someone working against the Committee from within.

A growing sense of frustration forced a noise of discontent from Joiner's lips and one of the soldiers glanced in his direction before resuming their vigil.

The sound from the helicopter's giant blades continued to pulse through the cabin and the flying procession veered left past the Egyptian-inspired obelisk that was the Washington Monument and away from The White House beyond it. Turning south, they sank lower to skim across the waters of the Washington Channel, the reflection of the black aircraft rippling on the surface before they regained altitude as they neared their destination.

Joiner pressed a button on his armrest and a transparent screen extended down from the ceiling. A holographic computer display blazed to life and a rotating image appeared depicting a man in Special Forces armour. Adjoining this 3D creation was a long and detailed service record that spooled down the screen behind. Above the text were the words:

COLONEL SAMSON
United States Army
Special Forces Subterranean Detachment
Brigade Commander

And across the moving image were three large, red letters:

M.I.A.

Joiner accessed the file and selected a field in the data's admin list. A tick appeared in the relevant box and two new words blinked into existence:

Presumed Dead

Joiner hit a button on his keyboard and sealed the file into the GMRC archive.

That Samson had not returned from his mission was a welcome relief. That he'd failed in his duty was not. When the expeditions had returned to base some three weeks after they'd left, Joiner had received the news immediately from his agents stationed at the SED. Neither the pendant nor the mysterious orb had been retrieved. As for Sarah Morgan herself, she and her friends had fallen victim to a devastating blast that had destroyed what was said to be an archaeological wonder of the highest order. Joiner had seen Ophion's subsequent report, such as it was. Large swathes had been redacted by the Committee's overly exuberant administrator – whoever that might be. So what was the result of the massively expensive exercise? The mission had failed in its entirety – although one good thing had come of it: Samson's demise. The colonel's knowledge of the pendant, the Anakim, Sanctuary itself and the asteroids was beyond unacceptable. In the hands of a rational mind the information was bad enough, but in the hands of a lunatic, who knew what chaos could be caused.

But with one problem solved another emerged. And with the pendant gone, so had the Committee's chances of furthering their mastery of Anakim technology. Joiner's summons to Tower Central had been swift and his dressing down complete. He had, of course, fought his corner with vigour. He had no love for the people who'd implanted the device in his head. And yet despite the failure, his position within the organisation's secret ranks served one useful purpose, it kept him alive. And as Selene Dubois had so eloquently put it, such a privilege was an opportunity ripe for redemption.

The memory of their meeting reminded Joiner of his surprise when he'd learnt that Richard Goodwin and his Darklight mercenaries were alive and well, scratching out an existence in the hidden depths. He'd presumed, like many others, that the ousted director of Steadfast and his merry band had long since succumbed to the unforgiving landscape that was Sanctuary Proper. How they'd survived for so long was a mystery, but whatever the method, they continued to pose a threat to Joiner, the Committee and the USSB itself. They would, at some point, have to be dealt with. If nothing else, the Committee was keen to investigate the massive underground city that Goodwin now called home. And whatever Joiner might have been told, or not as the case may be, he knew that whatever had caused Sanctuary's ceiling to activate most likely originated from that location. And if he was to determine the true source, as the Committee desired, he would at some point need to find out more, much more.

Inevitably, Joiner's thoughts returned to the most pressing matter that required his attention. If he was to regain control of his life he needed help, and that meant he needed someone he could rely on and trust. It had been some time before he'd even considered asking the question that needed to be asked, but when it had come and the answer had been yes, then he knew what he had to do. Most would have not even considered the course of action he was about to undertake. They would say when your bridges were burnt, that was it, there was no going back, but Joiner knew what it took to convince a person even when everything was stacked against him. And this time was no different ... at least, that was his hope.

A red light flashed on a communication headset that hung from the ceiling and Joiner powered off the computer and placed one of the headphones to his ear.

'Sir, we've reached our destination,' said the pilot.

'And you're telling me this, why?' Joiner said, irritated. 'Set us down.'

'That's the problem, sir, there seems to be a game in progress.'

Joiner peered out of his window to see a crowded stadium below and forty thousand pairs of eyes staring up at the helicopters that now circled the skies above. Nationals Park baseball stadium was home to a Major League Baseball franchise, the Washington Nationals. Joiner hadn't considered the facility might have been in use. Why would he? He went where he wanted and did what he liked.

The pitcher and the rest of the players stared up at the intrusion; many had the audacity to wave them away and a couple produced obscene gestures, one of them being the coach.

Joiner gave a sniff of disinterest and put the microphone back to his mouth. 'They'll move.'

'Sir?'

'You heard me, pilot.' Joiner hung the headset back on its hook and turned to his subordinate. 'Lock it down.'

The man nodded and gave the order to jam all communications. A second later all local transmissions failed and worldwide TV audiences suddenly experienced a ubiquitous on-screen message that read: 'No signal.'

The roar of the helicopter's jet engines increased and the baseball players scattered for cover, much to Joiner's satisfaction.

His helicopter landed on the field soon after, with five more craft landing in quick succession.

Joiner's door slid open and he stepped out of his GMRC transport and down onto the specially cultivated grass of the pitch.

Armed GMRC soldiers fanned out before him while the U.S. Army gunships continued to patrol the airspace above.

As the noise from his landed aircraft died down, Joiner could hear catcalls and boos ringing out around the stadium. *Like I care*, he thought and flipped down his sunshades, *these idiots will all be ash and bone within the year*. He strode forward with his armed escort as protection and made his way up to the stands, where his men cleared a way through those gathered with brutal efficiency. The crowd turned ugly, bottles were thrown, and Joiner ducked as one whistled past his head.

Joiner gestured to his closest agent. 'Show these peasants some manners.'

The operative gave a nod, cocked his weapon and fired a shot into the air. More gunshots rang out as Joiner's soldiers sent people scrambling back in panic.

Joiner surveyed the scene and saw that his heavy-handed tactics had also served to isolate the man he sought. He moved towards the lone person sitting still in a sea of rapidly emptying seats.

A moment later Joiner eased himself down onto one of the chairs and sat staring out at his helicopters, which adorned the field of play.

The man next to him stayed silent and Joiner decided to speak first.

'You're probably asking yourself why I'm here.'

There was no response.

'I'm putting together a special taskforce,' Joiner said, undeterred.

'I need you to lead it. It'll mean longer hours; triple your previous pay and a slew of benefits you wouldn't believe.'

Silence ensued and both men remained looking straight ahead as the uncomfortable atmosphere increased.

'We both know retirement isn't for men like us,' Joiner said, 'we live to work, to make things happen, to make a difference.' He gestured at the milling baseball fans. 'We aren't built to live amongst the herd, to play by the rules. Come back into the fold and your life will mean something again.' Joiner glanced left. 'Accept my offer and I guarantee you'll be shaping not just the future of our country, but of the whole world.'

The man crossed his arms and sat stony-faced.

'What do you say?' Joiner said.

'I asked for one thing,' Agent Myers said, 'that I be allowed to live on the surface in peace before relocating to New York.' He turned to face Joiner. 'And you couldn't even give me that, could you?'

'You're bitter,' Joiner said. 'I understand.'

'Do you? I give you the best years of my career and unflinching loyalty and you repay me with what? A bullet to the gut.'

'I won't apologise for my actions,' Joiner said.

Myers gave a snort of disbelief.

'But – BUT,' Joiner said, 'I will admit to misreading the situation. Debden was the leak.' Joiner removed his glasses. 'I should have seen it, the man was always too keen. Did you notice?'

Unimpressed, Myers didn't answer and Joiner allowed the agent his moment of control.

'And that's it?' Myers said, when Joiner failed to continue. 'That's your pitch? That's what I get, no apology and a pay rise?' He gave a shake of his head. 'You've got some nerve.'

Joiner motioned to one of his armoured agents. 'Nerve has nothing to do with it,' he said, accepting a steel briefcase. 'I need you; it's as simple as that.'

'And you thought I'd just come running?' Myers said. 'When I got your message that you wanted me back on duty, I had to know, what could possess a man to ask such a question of someone he'd tried to kill?'

'I didn't try to kill you, I meant to wound. My aim was off. But I had to know if you were the leak and I had to force Stevens into fessing up. It was my only option.'

'Your only option?'

'Look,' Joiner said, keeping up the pretence, 'I realise I was wrong, but you know as well as I there are more pressing matters than your grudge. But if you need me to apologise, I do so, unreservedly.'

Myers expression remained fixed in a glowering mask of distrust.

Joiner gestured at the grey-clad intelligence operatives that patrolled the area. 'Look around you,' he said, 'armoured agents inside our own borders. I take it you noticed?'

Myers glanced at the menacing figures. 'How could I not?'

'Then you should know that even back at Sanctuary, the securest facility on the planet, we have factions arrayed against us, factions that should not exist.'

'I heard about the abduction.'

'Then you will know that the game has changed. All bets are off. The world is changing, old alliances are collapsing and new ones rise. If the GMRC and our country is to survive we must adapt, we must react. The information you uncovered about the secret organisations operating inside the GMRC was invaluable, but what I didn't tell you at the time was that I've been trying to infiltrate one of these organisations for decades.'

Myers looked at him and Joiner refrained from smiling. *I'm getting to him.* He popped open the catches on his briefcase and withdrew a printed image of an X-ray and held it out to Myers.

'Look at it,' Joiner said.

Myers flicked his eyes in its direction.

'Do you see the device,' – Joiner pointed to a spot on the photo – 'next to the brainstem?'

'Who is it, another mark for termination?'

'The X-ray is mine.'

Myers face registered a look of shock and he couldn't stop himself from taking the image to inspect further.

'Do you see now why I'm here? I've been compromised. My position at the GMRC is under threat, and without me our government will have even less influence over global affairs than it already does.'

Myers continued to study the X-ray. 'Can it be removed?'

'Without damage? Unlikely; Sørensen was behind the procedure.'

'Then it's not just your tenure at the GMRC that's at stake,' – Myers passed the image back to him – 'but your position as U.S. Intelligence Director as well.'

'And that's why I'm here. I can't do this alone. I need someone to mask my movements, to outthink those that seek to control me, to second-guess my decisions and to create a wall behind which I can function.' Joiner put the photo back into the case. 'I need to get this thing out of me, or at the very least disable or disrupt its activation, and I can't do that when everything is in upheaval, nor while the division is haemorrhaging information like a sieve. I need to clean house, and clean it good.'

'Then I wish you luck,' – Myers got to his feet – 'because you're going to need it.'

'You still need convincing,' Joiner said, also standing, 'after everything I've told you?'

'That you're surprised by that shows how little you know me.'

Myers walked away and Joiner saw his chance disappearing.

'Wait!' Joiner felt himself rooted to the spot. *I never follow, I always lead!* All his experience told him to stand his ground, to uphold his position of authority, but he knew if he did so now, Myers was lost and therefore so was he.

Myers stopped and looked back, his expression as guarded as ever.

Joiner continued to feel the tension of resistance before a glimpse of a disparate future made the decision for him. With his ego diverted, Joiner closed the gap between them. 'What if I tell you without your help I'll be unable to continue my duties? My next independent review is overdue, and if I'm removed from office no one will be able to stop what's to come.'

'And what's that?'

'A subversion of everything we hold dear.'

Myers' brow furrowed. 'By who?'

'They call themselves The Committee.'

'And they're responsible for sabotaging the Space Programme?'

Joiner hesitated before nodding his head.

'Who are they?' Myers said.

'A large collective of power elites operating above the law and backed by limitless funds.'

'You know their identities?'

'Some,' Joiner said, 'and you helped locate others, but most are faces without names, or names without faces or pasts. Even the ones who operate in plain sight have an untraceable history – digital and paperless dead ends. It's like they never existed. They are the ghost in the machine.'

'And you thought I was leaking information to this Committee?' Myers said.

'I did, and if you had the full picture you might understand why I reacted with such violence.'

Myers stayed silent and Joiner took it as his cue to continue. 'Do you remember why we had to remove Steiner from office?'

'You said he wanted to evacuate Steadfast against the Directorate's wishes.'

'I did. He'd become a liability and a security risk. However, it has since come to my attention that the professor may well have been working with this Committee and I believe it was they who were responsible for the Steadfast explosion.'

'You think they sabotaged the nuclear reactors?'

'It makes sense,' Joiner said, 'especially as they've also infiltrated the Directorate itself, and if Steiner hadn't escaped—'

'They would have covered their tracks,' Myers said. He shook his head. 'Jesus, can't you call an emergency summit?'

Pleased Myers continued to buy into his carefully fabricated tale,

Joiner remained grave. 'I don't have the proof, which is another reason why I need your help.'

'And it's this same Committee who possess the Anakim technology, this so-called God Device?'

'It's as we thought,' Joiner said, 'they're working with Sørensen and using the GMRC's R&D Division for their own ends.'

'Which is what?'

'I have no idea. All I know is Project Ares needs to be stopped and this God Device destroyed.'

'And that's the purpose of this special taskforce you're assembling?'

'It is, amongst other things.' Joiner could see Myers' resolve wavering. And that was always going to be his trump card. Whatever Myers thought of Joiner, whatever grudge he held against him, he knew as well as he what Ares represented; not just a threat to the United States and the GMRC, but to the whole of humanity.

'Tell me,' Myers said.

And there it is, Joiner thought, *I know him better than he cares to believe.* 'There's another faction that knows of the Committee; it was they who were responsible for my abduction. Your mission will be to seek them out, along with the hacker, *Da Muss Ich,* and Professor Steiner. You'll operate with total autonomy, zero oversight, no borders and no sanctions.'

'Budget?'

'Open book.'

Myers' pupils dilated at the thought and he held Joiner's gaze as he considered his options.

'I have three conditions,' Myers said.

'Name them.'

'One, don't expect me to respect or trust you.'

Joiner had never cared what his agents thought of him before so the concession was a given. 'Agreed.'

'Two, I want full disclosure. Everything you know, I know.'

Joiner knew that was never going to happen, but he nodded anyway. 'And three?'

'You submit to a physical exam—'

'Done.'

'And,' Myers said, 'a full psych test conducted by myself ... once a week.'

Joiner paused. Intelligence Division psychological assessments were a gruelling twelve hour slog where an agent was systematically worn down with targeted questions, sensory deprivation and enforced stress positions, all of which were sandwiched between a battery of scans and other neurological tests. They were gruelling, energy sapping affairs, as Joiner well knew – he'd helped design them. 'Monthly,' he said, 'excluding modules seven through nine.'

Myers shook his head. 'Fortnightly, excluding module seven, that's my final offer.'

Joiner waited ten seconds to make it appear he was mulling it over before holding out his hand, which Myers shook to seal the deal.

'You won't regret this,' Joiner said, as the noise from the surrounding crowd swelled louder. He reached into a pocket and handed Myers his agency I.D. and service issue sidearm.

'I already am,' Myers said. He checked the weapon, tucked it into his belt and attached the badge to his shirt. 'Just know that I'll protect you with my life, but I don't do it for you, I do it for the people we protect.'

Joiner didn't respond; he didn't care what Myers' motivation was, just that he had it. He put his glasses back on and surveyed the scene with a critical eye. A mass of sports fans remained in arm's reach of Joiner's ring of armed operatives, and many more hung further back as they waited for their pointless game to resume. *These people*, he thought, *what a waste of a life they lead, inconsequential in every way*. He didn't know how they could stand it, to be so oblivious to everything around them. *They are like sheep*, he thought, *blind, dumb, directionless sheep*. But Joiner knew there was one life that was worth living – his own – and it was long past time to reclaim it. With Myers onside and leading his new taskforce, it would surely be only a matter of time before his current predicament was turned in his favour. In fact, he couldn't envisage how it could not. He flipped down his sunshades and looked at Myers. 'Don't just stand there, Agent,' Joiner said, 'get this show back in the air.'

Myers expression switched alert and he stalked away to give out the necessary orders as if he'd never been away. Joiner watched him go with a sense of satisfaction, before his computer alerted him to an incoming call.

Joiner withdrew the device and put it to his ear. 'Yes?'

'Intelligence Director,' said a voice, its tone distorted deep, 'do you remember our last conversation?'

Joiner froze. 'How did you get this number?'

'That is the wrong question, Director,' the voice said.

'And what is the right question?'

'How am I making this call when you're jamming every signal for a half mile?'

Joiner searched his mind for an answer. 'Because you're overriding our system.'

'That's half the answer; keep going.'

Joiner suddenly realised what they were getting at. 'Because you're inside the stadium.' He whirled round to search the crowd.

The voice laughed. 'You won't find me, Director, and if you're thinking about locking everything down I'll be long gone, as will half the people in here.'

'What do you want?'

'We wanted to speak to you somewhere the Committee couldn't overhear us. We knew if we followed your agent long enough there was a chance you'd turn up, it just so happens it was later rather than sooner.'

Joiner's eyes narrowed. He hated being predictable. 'And how did you come to that conclusion?'

'Because you need all the friends you can get. Now, before you do something stupid like trying to catch me, look underneath the chair Agent Myers was sitting on. You'll find a sealed envelope. Open it.'

Joiner walked back to the seat in question, reached under and withdrew the envelope. Opening it, he pulled out a blank piece of card and a pen.

'Are you still listening, Director?' the voice said.

'Yes.'

'Then write down these numbers.'

The voice reeled out a series of digits which Joiner wrote down, but what the person behind the vocal disguise didn't know was that Joiner had opened the channel up to his security detail. Even now the helicopters above and the men below searched for the source of the call.

Joiner saw Myers pointing into the crowd and Joiner's operatives stormed forward. People screamed as the armed soldiers cut a swathe through the masses. Movement to the right caught Joiner's eye. A man pushed his way through the throng in the opposite direction to his pursuers. A moment later he emerged from the stands, leapt over a railing and ran onto the pitch. More operatives moved to block his escape and he came to a stop as the trap closed in. He put something to his ear.

'I told you not to do anything stupid, Director,' the man said, his voice still distorted.

'And I told you before; there's nowhere you can hide from me.' Joiner watched as his men bore down on their target. It was time to get some answers and he would make sure this individual suffered regardless of what he gave up. *No one controls me*, he thought, *no one!*

'Use the numbers, Director,' the man said, 'and our sight will become yours.' He held his arms aloft. '*EGO SUM REX GLORIAE!!*'

The man disappeared in a blinding fireball and a massive explosion rocked the stadium. The shockwave whooshed past with a rush of dust and Joiner staggered back.

When the air cleared, he found himself staring out at a large crater at the side of the pitch. Chunks of turf and dirt crumbled down from around its edge, while the bodies of his intelligence agents lay strewn in all directions, many of them disassembled into multiple parts. Somehow the helicopters had escaped unscathed.

'Sir,' an operative said, running up to him, 'are you hurt?!'

Still in shock, Joiner shook his head.

Agent Myers approached, gun in hand. 'We're clearing the

stadium; local emergency services are en route.' He glanced round. 'I'll issue a GMRC Alert for the media and our forensics will be here within the hour.'

'Good,' Joiner said, 'very good.'

'Do you have the numbers?'

Joiner held up the piece of white card and Myers removed it from his hand to inspect.

'It looks like a server address,' he said.

'That's because it is.' Joiner brushed a piece of dirt from his shoulder. 'And maybe an access code.'

Myers handed back the card. 'What did he shout before he went up? I didn't recognise it.'

'It was Latin. It translates something like, *I am king of glory*.'

'What does it mean?'

'It means he's a fanatic.'

'And the numbers,' Myers said, 'he said "*our sight will become yours*". Do you think the code links to a camera somewhere?'

Joiner took one last, lingering look at the carnage. Just when he thought he had these people cornered, he was left empty-handed – again. He looked down at the card. *Well,* he thought, *not completely empty-handed.*

As Myers waited for a reply that would never come, Joiner clenched his fist and crumpled the card. He was tired of reacting and defending, of the explosions and dead agents. *It's time,* he thought, *to change the game. It's time ... for action.*

CHAPTER EIGHTY-TWO

MALCOLM JOINER STRODE through the foyer of the GMRC's Washington building, with Myers and his armed operatives in close attendance. It had been some time since he'd last visited the Intelligence Division's D.C. branch and since the incident at the baseball park it was all systems go. As they emerged from the elevator agents scurried hither and thither, and the wallscreens were awash with data and footage of the stadium explosion and the terrorist at its heart.

A senior agent that Joiner knew well approached.

'Report,' Joiner said, as the woman fell into step alongside.

'Eight dead, ten more injured, three of them critical.'

'Profile?'

'We're working on tracing the terrorist's history, his route in to the stadium and his base of operations.'

Joiner stopped in front of the main wallscreen, which spanned one end of the office, and gave the agent his full attention. 'Identity?'

'We're working on it,' the woman said, her voice stressed.

Joiner withdrew his computer from a pocket and spoke into it. 'Patch me into the local speaker system.'

'Certainly, Director,' said the artificial intelligence.

A moment later a green light appeared and Joiner held the device before him like a microphone. 'Agents,' he said, his voice booming loud.

The office tumult died down and everyone paused to look in his direction.

'You know who I am, you know what I expect. I want this terrorist's movements traced to birth. I want to know what he ate, who his friends were, who he worked for, what he stood for, what he thought, where he went. All leave is cancelled, all agents recalled. You will work all night, you will sleep at your desk, and no one gets paid until I have the answers I seek. This is priority one; make it happen!'

Joiner switched off the mic and strode to his office suite, while behind him the department erupted back into organised chaos.

Joiner moved to his desk and motioned for Myers to close the door. Two armoured agents stood guard outside and Myers turned the transparent walls opaque.

Joiner dropped the piece of white card on his desk and flattened it out, then scanned the numbers into his computer. 'Identify and locate,' he said.

'Numerical values accepted,' a computerised voice said. 'Searching ...'

The office door opened and an agent handed Myers a suit of grey body armour.

'Data input verified, Director,' said the A.I. assistant.

'Put it on the wall.' Joiner turned to face the screen as the room's lights dimmed.

The display glowed into life and a central window appeared showing the numbers Joiner had written down at the terrorist's instigation.

> Server Address: 152.789.665.5.10.99

    > *VERIFIED*

> Wireless access code: 345990-888552

> *VERIFIED*

> I.P. Device
> *ACTIVE*

> Password
> *UNKNOWN*

> Access
> *DENIED*

'Password?' Myers said.

Joiner grunted. 'Computer, password input. Use all permutations and translations using the string: *Ego sum Rex Gloriae*.'

'Of course, Director,' said the A.I., 'processing ...'

Seconds ticked by before the same results displayed, except this time the final lines read:

> Password: Identified
> *REX GLORIAE*

> Access
> *GRANTED*

The image on-screen fluctuated and a message appeared:

SECURE SIGNAL REDIRECT

Joiner sat on the edge of his desk and waited as the message altered:

SOURCE VERIFIED
IDENTIFICATION: LIVE BROADCAST

'Looks like I was right,' Myers said, moving closer.

Joiner didn't reply. *What do these people want me to see?* His anticipation grew as the message changed again:

ACCESSING ...

Joiner leaned forward, his eyes boring into the screen.

ACCESSING ...

The screen darkened.

BROADCAST ACQUIRED

The image inside the window graphic flickered to life.

'What *is* that?' Myers said.

Joiner frowned. 'Zoom out.'

'Zooming out,' the computer said.

The image adjusted as it refocused and Joiner's eyes grew wide.

'Is that where I think it is?' Myers said.

'It's Sanctuary's military lab complex.' Joiner stood up. 'Dagmar Sørensen's secret playground.'

'And Project Ares' ground zero,' Myers said.

Without taking his eyes off the screen, Joiner pressed a button on his desk to lock his office door. From what he could see, the camera that streamed the image had been positioned inside a large chamber hewn out of solid rock, the exact same chamber from which Sarah Morgan had stolen the Anakim orb.

Inside this cavernous space ten self-contained laboratories dominated the perimeter. At two storeys high and with a host of oblong windows, each of these grey structures bustled with activity as lab technicians, dressed in their characteristic white coats, went about their duties, unaware that their movements were being spied on over two thousand miles away.

Whoever was trying to manipulate Joiner to their own ends had just provided him with an invaluable insight into Dagmar's, and thus the Committee's, secret operation. If he could rid himself of their hold over him, he could yet turn the situation to his advantage. His mind switched into overdrive as he played out possible scenarios in which he'd emerge victorious.

'Director,' the computer said, 'there appear to be multiple broadcasts streaming in parallel to the current image. Do you want to view them all at once?'

Joiner's pulse quickened. 'Do it.'

The window on the screen expanded and, one after another, new camera feeds appeared until the whole wall was full of moving images.

Myers gave a shake of his head in disbelief. 'It's their entire network. They've accessed their entire network. How can they not know they've been compromised?'

'Whoever's done this has more than one person on the inside,' Joiner said, 'and if that's the case they're deep cover agents. Dagmar would vet his people to the nth degree, but all organisations are susceptible; just look at Debden. He passed all our tests with flying colours and yet he was working for not one, but two, other employers. Which reminds me, I want your opinion on the procedural review I've instigated.'

Myers nodded. 'How are they getting the signal out of Sanctuary?'

It was a valid question. Underground-to-surface communications were strictly monitored. *So much for Sanctuary being the securest facility on the planet*, Joiner thought. He surveyed the array of images on show, scanning each one to see what he could see.

'What's that?' Myers said, pointing.

Joiner peered at the image in question. 'Computer, expand grid frame *D eleven*.'

The specified feed tripled in size and Joiner's blood ran cold. 'He must have brought it back on foot,' he murmured. He knew Ophion hadn't brought it through the SED; he'd had it under twenty-four hour surveillance.

'It's true then,' Myers said, 'it does exist.'

Joiner tore his eyes away from the shimmering form of the imprisoned Pharos to look at his agent.

'I may have been bleeding out when you shot me,' Myers said, 'but I'm trained to observe in extreme circumstances, as you are. I saw the video General Stevens showed you. I saw what you saw.'

Joiner turned back to the screen. 'Then you know as well as I that this ... *thing*, needs to be eradicated.'

'It looks secure.'

'Looks can be deceiving,' Joiner said, 'as well you know. They have no idea what they're dealing with.'

'And we do?'

'No,' Joiner said, 'and that's the problem.'

'Then whoever's seeking to coerce you may actually help us bring down this Committee you speak of.'

'Not necessarily; they want me to infiltrate them. For all we know they want this Anakim tech for themselves.'

'The Pharos doesn't look like any kind of technology I've ever seen.'

'Hmm,' Joiner said, 'biological tech, perhaps; whatever it is, it outlived the Anakim, and if that's not a lesson to heed then I don't know what is.'

'If it's more important to them than Morgan's pendant then I doubt we'll have much chance of getting to it. Those walls look reinforced; they could probably withstand a nuclear blast.'

Joiner knew he was right. The military that controlled the labs were beyond his control. And what with Dagmar and the Committee running things from behind the scenes, their chances of getting away with any attempt, successful or not, were slim to none. *We'll have to find another way*, Joiner thought, *and perhaps these live streams will give us that opportunity*.

He continued to watch the strange creature as its light glimmered in and out of existence inside the dark interior of its specially designed cell.

'What are you?' Joiner whispered. 'What do you want from us?'

As the two men studied the screen, an intrusive noise broke the silence.

Myers withdrew a coms device and put it to his ear. 'Myers,' he said.

There was a pause before he said, 'I'm on my way.'

Joiner unlocked the door. 'What is it? Have they found something?'

'I'm not sure, I'll keep you updated.' Myers scooped up his body armour and left the room.

'We have an incoming priority call, Director,' the computer said, 'do you wish to accept?'

'Who is it?'

'GMRC HQ, it is the Secretary General of Oversight.'

Joiner sighed. The Oversight Division was one of the few seats of power that rivalled his own. This was one call he couldn't avoid. 'Keep these broadcasts running,' he said, 'and ensure they're recorded and stored under top level encryption. My eyes only. Understand?'

'Of course, Director,' said the computer.

'Put the secretary general on-screen.'

The video footage from Sanctuary's laboratories vanished and a new window opened showing a grey-haired woman dressed in a power suit. She had sharp eyes and stood in front of an impressive desk bordered by two large flags bearing the emblems of the GMRC Directorate and the United Nations.

'Ah, Malcolm,' she said, 'I heard about the attack. I take it you're unhurt?'

'Madame Secretary, yes, everything's under control. Is this is a social call as we're pretty busy over here?'

'I wish that it were, Director. We require your presence in New York ... immediately.'

Joiner gave an incredulous snort at the request and the woman frowned.

'Forgive me, Madame Secretary, may ask I why?'

'Why?' She looked confused. 'Because the countdown has begun. Surface evacuation is just around the corner and with the dust cloud's early break up the next summit meeting has been brought forward. Didn't you get the memos?'

Joiner gave an inward groan. This was just what he didn't need, not now. *Did Debden hide this from me on purpose?* he wondered, ruing the fact that he'd yet to install his replacement. 'I've had some internal disruption.'

'That's unfortunate,' she said, unmoved, 'and despite your recent shock you will need to get here, if not today, then no later than noon tomorrow. This is not a request; the final summits are mandatory and I strongly suggest you liaise with your relevant departments as to the nature of the questions you'll be facing.'

'Questions?'

'There have been rumblings about your leadership, or absence thereof. Any failure to appear will only compound your problems. We also need your input on the Space Programme catastrophe, the Steadfast incident and the subsequent inquiries, and I've been told your independent review is overdue. I'm not sure what's going on over there, Malcolm, but to put it bluntly you need to get your house in order or you'll find yourself with a vote of no confidence, and we both know where that will lead.'

Joiner didn't know what to say and before he could think of something raised voices outside his office drew his attention.

'Director, are you listening to me?'

He turned back to the screen. 'I am, Madame Secretary.'

'No later than noon tomorrow,' she said. 'Don't be late.'

The woman's image disappeared from the wallscreen and Joiner remained staring at its blank surface before the disturbance he'd heard grew louder.

He collected his computer and emerged from his office to see his armed bodyguards engaged in a slanging match with a dishevelled analyst.

'WHAT IS THE MEANING OF THIS?!' Joiner said, furious.

'Sir,' – one of the operatives turned to face him – 'Agent Myers told us you weren't to be disturbed.'

'It was Agent Myers who sent me!' the analyst said.

Joiner gave a flick of his hand and the armoured agent stepped aside to let his plain-clothed colleague past.

'Director,' the man said, 'Agent Myers sent me to tell you he's following up a lead and he's taking a team to intercept.'

'Why didn't he tell me himself?'

'He said he tried, but your priority call blocked his attempts.'

'What sort of lead?'

'He wouldn't say.'

Joiner accessed his computer's contact list and tried calling Myers, but all he received was an unobtainable message.

'He said if you wanted an update you'd need to meet him on the roof in,' – the analyst checked his watch – 'two minutes.'

Joiner swore and headed towards the nearest elevator, with his bodyguards following close behind.

Moments later they were travelling upwards to the building's top floor.

What has he found? Joiner wondered, as their ascent slowed. The doors opened and Joiner strode down a corridor, up a set of stairs, past two sentries and out onto the building's roof.

A blast of wind buffeted him as three helicopter gunships prepared for take off. Two of the vehicles already had special ops forces inside, while to his left another group of grey-clad operatives moved towards the third.

Joiner saw Myers was amongst them. He called out to him, but the noise of the aircrafts' turbines drowned him out.

Leaning into the pulsating wind, Joiner made his way forward.

The roar of the engines increased as the team boarded the helicopter, but Myers had seen his director's approach and jumped back down to the roof.

'Sir,' he shouted as they met, 'we've had a breakthrough, a decoded signal; we're going to intercept!'

'Signal, what signal?!'

'The hacker, Bic, we've located his position; we think he's on his way to meet someone.'

Joiner grasped Myer's shoulder as one, and then another, of the helicopters took off. 'Are you sure it's him?'

'One hundred per cent.'

'Someone? Do you mean—'

'Steiner, yes, we think so!' He glanced back as he received a message through his headset. 'Sir, I have to go.'

'What's your ETA?!' Joiner said.

'Three hours, four tops, we're breaking a host of international and GMRC treaties; we're going dark as soon as we're airborne. Plausible deniability.'

Joiner moved to the helicopter and helped Myers board before climbing up to sit beside him.

'Sir!' Myers said, alarmed. 'What are you doing?'

'Coming with you!' An operative handed Joiner a communication headset which he put on before adjusting the mic towards his mouth. 'This is too good an opportunity to miss; just make sure you get me to New York by noon tomorrow.'

Myers gave him a nod, slid shut the door and gave a twirling motion with his finger as a signal for the pilot to take off. The roar of the blades increased and Joiner felt them go airborne while the forlorn figures of his bodyguards were left looking up at them from the rooftop below.

As the three helicopters reached a set altitude, a pair of wings unfolded from each craft, secondary jets activated and the main rotor slowed to a stop before folding away into the roof. Their pilot slid down a jet-black visor and their upwards momentum switched forward with a burst of power.

Joiner looked out of the window as first the GMRC skyscraper, and then the entire U.S. capital, disappeared behind as their speed increased. With matters no longer in his hands, he relaxed into his seat while the operatives around him checked their weaponry.

Myers saw him looking and he unclipped a pistol from his chest armour and held it out to him. 'Just in case.'

Joiner accepted the weapon, ejected the mag and locked back the slide to check it wasn't loaded. 'If Professor Steiner is with them,' he said, looking at Myers, 'you know what to do?'

'If he's there, he's as good as dead.'

Joiner flicked a catch and the slide on his gun snapped forward. Satisfied, he sat back again; save for the news about the summit meeting, this day was turning out to be one of the best he'd had in a long time. *Myers is back in the fold; I have full visual access to Sørensen's labs, and in just a few hours' time Bic will be in custody and Steiner put back where he belongs, in the ground. What's not to like?*

The drone of the engines continued to hum with a reverberating echo and Joiner closed his eyes as a single, uplifting thought made itself known, and he wondered how he could have ever doubted it. He smiled as the same thought came again: *it's still good to be me.*

CHAPTER EIGHTY-THREE

CLOUD FOREST BIOLOGICAL Reserve
Monteverde, Costa Rica

It was early morning in the small Costa Rican village of Monteverde and rolling mists blanketed green treetops like the ghosts of gods in the emerging light of dawn. Thick vines hung down beneath canopies of dew-laden leaves, while exotic birds sang in the beginnings of a new day. Indigenous insects buzzed and chirped with unending regularity and the hint of blue glistened in clearing skies. High above in the vault of heaven, tiny particulates continued to dissipate, and while some areas of the world still endured a darker existence, the peoples of Central America enjoyed the sun's life-giving rays in almost all their glory.

It had been many weeks since Sarah, Trish and Jason had fled the confines of the Honduran hospital, and slowly but surely they had worked their way south.

Keeping away from civilisation, they had driven from one small community to the next in order to avoid any authority or militia that might seek to do them harm. At the time Sarah had thought it ironic that three people who would do anything to further archaeological advance were being sought for damaging an ancient site they held dear. She had never intended to damage the Mayan ruins; why would she, when she strove to further human knowledge of the past? She wasn't a mindless vandal, but someone seeking the truth; it was just unfortunate that the truth she had searched for came into direct conflict with the remains of another.

But now, as Sarah stirred from sleep, the past was the past and full of trauma, like a nightmare-ridden fantasy. She didn't have the inclination to address the maddening deliberations of right from wrong, black or white, a lighter shade of grey from its darker cousin. All she wanted to do now was forget and heal, move on and live her life anew, but she knew that wish would never come true until she faced the demons she'd left behind.

The sun grew brighter and Sarah rolled over on her bed to face the other way. *The demons can wait*, she thought, and she relaxed her body to drift back into the comfort of mindless slumber.

♦

Time continued to pass in the Costa Rican wilderness, unhindered by the trials and tribulations of the residents living within its mellow realm. Sunrise had come and gone and Sarah let out a soft sigh as she awoke feeling tired and exhausted. Even the turmoil of her sleep was preferable to the reality of life; at least without cognitive thought she could be lost in another world without the feelings of continual torment and guilt that dogged her every waking moment.

She opened her eyes to stare out through the window of her log cabin at the forests beyond. Such beauty eased her spirit, from the darkness of the deep to the light of the surface; there was no better cure for the ache in her heart and the scars on her soul. Light streamed across the bed and a noise from the floor below alerted her to the presence of her friends.

A minute later a floorboard creaked outside her door and someone knocked with a feather-light touch.

'Sarah, are you awake?' Trish opened the door and Sarah closed her eyes. She didn't want to speak. It was always easier to hide.

Muffled footsteps padded across the room to the window. A groan of wood on wood preceded a subtle wave of fresh air and the faint scents of flowering plants washed over Sarah's senses. The sounds of the forest echoed into the room and despite what had gone before Sarah briefly remembered what it was like to feel safe.

'I know you're awake,' Trish said, 'I can see your eyelids moving.'

Sarah cracked open an eye to see Trish framed against a blaze of sunlight.

'We've already eaten breakfast; do you want Jason to cook you something?'

Sarah gave a shake of her head and Trish left without another word, she knew better than to force her friend into conversation. Sometimes people just needed peace and quiet, to be alone with their thoughts, or lack thereof, and right now that was exactly what Sarah needed.

With Trish departed, Sarah rolled onto her back to stare up at the thick, untreated timbers of the ceiling, her thoughts dwelling on the recent past.

♦

After leaving the hospital and travelling south through Honduras, it had been decided that crossing over into Nicaragua was the best course of action. And once this had been accomplished, they'd continued down the Atlantic coast in search of a suitable place to regroup and recover from their collective injuries. Trish and Jason had helped tend to Sarah's wounds which, apart from the one on her chest, had continued healing well.

Having stopped for a few days in a tiny fishing village, they'd resumed their journey only for the car to break down in the back of beyond. Fortunately the back of beyond in Nicaragua still enjoyed the benefits of a public transport system ... of sorts. Abandoning the stricken vehicle in the midday heat for a bus full of locals, livestock and the stench that entailed, they'd travelled inland before alighting at a small town where they managed to procure another car, which, if anything, was more beat up than the one they'd just left behind.

Keeping their southerly route, they crossed into Costa Rica twenty-four hours later, once again avoiding the official border crossing in favour of an unbeaten track, which slowed their progress to a crawl. After reaching another village, one that enjoyed the luxury of a single internet connection, they decided to bypass the relative well-populated centre of the country and head west to the once popular eco-tourist destination of Monteverde and its spectacular cloud forest reserve – and the decision had been a good one. With the GMRC limiting world travel like never before, the village was all but abandoned save for a few dozen families that had remained to eke out an existence with little material wealth. Not that such a life had dulled their spirit – from what Sarah had witnessed they seemed far happier than anyone she'd seen in the so-called advanced cities and their fractious urban sprawl. That said, their excitement at the arrival of the three explorers and the heartfelt welcome they'd given them had been overwhelming, so much so it had brought a tear to Sarah's eye, but it soon became apparent that such unbridled joy hadn't been completely altruistic in origin. Trish learned that their arrival was seen as a sign that things were returning to normal and the time of the *Cielos Oscuros*, or 'Dark Skies', had finally ended. Not wanting to dash their hopes by explaining they weren't the first wave of new tourists they believed them to be, they enjoyed the initial week of being treated like royalty before settling into a more frugal lifestyle as they conserved their funds for the weeks ahead. Despite the white lie, or rather an avoidance of the truth, Jason had pointed out it probably wouldn't be long until real tourists did start arriving now that the dust cloud had receded. The GMRC couldn't keep people locked up forever, he'd reasoned, and Sarah had to agree. With the worst of the impact winter already behind them the world would gradually return to normal and the rebuilding process would begin. She'd wondered what would happen to all the underground bases now that their primary purpose had not reached fruition. According to Jason, they'd carry on regardless; what else could they do with such an investment? And he had a point; Sanctuary notwithstanding, the other bases would not just be abandoned by their respective governments. And when the GMRC disbanded, they would revert to full autonomy, ready and waiting for when the human race needed them again.

And so, in their idyllic locale, the hours, days and weeks had passed and there they had stayed, living out a simple existence in remote isolation, cut off from the outside world, and surrounded by the perpetual beauty of the islands of forest in the clouds.

An itching sensation brought Sarah back to the here and now and she reached down to scratch beneath the bandage that still encircled her chest. Whether due to the pendant nestled beneath, or for another reason entirely, that particular wound had failed to heal like those on her hands, feet and head. The last time she'd summoned the courage to look at it was back in hospital and that was one time too many. Ever since she'd refused to acknowledge its existence, averting her gaze and denying the intense emotions that were inextricably linked to its creation.

A couple of days earlier, when Trish had redressed it for her, Sarah had been informed that there was only a small section of scab left and that the bandages were no longer necessary. Sarah, however, wanted the covering left on for as long as possible, even if it meant showers and baths continued to give way to irregular cleaning with a damp flannel. There were too many mirrors in the bathroom, too many ways to catch sight of that which she wished to avoid.

Unable to deny life any longer, Sarah sat up and rubbed her tired eyes. She hated the sensation of oversleeping, but it helped dull the pain inside and so she persisted. She just wished she could go back on the morphine she'd had back on the ward.

Movement made her glance up, startled.

She relaxed. Her friend was back. A ginger cat ambled across the floor before jumping up onto the bed. Sarah held out her hand and the animal pushed its face against it while purring in blissful satisfaction. She stroked the cat for a while longer before getting up and pulling on yesterday's clothes. As she went to go downstairs a sudden pain in her chest made her pause. She grimaced and held up her hand to see it trembling. She clenched her fist and willed the sensation away. *It will pass*, she thought, *it always does*. She took a deep breath, and then another, deeper and slower than before, and the tremors subsided. Gathering herself, she opened the door to begin another day of numb distress.

◆

It was late afternoon by the time Sarah decided to eat. She returned after a long walk through the treetop boardwalks to join Trish and Jason at the kitchen table to tuck into a modest spread of bread, rice and beans.

The three friends ate in silence while the sound of distant laughter from the local children at play drifted through the open door. Sarah caught Trish giving Jason a look that suggested she wanted him to say something. The noiseless exchange continued back and forth with increasing intensity before Sarah could take it no longer.

'If you have something to say, just say it.'

Jason gave her a guilty look, his mouth half full of food. He pointed at Trish who gave a tut of annoyance.

'Well?' Sarah said, turning to her.

'We've been thinking—'

Jason cleared his throat.

'*I've* been thinking,' Trish said, giving Jason a withering look, 'that we need to start planning what to do next.'

'Now that you're better and everything,' Jason said.

Sarah looked from Trish to Jason and back again. 'What's there to talk about?'

Trish frowned. 'Err, quite a lot. Like where do we go from here? How do we get there? What do we do when we get there? Do we try to go home, or go some place else?'

Sarah tensed at the barrage of thoughts that such questions dredged up and instead of answering she concentrated on the piece of bread in her hand. She tore a lump off with her fingers and placed it in her mouth to chew.

'We can't avoid this forever,' Trish said. 'Sooner or later we'll run out of money and then we won't be able to go anywhere.'

'So why not just stay here, then?' Jason said. 'That's an option, isn't it?'

Trish looked at Sarah, who shrugged and continued to immerse herself in the task of eating lunch.

'If we tried to go home,' Jason said, 'they could be waiting for us, couldn't they? I mean, even if we got through the GMRC checkpoints without any papers, we could wind up walking into a trap, don't you think?'

'Probably,' Trish said. 'The more I've thought about it, the more I've come to believe that there's no way we could go anywhere that has any type of CCTV, traffic cameras or any device that has face recognition. As soon as we went through an airport or a checkpoint they'd be alerted to our presence. And if they thought we were dead and buried, images of us wandering around alive and kicking would soon tell them otherwise.'

'Then we do stay here,' Jason said, 'there's no cameras for miles around.'

Trish made a face. 'As much as I like this place, I don't think I can stand it forever. I'd go nuts and you probably would, too.'

He sipped at his drink of water, deep in thought. 'We could wait until the GMRC gets broken up and the border crossings return to normal. Then we could sneak back home with no one the wiser.'

'Maybe,' Trish said, 'anything will involve risk; it's just how much we're willing to take. The main problem will be funding any travel. Bypassing immigration into any country will be expensive, regardless of whether the GMRC are operational.'

'We could sell some of the artefacts,' Jason said. 'What do we have left? Parchments, the Mayan tablet – what about our Deep Reach helmets? Even bashed up they must be worth something to the right dealer.'

'It's worth considering.' Trish leaned back in her chair. 'We don't have much else to bargain with. Either that, or we try and get some work in one of the smaller towns.'

Sarah listened as her friends continued to discuss their options before talk turned to a more painful subject.

'I'm telling you,' Jason was saying, 'there must be a link between the Sphinx in Sanctuary and the one in Egypt. The resemblance was uncanny.'

'As I said before, it could be coincidence,' Trish said, 'and it wasn't that similar. There were some big differences, the head for one, the headdress, and of course its size.'

'I can't stop wondering how old it was; those standing stones looked far older than Stonehenge.'

Trish nodded. 'You could spend your entire life documenting the site and not even scratch the surface.'

'*Could have*,' Jason said. 'There's nothing left of it now.'

As the conversation continued, Sarah found herself listening with greater interest, the subject of archaeology pulling her in despite her desire to do otherwise.

'We never did find out what it was all for,' Jason said, 'the device, the power it unleashed. What did it do? Where did it go?'

'We've gone over this before,' Trish said, 'there's no point going on about it again; we need to accept that we'll never know.'

Sarah looked at the scars on the palms of her hands. 'Sometimes I wonder if it ever happened.'

Trish looked at her in surprise, perhaps wondering why she'd decided to comment for the first time since they'd returned to the surface. Truth was, Sarah didn't know either.

'But it did happen, though, didn't it?' Jason said.

Trish waited for Sarah to continue, but when she didn't she gave a shudder. 'I still have nightmares about those creatures.'

'You didn't see it when it was right over you,' Jason said. 'I nearly crapped myself. Sometimes I wake up and think it's in the room with me. I never really knew what it meant when people said they had night terrors. Now I do.'

'I saw something,' Sarah said, 'when I was there.'

Trish leant forward when she failed to elaborate. 'Something?'

Sarah stroked the top of her thigh, unconsciously comforting herself as she tried to tread between the fine lines of subjects she wished to avoid. 'It was like a window into somewhere else.' She looked up at them with haunted eyes. 'Didn't you see it?'

Trish shook her head.

'Somewhere else?' Jason said. 'What, like a projection of the past?'

Sarah struggled to recall what she'd seen. A memory of fire made her wince and she squeezed her leg in anguish.

'Perhaps we should talk about this another time,' Trish said, concerned.

'No, not a projection,' Sarah said, feeling compelled to continue, 'it was real; I could see it, beneath the spinning pentagram, like a—' She stopped, knowing how it would sound if she said it.

Trish reached out to her. 'Go on.'

'It was like a portal ... to another world.'

Jason looked doubtful. 'I saw the pentagram, but I didn't see anything like a portal.' He turned to Trish. 'What about you?'

'No, but then we didn't have that black slime all over us. Goodwin said it was hallucinogenic, or a neurotoxin, and the hospital said you had high toxicity levels, they thought you'd been poisoned.'

Jason snorted. 'Which is why they didn't trust us, they probably thought we did it.'

'I did see things,' Sarah said, recalling the horrific images and sounds she'd experienced as she'd worked her way towards the altar. She shut her eyes to dispel the fear that remained trapped inside. 'But this was different,' – she opened her eyes again – 'more real.'

'I did wonder where we'd end up after we transported,' Jason said. 'For all we knew we could have landed on another planet.'

Trish laughed.

'What?' Jason said, aggrieved. 'We could have.'

'You'll be saying we're in a parallel dimension next.'

Jason grumbled something that sounded like, '*We might be.*'

'Whatever it was,' Trish said, looking back at Sarah, 'real or not, it doesn't matter now.'

'It does if she tries to go through any checkpoints,' Jason said, trying to redeem himself.

Trish folded her arms. 'How so?'

'Metal detectors; with that thing in her chest they'll go haywire.' He looked at Sarah. 'They'll probably think you're carrying a bomb or something.'

Sarah's hand went to her chest.

'Even if they did,' Trish said, 'there's nothing we can do about that, either.'

'What happened to the smaller pendant?' Jason said. 'Is that in there as well? The surgeon didn't mention it.'

'I guess so,' Sarah said, not wanting to discuss it any further.

Trish gave him a look of reproach.

He touched Sarah's arm. 'Sorry, I didn't mean to ... you know.'

She gave him a tired smile and got up to retire to the living room of the two storey luxury cabin. As she sat in silence, the cat she'd befriended came up to sit on her lap while Trish and Jason continued to talk in low tones in the next room.

It was some time later, after Sarah had fallen asleep, that the sound of a TV broadcast woke her from a forgotten dream.

The cat no longer occupied her lap and Trish and Jason sat on the sofa to her right, watching the large display that had been built into the fabric of the wooden wall. She noticed her two friends held hands. Whether the action was romantic or out of an unconscious need for human contact, she didn't know, but regardless of the intent, it was heartwarming to see.

Trish noticed she was awake and withdrew her hand from Jason's as if embarrassed, or like she'd been caught committing a deadly sin.

Jason, feeling the movement, looked at Trish and then at Sarah. 'Have you seen this?' he said, gesturing to the screen. 'This could work in our favour.'

Sarah focused on the image. It was the BBC's worldwide news service, which was unusual as normally they only received local stations.

The news anchor was prattling on and it took a moment for Sarah to understand what she was saying. 'Is this true?' she said, looking at her friends.

'Looks that way,' Jason said. 'They say he won it some months back in a landslide. An independent, can you imagine?'

Trish sat up straighter, excited. 'The good news is, he wants to oust the GMRC, and not just their protocols, he wants to stop their operations in the whole of the United States, and not just there, he wants its allies to follow suit. Which means—'

'The UK too,' Sarah said.

Jason grinned. 'Give it six months and we could be going home.'

Sarah stared at the newsfeed and the image of the next President of the United States. 'John Harrison Henry,' she murmured. *Could he be our ticket to a new life?* She wondered. *Will he live up to his claims?* Who knew, he was after all, still a politician and if the past forty years were anything to go by, the leaders of the world's supposed greatest democracies said one thing and then did the total opposite. *No wonder people become disaffected*, she thought. *But perhaps this man is the start of a new beginning, someone to stand up to the banks, corporations and elites that serve themselves over the people.* Sarah shifted in her seat. *Or will he turn out like all the rest? Kept in line by the hidden powers that remain regardless of who enters office.* Her gut instinct favoured the latter, but like all things, only time would tell. It changed things though, that much she knew; it gave some semblance of hope in an otherwise bleak future, even if that hope wasn't her own. She looked at her friends, who eyed her with wary optimism.

'We're going into town tomorrow to get supplies,' Trish said. 'Do you want to come?'

Sarah thought about it. With the road network in a state of disrepair, the nearest town worthy of the name was a long way away. 'Isn't the GMRC curfew still in effect?'

Trish nodded. 'We'll stay overnight and come back the following day.'

'What time are you leaving?'

'Early, 'bout six.'

Sarah made a face.

Trish laughed. 'I didn't think you would.'

'Do you want us to get you anything?' Jason said.

'Chocolate bars, cakes, maybe.' Sarah paused to think. 'Anything sweet.'

He nodded and went back to watching the TV.

Sarah continued to listen for a while as the different reports from around the world came and went before she got up and moved to the balcony. The net curtains rustled in the light breeze as she parted them to walk out into the open air. She looked down at the steep drop over which the cabin had been built. The elevation ensured the tops of the nearest trees were just below her, offering a clear view of the wisps of cloud that hung suspended over the rejuvenated forest which spread out for as far as the eye could see. She breathed deeply, sucking in the fresh air and soaking up the rays of the sun, which already drifted towards the horizon and a distant mountain beyond.

Sarah stayed leaning on the balcony's rail as the sun dipped lower in the sky, her mind drifting without direction.

A noise from behind made her glance round to see Jason and Trish coming to join her.

'The days are drawing in,' Trish said, as she came to stand next to her.

Jason moved to Sarah's other side and leaned on the balcony rail in similar fashion. 'At least we have days again. This time last year this would have been pitch-black.'

'I still have trouble getting over how everything's grown again,' Trish said. 'It's amazing, don't you think?'

Sarah nodded and Jason grunted his agreement as they each enjoyed the beautiful vision that surrounded them. More moments of silence passed. Day turned to dusk and the sun set over the majestic vista, sending beams of light cascading through the trees and casting fascinating shadows through the slow, spiralling mists. A single bird repeated its distant call while the sound of insects increased as nocturnal life replaced its diurnal kin.

'We are going to have to make a decision soon,' Trish said, breaking the spell, 'about what we do next.'

Sarah could see her friends looking at her and knew they wanted to know if her convictions remained. And from their earnest expressions she knew she would have to say something sooner rather than later or her pain would spread to them, and that was something she couldn't abide. *Why should they suffer because of me, after all I've put them through already?* She stood up straight. *At least the future isn't the past*, she thought and expelled a deep breath. 'I still want to find out,' she said, 'once and for all.'

'About your mother?' Jason said.

Sarah nodded. 'I need to know ... if it was my fault. I can't move on with my life until I do.'

'And that means finding out who set the fire,' Trish said.

'The military had my map in Sanctuary's vaults,' Sarah said, her voice quiet but determined, 'which means it was taken before the fire was lit.'

'If it was the U.S. government,' Jason said, 'then you may never find out.'

'Then I'll never find peace.'

'If we couldn't find out while we were in Sanctuary,' Trish said, 'what chance do we have now?'

Sarah didn't want to think about it, but Trish was right, regardless. Her best chance of finding out the truth had disappeared as soon as she'd left the underground base. *It's strange*, she thought, *things are so much clearer in the light of day*. The dark, she realised, much like secrecy, always had the ability to affect judgement.

'What about Homo gigantis – the Anakim – and Sanctuary itself?' Jason said. 'Do you still want to expose it all?'

'The world has a right to know.' She looked at them. 'Doesn't it?'

Trish gave a nod.

'I would say so,' Jason said.

'And there's no way we could go back to the way we were before,' Sarah said, 'and pretend like nothing happened.'

Jason shook his head.

'Not a chance,' Trish said.

'Then that means only one thing, we gather our evidence and when we have enough, we go public.'

Jason didn't look convinced. 'That could take years.'

'Not necessarily. We have the parchments,' – Sarah steeled herself and touched her chest – 'and we still have the pendant; we just need to find some more bones.'

'That's a big *just*,' Jason said.

'Is it? We found them before and I know a place that is still ripe for potential burial sites.'

Trish's expression turned confused. 'You do?'

'The Cradle of Humanity,' Jason said, 'of course!'

'But the meteorite,' Trish said, 'South Africa was obliterated.'

'The surface was,' Jason said, looking to Sarah for confirmation, 'not underground. There may have been quakes, but something will remain and we know exactly where to look.'

They all fell silent as they contemplated what they would need to do to bring about their goal.

'It's a big decision, though,' Sarah said, 'life changing, and considering what I've put you both through, I wouldn't blame you if neither of you wanted anything to do with gigantis ever again. Perhaps the question should be – can you even trust me after everything I've put you through?'

'Of course we can,' Trish said, 'don't be silly. We knew what we were signing up to, and despite what you might think we do have minds of our own, you know.'

'I know that, I just feel ... responsible, that's all.'

Jason gave her a nudge. 'We know, but you don't have to. I'm big enough and Trish is ugly enough that we can take care of ourselves.' He looked past Sarah and waited for a reaction, and when none came he said, 'Did you hear me?'

'I did,' Trish said, her expression smug, 'but I'm choosing to ignore you.'

'It's a shame we can't say the same for your smell.' He sniggered and gave Sarah a wink. 'The local kids call her *el hedor*, it means—'

'*The stink* and it was you who taught them to sing it!' Trish leant round Sarah and cuffed him round the head, which made him laugh and brought a brief smile to Sarah's face.

'I thought they were just pleased to see me first of all,' Trish said to Sarah. 'They were running all round me, dancing and whooping and singing this song and it wasn't until I listened to it that I realised what they were saying. I got my own back though didn't I, Jas?'

'Pigs wee tea, I thought it tasted quite nice until I found out what it was.'

Trish giggled and Sarah's face turned serious. She found it difficult to maintain a smile these days and keeping up a fake façade was nigh on impossible.

'So, what do we do, then?' Jason said. 'How do we go about exposing the biggest cover up in history?'

'We need money,' Trish said. 'It's like we said before, fake paperwork and passes will be key.'

'Well, we won't have to worry about controls in South Africa,' Jason said, 'that's for certain. And we know the rest of Africa can be navigated below the radar if need be, and half of Asia will be just as slack.' He reached up and stretched. 'I'll take the Deep Reach helmets with us tomorrow, see what I can get for them.'

'No parchments though,' Sarah said, 'or the Mayan tablet; they're priceless.'

He nodded.

'And I'll go on the net,' Trish said, 'see what's what.'

Jason yawned. 'I still can't believe they don't have it out here. Although at least they have electricity, that's something, I suppose.'

'You wanted remote,' Trish said. 'And besides, they used to have it; one of the elders told me when the dust cloud hit, a gang of outsiders stole all the infrastructure – masts, cables, the lot.'

'I suppose the satellites will start working again soon,' Jason said. 'Better get hold of a cheap sat-phone if we can, might come in handy.'

'I'm just glad it's all coming to an end,' Trish said. 'The impact winter, I mean. I've had enough excitement to last me a lifetime and from what the news has been saying, it was getting pretty scary up here, and that was without all the wars.'

Jason murmured his agreement. 'Civilisation is more fragile than we think.'

Sarah remained silent, immersed in a swirl of thoughts. Even talking about what was to come stirred up powerful emotions. And yet the same questions remained, and along with them, the same problems she'd faced before she'd left London all that time ago. It seemed like a lifetime, but when she thought about it was actually less than two years since she'd embarked on her journey into the unknown. *Would I have swapped it all for a life with Mark, a life of veiled threats and drunken abuse?* She would like to think not, but then that meant accepting the rest as preferable, which was hard to take. She wiped her eye with the back of her hand as it teared up.

Jason, perhaps sensing her melancholy, put his arm around her shoulders and gave her a hug. 'Don't worry, Sazza,' he said, 'we'll look after you, ain't that right, Trish?'

'Of course we will.'

'And you'll never walk alone, you just have to keep hope in your heart,' – he pointed into the distance at the final rays of light – 'don't be afraid of the dark, at the end of a storm is a golden sky.'

'That's really beautiful, Jas,' Trish said and linked arms with Sarah.

The three friends gazed into the setting sun and Sarah felt her tension ease. 'It sounds familiar, isn't that a football song?'

Jason chuckled. 'I was hoping you wouldn't recognise it, I think Rodgers and Hammerstein were the ones who actually wrote it. I like the words, they have power.'

'And we still have each other,' Trish said, 'that's what counts.'

The sun flared bright before it finally disappeared beneath the horizon and the inevitable darkness closed in.

Trish gave a shiver. 'I'm going back in; it's a bit nippy out here.'

Jason followed her inside before stopping to hold the curtain open. 'You coming?'

Sarah shook her head. 'I'll be in in a minute.'

He gave her a look of understanding and let the curtain drop back to leave her standing alone on the balcony. A moment later a light inside the cabin switched on and Sarah returned her attention to the trees and the forbidding dark that lurked in their midst.

The sounds of the night intensified, the resonant chirp of crickets prevalent amongst the squawks and croaks of the various creatures that called the cloud forest home. Nearby, a local couple strolled along a wooded path, their low tones drifting up through the foliage, and Sarah wondered what it would be like to live in such a place your whole life. *I'll never know*, she thought and looked up at the sky where the shimmer of the brightest stars shone through the dust cloud's fading shroud. It was good to be back on the surface, and while her sense of safety had left her, she knew, at some point, it would return.

A shooting star arrowed across the sky, its blazing arc of light fading away like a forgotten soul. Sarah closed her eyes and made an impossible wish before opening them again to gaze out at the blackness.

Her mind echoed empty before another meteor streaked across heaven's empyrean vault and she wondered, *What does the future hold for me now?* She did not know, but one thing was for certain, the life she'd known and the person she'd been would never return. With one last look at the wilderness, Sarah Morgan re-entered the cabin to rejoin her friends, the two people she could rely on more than any other in the world, who she cared for above any other and who epitomised one unifying and emotive word ... *family*.

CHAPTER EIGHTY-FOUR

THE THUMP of a car door closing woke Sarah from a troubled dream. She opened her eyes to darkness and realised Trish and Jason were leaving for town. Full of anxiety, she knew she didn't want to be left on her own, and she rushed to the window and heaved it open, only to see a set of red taillights vanishing down the un-surfaced road. The cry of '*wait!*' died in her throat and she stood staring in forlorn disappointment at the emptiness without.

Closing the window, she returned to bed, pulled the sheets up around her and curled into the foetal position. Left all alone, she felt on the verge of tears.

She fought back the sensation, angry and disturbed by her weak resolve. *What's wrong with me?* she thought. She tried to reclaim her hold on unconscious sleep, but her limbs felt cold and shaky and the idea she could be suffering from some kind of illness increased her concern. *You had a brain operation*, said a voice in her head, *you could have an infection, a bleed – or worse – both! I haven't got a bleed*, she told herself, *don't be crazy, I've been fine for weeks. But what if you needed drugs to suppress the chance of infection? If you haven't been taking any, you've put yourself at risk.* And so the thoughts went on, round and round in her head until her stomach clenched into a knot and the taste of bile entered her mouth. Unable to get back to sleep, she lay in bed until the sun streamed into the room and her sheets clung to her with the damp cold of sweat.

As Sarah lay in a semi-catatonic state, the combined sensations of the itchy bandage round her chest and the clammy, dirt-ridden bedclothes overwhelmed her mind. Unable to stand it any longer, she flung off the covers and slid to the edge of the bed, where she sat staring at her hands, which continued to tremble and shake. Clenching her fists, she stood up and a wave of nausea made her head swim. She breathed deeply to expel the feeling and stumbled out of the room and into the dingy bathroom, with its blackout blind and closed shutters. In semi-darkness, she splashed cold water over her face and then cupped her hands to allow the cool liquid to pool before drinking it down with great, gasping gulps. She tucked the strands of hair that clung to her face back behind an ear and struggled out of her pyjama top, which she dropped to the floor in a sodden heap. Naked apart from her bandage, she moved back to the bedroom, feeling light-headed from the lack of sleep. *At least my hands have stopped shaking*, she thought, and she pulled on some clean knickers and an old T-shirt before sitting back down on the edge of the bed, which felt damp to the touch.

She ran her hands over her face and then bowed her head. Is this my life now, she wondered, too scared to be on my own, a nervous wreck? What do I have to look forward to? The prospect of failing to find Mum's killer and revealing the truth to a world too busy to care. And what difference would it make, anyway, if everyone knew about the Anakim? Will it change my life? No. Will it endanger Trish and Jason? Yes.

She knew they said otherwise, but could she really drag them back into the mire? Or should the question be, am I even capable? Can I function in the real world? She held out her hand which trembled in response. I don't even know who I am anymore. Am I Sarah from London, daughter of a murdered mother? Am I Sarah the childless spinster, cursed to live alone? Or am I the archaeologist who's ridiculed by her professional peers? You're Deep Reach, said another voice, don't you remember?

She didn't want to remember and her brief life in Sanctuary was fading fast; it was almost like it had never happened. But ever since she'd decided to leave London behind in search of Homo gigantis, she'd been either chasing secrets or fleeing from those who wanted to protect them. *Perhaps I should just give up and live a quiet life? Go back to the soul-sucking boredom of my nine-to-five*. It sounded nice, it sounded safe.

A scratching noise at the bedroom window caught her attention. She got up and walked over to open it and the ginger cat jumped down to rub round her legs. Sarah watched it wander away to investigate beneath the bed and that's when she remembered her drawings. She moved to the bed and peered underneath. The cat's face popped out and kissed her face with its nose. She stroked its head before gently moving it aside as she reached out to locate the cardboard box she'd hidden away. Sliding it out, she carried it downstairs to the kitchen while the cat continued to worry around her.

She placed the box on the dining table, withdrew the sheets of white paper and spread them out. Sitting down on a creaky chair, she chose one of the pencils at random, selected a blank sheet and paused as her hand trembled. She reached out and held it with her other hand and waited until the disturbance eased. Able to continue, she drew a straight line, and then another, and soon she was immersed in the task, connecting series after series of bisecting lines. She didn't know why she was doing what she was doing, but it felt right somehow.

She hadn't told Trish and Jason about her midnight preoccupations, the time when she usually succumbed to the compulsion to put pencil to paper. She felt guilty for not telling them, but she knew they wouldn't understand, or would ask questions she didn't want to consider. She finished shading the drawing and held it out to assess. It wasn't quite right. She moved it aside and started afresh on a new sheet.

Hours passed and Sarah didn't realise how long she'd been lost in her artistic fervour until the lack of illumination halted her progress. Frustrated at the interruption, she got up and switched on the light. The ginger cat stared at her with green eyes from where it sprawled on the kitchen counter. Sarah gave it a quick stroke before deciding to take on some food and drink.

After she'd nourished herself she looked at the fruits of her labour and frowned. Representations of pentagrams and sphinxes lay strewn around the kitchen. Many of them included detailed symbols and depictions of various constellations she had no right to know, let alone draw. She picked one up from the floor to examine and wondered why, when she wanted to forget the past, was she unable to stop drawing it? But it wasn't these pictures that concerned her most; the other element of her artwork was a single image, repeated over and over again: the symbol of a cross. But none of the slight variations she'd drawn matched what she'd been striving to get down on paper, and it was perhaps for this reason that she'd been unable to cease the task for so long.

She picked up some of the papers from the table and leafed through them. 'None of them are right,' she murmured, her anger rising. 'None of them match!' She threw them to the floor and then swept the rest from the table in a rage before she stopped and stood breathing hard in confused despair.

She sank down onto a chair and looked over at the cat, who remained unmoved by the commotion, the docile feline just stopping to gaze at her before resuming its never-ending chore of washing.

Sarah knew why she'd drawn the cross; how could she not when the constant reminder of her last hours in Sanctuary had left such an indelible imprint on her flesh?

She turned her palms up to stare at the marks she normally tried so hard to ignore. An image of the bloody Anakim altar appeared in her mind's eye and she grimaced at the remembered trauma. Thrusting the thought away, she continued to inspect the scars and the white tissue at their centre. Around each one the skin had blackened into a circular patch, perhaps induced by the device that had also fused her shoes to her feet. She glanced down at the marks where the metal clasps from her climbing boots had conducted the heat to leave their brand on her skin. She'd hoped, after all this time, that the ugly welts would have healed better, but it seemed she was destined to endure a visual reminder of the past for as long as her body deemed fit.

The sound of distant thunder brought back more unwanted memories and soon the first raindrops fell, their strength and frequency increasing into a deluge. The rattle of the downpour filled the cabin's interior and she wondered if Trish and Jason were okay. *If it continues like this*, she thought, *they might even turn back*.

Sarah looked around at the drawings scattered all over the floor, her madness on display for all to see. A sense of urgency gripped her. She bent down and scooped up a handful and stuffed them into the box before repeating the process again and again until the container bulged with the crumpled mass of paper.

She went to return upstairs, but something caught her eye. A single piece of paper had evaded her purge and hung in wedged suspension between the cooker and fridge. She stooped down and pulled it out. The image of the cross was bent in half and she flattened it out to see a single crease remained through its centre. Another image seared into her mind. An image of a bloody wound and beneath it the tattoo of a crucifix. Shaken by the sudden insight, she lowered herself back to her chair and picked up the pencil to sketch in what she'd been missing all along.

When she'd finished she held up the image of the crucifix and realised the man she'd drawn in sacrifice was the very one she was refusing to think about. In her attempt at divorcing herself from the pain, she'd lost sight of the very thing, the very person, who caused it. She closed her eyes and held the paper to her chest and her heart beat faster. She knew she had to release the pain to be free, but it was so hard, there was so much and she'd been holding onto it so tightly she didn't know how to let it go. She didn't even know if she wanted to, because if she did, she'd accepted it was over, and he was really – truly – gone.

Thunder cracked loudly overhead and Sarah's stomach clenched tight, jerking her out of her inner conflict. The cat jumped down to the floor to retreat to cover and she felt her throat constrict as her heart thumped fast and erratic. Feeling like she was going to be sick, she stood up, went dizzy and clung onto the countertop. Her heart continued to beat faster and faster, her breathing coming in short, rapid bursts as a steady pain built within her chest. She looked down at her hands, which curled into spasm. Scared, she stumbled into the living room as lightning lit up the night. More thunder boomed loud and she lost sense of time as she staggered up steps and eventually made it into the darkened bathroom. She prised open the cabinet and fumbled inside, sending bottles of medicine clattering into the sink below. Unable to see, she searched for the pull cord and switched on the light. Grasping the bottle she desired, she popped open its lid and emptied a few pills into her still shaking palm. Turning on the tap, she put hand to mouth, scooped up some water and flushed the tablets down and waited for her suffering to ease. When this failed to happen, she hugged her arms to her chest and sank down to the floor, where she curled up in a ball to shiver and shake in feverish delusion. The storm outside continued to howl and shutters banged loose as the wind whipped up a gale. Lightning flared bright and the cabin's lights flickered out, and everything plunged into darkness.

CHAPTER EIGHTY-FIVE

MID-MORNING SUNSHINE FILTERED in through the fresh air of a new day and Sarah stirred from a deep, uninterrupted sleep. Something soft tickled the flesh of her cheek and she opened her eyes to see the face of the ginger cat filling her vision from her position on the bathroom floor. The friendly creature meowed and brushed against her a final time before moving away to sit in the doorway to act as a small, furry guardian in an otherwise empty house.

Wincing at the discomfort of sleeping on hard tiles, Sarah sat up and allowed her mind to clear. Bottles lay strewn on the floor around her and the drawing of the crucifix lay close by, the paper crumpled and torn. Pulling herself up, she stared at her reflection in the mirror. Her hair clung to her face and one end of the bandage that encircled her chest hung down below her T-shirt. 'Who am I?' she whispered to the stranger who stared back at her. 'Who are you?'

The question and her mute reflection reminded her of a moment back in Sanctuary when she'd stood in a certain apartment and questioned her own sanity. That night she'd asked her mother if her death had made Sarah seek her own. Now she just wanted to know who she was and where she was going.

She reached round and pulled her hair to one side to look at the scar where the surgeon had opened up her skull. Yet another reminder of the dangers she'd inflicted on an already damaged body. *Will I ever learn?* she asked herself. *Will I ever stop?*

She glanced down at her drawing and the figure of the man on the cross and realised she couldn't even bring herself to say his name.

She returned to gazing into her own eyes. 'Am I that much of a coward?'

As usual her doppelganger didn't reply and Sarah removed her T-shirt to consider the wrapping that masked her wound. *I'm not a coward*, she thought, and as she reached up to the bandage, she realised her hand no longer shook. Grasping one end, she unfurled the white gauze, once, twice, from around her chest. The last section appeared and the fine fabric stuck to her skin, but with a final tug it came free to reveal the area beneath.

No longer was the injury scabbed over or weeping. Smooth, alabaster skin covered her breast bone and the Anakim pendant embedded beneath. Of course, she hadn't escaped the ordeal without a mark, there was a scar, how could there not be? The red hot metal had left a permanent striation in the shape of a distorted star. But the thing that stood out the most was something Sarah would never have suspected. Overlaying the healed wound was a discolouration of the skin. And it was far from ordinary.

She reached up to run her fingers over the bronzed arms of a faint, yet readily discernable, cross. Somehow, when it had melted atop her pentagonal artefact, the golden keepsake given her by Trish had left a permanent stain on her skin. Strangely, the cross was also offset from the rest of the scar so that it was positioned slightly to the left, towards her heart. She couldn't help but wonder about the location and form of the mark which was, to all intents and purposes, a tattoo, albeit one created by unusual means. *Has my wish come true after all?* She recalled the wording from two nights before. *Please bring him back to me*, she'd wished, *I'll take whatever you can give me, just give me something, anything.*

'Are you with me?' She looked up and closed her eyes. 'Are you still with me, Riley?' she whispered and pressed her hands against the cross on her chest.

No answer came from within the vaults of her mind.

She looked back into the mirror to marvel at the similarity of her new mark to the tattoo of a crucifix that had adorned Riley's chest. It was like they were linked somehow, between worlds, and she wished she'd had the courage to look at the wound sooner. The imagining eased her suffering and strengthened a fragile resolve. It was like a part of him remained embedded within her, much like the pendant itself, a single powerful connection that could never be removed.

She looked down at her chest and traced the mark with her finger, before her hand strayed back to the place where the pendant lay hidden. She pressed hard against her skin and thought she could feel the metal beneath. It was a strange feeling to know that something foreign was inside her. Something not just foreign, but a device of power forged by non-human hands. And while the rest of her life remained uncertain, there was one thing Sarah knew for sure; that feeling wasn't a good one.

Suddenly feeling unclean, inside and out, Sarah moved to the shower and turned on the taps. A moment later she'd slipped out of her underwear to stand beneath the hot jets of water, which cascaded over her body in a cleansing wave. She stood, head bowed, to let the rushing flow wash away the grime of the past. But the more she allowed herself to relax, the stronger her sense of loss became. *Riley is gone. He's dead, because of me! I could have been happy with him back in Sanctuary and I threw it all away for what? This? This isn't freedom* – she put her hands to her face as reality kicked in – *this is hell!* A tear rolled down her cheek, and the tear turned into a sob, and the sob into heartrending grief for the loss of the man she'd loved and for the life she could have known. Her mouth gaped in silent agony and she sank down in the shower and cried, deep, gut-wrenching tears of self-loathing pity, which racked her chest and burned her throat until she could cry no more.

♦

Sarah didn't know how long she'd stayed in the shower, but it was long enough that her skin had reddened from the continual heat and day had turned to dusk. When she'd finally emerged, it was as a spent, hollowed out shell of the person she once knew.

Unthinking, she pulled on her dirty T-shirt and underwear, before wiping her hand across the steamed up mirror to stare at the person within. It was then, when she contemplated the worst, that she glimpsed a shadow in the reflection, hovering behind her in the corner of the room. Terrified, she swung round.

Nothing was there.

She opened the bathroom door and the cat, which had been sitting on the other side, jumped up before staring past her and letting out a terrified hiss. Sarah could sense ... *something*, in the room behind her. The cat let out a horrific howl and the TV in the living room switched on.

Sarah leapt forward and rushed downstairs, glancing back over her shoulder at the forbidding doorway of the bathroom. Scared out of her mind, she expected to see her friends, but no one was there. Another indistinct form moved on the balcony and Sarah fled out the front door and screamed as she rebounded off someone coming in the other direction.

'Jason?' she said, dazed.

Her vision cleared and the figure at the bottom of the steps raised a gun.

Not Jason!

Glancing back, another armed man entered the house from the balcony. With nowhere else to go, Sarah vaulted over the railing, landed in mud and sprinted away.

Shouts of pursuit chased her down a forest path. Her bare feet slipped and skidded on the sodden soil and she emerged into an open field. Floodlights blazed on and she slithered to a stop, half-blinded.

Red lasers traced dots all over her body and Sarah raised a hand to her eyes and squinted against the glare. 'Who are you?' she said, her voice trembling. 'What do you want?!'

'DON'T MOVE!' A blurred form emerged from the light, rifle raised. 'On your knees! Put your hands on your head!'

Sarah did as she was told before another voice said, 'You're a hard woman to find, Sarah Morgan.'

The soldier moved aside and another person appeared in the glare. He gestured for the soldier to lower his weapon and he held out his hand and helped Sarah to her feet.

'Who are you?' she said, confused.

'Who am I?' His grip clamped tight. 'I'm someone who is pleasantly surprised.' Malcolm Joiner removed his dark glasses. 'And you, Ms. Morgan,' he said, staring down at her with cruel, hungry eyes, 'have something I want.'

CHAPTER EIGHTY-SIX

One after the other, three unmarked helicopter gunships lifted into night skies with a great roar and a rush of air. Trees and plants, lit up by the aircraft's floodlights, bent and twisted in the downdraft before disappearing into darkness as the aerial convoy gained altitude.

Malcolm Joiner looked across at his prisoner with calculating eyes. Sarah Morgan, the woman who'd started it all. *She has no idea*, he thought, *how much trouble she's caused me*. He glanced to his right. 'Show me.'

Agent Myers reached out and pulled down Morgan's T-shirt, exposing her chest.

Joiner leant forward to inspect the wound before looking up into her defeated eyes. There was no fight left in her, which was why she'd capitulated to his agents' interrogation in a matter of moments. He gave Myers the nod and he released his hold.

Joiner sat back in his seat. It was a curious turn of events. They both had something inside them that didn't belong. He resisted the temptation to touch the scar on the back of his neck and frowned. Regardless of their shared circumstance, that she knew nothing about the hacker or Steiner was vexing. *Why had she been here at all?* Joiner wondered. *And where are Bic and the Professor?*

Myers had no answers and Joiner was left to ponder the puzzle that was left. Every piece of intel indicated the hacker should have been there. Was it a false trail? Did Bic lead us to Morgan on purpose, or is some other power at work? Those were the questions he needed answering. Or was the hacker alerted to our presence? Or did he somehow detect our arrival and abandon his plans? If so, then he might have been on his way to meet Morgan himself – a worrying prospect.

Or does the hacker know more than he's letting on? Does he know the importance of the Anakim artefact? Or was it Steiner that arranged the meeting?

Joiner interlaced his fingers and placed them on his lap. Whatever the case, he thought, I'm in possession of the most powerful object on the planet. The question isn't how I came to have it – he continued to study Morgan as she gazed out the window – but what am I going to do with it next.

CHAPTER EIGHTY-SEVEN

SARAH LET the whine of the aircraft's engines vibrate through her body without resistance as she stared out into the brightening night sky. She had no idea where they were heading and quite frankly, she didn't care. Everything had been for nothing. All the fighting, all the trauma, all the death, where had it got her? It was as she'd known all along. *Everything I touch turns to dust. The world is better off without me.* But even though she'd accepted defeat, she knew there was one good thing that would come from her capture. Without her influence, Trish and Jason could live out the rest of their lives happy and content in the light of day.

She looked left and caught one of the soldiers staring at her bare, mud-splattered legs and she pulled her T-shirt lower. The man with the glasses, whoever he might be, saw the movement and glanced in her direction before turning to look back out of the window. Sarah knew there was only one thing on his mind, and it had nothing to do with libidinous lust.

She drew her hands to her chest and pressed them against the hidden cross beneath and embraced the only comfort she had left, that the man she loved would forever be in her heart.

Dazzling sunlight appeared over the horizon and Sarah turned to gaze out at a new dawn over empty seas and asked herself, *what is it all for? What is the point of living?* But as the aircraft banked left and Sarah glimpsed the flag of the United States fluttering free over its capital city, there was only one question left in her mind ... *when*, she wondered, *will it all end?*

CHAPTER EIGHTY-EIGHT

MALCOLM JOINER SAT at his desk inside the Intelligence Division's D.C. branch and stared into space, deep in thought. He'd been left with a big decision regarding the Anakim pendant and its human host, perhaps the biggest decision of his life. Should he hand over something that might be capable of imbuing its owner with near limitless power, or keep it for himself and risk the Committee terminating his life with the flick of a switch? There was another argument against keeping the artefact; it would also mean he sacrificed the upper hand. The Committee thought he was under their thrall; if he broke ranks now that edge would be lost. But despite the pros and cons, the whys and wherefores, neither option had been particularly appealing, and relinquishing something he deserved – the chance of greatness – went against everything he knew.

The wallscreen opposite brightened and the figure of a woman appeared, surrounded by a corporeal glow. 'Director,' the artificial intelligence said, 'I have detected an untraceable, incoming call routed through an unofficial channel. Do you wish me to transfer it to your desk?'

Joiner looked at the shimmering image of his A.I. assistant and nodded.

A moment later a green *answer* button materialised on his tabletop screen and he tapped it with a finger.

'Director,' said a voice, its tone disguised deep, 'you have seen what we see and now it is time to earn your keep.'

'I wondered when I'd hear from you again.' Joiner checked his watch. 'Your timing couldn't be better. What is it you want?'

'The woman, we know you have her.'

'Do you?' he said, his tone scathing.

The voice hesitated. 'You have already given her to the Committee?'

'Did I say that?'

'Do not play games with us, Director, you have already taken the life of one of our people, we will not tolerate anymore defiance.'

Joiner's eyes narrowed. 'Your *fanatic* took his own life and if you wanted to take mine you already would have. Do what you must.' He hung up and sat back in his seat. He was done playing games. He'd never shied away from making big calls and he wasn't about to now, it was time to call their bluff.

He waited for the caller to ring again, but no transmission arrived and Joiner was left wondering if he'd made a mistake.

Someone knocked on the office door and Agent Myers entered at Joiner's behest.

'Your transport has arrived,' Myer said, 'you'll be in New York within the hour.'

'Do you have it?'

Myers nodded and placed a small device on the desk. 'It should block any signal from activating the kill switch, but without testing it I can't be a hundred per cent certain.'

'Then how certain can you be?'

'Ninety-nine point nine per cent.'

'Good enough,' Joiner said.

'It's already active; you just have to keep it within ten feet at all times.'

'And no one else knows but you?'

'No one,' Myers said.

Joiner picked up the jammer, examined it and then slipped it into his pocket. It was always a good idea to have a back up and now he had someone he could trust, the Committee would be none the wiser – until that was, they made an attempt on his life.

Joiner turned to his A.I. assistant. 'Activate protocol *Overwatch*.'

'Activating ...' the computer said.

The office door locked and the wallscreen filled with the live images from Sanctuary's secret laboratories.

'Locate Dagmar Sørensen,' Joiner said.

'Locating ...' said the computer.

A red rectangle moved across the video grid in search of the specified parameters before stopping and switching to green.

'Sørensen, Dagmar,' the A.I. assistant said, 'located.'

A single image moved to the centre of the wall and Joiner saw the familiar figure of the R&D director, dressed in a white lab coat, waiting at an elevator.

'Shouldn't we be heading to the roof?' Myers said. 'If you want to get to the summit by noon ...'

'In a moment.' Joiner watched as a scientist approached the R&D director. 'Computer, activate audio sync.'

'Lip reading conversion, processing,' said the computer, 'estimated accuracy ... ninety-six per cent.'

Joiner waited for the conversation to start. *What are you up to Dagmar?* Joiner thought. *What secrets are you hiding from me?*

♦

Two thousand miles away, deep beneath the mountains of Mexico, Dagmar Sørensen, the GMRC's R&D director, stood before the elevator doors in anticipation of his guests. An unusual thrill of excitement flooded his pain-riddled body. Soon he would be able to begin the first stage of what he'd worked for so many years to achieve and Project Ares would finally soar to the heights he'd always envisaged.

He turned as one of his scientists approached. 'I said no interruptions.'

'Yes,' – the man gave a nervous smile – 'forgive me, Director, but we believe we've located the source of the data anomaly.'

'And?'

'It's a signal, and its signature is virtually identical to readings we've taken from functioning Anakim technology.' The scientist passed his superior a sheet of printed paper before continuing. 'We were able to use satellite replacement relays to extrapolate and verify the global positioning and narrow the time of the event to a twenty-four hour window.'

'Which was?'

'Two months ago, at roughly the same time when the energy wave activated Sanctuary's ceiling.'

'And the location?'

'It's as we thought, the event occurred on the surface, approximately a thousand miles south east of what we believe to be Sanctuary Proper's southernmost border.'

Dagmar wiped a handkerchief over his sweating brow. 'And the instrumentation is functioning within parameters?'

'We ran a full diagnostic, there can be no mistake.'

Dagmar considered the news. *Functioning Anakim tech on the surface? It's unprecedented. Well,* he thought, *almost unprecedented.* 'Do we know what lies a thousand miles south east?'

The scientist nodded. 'We do, it appears to be a disused settlement, ancient by human standards. It's a well-documented site of Mayan creation; they call it the ruins of Copán.'

'Send a team ...' – Dagmar inhaled a rattling breath – 'to the surface to investigate.'

'You might want to make that three,' the scientist said, 'we have yet to confirm, but it looks like two more distinct signals occurred at the same time as the first.'

Dagmar grasped the scientist's arm. 'Two more? You're sure?'

The man winced as his director's fingernails bit into his flesh. 'Quite sure. One looks to have originated in the Amazon rainforest, while another was in central China.'

A bleep from the elevator indicated someone was descending from a level above, and Dagmar released his hold. 'Update me when our guests have left.'

The scientist bobbed his head to acknowledge the request and scuttled away just as the elevator pinged and the doors slid open.

Selene Dubois and two other, equally tall, Committee members, a man and a woman, emerged into the brightly lit, white corridor. Behind them, four S.I.L.V.E.R. assassins shadowed their masters' movements, their chrome armour and formidable weaponry glittering under the lights.

Dagmar mustered an expected subservient bow. 'Your bodyguards are not necessary,' he said, indicating the four warriors. 'This facility is entirely safe, I can assure you.'

'Dagmar,' Selene said in greeting as she and her two companions surveyed their new environment. 'Considering what it is you have down here,' – her gaze settled on him – 'I doubt anyone of us is *safe*.'

'Of course, as you wish.' Dagmar gestured at two Special Forces commandos who guarded a nearby entrance. 'But rest assured we have a hundred such soldiers on standby in the event of a ... situation.' He gestured down the hallway. 'Shall we proceed with the tour?'

♦

Malcolm Joiner watched from his distant vantage point on the surface as Dagmar led Selene and her delegation down the corridor of the laboratory complex. *So*, he thought, *it's as Morgan said, she escaped Sanctuary using some kind of Anakim device, which also answers the question of how she broke into Sanctuary in the first place.* He pondered what he'd just learnt before the group disappeared from view as they passed into another area of the facility.

'Sir,' Myers said, stepping closer, 'we have to go – the summit ...'

'The summit can wait, this is too important.' Joiner searched the other camera streams to see if he could find where Dagmar had taken them. 'Computer,' he said, 'expand grid frame *K five*.'

The image expanded to the centre of the wall to show the delegation stopping to inspect the skeletal remains of an Anakim man.

'Computer, re-create audio,' Joiner said, 'and track and record Dagmar Sørensen and his group from camera to camera, I want to see and hear *everything*.'

'Certainly, Director,' said the A.I. assistant, 'actioning.'

♦

Dagmar waited for Selene and her associates to finish discussing the Anakim skeleton before leading them through another doorway and into an adjoining laboratory.

'What news of the space station?' Selene said, 'you mentioned an issue.'

'We lost contact for a few days,' – Dagmar paused to cough – 'but everything is fine now, communications have been fully restored.'

'Have any new predictions been made?'

Dagmar saw the other two Committee members listening with interest. 'Not as yet. The technology is complex and the images provided are jumbled and nonsensical, to our minds, anyway.' He paused for breath. 'When we find something new – as always – the Committee will be the first to know.'

'And the ... *God Device*, it continues to function as expected?' Selene said. 'If I remember rightly you were concerned about its long term exposure to a micro-gravity environment.'

'Space seems to optimise its power output,' – Dagmar guided them into another hallway – 'the source of which we are yet to determine. The quantum realm continues to surprise in its complexity.'

♦

Back in Washington D.C., Agent Myers looked to his director. 'I thought all the space stations were destroyed?'

'So did I.' Joiner grimaced. 'Their operation is even bigger than we thought.' He returned his attention to the wallscreen.

'—seems to be a success,' Selene was saying, 'he continues — as you envisaged.'

Dagmar smiled. 'The implant and retraining — powerful — Joiner — continue to — compliant.'

'Computer, switch to another camera,' Joiner said, 'now!'

'I'm sorry, Director, no other view is available; audio creation requires line of sight, lip-reading conversion is fifty per cent and falling ... thirty per cent – ten – five – two. Conversion lost.'

Joiner swore in frustration as Dagmar and Selene moved away from the camera.

♦

'When will you tell him about the implant?' Dagmar said.

'There is a strong possibility he already knows.' Selene paused as the R&D director unlocked a set of doors. 'Malcolm Joiner is nobody's fool. However, whether he knows or not will not reduce our hold over him, it may even strengthen it.'

'And the abduction?' Dagmar said. 'You still haven't found out who may have compromised him?'

Selene frowned. 'No, but we will. There has been another incident since, at a baseball stadium. We will wait for them to overreach themselves, or until Malcolm hunts them down, and then we will erase them from existence – together.'

'Joiner will obey your commands to a point,' Dagmar said, 'but he is not without autonomy; he may learn to resist in other ways. There might come a time when you have to flick the switch and activate the implant.'

'Malcolm is one of us now, whether he likes it or not,' Selene said, 'and he has a part to play in what is to come, of that we know. How long that part will last remains to be seen.'

Dagmar nodded and refrained from further comment. He knew a rebuttal when he heard one.

They reached a massive pair of blast doors and a contingent of ten Terra Force soldiers standing guard before it. Dagmar approached a panel on a nearby wall and swiped his card across a reader, tapped in a code, and inserted his hand into a biometric scanner which analysed his fingerprint, heart rhythm and DNA. Overhead, a red light turned to green and a siren sounded before the blast doors inched apart.

♦

The delegation entered a new area and Joiner's computer switched to the next available camera. A few seconds after that, the audio creation resumed.

'What have you learned?' Selene said to Dagmar.

'So far? Unfortunately not a great deal, it seems to be able to avoid our attempts at investigation.'

'It's caged, is it not? What is the difficulty?'

'There is a well known and bizarre process in quantum mechanics whereby a particle can pass through solid barriers. It's called quantum tunnelling and while—'

'Spare me the physics lesson, Director,' Selene told him.

Dagmar nodded. 'The upshot is that the creature has the ability to phase through our reality. For something of its complexity and size it should be an impossibility, and yet—'

'It can,' Selene said.

'It appears so; there is still so much we have to learn.'

'And that is why we are here, not to see this,' – she made a gesture at something off camera – 'but the next evolution of your work.'

Joiner leaned forward. *Next evolution? What are they there to see, if not the Pharos?* 'Computer,' he said, 'expand and centre all streams within one hundred feet of Dagmar Sørensen's current location.'

Five more images moved to the wallscreen's centre. Only one showed anything of interest and that was the massive, reinforced enclosure designed to keep the mysterious creature contained. Joiner gazed at the dark interior, searching for the beast that lurked within.

Selene Dubois approached a railing to look down into the manmade prison. 'Are you sure it's in there?'

'It's there,' Dagmar said, 'it's just shy. Come,' – he beckoned them forward – 'we're almost there.'

The R&D director ushered the three Committee members ahead of him while the four chrome-clad assassins followed behind, their weapons now firmly in their hands.

The party of eight approached another set of blast doors and Dagmar went through the same entry procedure as before. Joiner saw another red light switch to green and the huge mechanism crept open to reveal a safety barrier and the large, empty blackness of an elevator shaft beyond.

'I thought this was the tour,' Joiner said, transfixed, 'but it's just the route in.'

Myers glanced at him. 'In to where?'

Joiner didn't reply as the A.I. assistant centred on a new camera and the audio conversion resumed.

♦

'It allowed us to observe how the energy is transferred,' Dagmar said, his breathing laboured, 'it was a fortuitous event to happen now, just when we were about to begin.'

'The ceiling's activation is more than a scientific discovery,' Selene said, 'much more, and whatever you may think it was not by the fluke of chance that Sanctuary has awoken.'

Dagmar's expression was dubious. 'You believe it was by design?'

'That you doubt it,' Selene said, 'shows how wedded you are to the material world. I'm surprised you haven't realised by now, Director, working with your quantum mechanics, that the world beyond our senses,' – she laid a hand on his shoulder – 'is there for us to control.'

Dagmar stared into her mismatched eyes and then gave a shake of his head. 'The occult is not science. And whatever you may think, the ceiling is not some kind of sign.'

'But that is exactly what it is.' She released her hold. 'Sanctuary's vast vaults have reactivated now, of all times throughout history, when the skies rain fire and the world and every living thing is faced with annihilation. These are momentous days, foretold before your God Device was even found.'

'Prophecy and hearsay are no substitute for observational experimentation and hard data,' Dagmar said, his temper rising, 'but the fact remains, something turned the ceiling on, and something else will turn it off.'

'Says the uninitiated man.' Selene looked down on him with something akin to pity. 'But you are quite right, it is simple cause and effect. And if – *when* – you decide to suspend your belief and embrace ours, you will come to see that the human mind, if harnessed, is more powerful than you could ever have imagined.'

The high-pitched whine of an electric turbine drew their attention and a large platform arrived beyond the barrier, which automatically began to rise.

Dagmar led the delegation forward and held his hand over a large, red button as he waited for everyone to board. He looked at Selene who gave him a nod.

'Take us down, Director,' she said.

Dagmar Sørensen depressed the button and they descended into the depths.

♦

Joiner scanned the images and waited for Dagmar and the Committee members to reappear, but seconds came and went and the wallscreen remained unchanged.

'Computer,' Joiner said, 'get them back! Re-locate Dagmar Sørensen.'

'Re-locating,' the A.I. said.

Joiner walked along the wall, searching for any sign of the R&D director, the Committee members or the four chrome-clad assassins, but seconds turned to minutes and there was still no sign of them.

'Where are they?' Joiner said, agitated.

Myers peered at the screen, waiting. 'Perhaps they've gone beyond the network.'

'Computer,' Joiner said, 'where is Dagmar Sørensen?'

'Re-locating ...'

Joiner stalked back across the office, his eyes boring into the screen as he continued to seek the missing delegation. 'Where are they?!'

'There is a ninety-eight point nine per cent probability,' the computer said, 'that Dagmar Sørensen is no longer inside the facility. Shall I search for his companions?'

'Do it!' Joiner slammed his hand down on the desk. 'FIND THEM!'

CHAPTER EIGHTY-NINE

DAGMAR SØRENSEN EMERGED from the elevator ten levels below the main laboratory complex and entered a large, oval chamber made from dark, grey concrete. Selene Dubois and her entourage followed him out and peered round at the sealed room in which they now found themselves.

'This way, please,' Dagmar said, and he walked forward to stand on a section of the floor segregated from the rest by a single, circular channel.

When everyone was inside the circle Dagmar pressed a button on his collar. 'We're ready.'

A white light appeared above and a glass cylinder rose up out of the floor as an identical one slid down from above to meet it.

Dagmar removed a breathing mask from the pocket of his lab coat and placed it over his nose and mouth. 'You may feel a slight pressure in your ears,' he said to Selene, 'don't worry it's just part of the decontamination process.' He gestured to the armed assassins. 'Tell them once they're inside not to remove their helmets or they'll compromise the air.'

Selene turned to one of the armoured figures. 'Did you hear that?'

The man behind the mirrored visor gave a slow nod of his head.

A loud buzzer sounded and Dagmar said to the Committee members, 'You may want to hold your breath!'

A moment later a whoosh of mist engulfed the cylinder and the people within. Three seconds after that, the vapour turned a faint shade of yellow before the metallic clunk of a heavy mechanism sent the concrete pad on which they stood gliding up through the giant transparent tube and through an opening in the ceiling above.

The concrete platform came to a stop with a pneumatic hiss and five clamps snapped down to secure it in place. The yellow haze dissipated and Dagmar stepped down a set of steps and into a hive of activity.

♦

Selene Dubois and her associates followed the R&D director into a vast underground atrium one hundred feet wide and thrice that in length. Technicians, doctors, scientists and military personnel bustled throughout the large expanse, which acted as an oversize laboratory full of medical apparatus, operating tables, a strange array of robotic equipment, and a host of workstations similar to those found in Sanctuary's Exploration Division, the legendary SED.

Towering glass windows lined both sides of the expanse, behind which multiple floors separated residential areas from offices and more high-tech labs. While those working in the atrium's centre remained focused on their finely tuned equipment, skilled labourers toiled on the levels above, sending showers of sparks cascading to the floor as they welded in new sections of an overhead crane.

'All the staff you see,' Dagmar said, raising his voice over the clamour, 'live and work in this compound and are totally independent from the rest of the complex and the base beyond.' He paused to cough into his handkerchief. 'No one comes in and no one goes out without my express permission.'

'How long are they here for?' Selene said.

'As long as it takes.' Dagmar skirted round a vat of foul-smelling liquid and headed towards a quieter section of the compound.

The noise behind died away and the group entered a long, silent corridor that echoed to the sounds of their footsteps. At the end, two armed sentries stood aside to allow them through a large reinforced metal hatch and they emerged into a structure similar to the giant cell that housed the Pharos. However, rather than having a spartan interior, this prison had been partitioned into five sections by thick, semi-transparent curtains that hung from the ceiling above. Around the tops of the walls, more scientists worked at a host of holographic workstations that ringed the entire perimeter.

Dagmar paused before the first curtain. 'Your bodyguards will have to stay here, unless they plan on living out the rest of their days in Sanctuary.'

Selene gestured to the assassins' leader, who halted his team's advance.

Reduced to a party of four, Dagmar and the three Committee members pushed past the first curtain.

On either side, shrouded by the plastic sheets, the indistinct forms of lab technicians worked in silence around large pieces of similarly obscure apparatus.

Dagmar moved aside the final partition and motioned to three scientists to vacate the area. Left alone with the R&D director, Selene and her two associates assembled on a platform to gaze up at what they'd journeyed to see.

A minute of reverential silence followed before Selene said, 'How long until you begin?'

'As soon as they arrive.'

'Ophion has been despatched to ensure safe passage,' she said. 'They will be here within the hour.'

'What about the ... complication?' said one of the other Committee members. 'Will it not cause a delay?'

Dagmar shook his head. 'The surgery will be swift.'

'Will it cause permanent damage?' Selene said, concerned. 'There is much we need to know.'

'It will be invasive, but we will try to ensure there is no lasting impairment, at least in terms of cognitive ability.' Dagmar wiped spittle from the corner of his mouth. 'The timing, though,' he said, 'it couldn't have been any better; the chance of success has increased dramatically.'

'The timing is the chime of destiny,' Selene said, returning her attention to the focus of their fascination. 'Powerful forces are at work and thousands of years of disconnected events have transpired to bring us to this point. A new age of humanity has begun and we will shape its future for millennia to come. The work you do today, Director, will echo an eternity.'

She reached out to run her fingers over a dark, coral-like surface, while her gaze remained fixed on the rest of the monolithic structure that soared above their heads.

Retrieved from deep within Sanctuary Proper's forgotten reaches, the primordial edifice glinted and glistened beneath powerful lighting rigs and those that laid eyes on it knew they were looking at something conceived beyond the machinations of man. A mass of state-of-the-art monitoring equipment surrounded the fifty foot high monument, which had five vertical sides to form a pentagonal prism twenty feet in width. Attached to this wealth of technological hardware, thick black cables sprouted like many lifeless snakes to wend their way to the artefact's rocky substrate, where they terminated. But it was the forward-facing and singularly unique frontage of the ancient architecture that captivated the eye. Some ten feet wide and thirty high, a single, rectangular void had been fashioned deep into the relic's core. And recessed into the front edge of this depression, framed by a corroded metal surround, was a glass-like panel that held back a pale, viscous liquid which swirled in slow, lazy eddies as it merged with darker fluids disturbed from within. At the base of the aperture a ceramic panel had been installed by Anakim hands eons past, and sunk into its centre were three perfectly formed circles.

Dagmar entered a command into a nearby computer and the

platform on which they stood rose up into the air to bring them level with the artefact's centre. Another command activated a mechanism high above and a large, black panel dropped down to cover the monolith's transparent case and the fluid within.

'Our new ally has proven his worth,' Dagmar said, savouring his success, 'and to relinquish something he craved confirms his allegiance is – for now – beyond doubt.'

'Malcolm Joiner has done well.' Selene glanced at him. 'The imminent arrival of the elusive Ms. Morgan and the pendant will be the final piece in our puzzle.'

'Are you ready to see the fruits of our labour?' Dagmar said.

Selene nodded and the R&D director flicked a switch, causing the black panel to shimmer. A wave of electricity swept over its surface and the onlookers were bathed in a flickering glow.

Where the relic's interior had been shielded from view, the bespoke scanner, designed to penetrate the dense liquid within, laid bare its secrets. Immersed in what now looked like clear, sparkling water, not one, but three forms hung suspended around a central core. Each one of the figures, mouths agape and naked as the day they were born, remained devoid of movement, except for their eyes which occasionally moved as if asleep. And what a sleep it had been; for hundreds of thousands of years these citizens from another age had remained in a state of eternal hibernation, waiting for someone, or something, to wake them from an endless dream. And that wait had – *finally* – come to an end.

Selene stepped closer to the flickering image. 'It is time,' she said, mesmerised by the vision of the three Anakim giants, 'to awaken … the gods.'

EPILOGUE

THE LAUGHING CALLS of boisterous howler monkeys echoed out through the lush jungle of the Amazonian rainforest, while the midday sun beat down with a ferocious heat. Close by, hosts of exotic birds roosted in the lofty vaults of towering trees, their many squawks and whistles mixing with the sound of the millions of creeping, crawling, buzzing insects that scuttled and flew through the dense undergrowth.

Immersed in the midst of this scene of natural wonder, hundreds of miles from civilisation and deep within the forest's heart, strange shapes lurked hidden beneath the verdant greens of resurgent foliage. Lost cities and forgotten civilisations, buried by time and with links to a past far older than many would believe, lay waiting to be discovered by those that sought to reclaim it. But where there was the old there was also the new, and while the dead were gone, the living continued to fight for survival in an uncertain world.

Next to a small tributary of the mighty Amazon River, some distance from the ancient realms, a small group of huts had been built by human endeavour. Within this tiny compound, a plume of smoke drifted up into the stifling, humid sky and the smell of roasting meat wafted upstream on a subtle breeze. Drawn in by this succulent aroma, wild animals sniffed the air and prowled closer to see what they could see. But amongst these creatures large and small, another animal, a super-predator, stalked its prey.

A branch cracked and the top of a small tree shuddered, sending a flock of birds flying screeching into the skies. Monkeys chattered in warning and a big cat growled, and yet it was an indigenous infant that stood in danger's way. Sitting on its own, the young child played at the edge of a clearing, its parents momentarily distracted elsewhere. Another twig snapped, the bushes rustled and a dark shadow blocked out the sun. The child gazed up into a pair of glowing green eyes. An armoured hand grasped the limb of a tree and the figure swayed on its feet before moving from the forest and out into the open.

The man reached up and removed his helmet to reveal the back of a close-shaven head glistening with sweat. Staggering forward, the interloper managed ten more steps across dusty soil before dropping to his knees. The helmet fell from lifeless fingers and a moment later he keeled over with an audible crash that brought the natives running. The leader of the tribe approached and prodded the lifeless form with a stick before rolling the body over to reveal the face of a foreigner. More people gathered round to observe the oddity and a woman crouched down and touched the metallic suit with a tentative hand. She looked up at her husband and pointed at a symbol on the man's armour before holding up a circle of wood with a hole in the middle that hung round her neck. 'It is a sign,' she said in her native tongue.

The chieftain considered the man's shallow breath before making a decision. 'Then we shall help him.' He bent down and picked up the discarded helmet and ran his fingers over the strange design before gazing back down at the symbol that had saved the man's life:

U.S.B. STEADFAST

He didn't know what the images meant, but whatever they were they had not served its owner well. He dropped the helmet to the ground and helped his kin drag the man into shade.

The child who'd first encountered the intruder picked up the forgotten headwear while his parents attended to the demon's health. He ran his fingers over black markings and wondered, like his father, what they could mean. But if he'd had the relevant schooling, he would have known they were sets of letters that spelt out two, simple identifying words:

Colonel Samson

The boy placed the helmet over his head and a dazzling blaze of light lit up the interior. Amazed and scared in equal measure, he stood transfixed as an image appeared on the visor, an image of the man to whom the headwear belonged.

The image fuzzed and crackled. 'My name's Colonel Samson, U.S. military Special Forces.' He glanced up at the sky as beads of sweat trickled down his face. 'I have been lost in this wilderness for two months and a day. My navigation systems are down. My sense of direction—' He gave a shake of his head, his eyes haunted with fever. 'If anyone sees this, find my daughter, find Brett Taylor. Tell her – tell her there's no time left, the world as we know it is at an end.' He dragged the camera closer until only his maddened eyes filled the screen. 'Listen – listen to me now; this is what I know ...'

♦ ♦ ♦

Cloud Forest Biological Reserve
Monteverde, Costa Rica

A lone car, splattered with mud, bumped and rolled across a sun-dappled dirt track road before coming to a stop outside a dilapidated cabin surrounded by trees. The driver's door creaked open and banged shut an instant later.

Jason stretched his legs, arched his back and gave a groan of relief. 'Next time we need to go to town, I'm staying here.'

Trish grunted something in response and collected a bag from the back seat before clambering out and hooking the door shut with her foot. She walked up the porch steps and stopped in the doorway. 'Jason,' she said, 'come here, something's wrong.'

Dropping the bag, Trish ran inside with Jason following close behind.

The scene inside the cabin was one of disarray. Upended furniture, cushions torn apart and floorboards prised up.

'Sarah!' Trish ran to the kitchen. 'Sarah!'

Jason sprinted upstairs and burst into Sarah's bedroom, which had been similarly trashed. He rushed back out to search the other rooms.

After more frantic moments, Trish came to a halt on the landing and stared at Jason in despair. 'Oh my God, where is she?'

Jason shook his head. 'They took the parchments and Mayan tablet, too. They knew what they were looking for.'

'Do you think ...?'

'It must be,' he said, 'they must have found us somehow.'

Trish wiped a tear from her eye, her face stunned by shock and Jason walked over and hugged her to him.

'What do we do?' she said.

He kissed the top of her head and stared out of a window at the forest beyond. 'We'll find her. Even if we have to break back into Sanctuary itself, we'll find her.'

♦

'All the locals agree, they had helicopters,' Trish said, 'and they heard voices, American accents. Some even saw the men that took her, they wore black tactical gear and others the grey armour used by the GMRC.'

Jason righted the kitchen table and spread a map across its surface. 'Did they see what direction they headed?'

'North.'

'Then that confirms it. If the GMRC are involved, they've taken her back to Sanctuary. We have to go back.'

'But we just sold our Deep Reach helmets.'

Jason jabbed his finger at the town they'd just visited. 'Then that's where we start.'

'But how will we get back into the base when we get there? We don't have the pendant and there's no way we can breach their security.'

Jason stuffed more supplies into a holdall and zipped it closed. 'We'll find a way, or find someone that can.' He shouldered the bag and walked back into the living room where the TV fuzzed and flickered behind cracked glass as it searched for a signal. 'Have you got everything?'

Trish nodded and Jason's face hardened into determination. 'Then let's go.'

The two explorers left the cabin and returned to the car. With their supplies loaded, and direction set, Jason revved the engine and reversed round before slamming the gear stick in first and flooring the accelerator. Wheels spun, dirt and stones sprayed out, and they surged forwards back the way they'd come, the car slipping and sliding as it struggled to gain traction as they sped towards civilisation and the mission to come.

♦

An hour out from the cabin and they tore along the gravel road at breakneck speed.

'Which way?' Trish said, looking at the map.

Jason recognised the T-junction ahead. 'It's left.' He dropped gears from fourth to second and slid the car round the corner.

Trish screamed. 'Watch out!'

An oncoming four-by-four swerved off the road and the fleeting glimpse of its passengers' shocked faces vanished behind as Jason regained control.

Trish glanced back as the other vehicle rejoined the narrow highway. 'Was that a police car?'

'I hope not; are they turning round?'

She shook her head. 'Not yet they haven't. You need to slow down; we're no good to Sarah dead.'

'Or in prison.' Jason dipped the clutch, slammed it into third and accelerated. 'If that was the police, let's not give them the chance to catch up.'

The engine roared and the car barrelled on through the forest and, if she could have seen, Sarah would have known ... her friends were on their way.

♦

Two hours later, back at the abandoned cabin, night had fallen and a foreign wind rustled through the cloud forest's trees. The front door creaked open and banged shut in the breeze before repeating the process again and then again, in unending percussion. A vehicle crept along the nearby road, its fat, off-road tyres cracking and popping the gravel underneath. Main beams streamed bright and the shadows swung round as the four-by-four parked up to highlight the surrounding area in a blaze of headlights. The gasoline engine stuttered to silence and the illumination dimmed. Suspension creaked and car doors slammed as four people emerged into the dark of night.

Footsteps thumped up wooden steps and into the cabin, where the TV continued to flicker in the living area with an ethereal glow. Broken glass crunched underfoot and someone switched on the light.

'Search the rooms,' a woman said, 'this happened recently.'

The newcomers spread out into the cabin to search for signs of continued habitation, but when they'd quickly exhausted all avenues they regrouped back in front of the TV.

'It's totally cleaned out, no food, no clothes, nothing.'

'Whoever was here had something of great value; you wouldn't go to these lengths for anything else.'

'So what's next? What do we do now?'

The three who'd spoken looked to their leader, who had, up until now, remained silent.

'He told us we were to meet someone here,' the man said, concerned. 'It looks like someone beat us to it, or he got it wrong.'

The woman who'd been the first to speak gave a snort of derision. 'Of course he got it wrong. I don't even know why you keep trusting him.'

The young man next to her made a rude gesture. '*Ach*, what do you know.'

'More than you, little man.'

The bickering continued and the voice of another woman joined in before the leader stepped between them.

'Enough! Enough!!' Professor Steiner said, his voice ringing with authority. 'This is getting us nowhere.'

Brett Taylor laughed. 'Nowhere? Look around, nowhere is exactly where we are.'

'We agreed we had to come,' Steiner said, 'you included.'

The disgraced FBI agent glowered at him and the young man chuckled and made a derogatory remark.

Jessica Klein touched his arm. 'That's not helping, Eric.'

The young German made a face and wandered away to the kitchen.

Jessica watched him go before turning back to the professor. 'And Bic didn't say who was supposed to be here?' she said. 'You're sure?'

Steiner nodded. 'He said he didn't know, only that the GMRC were interested in her.'

'And some random woman would have helped us, how?' Brett said. 'If we'd have got here sooner it could have been us in harm's way. I thought he was supposed to be helping us *avoid* the authorities, not lead us to them.'

'He obviously thought the risk was worth it,' Steiner said.

'That's because we're the ones in the firing line!' Brett shook her head in disbelief and stalked out of the front door.

Steiner sighed. 'She's got a point.'

'Bic has got us this far,' Jessica said, 'we have to trust him.'

Steiner wanted to agree, but relying on a man regarded as the world's foremost terrorist was still something he was finding hard to accept.

A message on the TV flashed up reading: *Satellite signal acquired.*

The screen crackled to life and the fractured image of a woman in a yellow power suit appeared.

'This is the BBC's World News Service, reporting to you live from—'

Jessica hit the off button and the damaged screen went blank. 'I can't stand that woman,' she muttered and then looked back to the professor. 'I'll go ask some of the locals if they saw anything, it might give us a better idea of what's going on and who it was we were supposed to meet.'

Steiner gave a nod and adjusted his spectacles. 'I'll have another look round in case we missed anything. I'll meet you out front.'

'Eric!' Jessica said.

The young German poked his head out from the kitchen. '*Ja*?'

'Are you coming?'

He glanced at Steiner and then gave a nod and the two of them left the professor alone in the cabin to mull over his thoughts.

The sound of frogs croaking and crickets chirping drifted in from the balcony and Steiner removed his glasses to massage tired eyes. This was not how he'd envisaged spending his twilight years, going from country to country branded as a murderous fugitive. *Perhaps it's Bic who finds it distasteful working with me*, he thought. The irony brought a wry smile to his face. Putting his glasses back on, he trudged upstairs to give the rooms a second look and it was in the bathroom where he spied something of interest. He bent down and slid out a sheet of paper that had become trapped in the crevice between sink and wall. Smoothing it out, he held together its torn sections to reveal the drawing of a crucifix. He turned it over and found more drawings on the back, but unlike the single image, these were stylised constellations and letters, or more accurately, symbols. And they were familiar enough to make him frown. He glanced round to make sure the others hadn't returned before running his fingers over the images. He was by no means an expert in historical matters, but having been in Sanctuary on numerous occasions, and having visited its fabulous Smithsonian museum, he knew Anakim inscriptions when he saw them. *The question is*, he thought, *what are they doing here?*

He shivered. The room suddenly felt cold and the hairs on the back of his neck bristled. He looked round in unease and tucked the paper into a pocket before retreating downstairs. The balcony's net curtain fluttered in the air and a chill breeze blew through the cabin. Steiner pushed the curtain aside and moved out to look up into the night sky. His eyes drifted out of focus as he delved into memories past before a distant flash drew him back to the present. Another shooting star zipped across the heavens, and then another, and another after that. The light show continued, but rather than enjoying the spectacular vision of the distant meteor shower, Steiner saw it for it was, a premonition of what was to come.

The sound of the staircase creaking made him turn just as a flurry of wings erupted in his face. Steiner yelped and jumped back as a bird flew squawking into the sky. Spooked, he ducked back into the cabin and glanced up at the bathroom's dark doorway before switching off the light and hurrying outside.

A second later he was climbing into the front passenger seat of the four-by-four and slamming the door shut behind him.

Brett, who sat in the driver's seat, gave him a quizzical look.

Steiner slowed his breathing and tried to ignore the strange sense of dread that had descended on him in the cabin. He peered up at dark shutters that concealed the bathroom window and told himself, *it was just the bird. Stop being an old fool.*

He jumped as the back doors opened.

Jessica and Eric clambered inside.

'So?' Brett said, turning round.

'They were reluctant to talk,' Jessica said, 'I think they were protecting someone.'

'Figures,' Brett said. 'Perhaps I should have spoken to them.'

Eric made a face. 'You'd just make it worse.'

'You could try,' Jessica said, 'but I think Eric's right; if they were reluctant to talk to us you'd stand no chance.'

Brett's expression showed doubt about that statement, but she refrained from relinquishing her seat, perhaps because she knew Jessica's journalistic past made her a credible interrogator, or more likely, she wanted to ensure she retained control of the vehicle.

'So, what now, then?' Jessica said.

Steiner looked at her. 'We keep heading north, as before, nothing's changed. Whoever was here has gone and we need to get back to the States.'

Eric nodded. '*Ja*, we have a world to save.' He tapped Brett's shoulder. 'Let's go, *fräulein*.'

Brett scowled and turned the key in the ignition. The vehicle's engine rumbled to life and the headlights blazed bright.

Steiner took one last look out of the window. Eric was right; they had a world to save, billions of lives were in their – *his* – hands. He was used to power, but this was the first time he'd ever had so much riding on the decisions he made. One wrong move and the entire planet would burn. *I just hope I can make a difference*, he thought, as more shooting stars skimmed across the celestial sphere, *because our time is nearly up*.

♦

The four-by-four drove away into the night, its red taillights disappearing down the road. But back inside the cabin, the darkness lingered and the TV switched back on as its system searched for broadcasts. One by one, the aerial picked up a new channel which displayed on-screen as it saved the frequency in its memory bank. After some moments it entered a new category and the first international news channel appeared.

'—have been made of this strange phenomenon in the Chinese city of Xi'an,' a reporter said. 'Some are claiming it's a UFO, but as yet, all sightings of the mysterious, gliding light have been – not in the air

– but on the ground, causing some sceptics to call it an MOB, or what's more commonly known as, *man on bike*.'

The TV fuzzed into black and white pixels before the next channel displayed.

'—celebrations continue into the night throughout the world's major cities as leading experts declare the impact winter is in full retreat. And as weather patterns return to normal, crop yields continue to rise—'

The TV searched for the next signal.

'And good evening from Los Angeles, I'm Hunter Davies. This is a Fox News special report. As the GMRC announces a timeline for talks on water rationing, we ask viewers and panellists what they think this will mean for them and why some citizens appear to be more equal than others.'

The picture vanished and the previous graphic displayed:

Searching ...

The message changed:

Signal acquired ...

'President elect, John Harrison Henry, has offered an olive branch to the Chinese amidst escalating tensions with the West. But with the Japanese still calling for the U.S. and its allies to launch a full scale attack, it's unclear whether meaningful relations can be maintained ...'

Searching ... Signal acquired

Channel 107
CNN
{Cable News Network}

'— first pictures from inside the impact zone have been released today as news crews were allowed back in as South Africans attempt to rebuild their shattered country. No one knows how long it will take before people can return to the African nation, but if the footage is anything to go by, one thing is certain, it's not going to be anytime soon.'

Searching ...

Channel 108
Chinese Central Television
CCTV News
{Subtitled}

'The Pope has once again called for calm as Italy's capital saw pitched battles erupt late last night between various religious and political factions. This comes after a recent spate of suicide bombings that has rocked the Eternal City. Some are blaming Catholic fundamentalists, although it has been cited elsewhere that at least some of the violence was—'

Searching ...

Channel 109
NDTV India

'—tensions continue to rise in the Chinese province and questions remain as to what is causing this rash of disappearances. So far only two bodies have been recovered, but city officials are reluctant to release the circumstances surrounding the deaths. Some believe a serial killer is on the loose, or that a terrorist organisation is to blame. However, a member of the Xi'an city police administration, said, categorically, '*there is no connection between these occurrences and the strange light captured on camera by local residents and UFO hunters.*' A light, which you can see in this footage, appears to float across the ground and has the ability to pass through solid walls—'

Channel 110
BBC World News Service
{Channel Search Complete}

'—but before we go, did you want to make a closing statement to our viewers around the world?'

'I would, thank you, Keira.' The man faced the camera. 'I don't pretend to have all the answers; God knows I've made my fair share of mistakes in life—'

'Haven't we all,' Keira said with a smile.

'—and who knows what the future holds. But, for me, there is one thing that is crystal clear. We must find a way to protect this planet and the precious life that clings to its surface. The next asteroid strike might be the one that wipes us out and everything humanity has striven to achieve will be gone in an instant. And not just humanity's achievements, but all life on this planet, all the billions of years its taken us to get this far will vanish and when that day looms large and we look back and realise we had the chance to do something before it was too late, how will we feel knowing everything is going to end, that everyone and everything we've ever loved, or ever will love, will cease to be?

'In 2015, Russell Schweickart, an Apollo astronaut who travelled the world to encourage a coordinated global response to the asteroid threat, conducted a Newsweek interview with author, Nina Burleigh. In that interview he said the following, 'I fear there's not enough of a collective survival instinct to really overcome the centrifugal political forces. That is, in a nutshell, the reason we'll get hit. Not because technically we don't know it's coming, or we can't do something about it.'

'When I first heard that I realised, as a species, how stupendously dumb we really are. Can we really let this happen? This is not fiction; this is real life, a real threat. Can we continue to sleepwalk through life now that we know what's out there? Is it really that difficult for humanity to unite in a single cause? Are we so chained by money and blinded by material desire and personal gratification that we will rush headlong into oblivion?'

The man glanced at Keira before looking back at camera. 'What do you think? Yes, you, listening to me now, watching or reading my words on your computer or latest device, shall we just wait for our lives and every other human life to be extinguished? Because if we do nothing, that's what's going to happen; maybe not today, maybe not tomorrow, but at some point in the future another asteroid will hit. So perhaps the question should be ... what are you going to do about it? All life on this planet rests in Homo sapiens' hands and there's an asteroid out there with our name on it[*], and whether we like it or not ... the clock is ticking ...'

NEXT BOOK IN SERIES

To be continued in ...

Ancient Origins: The Tenth Protocol
(Book Five of *Ancient Origins*)

available at
amazon

https://geni.us/tenthprotocol

ABOUT THE AUTHOR

Robert Storey began work on what would become the Ancient Origins series in 2013. The series of six novels was completed in 2018.

Robert died a year later in March 2019.

For more information about Robert and his work, please visit:

fuse-books.com/robertstorey

ALSO BY ROBERT STOREY

Ancient Origins: Revelations

(Book One of *Ancient Origins*)

Ancient Origins: Dark Descent

(Book Two of *Ancient Origins*)

Ancient Origins: Let There Be Light

(Book Three of *Ancient Origins*)

Ancient Origins: Genesis

(Book Four of *Ancient Origins*)

Ancient Origins: The Tenth Protocol

(Book Five of *Ancient Origins*)

Ancient Origins: The Lost Prophet

(Book Six of *Ancient Origins*)

https://geni.us/robertstorey

APPENDIX A - GMRC CIVILIAN PERSONNEL

Professor George Steiner

Director General of GMRC Subterranean Programme
Nationality: American
GMRC Clearance – Level 10 Alpha
Designation – Civilian
Deployment: GMRC Directorate (Oversight) / Transient
GMRC Division: Subterranean Programme
Skill set:
Subterranean structural engineering
Management and leadership
Planning, design and development
Mathematical modelling and forecasting
Computer programming and software development

Malcolm Joiner

Director of U.S. and GMRC Intelligence
Nationality: American
GMRC Clearance – Level 10 Alpha
Designation – Civilian
Deployment: GMRC Directorate / Transient

GMRC Division: Intelligence Division
Skill set:
Espionage and covert intervention
Intelligence gathering, restriction and dissemination
Information pathways / Management and leadership
Psychological warfare

Richard Goodwin
GMRC Subterranean Base Director
Nationality: American
GMRC Clearance – Level 9 Alpha
Designation – Civilian
Deployment: U.S.S.B. Steadfast [U.S.S.B. Sanctuary – unofficial]
GMRC Division: Subterranean Programme
Skill set:
Management and leadership / Planning, design and development

Dr. Kara Vandervoort
Ecosystem Director
Nationality: South African
GMRC Clearance – Level 8 Alpha
Designation – Civilian
Deployment: U.S.S.B. Steadfast
GMRC Division: Subterranean Programme
Skill set:
Biomechanical engineering / Management / Data analysis

Special Agent Myers
CIA Agent and GMRC Intelligence Operative
CIA Special Operations Group (SOG)
Nationality: American
GMRC Clearance – Level 9 Delta
Designation – Civilian
Deployment: Transient
GMRC Division: Intelligence Division

Skill set:
Covert military intervention / Leadership / Strategic planning
Close quarters and unarmed combat

Dagmar Sørensen

Director of GMRC Research & Development
Nationality: Norwegian
GMRC Clearance – Level 10 Alpha
Designation – Civilian
Deployment: GMRC Directorate / Transient
GMRC Division: Research and Development
Skill set:
Scientific exploration and advance
Black project development and integration
(Special access programmes: acknowledged and unacknowledged)
Information pathways / Management and leadership

Grant Debden

Primary Aide to Malcolm Joiner
Nationality: American
GMRC Clearance – Level 8 Delta
Designation – Civilian
Deployment: Transient
GMRC Division: Intelligence Division

Ms. Sylvia Lindegaard

GMRC Delegate
Nationality: Danish
GMRC Clearance – Level 10 Alpha
Designation – Civilian
Deployment: U.S.S.S. Archimedes
GMRC Division: Space Programme / Oversight
Skill set:
GMRC integration specialist

Management and leadership / Planning and development
Information pathways

Dr. Vladan Marković

Senior Research Scientist
Nationality: Ukrainian
GMRC Clearance – Level 10 Delta
Designation – Civilian
Deployment: E.U.S.B. Sentinel (reassigned to E.U.S.B. Superior)
GMRC Division: Research and Development
Skill set:
Bio-technology, research, design and development
Quantum mechanics, application and research
Anakim technology specialist

Dr. Laurent

Doctor of Medicine (Surgeon)
Nationality: Belgian
GMRC Clearance – Level 9 Delta
Designation – Civilian
Deployment: U.S.S.B. Sanctuary
GMRC Division: Research and Development
Skill set:
Bio-technology, application and development
Neurology and neurosurgery
Neural-implants specialist

APPENDIX B - S.E.D. PERSONNEL

Deployment: U.S.S.B. Sanctuary
Designation: GMRC Civilian

Dresden Locke
S.E.D. Facility Commander
Nationality: American
Profession: Explorer

Riley Orton
Deep Reach Team Leader
Team: Alpha Six
Nationality: American
Profession: Explorer

Jefferson Church
Deep Reach Team Member
Team: Alpha Six
Nationality: American
Profession: Explorer & Lead Archaeologist

Cora Islanovich (Deceased)

Deep Reach Deputy Team Leader
Team: Alpha Six
Nationality: American
Profession: Explorer

APPENDIX C - U.S. MILITARY PERSONNEL

Colonel Samson

United States Army SFSD Brigade Commander
Special Forces Subterranean Detachment
(Codename: Terra Force)
Nationality: American
GMRC Clearance – Level 8 Alpha
Designation: Military – Special Forces
Deployment: U.S.S.B. Steadfast
Skill set:
Overt military action / Sniper tactics and marksmanship
Covert military intervention and counter-insurgency
Close quarters & unarmed combat / Leadership & strategic planning
Subterranean warfare / Subterranean transit

General Stevens

United States Army Commanding General
Special Operations Command Sanctuary
Nationality: American
GMRC Clearance – Level 10 Beta (Special Access Personnel)

Designation: Military
Deployment: U.S.S.B. Sanctuary
Skill set:
Overt military action and unarmed combat
Leadership, logistics and strategic planning
Subterranean warfare

Corporal Adam Walker

United States Army Decontamination Team
Nationality: American
GMRC Clearance – Level 5 Beta
Designation: Military
Deployment: U.S.S.B. Sanctuary
Skill set:
Overt military action / Unarmed combat

Major Delph Armstrong

United States Army SFSD
Special Forces Subterranean Detachment
(Codename: Terra Force)
Nationality: American
GMRC Clearance – Level 8 Delta
Designation: Military – Special Forces
Deployment: U.S.S.B. Sanctuary
Skill set:
Overt military action / Multi terrain warfare
Close quarters and unarmed combat
Subterranean warfare

Sergeant Alvarez (Deceased)

United States Army Decontamination Team
(Staff Sergeant)
Nationality: American
GMRC Clearance – Level 5 Alpha
Designation – Military

Deployment: U.S.S.B. Sanctuary
Skill set:
Overt military action / Unarmed combat

Brigadier General Ellwood

United States Army Commanding General
(Division Commander)
Nationality: American
GMRC Clearance – Level 10 Delta
Designation – Military
Deployment: U.S.S.B. Sanctuary
Skill set:
Overt military action / Subterranean warfare
Covert military action and unarmed combat
Leadership, logistics and strategic planning

APPENDIX D - ARCHAEOLOGISTS

Sarah Elizabeth Morgan

Nationality: English

Profession: Archaeologist, Anthropologist

Current location: USSB Sanctuary

Trish Brook

Nationality: English

Profession: Archaeologist

Current location: USSB Sanctuary

Jason Reece

Nationality: Welsh

Profession: Archaeologist

Current location: USSB Sanctuary

APPENDIX E - S.I.L.V.E.R. OPERATIVES

Ophion Nexus

S.I.L.V.E.R. Operative (Taskforce Leader)
Nationality: Classified
GMRC Clearance – Classified
Designation – Civilian / Private Contractor
Deployment: Classified
Skill set: Classified

Zhang Bai

S.I.L.V.E.R. Operative
Nationality: Classified
GMRC Clearance – Classified
Designation – Civilian / Private Contractor
Relatives: Tien Bai (sister – see below)
Deployment: Classified
Skill set: Classified

Tien Bai

S.I.L.V.E.R. Operative
Nationality: Classified

GMRC Clearance – Classified
Designation – Civilian / Private Contractor
Relatives: Zhang Bai (sister – see above)
Deployment: Classified
Skill set: Classified

Contador Valantis

S.I.L.V.E.R. Operative
Nationality: Classified
GMRC Clearance – Classified
Designation – Civilian / Private Contractor
Deployment: Classified
Skill set: Classified

APPENDIX F - ASTRONAUTS

Tyler Magnusson

Pilot Commander (acting Captain of Archimedes)
Nationality: American
Rank: Commander
NASA Clearance Level: AMBER 1 (Segregated Personnel)
Deployment: U.S.S.S. Archimedes

Astrid-Hélène Pichon

Flight Engineer
Nationality: French
Rank: Mission Specialist
ESA Clearance Level: JADE 1 (Segregated Personnel)
Deployment: International Space Station (I.S.S.)

Alexei Denisov

Pilot Cosmonaut
Nationality: Russian
Rank: Second Officer
RFSA Clearance Level: JADE 1 (Segregated Personnel)

Deployment: International Space Station (I.S.S.)

Bo Heidfield (1990 – 2041)

Space Station Commander
Nationality: American
Rank: Captain (Deceased)

APPENDIX G - DARKLIGHT PERSONNEL

Commander Hilt

Darklight Officer

Nationality: American

GMRC Clearance – Level 8 Delta

Designation – Civilian / Private Contractor

Deployment: Classified

Current location: Sanctuary Proper

Skill set:

Overt military action / Multi terrain warfare

Covert military intervention / Sniper tactics and marksmanship

Hostage retrieval and counter terrorism

Close quarters and unarmed combat

Leadership and management / Strategic planning / Reconnaissance

Major Offiah

Darklight Officer

Nationality: Nigerian

GMRC Clearance – Level 7 Alpha

Designation – Civilian / Private Contractor

Deployment: Classified
Current location: Sanctuary Proper
Skill set:
Overt military action / Multi terrain warfare / Leadership
Covert military intervention / Close quarters and unarmed combat
Hostage retrieval and counter terrorism / Strategic planning

Captain Winter
Darklight Officer
Nationality: American
GMRC Clearance – Level 7 Alpha
Designation – Civilian / Private Contractor
Deployment: Classified
Current location: Sanctuary Proper
Skill set:
Overt military action / Multi terrain warfare / Reconnaissance
Covert military intervention / Close quarters and unarmed combat
Leadership and strategic planning

Lieutenant Gabriela Manaus
Darklight Officer
Nationality: Brazilian
GMRC Clearance – Level 7 Gamma
Designation – Civilian / Private Contractor
Deployment: Classified
Current location: Sanctuary Proper
Skill set:
Overt military action / Multi terrain warfare / Reconnaissance
Covert military intervention / Close quarters and unarmed combat

APPENDIX H - OTHER PERSONS

Jessica Klein

BBC Newsreader and TV Presenter
Nationality: English
Profession: Journalist
Relatives: Daniela & Victoria (daughters) / Evan (husband)
(Pseudonym: Eliza Sterling)

Brett Taylor

FBI Special Agent
Nationality: American
Profession: Federal Agent
Relatives: Colonel Samson (father)

Bic / Da Muss Ich

Computer Hacker / Cyber Terrorist
Nationality: Unknown
(Pseudonyms: DMI / *Da Muss Ich* / Because I Can /
Deforcement Insidious / D'Force / Elusive D / Oyakata / B.I.C.)

Eric Wolf

Computer Hacker
Nationality: German
(Pseudonym: *Das Gespenst*, the self-proclaimed Ghost)

Rebecca

Nationality: American
Profession: Mental health worker
Current location: Sanctuary Proper

Joseph

Nationality: American
Mentally handicapped man
Current location: Sanctuary Proper

Susan

Nationality: American
Mentally handicapped woman
Current location: Sanctuary Proper

Julie

Nationality: American
Profession: Mental health worker
Current location: Sanctuary Proper

Selene Dubois

Deputy Governor (Central Bank - USSB Sanctuary)
Nationality: Unknown
Profession: Banker
GMRC Clearance – Unknown
Designation – Civilian
Deployment: U.S.S.B. Sanctuary
Unofficial occupation: Member of 'The Committee'
Skill set: Unknown

Keira Jones

BBC News correspondent
Nationality: English
Profession: Journalist

Hunter Davies

Fox News Anchor
Nationality: American
Profession: Journalist / TV presenter

APPENDIX I - ORGANISATIONS

BBC (British Broadcasting Corporation) – Television, radio and multimedia network broadcaster operating in the United Kingdom and globally / www.bbc.co.uk

CNN (Cable News Network) – American television news channel / www.cnn.com

Fox News Channel (FNC) – American television news channel / www.foxnews.com

CTV News – Division of CTV Television Network, Canadian television news channel / www.ctvnews.ca

CCTV News – Chinese Central Television / Chinese state television broadcaster / www.cntv.cn

NDTV India – New Delhi Television / Leading Indian news channel / www.ndtv.com

United Nations (UN) – International organisation for law, security, human & civil rights, political freedom and world peace / www.un.org

GMRC (Global Meteor Response Council) – International organisation set up by the world's nations for the protection and preservation of humanity, civilisation and all life on Earth. Consisting of twenty-five divisions, the majority of the GMRC's policies and actions are carried out by a core of twelve divisions (see table below). Each of these divisions operates under one or two of the following three criteria:

PUBLIC: Activities disclosed to society
COVERT: Activities not disclosed to society
CLASSIFIED: Existence not disclosed to society

		OPERATIONAL CRITERIA		
		Public	*Covert*	*Classified*
GMRC DIVISON	Subterranean Programme		•	•
	Space Programme	•	•	
	Research & Development		•	•
	Intelligence		•	
	Population Education	•	•	
	Population Control		•	•
	Economic Control	•	•	
	Conservation	•	•	
	Resource Control	•	•	
	Operations & Military	•	•	
	U.N. Integration	•		
	Oversight	•	•	

NASA – The National Aeronautics and Space Administration (civilian space agency of the United States government) / www.-nasa.gov

CNSA – The China National Space Administration (civilian space agency of the People's Republic of China) / www.cnsa.gov.cn

ESA – The European Space Agency (civilian space agency of Europe) / www.esa.int

RFSA – The Russian Federal Space Agency (civilian space agency of Russia) / www.federalspace.ru

Smithsonian Institution – World renowned collective of research centres and museums in the United States of America / www.si.edu

[Author note: I always thought the Institution was called the Smithsonian Institute, but apparently this is a common misnomer.]

Smithsonian Museum of Sanctuary (SMS) – Located in USSB Sanctuary and administered by the Smithsonian Institution, the Museum of Sanctuary is a vast resource on the extinct species, Homo giganthropsis (commonly referred to as the Anakim).

BND – The German Federal Intelligence Service, also known as the Bundesnachrichtendienst.

The Committee – A secret society of power elites operating outside the law. Little is known about the global organisation, its members, structure or purpose, however, its near limitless wealth and influence hints at a long and illustrious heritage.

APPENDIX J - FACILITIES, UNITS & DESIGNATIONS

U.S.S.B. – United States Subterranean Base

U.S.S.B. Steadfast – A Class subterranean base

Footprint: circa 20 sq. miles (52 sq. km)
Height: 7,500 ft (2.3 km)
Depth from surface: 3,000 ft (0.91 km)
Deepest point from surface: 10,500 ft (2 miles / 3.21 km)
Cubic capacity: 28.7 cubic miles (119.6 km^3)
Year of build: 1996 – 2035
Population: circa 500,000

U.S.S.B. Sanctuary – A Class subterranean base

Footprint: > 314 sq. miles (813 sq. km)
Height: 21,120 ft (6.4 km)
Depth from surface: circa 10,000 ft (1.9 miles / 3.1 km)
Deepest point from surface: 31,120 ft (5.9 miles / 9.5 km)
Cubic capacity: 1,256 cubic miles (5,203 km^3)
Year of build: 2016 – ongoing
Population: circa 20 million
Motto: '*Protegere Et Conservare, Civilitatem, Humanitas Et Omnes*

Vitam In Terra' ('To protect and preserve civilization, humanity and all life on earth').

Sanctuary Proper – Ancient subterranean structure
Footprint: > 20,000 sq. miles (51,800 sq. km)
Height: circa 20 to 30 miles (32km to 48km)
Depth from surface: circa 10,000 ft (1.9 miles / 3.1 km)
Deepest point from surface: circa 22 to 32 miles
Cubic capacity: 400,000 to 600,000 cubic miles
Year of build: circa 900,000 yrs B.C.

E.U.S.B. – European Union Subterranean Base

E.U.S.B. Deutschland – A Class subterranean base
Footprint: circa 40 sq. miles (104 sq. km)
Height: 8,500 ft (2.6 km)
Depth from surface: 2,500 ft (0.76 km)
Deepest point from surface: 11,000 ft (2.1 miles / 3.36 km)
Cubic capacity: 28.7 cubic miles (270.4 km^3)
Year of build: 2015 – ongoing
Population: circa 2,250,000

Darklight – Private security firm operating around the world and utilised by various organisations, corporations and governments. Primary client: Global Meteor Response Council.

SOG – CIA's Special Operations Group

NCO – Non-commissioned officer.

XO – Executive officer.

SFSD – Special Forces Subterranean Detachment
Division of the United States Army
Member of Subterranean Command

Codename: 'Terra Force'

Active: 2013 – present

Type: Infantry / Special Forces Commandos

Motto: 'No Depth Too Difficult, No Height Too Great – Honor and Country!'

Battle cry / affirmation: 'Ooyah!'

Deployment: United States Subterranean Bases

S.E.D. (Sanctuary Exploration Division) – Founded in 1826 by the sixth President of the United States, John Quincy Adams, the SED has a unique position within USSB Sanctuary in that it has a certain amount of autonomy despite its military oversight. The reason for this independence is mainly due to two factors. Fact one, the SED was operational long before the USSB was built or the GMRC ever conceived. Fact two, the SED was also instrumental in helping the United States government and GMRC create USSB Sanctuary, their knowledge of Sanctuary Proper an invaluable resource to the subterranean engineers during the planning, design and development of the enormous multilevel, underground structure / city.

Types of Team: Mapping, Structural, Archaeological, Scientific and Deep Reach.

Motto: 'Into the dark, into the light, pioneers for life.'

Sancturian – name given to residents of USSB Sanctuary.

Project ARES – Unacknowledged Special Access Programme, or black project, utilising ancient Anakim technology. A collaborative venture between the GMRC's R&D Division, United States military and NASA.

GMRC Directorate – Executive body ruling over the GMRC. Comprising Directors from the twelve major divisions within the GMRC, the Directorate helps to shape the council's policies and actions around the world.

Motto: '*In Veritate Scientia*' (In Truth, Knowledge).

Deep Reach – Special unit working within Sanctuary's Exploration Division (S.E.D.).

Team Alpha Six – S.E.D. Deep Reach unit.

U.S.S.S. Orbiter One – United States Space Ship. Co-funded and managed by NASA and the U.S. military. Small, modular craft designed for orbital observation and scientific research.

U.S.S.S. Archimedes – United States Space Station. Co-funded and managed by NASA and the U.S. military. Large, modular craft designed for orbital observation, scientific research and classified military applications.

I.S.S. – International Space Station. Co-funded by the world's major spacefaring nations. Large, modular craft designed for orbital observation, scientific research and classified military applications.

E.S.S. Guardian – European Space Station. Co-funded and managed by the ESA (European Space Agency) and the EU (European Union). Large, modular craft designed for orbital observation, scientific research and classified military applications.

C.S.S. Jiùshìzhǔ – Chinese Space Station. Co-funded and managed by the CNSA (Chinese National Space Administration) and the People's Republic of China. Large, modular craft designed for orbital observation, scientific research and classified military applications. Jiùshìzhǔ translates as '*the Saviour*'.

Three Sisters – A phrase used to describe the collective of the three space stations, Archimedes, Jiùshìzhǔ and Guardian.

S.I.L.V.E.R. – A multidisciplinary elite taskforce comprising twenty-two highly skilled individuals, or operatives, available to the highest bidder. Masters of various styles of combat, each member has access to the best military hardware the world has to offer and can function as a lone agent, or as part of a greater whole. S.I.L.V.E.R. is an acronym for: Stealth, Infiltration, Liquidation, Verification, Extraction and Reconnaissance. Their existence is hidden from public eye and they are regarded as mercenaries by some, assassins by others, and necessary by those who employ them.

APPENDIX K - WORDS, TERMS & PHRASES

Anakim – Ancient and extinct race of Hominids living on Earth circa 1.2 million to 20,000 years before present-day. Scientific name: Homo giganthropsis (unofficial: Homo gigantis). Alternative plural: Anakai.

Nephilim – The word *Nephilim* is found in the Hebrew Bible. Its true meaning, as far as I can tell, still seems to be contested to this day. Some suggest it derives from the word, *nephal* or *naphal*, which can mean 'to fall', which some then interpret as the 'fallen ones'. Another, and perhaps more reasoned argument, is that *Nephilim* is derived from the word *naphil* which means 'giant'. When researching this, I found that Dr. Mike Heiser gave a well-reasoned argument for the latter hypothesis mentioned above.

Mesoamerica – A region in Central America in which pre-Columbian cultures thrived between approx. 10,000 B.C. and 1700 A.D. Modern day countries contained (partly or fully) within the Mesoamerican area include: Mexico, Guatemala, El Salvador, Honduras, Belize, Nicaragua and Costa Rica. The most well known civilisations/tribes in Mesoamerica include: Inca, Aztecs, Maya, Olmecs, Mixtecs and Zapotecs.

Ooyah – SFSD commandos' affirmation / battle cry.

The Deep Web – Term for the part of the World Wide Web not appearing on regular search engines. Unindexed content not seen by regular Internet users who frequent the Surface Web. This content can take many forms; some is benign while other content can be more sinister in origin and use, resulting from illegal activity by individuals, criminal gangs, corrupt organisations, companies and sovereign nations, although the latter may argue this is just offensive national defence conducted in their country's best interests. Also known as: Deep Net, Dark Net, Dark Web, Invisible Web, Under Web, Under Net, Hidden Web etc.

Scheiße – Vulgar German word for shit, faeces or something rubbish / worthless (alternative: *Scheisse*).

CPR – Cardiopulmonary resuscitation.

KIA – Killed in action.

MIA – Missing in action.

Brine Pool – A high salinity body of water found on the seabed of deep oceans which give the impression of an underwater lake or pool.

Intercept missions – Planned missions by the GMRC's Space Programme to prevent four of six approaching asteroids from impacting planet Earth.

Caste – Word used by *The Committee* to distinguish between the hierarchical ranks of its members. There are thirteen castes within The Committee, and only nine people can hold the top, and thirteenth, caste.

EVA – Extra vehicular activity is a term used by astronauts and cosmonauts when they operate outside of their spacecraft in a pressurised suit when in the vacuum of space or other unpressurised environments.

Obsidian – Is a volcanic glass which has a shiny black appearance and naturally occurs in nature.

Das Gespenst – The name used by the computer hacker, Eric Wolf, which translates from German as: 'The Ghost'.

Da Muss Ich – One of many names used by, and assigned to, the cyber terrorist, B.I.C., which translates from German as: 'Because I Must'. Although, the acronym B.I.C. stands for the better known name of: 'Because I Can'.

Rodgers and Hammerstein – A well known, multi-award-winning musical theatre writing duo from the United States. Considered by some to be the greatest writing team of the twentieth century, they wrote the song 'You'll Never Walk Alone' for their musical *Carousel.* This song has since been covered numerous times all around the world and is used by supporters of Liverpool Football Club (Liverpool, England) on match days, as a rousing anthem.

'There's an asteroid with our name on it' – When I originally wrote the last sentence of this book, I didn't realise I had paraphrased a well known scientist. Rather, I was sitting back in relief that I had finished the manuscript and quite pleased with my final paragraph. However, when I read back over my work a nagging doubt crept into my mind that perhaps the words were not my own. After some investigation I found that my fears were true – and there was I believing I'd come up with the perfect line ... I should have known [sigh].

Anyway, there was a slight chance I had come up with these words independently on my own, but considering I am a big fan of the man who originally said them, it was clear to me I must have read or heard these words spoken previously and just believed I'd had a flash of inspiration, when in fact … I hadn't. So who said 'There's an asteroid with our name on it'? The man in question is the English physicist, **Professor Brian Cox, OBE**, who currently works as a professor of particle physics in the School of Physics and Astronomy at the University of Manchester, England. When speaking to the MailOnline he said:

'There is an asteroid with our name on it and it will hit us,' Professor Cox told MailOnline. In fact, the Earth had a 'near-miss' only a few months ago.

'We didn't see it,' says the 46-year-old. 'We saw it on the way out, but if it had just been a bit further over it would have probably wiped us out. These things happen.'

(Source: http://www.dailymail.co.uk/sciencetech/article-2740010/There-s-asteroid-Brian-Cox-warns-space-rock-wipe-humanity-robots-don-t-first.html)

Official website of Professor Brian Cox and Gia Milinovich: www.apolloschildren.com

Russell Schweickart – A retired NASA and Apollo astronaut, and founder of the B612 Foundation.

B612 Foundation – A private organisation dedicated to protecting Earth from asteroid impacts. The non-profit foundation also informs decision-making on planetary defence issues. B612 provides a non-governmental voice on the risks, options, and implications of asteroid data.

(Source: http://b612foundation.org/our-mission/)

Website: b612foundation.org

Newsweek – Has been a staple of American media for over 80 years, bringing high-quality journalism to millions of readers around the globe. Newsweek publishes print editions in Japanese, Korean, Polish, Spanish, Arabic, and Turkish, as well as an English language international edition, but is a primarily digital property available across platforms and devices. Newsweek provides in-depth analysis, news and opinion about international issues, technology, business, culture and politics /

www.newsweek.com

Nina Burleigh – An award-winning investigative journalist and the author of five books. Her last book, *The Fatal Gift of Beauty*, was a *New York Times* bestseller. She is currently National Politics Correspondent at Newsweek (see above) and has written for numerous publications including *Rolling Stone*, *Businessweek*, *The New Yorker*, *Time*, *New York* and *The New York Times* / www.ninaburleigh.com

'It is not in the stars to hold our destiny but in ourselves' – A famous saying from Shakespeare's play, *Julius Caesar* ... or was it? After doing some digging it appears these words may be a paraphrase of the bard's work, rather than the words of the man himself. The words Shakespeare actually wrote, as far as I can tell, are as follows: 'The fault, dear Brutus, is not in our stars,

'But in ourselves, that we are underlings.'

'Not even the gods, fight necessity' – A quote from a famous Greek poet: Simonides of Ceos. Used by Contador Valantis when he addresses the captured Pharos.

Judeo-Christian Bible – The basic text of Judeo-Christianity is the Bible, as preserved in Jewish and Christian tradition. It consists of two parts: the Hebrew Bible and the New Testament /

(Source: http://www.judeochristianity.org/judeochristianity_principles.htm)

UCI – The Spanish abbreviation for Unidad de Cuidados Intensivos, or in English, Intensive Care Unit (ICU).

Vitruvian man –A famous drawing by Leonardo da Vinci.

APPENDIX L - LOCATIONS, BUILDINGS & MONUMENTS

Sanctuary Proper – Ancient underground structure built by an extinct species of Hominid, Homo giganthropsis. Located beneath the deserts and mountains of central and northern Mexico.

Dulce – Small town located in Rio Arriba County, New Mexico, United States.

Ruins of Copán – ancient Mayan city located in the Copán Department of western Honduras.

Sterkfontein Caves – Also known as the Cradle of Humanity. Located near Johannesburg, South Africa.

City of New York, State of New York, USA – Most populous and arguably the most iconic city in the United States.

Smithsonian Vaults – Secure facilities used to store ancient Anakim artefacts and remains. The vaults are located inside USSB Sanctuary and beneath the Smithsonian Institution's sprawling Museum of Sanctuary.

Military Vaults – As above but with extra security and limited access.

U.S.S.B. SANCTUARY United States Military Scientific Laboratory Complex – High security facility run by the U.S. Army. Utilised by NASA and the GMRC'S R&D Division, the complex contains projects and research based on artefacts of Anakim origin.

Shuttle bay – Area inside the S.E.D. from where air-shuttles are launched.

Departure lounge – Nickname given to the staging area in the S.E.D. used by teams prior to launch.

S.E.D. Control Station – Area inside the S.E.D. Command Centre that controls the launch and return of air-shuttles into Sanctuary Proper.

S.E.D. Command Centre – Area inside the S.E.D. complex that houses the Control Station (see above), shuttle bay and the offices for high ranking S.E.D. personnel.

Tower central – Is an ancient Anakim tower located at the heart of U.S.S.B. Sanctuary. At three miles high the spectacular structure was built to last and it was decided – for reasons both structural and aesthetic – to construct the human subterranean base around it.

GMRC Command Complex – A large office complex with a central skyscraper (or domescraper) located on the Dome level of U.S.S.B. Sanctuary

Dome Level – The topmost level of U.S.S.B. Sanctuary and the most exclusive, due to the health benefits (both mental and physical) of living, and/or working, in a more open and natural environment.

New Park District – Located on the Dome level (see above), the New

Park District is as the name suggests, an area within U.S.S.B. Sanctuary that is filled with various picturesque parks and forests; it also contains within its borders the subterranean base's museum complex

Mission Control Center (NASA) – Located in the Lyndon B. Johnson Space Center, Houston, Texas, USA, the Control Center acts as the hub of operations conducted by NASA.

The Auditorium – The largest space module ever built, prefabricated on the surface in the year 2032, and assembled in space a year later, it acts as the central node of the International Space Station (ISS). It has multiple uses including: a mission centre, conference room and viewing gallery.

ALMA – The Atacama Large Millimeter/submillimeter Array in Chile, South America. The array consists of sixty-six radio telescopes which have two sizes of dish, twelve and seven metres in diameter. ALMA has many uses, once of which is the study of comets.

TSKA The Two Square Kilometre Array. Built in the year 2025 in Peru. An array of radio telescopes spread out over two square kilometres.

Anakim Sphinx – An ancient monument located beneath the surface of a deep lake inside Sanctuary Proper. Date of construction: unknown.

Anakim Arch – A massive crystalline structure located in Sanctuary Proper.

Cloud Forest Biological Reserve – A stunning and biodiverse preservation area located in Monteverde, Costa Rica. Also known as: Reserva Biológica del Bosque Nuboso de Monteverde.

Monteverde – Small town in Costa Rica (approx. four and a half thousand feet above sea level).

Washington Monument – Is located in Washington D.C., USA and stands at the centre of the National Mall as a tribute to its country's first president, George Washington. Unlike the ancient Egyptian obelisks it was inspired by, the monument was constructed rather than carved from a single piece of stone. However, due to this, the structure dwarfs anything created in Egypt and clocks in at a towering one hundred and sixty-nine metres, or five hundred and fifty-four feet.

San Pedro Sula – A major city in the country of Honduras. Population, circa 500,000.

Hospital del Valle– A large hospital in the Honduran city of San Pedro Sula.

Nationals Park – Is a baseball stadium currently used by the Major League Baseball franchise, the Washington Nationals. It is located close to the Anacostia River in Washington D.C., USA.

APPENDIX M - TECHNOLOGY, ARTEFACTS & OBJECTS

Thermal Density Reduction (T.D.R.) – Excavation technology utilised in the creation of large scale subterranean chambers.

Netcube – A storage device for computers using a state-of-the-art fluid drive instead of the cumbersome hard disc drives which preceded them. Used to store massive amounts of data, a Netcube is capable of storing the majority of mainstream data held on the World Wide Web. (Also known as a 'webinabox'.)

RV – Acronym used by the military for a rendezvous point. Also used as an acronym for a 'remote vehicle'.

Thermal sword – Darklight personal weapon.

SABRE – Synergetic Air-Breathing Rocket Engine, an engine that operates in both air-breathing and rocket modes. Developed by Reaction Engines / www.reactionengines.co.uk.

DPD – Digital Parchment Paper.

T.I.I. – Thermal Image Intensifier.

Stelae – Carved stone monuments, singular *stela*.

Rosetta Stone – An ancient stele created in Egypt over two thousand, two hundred years ago. Its inscriptions – which were carved into its dark grey (or *black*) granite surface – comprised two languages, Greek and Egyptian, and utilised three scripts, Greek, demotic and hieroglyphic. This mixture of texts allowed Jean-François Champollion to decipher the previously lost secrets of the ancient Egyptians' hieroglyphic language.

T.I.I. – Thermal Image Intensifier.

Air-shuttle – A specially designed vehicle which travels on rails and through a large transparent tunnel / tube. An air-shuttle is the fastest way out of the USSB and into Sanctuary Proper (and vice versa). Propulsion is in the form of gravitational pull, staged rocket burns and strategically placed air-jets (assisted by a low-resistance cushion of air).

Computer phone – Advanced mobile phone with the processing power to run advanced software packages. Acts as a personal computer as well as a smart phone. Computer phones are able to connect to wallscreens and monitors via induction ports.

United States Credits (USC) – Currency used in United States subterranean bases. One USC is equivalent to one U.S. dollar.

The Centipede – Remote operated all-terrain supply vehicle. Multiple wheels, low ground clearance and an articulated chassis enable the machine to scale near vertical climbs and all manner of obstacles.

Quantum processor – Super powerful computer processor based on a qubits (quantum bits) rather than bits. These processors can carry out a far greater number of computations than computer architecture utilised in the first two decades of the twenty-first century.

UAV – Unmanned aerial vehicle, also known as a drone.

Wallscreen – Large, interactive monitor attached to a wall, usually taking up the entire surface.

HUD – Head-up display, or heads-up display. Data projection onto a transparent screen / visor / window allowing a user to continue looking in the desired direction while being kept apprised of real-time information.

Deep Space Detection Array (D.S.D.A.) – NASA and U.S. military satellite in high Earth orbit. Categorised as an unacknowledged Special Access Programme / black project. Capabilities: satellite disruption technology and deep space surveillance imager.

OLED – Organic light-emitting diode. Utilised in monitors, televisions and other visual displays.

Monotube – Public metro transportation system in USSB Sanctuary. Utilising a high-speed mono rail configuration, the train navigates the subterranean base via a network of transport channels and tunnels.

MX4 assault rifle – Advanced projectile weapon used by the U.S. military and Darklight security firm.

Beam rifle – Sophisticated non-projectile weapon capable of unleashing high-powered energy in the form of a beam.

Vacuum Lift – Super fast mechanism used to transport people up or down within a structure / facility.

Deep Reach helmet – High-tech headwear worn by S.E.D. Deep Reach personnel.

Multifunction card (M.F. card) – Given to permanent USSB residents, the MF card acts as a door key, sector pass, credit / debit card, data storage device and identity badge.

Mayan map – Dated at over a thousand years old, the dense metallic tablet was unearthed by Sarah Morgan in 2040 at the Ruins of Copán in Honduras. Consisting of Mayan hieroglyphs around a single line, the simple inscriptions portray a map linking together the ancient Mayan cities.

Anakim parchments – Collected by Sarah, Trish and Jason from a number of sources, these ancient scrolls are made from an unknown material which fails to degrade over time. They also have the capability to store large amounts of data and act like a digital display when activated using Sarah's pentagonal pendant.

Anakim orbs – Ancient relics unearthed in Sanctuary Proper by an S.E.D. archaeology team.

Anakim pendants – two metallic pentagonal pendants found by Sarah Morgan during previous archaeological digs. The larger of the two, measuring two and a half inches in diameter, enables the wearer to activate Anakim technology, although its use is limited by the operator's physical size.

Pentagon – Five-sided polygon.

Pentagram – A five-pointed star contained within a circle.

God Device – A piece of ancient technology of unknown origin.

Pharos – An entity, or creature, that inhabits the dark halls of Sanctuary Proper. Also referred to as 'the light', it was named after the ancient Lighthouse of Alexandria, which was built by the Romans on the tiny island of Pharos, Egypt, around two thousand, three hundred years ago. The lighthouse was one of the Seven Wonders of the ancient world and no longer exists, save for the odd stone recycled at other sites.

Like its namesake, the pronunciation of the beast's epithet, 'Pharos', is pronounced as follows: 'fair-os'.

Anakim monolith / prism – Massive fifty foot high artefact removed from a 900,000 year old building. Unearthed and recovered by SFSD soldiers under the command of General Stevens. The monolith contains a single chamber full of a viscous liquid which is protected by a transparent material.

Anakim shield – Another ancient relic unearthed in Sanctuary Proper by S.E.D. personnel. Found in the same hoard as the orb (see above) and stored in the military vaults beneath the Museum of Sanctuary.

APPENDIX N - MAPS, DIAGRAMS & REFERENCE

GMRC SUBTERRANEAN PROGRAMME

Country / State of Origin	Suffix	Number of Subterranean Bases
UNITED STATES SUBTERRANEAN BASE	USSB	10
EUROPEAN UNION SUBTERRANEAN BASE	EUSB	10
PEOPLE'S REPUBLIC OF CHINA SUBTERRANEAN BASE	PRCSB	9
RUSSIAN FEDERATION SUBTERRANEAN BASE	RFSB	5
SUBTERRANEAN BASE BRAZIL	SBB	4
SUBTERRANEAN BASE *(Independents)*	SB	3
JAPAN SUBTERRANEAN BASE	JSB	2
SUBTERRANEAN BASE INDIA	SBI	2

TERMINOLOGY / MAP

USSB – United States Subterranean Base
GMRC – Global Meteor Response Council
Darklight – World's largest private security contractor
SFSD – Special Forces Subterranean Detachment (*Terra Force*)
SED – Sanctuary Exploration Division
Deep Reach – Special survey team working within the SED
S.I.L.V.E.R. – An elite military unit available to the highest bidder
Sanctuary Proper – Ancient underground structure built by an extinct species of Hominid, Homo giganthropsis (the Anakim)

USSB
STEADFAST
NEVADA
UTAH
COLORADO
CALIFORNIA
Las Vegas
USA
Los Angeles
ARIZONA
NEW
MEXICO
TEXAS
MEXICO
USSB
SANCTUARY

POEM - I SEE YOU

I write
I sigh
I can
And do
Hope and pray
That someone
At some point
May brighten my day

At once
At night
The dark
No light
My mind a blur
Confusion astir
Words not worth writing
Some might say

It's clear as I create this verse
That poetry can be

As deep or light as I want to see
Whether or not it has meaning to me
To you, to them, to everyone
I sigh
I write, I ...
Pray

POEM - ENTER THE LIGHT

Darkest shores
Temptations past
I'm still to live
To breath, to love

I used to think
Motivation elusive
And yet ... now
Negative is conducive

My jealously, my failings
Another's complainings
A comment, belittling
I feel it, so crippling

And yet despite my yearning
I believe in my learning
That one or two failings
Can propel me up high

Determination afire
Heart aching desire
To reach dream's destination
My compassion now real

And so, as such, with clarity enhanced
Answer this question
Have I had my day?
Have you, what say?

Ancient Origins: Genesis is dedicated to those who fight the good fight.

ACKNOWLEDGMENTS

A massive thank you as ever to my parents for helping me stay the course and for their invaluable editing and insight into what works and what doesn't. Also, another big thank you to my copy editor, Julie Lewthwaite, who continues to keep me on the straight and narrow.

Furthermore, thank you to everyone who has given me their support and encouragement, which includes anyone who's been kind enough to contact me or leave a review for my books online or otherwise. It's your kind words and feedback that has kept me motivated through difficult times, both professionally and personally.

Robert Storey

2015

ADDENDUM

Fuse Books partnered with Terry and Maureen Storey, following the tragic death of their son Robert. It is our privilege to bring his Ancient Origins series to new readers.

In these books, Robert lives on.

As Rob himself noted above, and we can confirm from our time working together, these books would not have made it to publication without the support of Terry and Maureen.

Wonderful, devoted parents who could not have done more for their son.

James Blatch & Mark Dawson
February 2020

First published in Great Britain in 2015

2nd Edition

Fuse Books

Printed in Great Britain
by Amazon

49293320R00330